SUBVERSIVE

SUBVERSIVE

Book One of the Subversive Trilogy

RAENA ROOD

One Foundation Publishing
Freeburg, Pennsylvania

ISBN: 978-1-952431-00-5

ISBN: 978-0-692-61860-8 (e-book)
ISBN: 978-1-952431-00-5 (paperback)

Cover Design by Rossano Designs
Edited by Teresa Crumpton

One Foundation Publishing
P.O. Box 294
Freeburg, PA 17827

http://raenajrood.com

"Then they will hand you over for persecution, and they will kill you. You will be hated by all nations because of My name. Then many will take offense, betray one another and hate one another."
--Matthew 24: 9-10

CHAPTER ONE

At the edge of the cornfield, Gemma Alcott stood in front of the withered body hanging from the cross.

Hot bile climbed her throat. She clamped a hand over her mouth to contain it.

The storekeeper's leathery skin distorted the faded tattoo of a blue whale on his forearm, making the mammal appear to be fleeing the weather-beaten flesh. Nails as thick as her middle finger bound each of his gnarled hands to the crossbar, the weight of his body dragging at the open wound. A third nail protruded from his crossed ankles, and beneath this final, terrible mutilation, hung his feet—bare and black—from the grotesque combination of gravity and pooling blood. His head sagged on one emaciated shoulder, and his eyes were glazed over and vacant, like windows of an abandoned house.

She dropped her hand. Took a few cautious steps closer. "Henry?"

SUBVERSIVE

The stench—sickly-sweet and nauseating—overpowered her, and she covered her mouth and nose with both hands to keep from vomiting. But the smell leeched through her fingers, bringing to mind rotting husks of raccoons and deer. Only this was worse. Far worse.

Maybe it's not Henry. It doesn't really look like him.

Gemma seized onto this tiny measure of hope, choosing to ignore the whale tattoo. And the fact that she was currently standing in Henry's backyard, staring at a crude version of a cross fashioned out of boards that perfectly matched the crimson shade of Henry's barn. Determined to know for certain, she pulled her jacket over her nose and inched forward, not stopping until she was directly beneath the body. When she lifted her head, the storekeeper's eyes came alive, and he glared down at her.

Like he was accusing her.

"No!" She turned to run but lost her balance and went down hard on her bottom. Instinctively, she grabbed for the hunting knife on her belt, struggling to free it from its sheath. Needing a weapon to defend herself in case the old man lowered himself down from the cross and staggered over to her, his breath sour with decomposition.

Finally, her finger found the clip and she flicked it open, freeing the knife. Sunlight glinted off the razor-sharp blade as she thrust it toward the body.

But when she looked up, Henry was still on the cross.

And he wasn't glaring at her.

He was dead.

No.

Henry couldn't be dead. He wasn't even supposed to be here. He was supposed to be at his grocery store in Ash Grove right now, meeting up with two men from her group—Allen Portzline and Max Yelchin. Their group had sent people into Ash Grove for food every month since arriving at the Station. Two people went to the store, while a third person stayed behind at the rally point—Henry's house—on the outskirts of town in case anything went wrong.

In two years, nothing had ever gone wrong.

A light breeze passed over the dead man's salt-and-pepper hair —which he always kept slicked against his skull with a peppermint-scented pomade—lifting and snapping it like a horse's tail at the thick swarms of blowflies surrounding his head. Then the breeze reached Gemma, and buried beneath the putrid stench of decay was the vaguest tang of peppermint.

She doubled over, retched, and a dark shadow passed overhead, briefly blotting out the sun. When she wiped her mouth on the sleeve of her jacket, an enormous black bird descended from above and settled on the old man's shoulder. A crow or a raven—she never could tell the difference—watched her with possessive eyes. Massive claws tore into tattered flannel and decaying tissue as the bird tightened its grip on the old man's shoulder. She could hear his flesh ripping.

With a shaking hand, she snatched up a stone to launch at the bird. But she hesitated at the last moment, terrified of hitting Henry, and the throw went wide. The creature didn't move, only cocked its neck and studied her with mild disdain. She hurled two more rocks at the bird before it finally grew irritated enough to unfurl its wings and fly away. But it seemed to go reluctantly, and with a parting glance that said *I'll be back later, when you're gone.*

Her stomach rolled, but she swallowed hard and forced the sour bile down. She pulled her handheld radio from its spot on her belt.

Her gaze fell to her watch.

6:15 a.m.

Why hadn't Max and Allen called yet? They must've reached the store by now and would be wondering where Henry was. The old man always waited for them outside the delivery entrance of his store, a lit cigarette dangling from his fingers.

But they hadn't called, which meant something was wrong.

Not just here, but *there.*

Gemma brought the Motorola to her lips.

A loud burst of static erupted from the speaker, and she cried out and staggered away from the body. She felt the radio slip through her fingers, and it disappeared into the high grass.

"No!"

Falling to her knees, she ran her palms through the grass, her breaths coming in panicky gasps as she desperately searched for the Motorola. Tears made it impossible to see. Minutes earlier, she'd easily found rocks to hurl at the repulsive bird. Now beneath the high grass, nothing existed but loose dirt and clumps of dried mud.

"Come on!" she muttered. *"Please!"*

Finally—yes! —her hand closed around hard plastic. The Motorola.

But the sound of fireworks exploded—a series of distant, rapid-fire cracks that echoed off the surrounding mountains and reverberated throughout the valley. Like black lava erupting from a volcano, a flock of birds burst from their hiding places in the tall grass. They sailed west, away from the sound, fighting the wind and cawing indignantly as they passed overhead.

Fireworks? In April?

Then her eyes fell on Henry, and as her jumbled mind put the pieces together, the truth hit her in the gut.

Not fireworks.

Gunshots.

Gemma leapt up and ran, abandoning the open field for the concealment of the forest. In her mind's eye, she could see the soldiers clearly, crouched inside their snipers' nests in the second-floor windows of Henry's farmhouse. Soulless drones tracking her progress through the scopes of their rifles. Toying with her. Waiting until she reached the protection of the forest—and believed she'd escaped—to pull the trigger. Already crafting the lies they would tell about how she'd left them no choice but to kill her.

She made it to the wood line, grabbed onto the sturdy mass of an ancient oak, and flung herself behind it. She buried her face in the tree and screamed. Beneath her grasping fingers, the tree's brittle bark broke loose and crumbled like tiny pieces of confetti. When she could no longer scream, she covered her ears and prayed—not a cohesive prayer, by any means, but a series of rambling and repetitive utterances, such as *Please, God* and *Oh God, help me* and *Don't let me die.*

Seconds later, the gunfire ended, but it was replaced by an unsettling silence. Forcing herself to take slow, deep breaths, she uncovered her ears and leaned around the tree to survey the field.

There were no soldiers. No open windows in the farmhouse.

Nothing.

The shots had been close, but not that close. Not directed at her. But what about Ash Grove? Fresh panic began to build within her. What about Max and Allen? What if they'd been ambushed at the store?

She had to help them, but she had no weapons. Nothing except a hunting knife and her father's old Leatherman. Even if she could somehow make it into Ash Grove without soldiers spotting her, she would only succeed in getting herself killed or captured. She couldn't even call the others back at the Station for help. Radio communications would put the rest of the group in danger. Besides, if Max and Allen had been ambushed and captured, the soldiers would've taken possession of the men's radios.

The first crippling wave of grief swept over her and threatened to crush her.

They're dead. They're both dead.

"Gem?"

A voice, strained.

Her gaze dropped to the Motorola in her hand.

Max.

Tears of relief welled in her eyes. Another breeze passed over her, carrying with it the nauseating combination of peppermint and decay, but she barely noticed and raised the radio to her lips. "I'm here. What happened?"

His muttered response cut in and out, but she heard enough to understand what was happening. *"Task Force...Waiting for us...Allen's dead..."*

Gemma leaned against the tree, her legs going weak beneath her.

Allen's dead?

"I ran upstairs..."

Henry kept most of his nonperishable inventory in the attic space above his store. Customers weren't allowed up there, but Gemma had followed Henry up the narrow staircase on other food runs to help him carry boxes of supplies downstairs. Dimly-lit and crammed full of cardboard boxes, the storage area offered plenty of places to hide. But she couldn't remember if there were any windows. Any way for Max to escape.

"What should I do?" she whispered. "Can you get outside somehow?"

"Quiet. They're coming..."

He must've kept the push-to-talk button depressed—probably to keep her from calling out to him and giving away his position— so she heard everything that followed. She heard soldiers thundering up the wooden stairs, not even attempting to be quiet. She heard a loud crash, followed by braying laughter. A mocking voice called out, *"Come out, come out, wherever you are!"*

She heard Max scream in her ear, *"Gemma! Run!"*

She didn't think, only dropped the radio and sprinted away from the field. Away from the cross. Away from the ruined body of Henry Castern. Away from Ash Grove.

Away from Max.

She leaned into the mountain, breathing heavily, unable to think of anything except making it back to the Station. Allowing fear to drive her forward even as her chest grew tight with the effort. Sharp pains spread through her abdomen, but she raised her arms over her head until they subsided. Her thighs burned, but she forced herself to concentrate on the trees, opened her stride and ran faster. The trees guided her home, each one in succession, and she followed the barely-perceptible pattern of shallow notches carved into their trunks. Tears blurred her vision, causing her to stumble and fall many times, but each time she pushed herself to her feet and kept moving.

For eleven miles, she never stopped running.

Hours passed before she finally glimpsed the Station through a gap in the trees. Only then did she stop, doubling over, hands on her knees, perspiration dripping onto the forest floor. After a few seconds, she tilted her head back and focused on the building in disbelief.

Named for its resemblance to an old train depot, the ramshackle building had once housed a ticket booth, gift shop, and café. With its natural-wood siding and slanted roof of forest-green shingles, it blended seamlessly into the canopy of pines above, providing the perfect concealment. After many years of neglect, the surrounding forest had reclaimed the building. An ankle-deep layer of dead leaves covered the front porch, and thick strands of ivy curled around each of the support posts, ascending all the way to the roof before disappearing into the building's full rain gutters.

From the outside, the Station appeared abandoned.

The inside was a different story.

Gemma used the sleeve of her jacket to wipe sweat from her forehead. What would she tell the others? They'd demand answers. Answers she didn't have. Allen had no wife—she'd left him years earlier—but Max had a fiancé.

Brie would never forgive her for leaving Max. Gemma knew this because, had the situation been reversed, she never would've forgiven Brie for leaving Gavin behind.

I left him there. She felt sick with the realization. *I didn't even try to help him.*

She considered turning around and heading deeper into the forest, wandering aimlessly until her strength gave out and she fell to the ground, meeting her end somewhere soft and quiet and without causing anyone more pain. But her feet betrayed her and carried her up the sloped ridge toward the overgrown parking lot where knee-high crabgrass and sow thistle seeped through cracks in the asphalt like blood oozing from a cut. She staggered along like a condemned prisoner on her way to the execution chamber, her dread increasing with every step. A wooden sign hung from a post at the edge of the parking lot. Red lettering over a canvas of chipped white paint, the words so faded they were barely legible.

Welcome to the Mammoth Mine!

Coal Mine Tours Every Hour, On the Hour!

Beneath a makeshift shelter composed of eight log support beams and a painted-metal roof, the entrance was nothing more than a large hole cut into the side of the mountain. An old coal car rested on the tracks, its canary-yellow exterior bleached white by the sun.

Dimly aware of an ache in her hands, she glanced down and saw bloody ruts carved into the soft flesh of her palms, the tips of her fingernails coated with dried blood.

She hadn't felt a thing.

A door slammed nearby, drawing her attention to the old bathroom pavilion, a squat, coffee-colored building once utilized by patrons of the mine tour. Despite the lack of electricity, the toilets worked, as the property included a private well and septic system. Pouring a jug of water into the commode triggered a flush. An old-fashioned water pump stood just outside the bathrooms. She headed toward the pumps, needing to wash the blood from her hands before anyone saw it.

At the pavilion, Gavin Bonnar emerged from the men's room and lifted the handle of the water pump. Suddenly, his head snapped sharply in her direction, his jaw rigid, his right hand grasping for the knife on his belt.

"It's okay." She held up her hands, bloody palms facing him. "It's just me."

Those words echoed through her soul.

Just me.

"Gemma?"

Gavin lowered the pump's handle and broke into a run, leaping over fallen logs, his tattered, blue chambray shirt sailing behind him like a superhero's cape. He reached her and pulled her into a tight embrace. One she didn't deserve. She inhaled the clean scent of Ivory soap. He must've bathed after she left this morning.

Gavin examined her hands, his thumbs smearing the blood. "What's this? What happened to you?"

She tried to speak, to explain what had happened, but the words wouldn't come. The only word she managed to get out was: "Max."

A small crowd emerged from inside the Station, blinking in the late morning sunshine. They looked like survivors of a nuclear holocaust surfacing after decades spent underground. Thin. Pale. Filthy remnants of sun-faded clothing hanging from too-lean limbs.

A young woman with pale features and a blonde pixie-cut stepped out of their ranks. She crossed her tattooed arms over her chest. A tiny diamond sparkled on her left hand.

Brie Douglas.

Max's fiancé.

"Gemma?" she called out. "What's going on?"

There shouldn't have been any water remaining in Gemma's body. During her endless run back to camp, she should have cried and sweated out every ounce of moisture.

8

But then Brie went up on her tiptoes, searching the forest for her love, and Gemma thought of Taylor. Just a flash.

Then she collapsed and sobbed into Gavin's waiting arms. Hot tears reached her mouth, and she swallowed them like bitter pills, loathing the salty taste of her own guilt.

"An ambush," she breathed into Gavin's ear between sobs. "They're gone."

CHAPTER
TWO

Gemma peered through the glass door into the old café, where patrons of the mine tour had once gathered after a chilly ride into the mine to consume grilled hot dogs, chowder, and hand-dipped ice cream cones. Twenty people—the majority of Gemma's group —filled the small space. Some milled about, while others crowded around the small tables, clutching cups of coffee that Gemma knew from experience tasted like dirty creek water.

The dry-erase board standing outside the café read *Group Meeting – 4 p.m.*

Oliver Barnes stood at the front of the room, hands clasped in front of his waist, wearing loose-fitting slacks and a faded button-down shirt that was three sizes too big. When no one reacted to his order, he ran a hand through grey hair that hung past his earlobes. In his previous life, Oliver had been a podiatrist. He also used to be much heavier. That's all anyone knew about him. Except for running all of the group's official meetings, he pretty much kept to himself.

A cross hung on the café's front wall, just behind Oliver. Soon after they'd arrived at the Station, someone—either Oliver or Coop —had fashioned the cross out of two thick branches and secured it together with twine.

To Gemma, it looked fragile. Easily breakable.

"Okay, everyone," Oliver said. "Find your seats so we can get started."

She slipped through the glass door, easing it shut behind her, and scanned the café for a place to hide. An inconspicuous corner. A group to blend into. Anywhere she wouldn't be noticed.

"Gem!"

Her best friend, Addie Hogue, waved at her from one of the tables.

"Over here!"

Half of the room turned to gawk at her, and Gemma imagined the floor opening up and swallowing her whole. So much for being inconspicuous.

Addie rose and tried to pull Gemma into a tight embrace, but her belly proved to be an insurmountable barrier between them. With two months remaining until her due date, the buttons on Addie's threadbare jacket no longer closed. "We were so worried about you. Sophia said you rolled around all night long." She dragged Gemma to one of the empty seats at her table. "You look like you got run over by an eighteen-wheeler haulin' a load of cattle."

Addie had grown up on a dairy farm in Lancaster County, and although she kept it under control most of the time, stress tended to bring the Pennsylvania Dutch out of her.

Gemma sank into her chair, doing her best to ignore the dozens of eyes currently boring holes into her skin. "Is that why everyone's staring at me?"

Addie put an arm around her. "Nobody's staring, Gem. You're just tired. We all are. I'd forgotten how much I hate sleeping in the mine. Even with the cots and blankets, it's freezing down there. All of that damp air can't be good for the baby." She dropped her hand to her stomach, rubbing it protectively. "How about you? Did you sleep at all?"

"Yes," Gemma lied, stifling a yawn with one bandaged fist. "Where are the boys? Oliver will have them thrown off the tower if they miss another meeting. Especially this one."

Addie nodded at the door. "They should be back soon. They wanted to scout the woods between here and Ash Grove in case Max got away but was too injured to make it back to camp." She shuddered. "I can't imagine what Brie's going through."

Gemma's eyes dropped to the simple gold band on Addie's left hand, so different from the elaborate pearl ring on her own finger. She had no idea how Gavin had gotten the ring, but she suspected Henry Castern had something to do with it.

Probably suspecting that she'd reject a marriage proposal, Gavin had presented the ring as a promise. A promise they would stay together. Look out for one another. And eventually—when *she* was ready—get married. Despite her reservations, Gemma had accepted the ring and kissed him and tried to be happy about it.

She really had.

"Quiet down!" Oliver's deep baritone thundered over the din, instantly quieting the room and drawing dozens of wide-eyed stares. "Sorry to shout, but we need to get started. We've got a lot of work to get done before nightfall."

There weren't enough seats for everyone, so the women filled the tables and most of the men stood. The group's only child, Sophia Dillon, sat on the floor in the back of the room, fiery-red hair spilling down her back. Hunched over a pile of construction paper and crayons, pale eyebrows furrowed in concentration, the ten-year-old appeared entirely disinterested in the day's proceedings.

But Gemma knew better.

"We lost two members of our group yesterday," Oliver began, his eyes briefly shifting in Gemma's direction. "Allen Portzline and Max Yelchin. Two good men, always the first to volunteer for supply runs. Before we begin, I think we should bow our heads for a moment of—"

The café door banged open.

Every head in the room swiveled as Kyle Hogue and Gavin Bonnar burst through the door, breathing hard, eyes hidden behind dark sunglasses. Mud and dirt caked the bottoms of their boots, and a series of grimy footprints extended behind them into the old gift shop. They removed their sunglasses and stood in the doorway like a pair of disobedient boys awaiting their punishment.

Oliver's jaw tightened. "Nice entrance, gentlemen. Late, as always, and I see you've brought half of the forest along with you." He gestured toward the mud they'd dragged in.

Kyle gave him a dirty look. "We're late because we had to sprint most of the way back up the mountain. If it were up to me, we would've kept looking for Max instead of rushing back for this pointless—"

Gavin smacked Kyle in the arm, silencing him. "We're sorry, Oliver," he said. "We'll clean the floor after the meeting's over."

Oliver glared at Kyle. "Sit down. Both of you."

Gavin unhooked his backpack and let it fall to the floor. Then he collapsed into the empty chair next to Gemma and offered her an apologetic smile. "Hey." He always smelled good. Like pine trees and soap.

"Hey." She took in his sun-darkened skin, green eyes, and perfect Roman features set beneath a mop of unruly brownish-blonde hair. Even after two years of dating, she found it impossible to believe that someone as perfect as Gavin could have fallen in love with someone as imperfect as her.

If only she could love him back.

Across the table, Kyle pulled his chair close to Addie and draped an arm around her shoulders. She rested her head against his, her long, brown waves merging with his disheveled blonde hair. "Stop getting into trouble," she whispered to her husband. "You daresn't talk to Oliver like that."

Kyle winked at her. "Oh, daresn't I?

She elbowed him in the stomach. "Shut up."

A familiar ache began to build in Gemma's chest. Watching Addie and Kyle interact was like forcing a bitter pill down her throat over and over again, multiple times a day. Hating the breezy effortlessness of her best friend's relationship, Gemma found reasons to not be around them, such as volunteering for every food run, much to Gavin's chagrin. Like Gemma and Gavin, Addie and Kyle hadn't known each other before going into hiding. Yet their relationship seemed unshakeable, built on a solid foundation of love and trust. The worse things got, the stronger they became as a couple.

Gemma's relationship, on the other hand, felt as tenuous as a candle flame in a hurricane.

At the front of the room, Oliver said, "Let's pray."

Everyone bowed their heads. Even Sophia placed her crayon on the floor and closed her eyes.

Beneath the table, Gavin's hand found Gemma's, and she reminded herself to not pull away. She wasn't betraying anyone. Gavin was her boyfriend. He comforted her. But she couldn't shake the guilt she felt every time he touched her.

"Father," Oliver prayed, "we thank You for the bravery and the sacrifice of Allen Portzline. We know that You were with him yesterday. Even in his final moments, You never left his side, just as You will never leave ours. We thank You for Henry Castern and the kindness he's shown us over the years. While we don't yet know Max's fate, we take comfort in the knowledge that You are with him right now, wherever he is. Please guide our meeting today. Make Your answers known to us. As always, we ask for safety, protection, and the courage necessary to continue despite the battles ahead of us. We ask these things in Jesus' name, Amen."

Gemma casually slipped her hand out of Gavin's, and the guilt of betrayal—her ever-present companion—returned to a manageable level.

Oliver cleared his throat. "Alright. I think we should start with —"

"Oliver?"

Halfway across the room, Celia Birch shot out of her seat like a missile, one hip slamming into the table hard enough to propel it several inches across the floor. The other women sitting there shifted it back into place. "The Task Force set up an ambush at Henry's store. So, they know about us? They know we're up here?"

"We don't know that, Celia," Oliver replied, stroking his beard. "They did ambush our boys, so they must know we're within walking distance. But the Dragon's Back is a big mountain, and we're—"

"Henry Castern was crucified, wasn't he? That's the truth, isn't it?"

15

His eyes widened. He nodded in Sophia's direction, but the girl was smart enough to keep her expression from fluctuating. She didn't want to be asked to leave the meeting.

Oliver returned his attention to Celia and lowered his voice. "Celia, I understand your concerns, but we're not going to discuss what happened to Henry. Not here and certainly not now. The purpose of this meeting is to consider our next steps in the wake of everything that's happened over the past twenty-four hours."

"But *was* he?" she demanded, the pitch of her voice increasing with each word. "Is the Task Force *crucifying* people now? I mean, my goodness, Oliver, we have a right to know what's going on out there."

The woman spun around and directed her next question at Gemma. "What did you see yesterday?" she demanded. "Tell us what happened to that man."

Gemma straightened in her seat, one boot tapping out a nervous Morse code on the floor. She grasped the thin chain around her neck and wound it between her fingers. She'd never tell them what she'd actually seen in that field. Henry's eyes frozen open, a silent scream disfiguring his once-kind features. How it had smelled standing there, beneath the cross. How the bird had fixed its black eyes on her, its claws tearing at bloated flesh. She wouldn't tell them because they didn't want the truth. None of them did. Not even nosey old Celia Birch, despite what she might think, because the truth was far worse than anything her imagination could conjure up.

"Go on, Gemma," Celia prodded, a hard edge finding its way into her voice. "Tell us what you saw out there. We have a right to know."

When she didn't respond, Gavin came to her defense. "They crucified him, Celia. What more information do you need?" He spread his arms wide. "If anyone wants more details, feel free to hike down to Henry's house and look for yourself."

Mia Weber, the group's designated mother hen, rose and joined Oliver at the front of the room. "Celia, I understand you're upset," she said, tucking a strand of brown hair tinged with grey behind one ear. "We're all upset about Henry. And about losing two of our friends. But there are other things we need to consider right now. With Henry gone, we've lost our only supplier. We burn through our food stores quickly, so our monthly supply runs are vital. Henry was our lifeline. With him gone..." She wrung her hands together. "Well, we need to find another sympathizer. Someone who will help us. And fast."

Tom "Coop" Cooper spoke up from his spot near the exit. "Summer's coming. We'll be able to hunt and grow as much food as we safely can without drawing attention to ourselves. But what about next winter? Are we willing to send people into town to purchase food?"

"Into town?" Red splotches appeared on Celia's cheeks. "With the Task Force in the area? The same Task Force who just crucified someone for helping us?" She turned to address the room. "None of us have valid I.D.'s. We can't legally purchase food. We'd be lucky to make it back here without being detained. Any volunteers?"

Gavin's hand shot up. "I'll go."

"Me, too," Kyle agreed.

"Everyone, please," Oliver said, shaking his head. "We must trust that God will provide for our group, as He always has. We have to believe that He will send someone else to help us."

Tabitha Crispin raised her hand. "I agree with you, Oliver. We *should* trust in God. But things are different now, aren't they? After what happened to Henry, who on earth is going to risk their lives to help us?"

"I don't know, Tabby. I really don't. But that's for God to decide, isn't it?"

Kyle stretched his legs out in front of him. "My biggest concern right now isn't our stomachs but our safety. Since no one else wants to bring it up, I guess I'll be the one. What if Henry gave up our location before he died?"

Gemma released the chain of her necklace, suddenly overwhelmed by the need to defend Henry. "He wouldn't have given us away, Kyle. Not ever. You *know* that."

"You can't be sure about that, Gem. If they tortured him..."

She swallowed hard, forcing the image of Henry from her mind. "If he'd given up our location, they wouldn't have ambushed us on our supply run. They would've shown up right here, on our doorstep."

SUBVERSIVE

A murmur traveled from one side of the room to the other, rising and expanding like a cresting wave. It appeared that many in the group hadn't allowed themselves to consider that they owed their freedom—and quite possibly their lives—to a man most of them had never met.

Brie Douglas rose from her seat and joined Oliver and Mia at the front of the room. The voices died down as she turned to face the crowded tables, looking both tough and beautiful—part fairytale princess and part video game heroine. "What about Max? What's our plan to rescue him?"

The air inside the café turned as thick as the coagulated blood beneath Henry Castern's feet. No one spoke at first, and then everyone responded at once, dozens of voices, talking over each other. Some incredulous. Others angry.

Celia: "Rescue him! Are we planning *rescue* missions now? Who are we...the Army?"

Kyle: "Even if he's alive, we have no idea where he is."

Mia: "I understand how you feel, honey. But this isn't the time to make rash decisions."

Tabitha: "Oh, bless your heart."

After a few minutes, Oliver waved his hands in the air. "That's enough, everyone. Let's keep order." The room quieted down, and Oliver turned to Brie. "We can't help Max now. Not with the Task Force actively searching for us. We would only be sending out more people to be detained. More people with the potential to compromise our camp. We simply can't take that risk."

"Risk?" Brie gasped. "But what if one of you had been captured? Would you want us to forget about you?" Her eyes fell on Addie, who sat with one hand over her stomach, purposefully not looking at Brie. "Kyle goes on supply runs all the time. What if it had been him in Ash Grove yesterday, instead of Max? Would you want us to just forget him?"

The question brought Kyle to his feet. "If I had been in Ash Grove yesterday," he spoke through clenched teeth, "and if—*if*—I was still alive, I wouldn't expect anyone in this room to risk his life to rescue me. Not my wife. Not my friends. No one." He shot Brie a look before Addie pulled him back to his seat. "And neither would Max."

18

The girl's beautiful face contorted into a mask of revulsion. "You're pathetic," she muttered. "You're all cowards." Then she turned her icy gaze on Gemma. "How could you leave Max out there? Why didn't you do something? You could've gone into town and watched the store. You might've seen them bring him out. You should've done *something!*"

"That's enough," Gavin said. There was a sharpness to his voice that Gemma hadn't heard before. "I understand you're upset," he continued, softening his tone. "But there's nothing Gemma could have done to save Max. And everyone in this room knows that."

Brie's eyes darted from face to face, searching for an ally and finding none. Then she ran, sobbing, to the back of the café, and shoved the door open so hard that it slammed into the adjoining wall. She disappeared into the old gift shop, followed closely by Tabitha Crispin.

The door drifted shut behind them, revealing a long crack in the lower pane of glass.

At the front of the café, Oliver dropped his head into his hands, thin fingers massaging his temples. "We're not going to figure anything out like this," he finally said. "Not when emotions are running so high. After a night in the mine, we're all running on empty. Let's plan on meeting again tomorrow morning. Bring cooler heads and bright ideas, please."

Everyone nodded, clearly relieved to be spared the task of making any real decisions for one more day.

"In the meantime, let's start rationing our food stores," Oliver continued. "No more special occasions. I don't care whose birthday or bar mitzvah it is. Nothing extra gets used. If you're looking for a way to help, go outside and pick berries, dandelions, anything edible. If you don't know what's edible, ask someone." He squinted at the back of the room and raised his voice. "What about the four hens that Mr. Castern gave you last summer, young lady? Are you taking care of them?"

Sophia's head jerked up, a bewildered expression on her face. Never before had she been called upon to speak during a meeting. "Uh...they're good. I mean...they won't lay as many eggs during the winter, or if they start to molt. But, as of right now, they're each still laying an egg a day."

"Good. Keep them well-fed and watered. Those hens are very important to us. Do you understand? We need those eggs."

The little girl nodded, her cheeks as red as her hair.

Mia put a hand on Oliver's arm. "What about tonight, Ollie? Where should we sleep? It's so chilly in the mine. Do you think it's safe to sleep downstairs tonight?"

Oliver's mouth drew into a thin line. "Not until we're certain the soldiers have left the area. That could be days or months. But for now, we have to be careful. Especially at night. Sorry, everyone, but we may as well hunker down and get comfortable in there." He walked toward the door, buttoning his wool coat. "Now, if no one has anything else, I'm going up to the tower to check on Kurt and Jerry."

With their leader gone, the group began to trickle back to the mine until only Gemma and Gavin remained in the café. A daddy long-legs ambled across the wooden tabletop, pausing briefly when it reached Gemma's folded hands before changing directions and maneuvering around the obstacle. She resisted the urge to unleash her frustration on the arachnid by smashing it into the table with her fist.

Gavin remained by her side, unspeaking, his callused hands clasped on the table in front of him. Despite Gemma's efforts at tamping it down, the tension between them grew a little each day. Now it felt as if a great chasm separated them, one they could never hope to cross. But during those first lonely months at the Station, when she'd only wanted to fall asleep and never wake up, Gavin had been her salvation. Her tether to the world.

Yet he'd been suffering, too. After his mother committed suicide when he was a toddler, Gavin had gone to live with his maternal grandmother. A Christian woman, she'd taken him to church every Sunday and introduced him to the faith. Two months prior to coming to the Station, his grandmother had been detained at an unauthorized worship service. A service Gavin had missed because he'd been working that night.

Gemma knew he blamed himself for not being there to protect his grandmother, but he'd put his own pain aside and tried to be exactly what Gemma needed.

And he *was* what she needed.

Just not what she wanted.

He gestured to the mud-streaked floor. "Well, since Kyle didn't stick around to help clean up this mess, I better start mopping."

"He should be with Addie right now," Gemma replied. "I'll help you."

Gavin went outside to fill a bucket at the water pump, and Gemma retrieved two old mops from the supply closet. Together, they set to work mopping the drying mud from the floors of the café and gift shop, mimicking Celia Birch's failed interrogation attempt, and complaining about the dampness of the mine. When they grew tired of those topics, they started recalling fond memories of Henry Castern, a man who'd often sworn like the sailor he'd once been, but who would've given any of them the shirt off his back.

When they ran out of things to talk about, they worked in silence until no water remained in the bucket, and the café and gift shop floors shone like new.

At least Oliver would be happy.

Outside, Gemma clutched the railing as Gavin dumped the dirty water and climbed the warped steps to the porch. "Thanks for standing up for me during the meeting. You didn't have to do that. You should've just let them toss me into The Wishing Well," she said, referring to one of the mine's old vertical shafts, which was covered by a flimsy metal grate. At the bottom, pennies glimmered on damp rocks.

Gavin wiped his brow on his sleeve. "Nah, you don't deserve The Wishing Well. If anyone deserves to be thrown down there, it's Kyle for not helping me clean up this mess." He winked at her, and there was something so comforting about him—so familiar—that she could almost picture herself being happy with him.

"Seriously, don't worry about it," he said. "Brie's grieving over Max and doesn't know what to do with all of her anger, so she aimed it at you. Not because it's your fault, but because you're the most convenient target."

"It's not just Brie, though. I feel like everyone hates me for leaving Max."

"They don't, Gemma." He bowed to tighten the laces on his boots. "Everyone's just upset. As for Brie, you need to give her time to process everything. She'll figure it out. There really wasn't anything you could've done for Max."

"I could've gone after him."

"If you'd gone after him, you would've been detained. Or worse. And then I would've had no choice but to rescue you." He pushed his sleeves up theatrically, exposing his fairly-impressive forearms. "Of course, such a rescue attempt would require me to go full-on Rambo on the Task Force. Red headband. Camouflage paint. The whole deal. I would've asked Sophia to help with my face paint. Can you imagine how ridiculous I'd look storming a detention center with camouflage kittens and hearts all over my face?"

Gemma suppressed a laugh. "If anyone can pull off camouflage kittens, it's you."

Gavin stood and kissed her forehead, then her cheek, his lips lingering there. Finally, he pulled away. "I'm going fishing. All this talk about food and rationing is making me hungry. If you come, I'll bait your hook. You don't even have to fish. You can just sit on the rocks and ramble on about girl stuff."

She smirked at him. "Can we talk about makeup and ponies and which boys are the cutest?"

Gavin's eyes sparkled. "I'm the cutest boy on this mountain. Obviously."

"Obviously." She struggled to hold back a yawn. "Actually, I was thinking about sneaking down to the basement and taking a quick nap before dinner."

"You *should* be practicing your defensive tactics. Not sleeping."

Gemma groaned. Loudly.

Gavin was a stickler for self-defense. Before his grandmother was detained, he'd been attending classes at a technical college with the intention of becoming a police officer. He and Gemma practiced their self-defense moves nearly every day, although she had no idea why. Hand-to-hand combat, take-downs, even ground fighting...none of those skills would matter if a Task Force soldier had a gun aimed at your face.

"Nobody's going to attack me today. Right now, I need some sleep." She waved him away. "Get out of here. Bring me back some fish."

"Yeah, yeah. Enjoy your sneaky nap. Hopefully no one tips Oliver off."

Gemma raised an eyebrow. "Nobody *better* say anything to Oliver." When Gavin turned to leave, she grabbed his arm and added, "Please be careful."

"I'm just going to the creek, Gem." He winked at her. "I'll be fine."

After he left, Gemma descended the unlit back stairwell, one hand gripping the railing, the other sliding along the opposing wall. Thirteen steps down, she bent over and searched until her fingers closed around a lantern. She switched it on, illuminating a massive room that had once been used primarily as storage space for gift-shop items. Typically, rows of cots would've stretched out along either wall like Army barracks, but now all of the cots were gone, temporarily relocated to the mine. At the far corner stood an old coal-burning stove, powerful enough to heat the entire building. Their group had access to an unlimited supply of coal, courtesy of the mine, and the stove itself produced almost no visible smoke.

Several wool blankets were scattered around the room. Gemma gathered them into a pile in the corner and crawled on top of them, curling onto her side. She wrapped her arms protectively around herself, relishing the idea of an hour or two of quiet, uninterrupted sleep.

But as soon as her eyes closed, her exhausted mind betrayed her, conjuring images of spiders emerging from cracks in the walls. With no other prey to be found, they surrounded her, their fangs dripping poison, their many eyes burning with a ravenous hunger.

Gemma grabbed her flashlight and shone it at the walls, expecting to see thousands of black eyes staring back at her.

Nothing.

She directed the beam at the floor.

Empty.

Either the spiders had returned to their hiding places, or they'd never been there at all.

Gemma hated most bugs, but spiders terrified her. Those fears had only intensified after arriving at the Station. The tiny spiders she'd encountered at her house in Ridgefield had done little to prepare her for the kinds of spiders that existed on the Dragon's Back Mountain. The daddy-long-legs from the café was nothing compared to some of the monstrosities she'd seen skittering around the basement on eight legs. They were huge, and furry, and *very* aggressive. And they traveled at an impossible speed, darting behind discarded blankets and rucksacks like well-trained soldiers advancing on an objective. Most would boldly stand their ground against any would-be assassins. She'd even seen one charge at Gavin when he tried to kill it.

Stop it, she told herself. There aren't any spiders. Just go to sleep.

She pulled one of the blankets over her head, as if a thin layer of wool could protect her from an army of determined arachnids. But it was better than nothing.

She closed her eyes again, expecting sleep to elude her. But she drifted off instantly.

Surprisingly, she didn't dream of spiders.

She dreamt of dragons.

Colossal, fire-breathing behemoths from another age, massive wings rippling with veins, soar across the gunmetal sky and cast enormous shadows on the scorched earth. They belch flames from the depths of their stomachs, incinerating any unfortunate souls who still occupy the desolate landscape below. Nothing remains but crumbling relics of cities, charred beyond recognition. Gone are the trees and mountains and rivers. What had once been the vast expanse of the Atlantic Ocean is now a dustbowl packed with ash.

But in a corner of the world, hidden deep beneath the ground, Gemma stands in a narrow passageway, at the escape ladder that leads to the world above. Everyone is dead, including Sophia. Not from the dragons but from malnourishment and dehydration. The food has run out and the water sources have dried up. Now she stands alone, spindly legs wobbling unsteadily beneath her like a newborn calf, the sole inhabitant of a mine that will soon become her grave.

Unless...

Unless she uses what remains of her strength to climb the ladder. The ladder that had once served as an emergency egress for the coalminers in the event of a collapse, and which she must now use to face the dragons, once and for all.

She might still meet her end, but at least she will meet it on her feet.

The passageway narrows around her, pushing her toward the ladder, forcing her out, expelling her as if she is a bone lodged inside its throat.

She climbs. Not because she is brave, but because she has no other choice. She ascends toward the surface, thick mouthfuls of smoke filling her lungs. The monsters above screech in anticipation. They've known of her hiding place all along, and they've been biding their time, waiting for hunger or thirst or madness to drive her from her hole. In her mind, she can see them, perched on the charred remnants of the old train tracks that used to carry the mine's visitors across the mountainside, black-tinged saliva dripping from their gaping mouths.

Gemma wonders, in an absent sort of way, the same way she might have, at one point, wondered what kind of weather the day might bring, what it will feel like to be burned alive.

When she reaches the top, her hand finds a rung that is cold and wet and yields to her grip. It comes alive beneath her hand, not a ladder at all but the tail of a massive, coiled serpent. All at once, it frees itself from the wall and coils around her, upper body first, then down to her waist, holding her in place and silencing her scream before it can leave her throat. Each time she exhales, it tightens its grip a little more. When she looks up, the ladder is gone (had it ever been there?) and something is lowering itself down from the darkness. Two glowing embers emerging from the shadows, bearing down on her.

Eyes.

The head of the snake, coming to claim its prey.

Only it isn't a snake at all but a dragon from the world above—one with the body of a serpent—that has found its way into the mine.

Its massive body tightens, sealing off her airway. Gemma tries to scream. The pitiful wheeze that emerges reminds her of the winter wind that assaults the Station's windows at night. And then she hears the distant, repetitive cracking of someone breaking sticks apart to build a fire.

But no one is alive to build a fire.

She is listening to the sound of her ribs snapping.

Without warning, the dragon unleashes a furious howl and releases its grip on Gemma. And then there is a wonderful and terrible weightlessness as she begins to tumble into the darkness, her delicate body smashing into rocks and ladder rungs, bones shattering inside emaciated flesh.

And then—at the last second—someone grabs her hand and pulls her roughly upward.

She opens her eyes.

It's him.

Taylor.

One arm linked through the ladder, the other clutching her jacket. She hasn't seen him in years, but she knows it's him. He's slain the dragon. A thousand shades of crimson stream through the open hatch above, colors more vibrant and beautiful than anything she's ever seen before. It takes Gemma a few breaths to realize that the mountain is on fire.

Everything is burning.

Dark shapes circle above, drawn like vultures to the death scene playing out below.

A faint cry of despair leaves her lips.

There will be no escape for them.

But Taylor isn't giving up. He continues to climb, pulling her upward, until they explode out of the hatch. They collapse onto their backs and suck smoke-thickened air into their lungs.

A dark shape passes over them, so enormous it blocks out the sun, accompanied by a horrifying, ear-piercing shriek.

And then Taylor rolls on top of her, shielding her body with his own.

"It's okay," he whispers into her ear. "It's just a dream."

But there is doubt in his voice.

Then she peers over his shoulder and sees it. The dragon that will end both of their lives. The beast soars in, outstretched wings rippling with veins, talons glinting like polished steel. And when it opens its cavernous jaws, the blue flame anchored deep within its throat ignites like a flare.

The blast hits them both. It's like being trapped inside a great furnace. Gemma can think about nothing but the pain. Terrible, endless pain.

But, through it all, Taylor's arms remain tight around her, his desire to protect her palpable even as his body catches fire.

CHAPTER THREE

She thrashed against the wool blankets, smacking frantically at her arms and neck to put out the flames, desperate to make the pain stop. Her eyes snapped opened, and instead of a blazing mountainside, she saw an empty basement, illuminated only by the pale glow of a Coleman lantern.

No fire.

No dragons.

Overhead, the Station's front door opened and closed, the screech of unoiled hinges playing like a familiar tune. Heavy footsteps crossed the café, heading for the rear stairwell.

Oliver.

Boots thundered down the stairs. Moments later, the dark silhouette of a man appeared in the doorway. He hesitated on the last step, his head on a swivel, as if searching the room for something. Probably for *her*. Gemma held her breath and sank deeper into the blankets.

"Yoo-hoo?" the figure called in a high-pitched voice. A voice she recognized. "You awake, Sleeping Beauty?"

Kyle.

Her relief gave way to irritation. "What are you doing here? You scared me."

He emerged from the shadows, a rucksack slung across his back. "Why? Did you think I was Task Force or something?"

"Worse. I thought you were Oliver."

"Yikes." He squatted beside her, his eyes falling on the pile of blankets. "Nice little set-up you've got here, Alcott. Apparently, someone didn't get Oliver's memo about not sleeping in the Station."

"He said we couldn't spend the *night* in The Station," Gemma shot back. "He never said anything about naps."

"Whatever you say, Rip Van Winkle." Kyle pushed a strand of blond hair behind his ear. "Your boyfriend asked me to wake you if you weren't up by the time I got back. It's almost eight."

"What?" She fumbled with the buttons on her digital watch. "There's no way I slept for three hours."

Kyle illuminated the display on his own watch and held it out for her. "Next time, set an alarm or something. You missed dinner."

Her stomach growled in protest. "Did you have fish?"

Kyle rubbed his bleary eyes. "Nope. Your boyfriend is a horrible fisherman, Alcott. You know that. We had canned beans. Dandelion soup. And the pièce de résistance...smoked venison. Tender as my boot and every bit as tasty."

She imagined chewing on Kyle's boot and her hunger subsided a little. "Why didn't Gavin wake me himself?"

"He's in the tower with Oliver until the morning. I hiked up there with him after dinner. Anything to avoid going crazy in the mine. Of course, your dullard boyfriend forgot his coat. He asked me to bring it up to him, but since *you're* the love of his life, and such a wonderful person, I thought maybe you could..."

"Ugh, shut up, Kyle," Gemma groaned, shoving the blankets away. "Where's the stupid coat?"

He punched her lightly on the arm. "That's the spirit. It's on a table in the café, right next to your backpack. I took the liberty of putting a few bottles of water in there, in case you get thirsty on your hike."

"How incredibly thoughtful, although I wouldn't expect anything less from you. You're always thinking about everybody else."

"That's just the kind of guy I am." When she vacated her spot on the blankets, Kyle collapsed into her place. "This is great, Alcott. You warmed it up for me. Probably wouldn't hurt if I rested for a few minutes, right? Us menfolk need to keep our strength up so we can protect you helpless ladies."

"Right. By the way, watch out for spiders. A big hairy one scurried past me right before you came downstairs."

"Wait...what?"

Gemma laughed and headed for the stairway. She sat on the lowest step, tugged her boots on over her trousers, and grimaced at the pain in her thighs. In her old life, she'd run cross-country in high school, and she'd always relished the feeling of sore muscles after a difficult run. Pain was the physical proof of her efforts, evidence of her body getting stronger.

Now, the pain only reminded her of Max. The friend she'd abandoned.

The trumpeting sound of Kyle's snores followed her as she climbed the stairwell to the café. The smell of smoked meat lingered in the air, but she knew better than to search the kitchen for leftovers. Anything not consumed would've been promptly taken to the mine, away from the bugs and animals, where the chilly climate kept food fresh much longer. She grabbed a long-expired granola bar from the stash in the cupboard, dropped it into her backpack, and stepped onto the porch.

Zipping her jacket against the chill in the air, she drew in a deep breath and inhaled the musty scent of dead leaves and damp soil. To the left of the bathroom pavilion, a set of wooden steps led down a steep embankment to a mustard and rust-colored playset. Sophia's four brown hens circled its base, clucking softly and pecking the ground. Enjoying a quick snack before bed. Soon, they would retreat inside the playset's lookout tower to roost.

After receiving the chicks from Henry Castern as a gift the previous summer, Sophia had immediately named one after herself.

Then, adhering to Kyle's gentle suggestion, she'd christened the remaining ones Blanche, Dorothy, and Rose, unwittingly earning them the nickname "The Golden Girls" around the Station and spurring people to sing, *"Thank you for being a friend..."* whenever they walked past the chickens.

Gemma leaned over the railing to get a view of the sky. The sun was almost gone. No matter how fast she traveled, it would be dark before she made it back to the Station. She hated the woods at night. Even after two years, she hadn't grown used to the all-encompassing darkness, the animals that prowled at night, the strange sounds. Once, coming back from the bathroom pavilion at night, she'd heard a child screaming. Thinking it was Sophia, she'd run to check on the girl, but Sophia was fast asleep. Later, Oliver said it was probably a bobcat, but Gemma couldn't imagine any animal making such an awful sound.

She gripped the railing tighter.

Why had she agreed to hike up to the tower alone? She wanted to march downstairs, wake Kyle up, and make him do it.

But...he was married to her best friend. And he was about to become a father.

He had more to lose.

Reluctantly, she left the shelter of the porch and started climbing the ridge toward the fire tower. Years of dead leaves crunched under her boots and fallen branches snapped like brittle bones beneath her weight. To her left, a chipmunk scuttled up a tree and perched on a low branch, expressing its irritation by chirping at her and flicking its thin tail. A steady, hollow popping sound disturbed the silence of the forest, drawing her eyes upward, and she scanned the darkened canopy above until she spotted the black-and-white body and flaming-red crest of a pileated woodpecker. The bird paused for two or three seconds, unnerved by the unnatural sound of her footsteps, before resuming its assault on whatever insect or grub lay buried within the tree.

She trudged upward, the crisp breeze stroking her cheek like a mother's hand, invoking memories of a different time. Random scenes passed through her mind, one after another, like disjointed images on a broken movie reel. Construction paper flowers dangling from the ceiling of her childhood bedroom. Her mother's wrinkled hands covered in soap suds as she pulled them out of the sink and shook them off. The first cold autumn night of the year when the baseboard heaters kicked on and the coils burned eight months of dust away, saturating the house with the distinctive scent of heat. And the sweet fragrance of her father's pipe smoke as she leaned against him on their front porch swing.

Selfishly, she'd been upset when her father eventually quit smoking, wondering if she would ever smell something so wonderful again.

After twenty minutes of hiking and daydreaming, the forest thinned around her, and a massive clearing appeared through a gap in the trees. A fire tower rose from its center like an abandoned monument, six flights of metal stairs leading up to a glass-enclosed lookout at the top. The lookout provided their group with a panoramic view of Ash Grove and most of the roads leading to and from the mountain. It wasn't perfect, but the tower gave them some sense of security, or control, over their situation.

Gemma wondered if it wasn't a false sense of security.

The ground sloped down slightly as she stepped onto a narrow access road overgrown with years of brush and teeming with wildflowers. The heavily-rutted lane wound its way through the woods, extending from the base of the tower all the way to the isolated gravel artery that cut across the top of the mountain. There, a chained metal gate prevented access by anyone curious or daring enough to risk their vehicle's shocks and struts on the access road's nearly-impassible terrain. Every few days, someone from their group would hike down to the gate to make sure it was still secure and that no one had been tampering with the lock. As long as the gate remained locked, the only way the Task Force could reach them would be on foot.

Gemma approached the clearing, and a branch snapped nearby. She stopped and listened, the beam of her flashlight flitting from one shadow to another as she searched for the source of the noise. But there was nothing. No rustling leaves. Only silence. Probably a deer. Spooked by her approach, the animal must've abandoned the field for the darkness of the woods.

She resumed walking, the clearing now only a dozen feet away. Close enough that she could see a faint light flickering at the top of the tower. She wondered what Gavin and Oliver would talk about, stuck together all night in that tiny glass house. Neither of them were great conversationalists, and they didn't much like each other.

She imagined the two of them in the tower, engrossed in a staring contest for the ages, or perhaps telling ghost stories with their flashlights directed up at their chins. Or maybe engaged in an epic dance-off. All equally-likely possibilities, but she chose to distract herself from the encroaching darkness by concentrating on this last one, imagining Oliver moonwalking across the tower's creaky wooden floor, while Gavin countered him with a surprisingly-good version of The Robot.

Silly with exhaustion, Gemma began to giggle. She covered her mouth to muffle the sound—

A soldier stepped into her path.

He blocked her from the field—and the tower—with his assault rifle.

The laughter died on her lips. She stopped dead, frozen, her legs useless stumps beneath her body.

RUN.

The word flashed red in her mind, blinking on and off like a neon bar sign in a forgotten alleyway. She tried to obey, but her body wouldn't cooperate, her muscles as stiff and unyielding as if affected by rigor mortis. The familiar sounds of the forest disappeared, drowned out by a strange ringing in her ears. Instead of running, she focused on the soldier's rifle, mesmerized by the way the glass sight reflected the moonlight.

Maybe he's not a soldier. Maybe he's just a hunter.

But enough light remained in the sky for Gemma to see the details of his olive-drab fatigues and black tactical vest. A patch the color of dried blood adorned his left shoulder. A patch which bore the insignia of the Federal Task Force: an eagle soaring over two intersecting swords which, ironically, resembled an upside-down cross.

"Don't move." His voice was deep but hushed. "And don't scream."

He meant it.

The tower was so close. If she screamed, Gavin and Oliver would both come running.

But they would never reach her in time.

"Who are you?" the soldier demanded. "What's your name?"

She couldn't scream—there was no point—so she remained quiet, her eyes fixed on the ground.

Anything you say could lead him to the Station. Say nothing.

"If you're not going to talk to me, should I ask your friends up in the tower?"

"No!" Gemma cried out. She couldn't risk more bloodshed, not after what happened to Max and Allen. And Henry. She whispered, "Please. I'll do whatever you want. Just leave them alone."

"All I want is your name."

It took everything she had to force her name from her mouth. "Gemma," she muttered. "My name is Gemma."

The soldier drew in a sharp breath, then took a cautious step toward her, lowering the barrel of his rifle slightly. She could no longer see the moonlight in the sight, so she focused on the eyes beyond it. Pale-blue eyes. Almost as familiar to her as her own.

She would've known them anywhere.

"What did you say?" He inched closer to her. The last vestiges of light in the sky pierced the canopy above and revealed the hauntingly familiar details of his face: angular jaw, unshaven chin, and a tiny mole low on his right cheek.

Gemma felt the blood drain from her face. Only by some miracle did she remain on her feet.

She saw recognition dawn in the soldier's eyes, and she forced herself to say his name.

"Taylor?"

CHAPTER FOUR

Ten Years Earlier

Her mother's bare right foot propelled them slowly back and forth on the wooden porch swing. The sun disappeared below the neighboring ridgeline, taking the heat of the day with it. Thick clouds of insects accompanied the darkness. They descended upon Ridgefield like an Egyptian plague, swarming every streetlight as far as Gemma could see. Their frantic throngs disturbed only by the occasional breeze carrying with it the sweet aroma of hand-spun cotton candy. The kind that disintegrates instantly on your tongue.

The distant sound of a rock band drifted up from the carnival grounds. It was the Mono-Tones, the last band of carnival week. Gemma could feel the night slipping through her fingers like water. By morning, it would all be gone. All of the rides and food and music. The traveling carnival would take its magic with it, leaving nothing behind but a muddy field strewn with crushed popcorn boxes and browning caramel-apple cores.

She lowered her voice in an effort to sound more mature. "If you don't want to go to the carnival, can't I just go by myself? I'm not a baby."

"That's true, Gem. But eleven isn't grown up, either."

"What do you think's going to happen?" she whined. "Do you think I'm going to get kidnapped or something?" Then, realizing her mom might see that as a distinct possibility, she quickly added, "Because I won't. I know all about strangers. We had a whole assembly on stranger danger in school. I still have the pamphlets in my room."

"That's wonderful." Her mother gave the swing a hard shove with her foot. They sailed forward, and Gemma's feet came within inches of touching the porch railing. "Those pamphlets should render you kidnap-proof."

"Mom. That's sarcasm. We don't do sarcasm."

Her mother groaned, probably wishing Gemma's father were home to put a quick end to the argument. "You're right, honey. I'm sorry." She examined her hands—long and slender fingers, nails clipped short and painted the palest shade of pink. "Look, I'm not worried about you getting kidnapped. I know you're a very responsible girl. That's not the problem."

"Then what is it? Why can't I go?"

A shadow passed over her mother's face. "It has nothing to do with you. It's this town. Things are...different than they used to be. You know that, right? Some people treat us differently because of what we believe. Your father and I think it's better if we just stay away from them. Do you understand?"

Gemma nodded, pretending to know what her mother was referring to, but she really had no idea. The truth was, things didn't seem all that different to her. There were some kids at school who wouldn't talk to her anymore, and others who called her mean names she didn't understand, but she still had plenty of friends. Something else must've happened. Something her parents didn't want to tell her. They whispered to each other when they thought she wasn't paying attention. She wanted to scold them for being rude, but it usually seemed best to stay quiet.

Down at the carnival, the band began to play "Old Time Rock n Roll." Gemma's father loved Bob Seger. If he were home instead of working late again, he might take her to the carnival to hear the band.

"If you're worried, why don't you come with me?" This wasn't Gemma's preferred option, but she was getting desperate. "I promise, we won't stay long."

"Absolutely not."

"But, why?" she whined.

"I have my reasons." Her mother used the clipped tone that said the topic was closed.

They remained on the swing, rocking back and forth in an uncomfortable silence until the Seger song ended. Then her mother muttered. "Alright."

Gemma lifted her head. "What?"

"One ride. I'm giving you enough money for one ride. Pick your favorite and ride it. I'll even give you a little extra for a bag of cotton candy if you promise to do exactly as I've asked. One ride. Then you come straight home. I expect you back here in a half-hour."

Gemma slid forward on the swing and stopped its motion with her flip-flops. "Thank you!" She threw her arms around her mother's neck and squeezed. "Thank you, thank you, thank you."

"One ride, Gemma. I mean it. And don't talk to anyone, okay? No one."

"Okay," she agreed. "I won't."

Although she wondered about the reason for this last command, she didn't bother to ask why.

She was already thinking of Taylor.

The carnival grounds sat on a marshy plot of land next to Baxter's Creek, which overflowed its banks after every rainstorm. Consequently, the surrounding ground was perpetually soft and muddy. Gemma's flip-flops sank into the mucky grass with each step before pulling loose with a wet sucking sound that made her think of the kissing noises some of the older boys on her bus made when pretty girls walked down the aisle.

They never did that for Gemma, of course. Probably because she wasn't pretty enough.

Out of fear of losing a flip-flop, she abandoned the grass for the stone-covered pathway that wound past the kiddie rides. The path wouldn't take her all the way to the bigger rides, but it would get her close enough to see what she was hoping to see.

Over at the bandstand, the cover band coaxed the crowd from their lawn chairs with the opening bars of Sweet Home Alabama. A mob of older women shrieked like excited birds and ran for the empty lawn in front of the stage, where they shook their bodies and danced in a way that made the men in the crowd hoot and cheer.

Gemma approached the kiddie rides. A squadron of large purple dragons sailed by, transporting their squealing passengers through the air like flying aces. Further on, an electric train endlessly circled a small track, its conductor slumped over and seemingly asleep on a lawn chair near the control panel while a legion of fruit flies swarmed his can of Coca-Cola. The train's only passengers—a pair of towheaded twin boys—sat jammed together inside the front car, looking genuinely bored.

Gemma bypassed the carousel, the funhouse, and the giant slide—she wouldn't waste her one ride on any of those snoozers— and kept her head low as she passed the never-ending row of game tents. She had no money for games, and most of the prizes were junk anyway: odd-smelling stuffed animals and inflatables that would spring holes before the night's end. But she made the mistake of locking eyes with a barrel-chested carnival worker. The man abandoned the fluorescent glow of his booth and stepped in front of her.

"Wanna give it try, girlie?" He gestured toward his balloon dart game, his grin widening to reveal several missing teeth. "Three throws for a dollar. Every balloon's a winner. Ya can't lose."

Gemma shook her head "No, thank you."

"Come on, kid. Did ya hear what I said? I said, ya can't lose."

"Sorry."

When he realized she wasn't going to change her mind, the man's grin vanished. "Go on, then," he muttered, jamming a hand into the pocket of his cargo shorts and pulling out a round can of Skoal. "Get outta here, ya little brat."

Gemma tried to pretend that she hadn't heard those angry words and that she couldn't feel his hateful gaze following her as she walked away. Without realizing she was doing it, she reached inside her tank top and pulled out the necklace she kept hidden beneath the thin fabric of her shirt. Her fingers closed around the tiny silver cross—a gift from her father for her tenth birthday—and squeezed it for comfort.

Maybe her mother was right.

Maybe coming to the carnival hadn't been the best idea.

She almost turned around right then and went home, although it would've meant risking another trip past the carnie. But she no longer cared about the ride or the cotton candy. She only wanted to get home.

Gemma turned halfway around...and stopped.

A few yards away, Taylor Nolan stood beneath the colorful arc of the Ferris Wheel, part of a group of eighth-graders that included another boy and two girls. Gemma never saw him anymore, not since he stopped attending services with his father, so she wasn't prepared for how different he looked. He'd grown noticeably taller, and his dark hair was longer than she remembered. So long that, as he talked to his friends, he was constantly pushing it out of his eyes.

The other boy had a military-style buzzcut and wasn't even trying to hide the fact that he was smoking. As for the girls, one was tall with dark hair, while the other was short and very pretty, with straight blonde hair that flowed to her waist. The complete opposite of Gemma's untamable auburn waves. She recognized the blonde as Amber MacLeay, and the only thing she knew about Amber was that she played the flute in the middle-school band. It seemed like the prettiest girls always played the flute. For her part, Gemma had made a half-hearted attempt at learning the alto saxophone before quitting in disgrace.

Amber leaned toward the dark-haired girl and whispered something in her ear. The girls disintegrated into a fit of giggles. The boys didn't seem to notice, however. They were too busy laughing at a pair of high schoolers who were aggressively making out at the top of the Ferris Wheel.

Gemma was trying to decide if she should walk over and say hi to Taylor when Amber reached out and took his hand.

She waited for Taylor to rip his hand away in disgust. To shove the girl backward, maybe hard enough that she fell over, muddying her jean shorts. Or even punch her. Boys should never hit girls, but Gemma wouldn't have held it against him. After all, he was only fourteen. Fourteen-year-old boys didn't hold hands with girls, did they? Especially in front of their friends.

But Taylor didn't pull away, and Gemma could do nothing but count off the seconds in her mind as she waited for something— anything—to bring the nightmare to an end.

Five, six, seven...

A pair of massive hands grabbed her from behind.

She cried out in surprise and tried to run, but the ground was wet and she promptly tripped, landing on all fours on the soggy grass. A sharp rock gouged a crevice into her right kneecap. Mud sprayed all over the front of her t-shirt and shorts. Some of it got into her mouth—it tasted like sucking on a penny—and she promptly spat it out. Hot tears of pain and humiliation flooded her eyes as she looked up at her attacker.

The carnival worker loomed over her, his lower lip jutting out unnaturally to accommodate the wad of tobacco in his mouth. "What's yer problem? Why ya tryin' to run from me?"

"Why'd you grab me?" Gemma tried to rub the tears from her eyes, but only succeeded in smearing more mud on her face. "You scared me."

Like a magician performing a trick, the carnie unclenched his palm and Gemma's necklace tumbled out of his fist and hung suspended in the air. "You dropped this. Chain must've broke."

The sight of her beautiful necklace, covered in mud and hanging from the carnie's oil-stained hands, made her want to cry harder. She reached for the necklace. "Thank you."

The carnie yanked the necklace away and spat a dark streak into the grass next to her. "Where're your parents? Ya shouldn't be wearin' somethin' like this in public. People don't like 'em."

By now, curious onlookers had gathered around, drawn to the drama playing out in front of them. A few pulled out their phones to record the incident. Gemma looked from face to face, silently pleading for help. But when they saw the silver cross dangling from the carnie's hand, several of the onlookers returned their phones to their pockets and walked away, shaking their heads.

But a few stayed behind to watch.

"Please," she whispered. "I'll go home. Just give it back."

The man guffawed. "Give it back? Why would I give—"

"Hey!" a voice shouted from behind Gemma. "Get away from her!"

The crowd parted as Taylor appeared, shoving his way past the few remaining onlookers. He stepped directly between her and the carnie. "Leave her alone, man. She's just a kid."

The carnie's dark eyes iced over. He strutted forward, chest puffed out like a rooster, and jammed a thick index finger into Taylor's chest. "Boy, you best not shoot your mouth off at me," he growled, barely loud enough for Gemma to hear. He gestured to the pouch tied around his waist. "Because, next time, I'm going to shove one of these darts down your throat."

Taylor didn't back down. Didn't even flinch. "Did everybody hear that?" he shouted to the onlookers. "This creep just threatened to shove a dart down my throat."

The carnie appeared to notice the few spectators still lingering around, and the glazed look in his eyes vanished. "Are ya nuts, boy? I didn't do anything of the sort." He took a step back, unfolded his fist, and showed Gemma's necklace to the spectators. "I was just sayin' how this girl's walkin' around in public wearin' this garbage, and how I ought to call the authorities and report her right now."

"When you call, don't forget to mention how you assaulted her."

The man returned his attention to Taylor. "What're you talkin' about?"

"Don't try to deny it. I saw the whole thing. You grabbed her and threw her to the ground. That sounds like an assault to me."

The carnie's face turned as red as the half-inflated balloons hanging in his booth. "I didn't throw her! She fell!"

"That's not what it looked like to me."

The carnie worked the tobacco in his lip, nostrils flaring, his gaze flitting from Taylor to Gemma and back again. After a few seconds, he shrugged and spat more tobacco juice into the dirt next to Gemma. She cringed away from it, but a few brown droplets hit her bare arm. She quickly wiped them away, her dirty hand leaving a streak of mud from her shoulder to her elbow.

"Ya know what? It ain't even worth it." He crumpled Gemma's necklace in his palm and tossed it into a nearby trashcan where it disappeared, absorbed into the overflowing pile of rubbish.

"No!" Gemma cried out. She launched herself to her feet and tried to run to the garbage can, but Taylor grabbed her arms and held her back.

"Just leave it," he whispered into her ear.

Her treasured necklace. The first real piece of jewelry she'd ever owned. Gone forever. And for what? Anger burned inside her, an unfamiliar but not entirely unwelcome feeling. She swung around to face the carnie. Imagined herself grabbing a handful of darts from his pouch and hurling them at his ugly face.

He dismissed her with a wave. "Get outta here before I have ya both thrown out."

"Yeah, somehow, I doubt you have that kind of power," Taylor said.

The carnie grunted and strolled away. With the action over, the rest of the crowd lost interest and began to disperse.

Taylor released his hold on Gemma's arms. "Are you okay?"

She nodded, holding back tears. "I just...I want to go home."

"Come on. I'll walk you."

Gemma wiped at her leaking nose, her tears instantly drying up. Taylor Nolan wanted to walk her home? In an instant, she forgot about the embarrassment. The anger. The unfairness of it all. She even forgot about her precious necklace. When Taylor put his arm around her shoulders, her heart inflated into a balloon of happiness, one the carnie could never hope to pierce, not even with his sharpest dart.

And then, like a beautiful blonde demon summoned by the devil himself, Amber MacLeay appeared in front of them. She stood with her palms on her hips, her perfectly tiny button nose wrinkling in disapproval as her eyes settled upon Gemma.

Under Amber's piercing gaze, Taylor's arm suddenly felt like a lead weight draped over Gemma's shoulders. Like one of those aprons the hygienist used whenever Gemma got x-rays taken at the dentist's office. Only Taylor's arm felt much heavier. Heavy enough to drive her slowly, inch-by-inch, into the ground.

But she didn't step out from under it.

"Um...?" Amber's heavily-glossed lips formed into an exaggerated pout. She was clearly trying to be adorable and succeeding. "Taylor? I thought we were going to walk around together."

"Yeah," he replied. "You guys go ahead. I know this kid, so I should walk her home. I'll be back in a few minutes."

Kid. That word always irritated Gemma when someone applied it to her, and it was especially annoying coming out of Taylor's mouth. But that was the least of her concerns right now. Instead, she watched as Amber's eyes left Taylor and settled on her. When their eyes met, the older girl's face hardened into something cold and unyielding. A marble bust of hatred. Icy fingers of fear wrapped themselves around Gemma's heart.

She was only eleven, but she was perceptive enough to know that she'd just made her first real enemy. Not counting the carnie.

"Come on, let's get out of here." Taylor guided her away from the game booths and down the pathway toward the exit. Although his arm remained around her, there was nothing romantic in the gesture. He was acting more like a protective older brother than a boyfriend. Which, she supposed, is exactly how he saw himself. But she was far too elated to be offended. Even Amber MacLeay slipped from her mind, her fear of the older girl's wrath thawing under the warmth of Taylor's embrace.

"Sorry about your clothes," he whispered. "I'd let you wear my t-shirt, but then everyone would be forced to gaze upon my amazing physique, and that's not fair to the other guys here."

Gemma giggled at this image, her face growing warm. "You're so weird."

He grabbed a few napkins from a nearby hot dog stand and handed them to Gemma, gesturing to the mud on her face. She wiped the mud away, humiliated.

"Hey, don't worry about that guy back there, okay?" Taylor said. "He won't bother you again. You saw how quickly he backed down when I confronted him, and he could've snapped me in half like a twig."

She tossed the napkins into the trash. "Weren't you scared?"

"Of *that* guy? No way. If all else failed, I could've outrun him."

Gemma laughed, imagining Taylor leading the overweight carnie on a chase through the carnival grounds. Past the Tilt-a-Whirl and the lemonade stand and the Bingo pavilion. When the man collapsed from exhaustion, Taylor would find Gemma and sweep her into his arms. And then, with everyone watching—including the blonde demon herself—they would share their first kiss. A long, passionate one, just like in the movies.

She turned away, trying to hide her face from Taylor. If picturing him shirtless had made her blush, she couldn't imagine what her cheeks must look like now.

They escaped the carnival grounds unnoticed, turned onto Low Street, and climbed the hill toward Ridgefield's main drag. Along the way, they passed several late arrivals, most of them teenage boy/girl pairs holding hands or otherwise clinging to one another. Perhaps it was only a coincidence, but as the couples passed by, Gemma felt Taylor discreetly withdraw his arm from her shoulder.

She immediately missed it.

"By the way, I'm sorry about your necklace."

"Thanks." She hated thinking about her beautiful necklace buried in a pile of garbage. "It's no big deal."

"You shouldn't wear stuff like that, you know," he offered quietly. "Even if you think you can hide it, it's better to not take the chance."

What did that even mean? Why couldn't she wear her necklace in public? And why had a little silver cross upset the carnie so much? None of it made any sense. She couldn't even ask her parents because they'd told her never to wear the necklace outside the house, and she'd disobeyed them by wearing it to the carnival. But even if she could ask them, they wouldn't tell her the truth. They were always trying to shield her from everything. They treated her like a baby. It wasn't fair.

They continued in silence until Gemma worked up the courage to ask Taylor the question she'd been wanting to ask him for months. "Taylor?"

"Yeah."

"Why don't you come anymore? To church, I mean."

He remained quiet for a long time, long enough that she thought he might not answer at all. And then he said, with a shrug, "That's my dad's thing, Gemma. Not mine."

"But...don't you miss everyone?"

Hidden meaning: Don't you miss me?

"Not enough to come back."

She tried not to let this admission hurt her feelings.

When they reached the intersection of Low and Main, Taylor raised his arm to stop her. There were very few cars on the road, but he still checked both directions before lightly touching her elbow as a signal for her to cross. When he touched her arm, she almost blurted out a dozen different things. How she missed him. How she hoped, every time she showed up at a worship service, that he might be there. How she thought about him and prayed for him all the time, especially since his mom died.

But she said none of this.

"Is your dad okay?" she finally blurted out. The moment the words left her mouth, she wanted to punch herself. What a dumb question. Of course, Pastor Nolan wasn't okay. He'd lost his wife— the love of his life—to cancer. Yes, it had been two years, and he was starting to smile during services again. But the sadness remained in his eyes.

"I don't know." Taylor brushed the hair away from his eyes. "He doesn't really talk about my mom anymore. At least, not with me." He sounded a little bitter.

"What about you? Are you okay?"

"Me?" Taylor seemed caught off-guard by the question, as if it was the first time he'd been asked about himself. He stuffed his hands into his pockets. "I'm fine."

He wasn't fine. Anyone could see that. But she didn't push him.

No other words passed between them until they reached her street. Gemma saw the two-story house ahead: pale blue with yellow shutters, like something out of a storybook. The downstairs was dark, but the lights were on in her parent's bedroom. Her mother would be reading a book in bed. One of her mystery novels. Her father's office light was also on, which meant, although he was home, he was still not finished with work for the day. If Gemma was lucky, she would be able to sneak up to her room and change into her pajamas before her mother saw her mud-spattered clothes.

She paused at the bottom of the porch steps. "Thanks for walking me home," she said. "And for...you know...everything else."

"Don't worry about it," he said. "But do me a favor and stay away from the carnival for the rest of the night. I don't need any more trouble."

"Okay." She didn't want to think about him returning to the carnival. Amber would be waiting for him. Waiting to hold his hand. Maybe even waiting to kiss him. "Bye."

"See you later, Gemma."

Taylor walked away.

She climbed the steps to her porch, remembering Taylor in a black suit several sizes too big for him, slumped in the front row of the funeral home. His head hanging so low that his chin nearly touched his chest. Pastor Nolan standing nearby, a few feet away from his wife's casket, shaking hands and accepting hugs and words of comfort. Getting all of the attention. All of the support. Everyone bypassed Taylor entirely, as if the sight of a grieving child was too difficult to acknowledge. But not Gemma. When her parents stepped forward to embrace Pastor Nolan, she slipped away from them and sat on a chair beside Taylor. After a few minutes, she placed her hand lightly on top of his. Only then did he seem to notice her, glancing up with red-rimmed eyes for a second before dropping his head back to his chest.

But he didn't pull his hand away.

Gemma released the doorknob and ran to the edge of the porch. "Taylor?"

He was already past her neighbor's house and about to cross the street, but when he heard her calling his name, he stopped walking and turned around. The street light directly above his head illuminated him like a spotlight. "Yeah?"

Gemma took a deep breath. "That girl from the carnival? Amber?" Her cheeks betrayed her, heating up again. Hopefully, he was too far away to notice her blushing. "I was just wondering...is she, like, your girlfriend or something?"

For a few seconds, Taylor seemed confused. And then, gradually, something like realization dawned in his eyes. He smiled at her. "No. She wants to be, but she isn't."

A butterfly of possibility fluttered in Gemma's chest, and she returned his smile with a brighter one of her own.

"That's good."

CHAPTER
FIVE

When the sun descended below the horizon, the wind picked up on the Dragon's Back Mountain, setting hundreds of dead leaves into orbit like colorful space shuttles. They sailed into the open field, gradually losing altitude and scuttling along the ground before coming to rest at the base of the lookout tower.

Cold air assaulted the back of Gemma's neck, chilling her skin and raising goosebumps on her arms. Her eyes drifted from the tower to the nametape on the soldier's uniform.

Nolan.

Taylor lowered the rifle the rest of the way, until the barrel pointed at the ground. "Gemma?"

And then—she couldn't have stopped herself if she'd tried—Gemma rushed forward, threw her arms around his shoulders, and buried her face in the dark fabric of his uniform. Despite the cold, beads of perspiration glistened on the back of his neck. His clothes smelled like charred wood, as if he'd recently spent time tending a campfire. She waited for him to shove her away—she could feel his internal struggle in the slight stiffening of his muscles—but then he relented, slinging his rifle over his shoulder and wrapping his arms tightly around her.

"I missed you." Her lips brushed the skin below his ear. Everything about him reminded her of home. Of that last night, two years earlier, just before she'd gone into hiding. "I didn't think I'd ever see you again."

Taylor held her close, his hands passing through her hair, his breath warm against her neck. "I didn't know it was you. I wouldn't have..."

"No, it's okay." She pulled away to examine his face. To convince herself that he was real. Flesh and blood, not just another dream. A fresh laceration and dried blood dotted his forehead, just above his left eye. She ran her index finger over the cut. "What happened?"

"Tree branch."

With their faces only inches apart, she found herself moving closer to him. His rough hands cupped her cheeks, guiding her lips toward his.

From the direction of the field came: "Kyle? That you?"

At the sound of her boyfriend's voice, Gemma shoved Taylor away. A single dark shape—Gavin—was halfway between the fire tower and the wood line and traveling swiftly in her direction.

Taylor unslung his rifle and slipped into the shadows of a nearby tree. "Your flashlight. He can see it."

She fumbled with the Maglite, trying to turn it off.

"Leave it. It's too late." Taylor's eyes remained fixed on Gavin. "Tell him you stopped to go to the bathroom. Make something up. But can we meet later? Around midnight? I need to talk to you."

She didn't hesitate. "Yes!"

"Can you get away without people realizing you're gone?"

Gemma's heart dropped. She could've slipped out of the Station easily. But Oliver wanted them to spend another night in the mine, where the main entrance was the only way in or out, and it would be guarded all night long.

Unless...

She tugged at the chain around her neck, considering another possibility. The idea terrified her, but if she wanted to see Taylor

52

tonight, it might be the only way. Before she could change her mind, she whispered, "Quick. Do you have a pen?"

Taylor produced a ballpoint pen from the pocket of his fatigues. "I don't have anything to write on."

"That's okay."

Gemma took his hand and pulled up his sleeve, exposing his left forearm and ten black numbers tattooed in small print on his inner wrist. "Taylor? What's—"

"Hurry up."

"Okay." She scrawled a crude map directly above the numbers, using the fire tower as a reference point. It was a horrible sketch—the distances between the various reference points weren't even close to being accurate—but she prayed it would be good enough to guide him to the right place.

He touched her arm. "Midnight."

She nodded.

And then he disappeared into the forest.

Gavin's eyes widened as she emerged from the woods. "Gemma?" He scanned the trees behind her. "What are you doing here? Where's Kyle?"

She dropped her backpack to the ground and crouched to unzip it. Dozens of tiny leafhoppers launched themselves out of a patch of goldenrod, several of them alighting on her arm. She pulled the coat out of the bag and handed it to Gavin. "Kyle needed a break, so I told him I'd bring you your coat."

His jaw tightened. "We *all* need a break. That doesn't give him the right to send you up here by yourself. Especially at night." He reached for the Motorola on his belt. Then, seeming to remember that their group was still operating under radio silence, he clenched his hand into a fist. "You know, Kyle never thinks. I'm sure he'd love it if I asked *his* wife to run an errand for me alone at night."

Before she could stop the words: "I'm not your wife, Gavin."

He opened his mouth to speak, but no words emerged, as if he'd been struck dumb. After a few seconds, he dropped his gaze to the ground, but she'd seen the pain in his eyes. Pain *she'd* caused. Pain he didn't deserve. He'd never been anything but good to her.

She closed the distance between them and brought her hands to his face. "I'm sorry," she whispered, lightly touching her lips to his. "I didn't mean it like that. All I'm saying is that I can handle myself. You don't have to worry about me."

Gavin wrapped his arms around her waist and pulled her close. "I know you can take care of yourself, Gem," he said. "I've seen you do it. But we're in this together, you and me. I *want* to take care of you, if you ever decide to let me."

If only it could be that simple. She loved Gavin; she really did. He was her best friend. But her bond with Taylor felt impenetrable, as if they were bound together not by invisible string but steel cables. Even now, she couldn't stop thinking about Taylor's hands on her face, the warmth of his breath against her neck.

What if he was watching her now, from the darkness of the forest?

The thought was jarring, and she gave Gavin a playful push to increase the distance between them. "Hey, speaking of taking care of me, what happened to my dinner? I thought we were having fish tonight."

Gavin passed a hand through his hair and laughed. "Yeah, about that..."

She stooped down to tighten the laces on her boots, her eyes searching the darkened woods. The forest stretched out below them, level for a few hundred yards before steeply dropping away. Ash Grove lay several miles to the west, the illuminated spire of the town's old church steeple visible over the slope of the next ridge. At the opposite end of town, the tip of Henry Castern's property jutted out from the trees like an accusatory finger.

She wondered if anyone had cut him down yet? Or was he still out there?

"What happened back there, by the way?" Gavin's voice interrupted her thoughts. "We saw the light from your flashlight, but then you stopped."

"Just going to the bathroom." She hated the bitter taste of the lie on her lips.

Gavin nodded, seeming to accept this answer, then picked up her backpack and held it as she shrugged her arms through the straps. He brushed her hair from beneath the straps before allowing it to settle on her shoulders. "You're so beautiful, Gem," he whispered into her ear. Then he spun her around and kissed her—a deep, passionate kiss. She kissed him back, all the while trying to push any thoughts of Taylor from her mind. Desperately hoping he wasn't still in the trees somewhere, watching her.

Finally, they pulled apart.

"I should get going," she said.

Gavin nodded. "I'll walk you back. Just give me a second to tell Oliver."

"No." She grabbed his arm before he could walk away. "Please. I'll be fine, I promise. You don't have to walk me back. If a bear attacks me, I'll use one of your fancy self-defense moves to fight him off."

He didn't look convinced. "Are you sure?"

"Positive." She went up on her tiptoes to kiss him on the cheek. "Be careful tonight."

"Always."

It was killing him to let her walk back alone—she could see it in his eyes—but he controlled himself. After one more kiss, they parted ways, heading in opposite directions.

"See you at breakfast," she called over her shoulder.

"Breakfast," he replied, then added, "I love you, Gem."

"You too."

But as she abandoned the moonlit field for the darkness of the forest, she found herself thinking of Taylor and of their meeting in a few hours. If she somehow managed to reach him tonight— because doing so without being noticed, or getting lost, or dying, would take an absolute *miracle*—would she really be able to leave him again? To turn away from him and go back to the miserable life she'd lived for the past two years? A life consisting of long days at the Station and cold nights in the mine?

Gemma already knew the answer.

She'd promised Gavin she'd see him in the morning. But what if she didn't?

What if she never saw him again?

CHAPTER
SIX

The entrance to the mine loomed ahead, a cavernous hole carved into the side of the mountain. It seemed to grow darker and wider as she approached, like the gaping mouth of some long-dormant monster. The dragon from her dream, waiting to draw her down its long throat and into its belly to consume her.

She pushed the thought from her mind.

The real danger wasn't inside the mine, but outside.

She descended into the covered shelter, passing by a series of wooden benches where tourists once gathered to await their ride deep into the old anthracite mine. Blocking the mine's entrance was a dilapidated coal car, its metal wheels choked by years-worth of overgrown weeds. Inside the car, Kurt Horst and Mia Weber sat hunched over what appeared to be a particularly-intense game of chess. They spared her the briefest of glances as she squeezed between the side of the car and the rock wall.

"Goodnight," she called out.

"Night," Mia muttered, barely looking at Gemma. "Ugh. Kurt, you're killing me tonight."

"I really am, aren't I? Should we switch to checkers?"

He ducked, deftly avoiding the pawn Mia hurled at him.

"*Pride cometh before the fall.* I'm just getting my second wind."

Gemma exhaled, her breath turning to vapor in the cold night air.

They were distracted. That was good. But neither Mia nor Kurt seemed interested in talking to her. And they weren't the only ones. Aside from Brie, several others had treated her coldly since the failed supply run and the loss of Max and Allen. She was starting to feel like an outcast. A pariah. And that made her miss her parents—and her old life—more than ever.

Gemma kept walking—passing beneath a sign reading *Mine Temperature = 57 degrees year-round. Bring a jacket!* —and entered a long tunnel lit by a series of battery-powered lanterns. A wooden board with faded white lettering announced the tunnel as the West Mammoth Gangway, named for the massive vein of coal that cuts through the mountain.

She followed the narrow-gage railway tracks for nearly a quarter-mile, passing additional coal cars once used to ferry tourists deep into the mine. She kept her eyes on the tracks, carefully averting her gaze from the props the mine's owners had left behind. But she didn't have to look—she could see them clearly in her mind. Pick-wielding mannequins clad in oversized denim. Fake donkeys straining against the weight of their carts. Plastic canaries teetering on perches inside metal cages.

They'd given her nightmares since her arrival at the Station.

At the end of the tunnel, she turned into another passageway. Wild ferns and moss sprouted from the tunnel's overhead support beams, finding nourishment in the artificial light provided by the lanterns. In certain spots, a fluorescent-orange fungus crawled up the granite walls. Nobody—not even the all-knowing Oliver—knew what it was, so everyone stayed away from it.

Kyle called it Mine Tang, which always grossed Gemma out. She imagined the makers of the orange drink traipsing through abandoned mines like this one, scraping the fungus off the walls and grinding it into powder.

Up ahead, a series of small caves and tunnels jutted off from the main passageway. Gemma's group used them as their impromptu sleeping quarters, but a century earlier, these same narrow tunnels had been filled with rough men, their faces and lungs blackened from hours spent striking the walls with pickaxes in their endless quest for coal that would make other men rich. Sometimes at night, she swore she could hear their deep, hacking coughs echoing through the mine as they chopped away at the walls.

All night long.

Chopping and hacking. Chopping and hacking.

She tried to walk quietly, so as to not wake the others, but the mine's gravel floor betrayed her, the tiny rocks crunching loudly beneath her boots. Her eyes drifted from one tunnel to the next. Packed rucksacks sat outside the entrance of every cave. Inside, she could see the long outline of cots, their sleeping occupants hidden beneath mounds of wool blankets.

Near the end of the passageway, she turned into the short tunnel she shared with Sophia. The little girl sat on her cot, red hair spilling down her shoulders. She was studying a tattered Action Bible by the light of her Coleman lantern. The book had been a gift from Henry Castern. But it was illegal to buy or possess any kind of Bible, so no one understood how he'd gotten it. But Sophia adored it. She'd recently begun drawing her own comics based on their lives at the Station.

Sophia frowned at her over the top of her Bible. "And where have *you* been?"

Gemma collapsed onto her cot and untied her boots, kicking them onto the gravel floor. "At the fire tower with Gavin." She pulled off her wool socks to examine the blisters on her heels. The raw skin appeared red and inflamed. The fresh Band-Aids she'd applied this afternoon had come loose during her hike up to the tower. Instead of rebandaging her heels, however, she lay back on her cot and propped her feet up. The cold air felt amazing against her wounds.

"Well, would it have killed you to tell me that?" Sophia dropped her book to her chest, her nostrils flaring. "No one tells me anything. You guys all treat me like I'm some dumb kid."

Gemma reached across the gap between their cots and placed a hand on the girl's leg. "I'm sorry for not telling you where I was going. I guess I've been a little messed up lately. But no one thinks you're a dumb kid, Soph. Quite the opposite, actually. I think you're brilliant. You're certainly much smarter than I am."

Because, she thought, I'm about to do something really, really stupid.

"Forgive me?" Gemma asked.

Sophia spun a red curl around her index finger, then allowed it to unfurl like a ribbon. "I guess so."

"Thanks, babe."

Sophia's gaze dropped to the open page in front of her. "Gemma? Was Jesus a sinner?"

Sudden topic changes were par for the course when it came to Sophia. Her mind traveled a hundred miles an hour. But Gemma was exhausted. And excited. And worried. And she had no desire to dive into a theological discussion with the girl, especially at this hour. She knew, however, that Sophia wouldn't go to sleep until she received a satisfactory answer to her question. "What do you mean?"

"Well, the last time Mia and I had Bible study, she told me that Jesus was the only human in the history of the world who never sinned. She said that's what made Him the perfect sacrifice for the rest of us." Sophia rolled over and propped herself up on one elbow, the Bible open in front of her. "Remember how the Israelites used to sacrifice lambs on the Passover? Well, Mia says that Jesus was *our* Lamb. One perfect sacrifice...forever. That's why we don't have to kill things anymore to make God happy."

Gemma beamed, impressed with Sophia's Biblical knowledge.

"But, tonight, I read about the crucifixion," Sophia continued. "I wanted to read about it because of what happened to Mr. Castern. And it says that, when Jesus was on the cross, He cried out to God and said, 'Father, Father, why have you forgotten me?' Or something like that."

Gemma ran her fingers through the girl's fiery hair, gently untangling it. "Yes. I remember that."

"But that sounds like He was mad at God, right? And if you're mad at God, doesn't that make you a sinner?"

One of the perils of engaging in a theological discussion with Sophia was that she often asked Gemma questions that were difficult to answer. But Sophia was living a life she hadn't asked for —one she still wasn't fully able to comprehend—and she was only trying to make sense of it all. Who could blame her for asking questions?

"Soph, I don't know a lot about the Bible," Gemma said. "I haven't read it in so long. But a wonderful pastor once taught me that, while Jesus was fully God, He was also fully human. And when He was suffering on the cross, He was in terrible pain—pain unlike anything you or I could imagine in our worst nightmares. When He cried out like that, I think it was the human side of Him reacting to that awful pain."

Sophia ran a finger over the illustration of Jesus on the cross. "I guess that makes sense." She brought her fingers to her lips, seemingly fighting back tears. "Poor Jesus. And poor Mr. Castern."

"I know, Soph." Something else Pastor Nolan once said during a discussion of the crucifixion popped into Gemma's mind. "You know what? I just remembered something else. That same pastor once told me that, while Jesus was on the cross, God had to leave Him so He could experience the full extent of God's wrath for our sins. So, if you think about it, when Jesus was on the cross, that was the first time in His whole life that He was separated from His Father. Maybe that's another reason why He said those words. I think He felt abandoned."

Sophia plucked at a random string protruding from the cuff of her ragged sweater, until she finally tugged the string loose, freeing the stitch and pulling several inches of thread along with it.

Gemma didn't bother to stop her.

"I know how Jesus must've felt." Sophia rubbed at her eyes. "My mommy abandoned me, too. Only it wasn't just for a few hours. My mommy never came back."

A fresh stab of pain, a tangible feeling, like a knife driven into Gemma's heart and turned sideways. When Sophia's mother—no longer able to deal with the fear, the hardships, or the loneliness— had slipped away from their group in the middle of the night, it had been horrible. Only eight at the time, Sophia had been inconsolable for days and cried herself to sleep nearly every night. Gemma had taken the girl under her wing like a little sister, determined to shield her from the horrors of the world for as long as possible. But Gemma couldn't hold back the world forever. No matter how hard she tried, she couldn't stop it from bursting through her carefully-prepared facade like weeds erupting through weakened asphalt. "Your mommy was afraid, Soph. She was tired of hiding and she knew you'd be safer with us. I can't imagine how difficult that decision must've been for her."

"Yeah, I guess." Sophia sniffed. "But I'm still mad at her."

"I know. But you should try to forgive her someday."

Sophia closed her Bible. "I'm kind of mad at God, too. Does that make me a sinner?"

A bead of water dripped from the old timbers and splatted on Gemma's cheek. She wiped it away, suddenly very tired. "We're all sinners, Soph. The only difference between us and the rest of the world is that we know it."

Sophia clutched her Bible against her chest, her mouth dropping into an uninhibited yawn. "Will you lay with me?"

Gemma checked the time on her watch. *9:37*

"Soph..."

"Just until I fall asleep?"

She had to meet Taylor in a few hours. Laying down for any length of time wasn't a good idea. What if she fell asleep? Or what if Sophia woke up when Gemma tried to leave? But she couldn't say no. Especially not tonight.

"Ugh, fine," Gemma groaned. "You're a pain, Soph."

The girl scooted over to make room for Gemma. "I know."

Gemma dimmed the lantern to its lowest setting and crawled into bed beside Sophia. The cot wasn't designed for two people— even if one of them was as small as Sophia—and it was a tight fit. Beneath the wool blanket, the girl's cold fingers curled around Gemma's. They closed their eyes and whispered prayers for Sophia's mother and Gemma's parents and the rest of their group. After the prayer, Sophia's eyes remained closed, her pale eyelids fluttering as she drifted to sleep.

Gemma lay awake, gazing at the timbers overhead and thinking. Meeting Taylor was a terrible idea. Maybe the worst idea ever. She could feel the *wrongness* of it. The sheer stupidity. Her father had once told her that making choices is all about weighing the risks versus the potential rewards. If she snuck out of the mine to meet Taylor, she would be risking everything that mattered—her safety *and* the safety of her friends—for what reward? A guy she hadn't seen in two years? What if Taylor wasn't the same person she remembered? Two years was a long time to fantasize about someone. To build them up in your mind. What if she'd built Taylor up to be something he wasn't?

Besides, she wasn't nineteen anymore. So much had happened since the last time she'd been with Taylor. Her entire world had changed. Not to mention that meeting Taylor would mean betraying Gavin, a wonderful guy who'd done nothing but give her love, even when she didn't deserve it.

No. She wasn't going to do it.

Her mind was made up.

Relief washed over her, and she was suddenly very tired. With the decision made, she felt the urgent pull of sleep, like sinking into a warm bathtub. She closed her eyes and prepared to drift into a dreamless sleep next to Sophia.

Memories of Taylor flooded her mind. The carnival. His arm around her shoulders. And—years later—their first kiss. How safe she'd felt when he held her in his arms, as if nothing bad could ever touch her again. And she knew she would never forgive herself if she didn't meet him.

Had there ever really been another choice?

At a quarter past eleven, in a series of cautious, painstakingly-slow movements, her legs nearly cramping up from the effort, she slid off the cot.

Sophia stirred and whimpered—a mournful sound—and Gemma froze, her breath catching in her throat.

But Sophia wrapped the blanket tighter around herself and rolled away. Within seconds, she started to snore, a sound as familiar to Gemma as the girl's voice. She hesitated beside the cot and memorized every detail of Sophia's face. With her fiery-red hair, porcelain complexion, and pouty lips, Sophia resembled her mother. The resemblance grew stronger every day. And yet it was Gemma who Sophia clung to after one of her nightmares. Gemma, who wiped away her tears and cared for her when she was sick. Gemma, who she called Mommy in the middle of the night.

And now Gemma was abandoning her, too.

The thought repulsed her.

No. She wasn't abandoning Sophia. She was coming back.

She considered leaving a note for Addie. *Please look after Sophia.* But there was no time. And she didn't need to leave a note because she was coming back. Yes. Of course, she was. In all likelihood, she'd be back before Sophia woke up. But, in the unlikely event she didn't return, Addie certainly wouldn't need a note to know to look after Sophia.

She dressed quickly, tugging on her boots and jacket, slipping her backpack over her shoulders. Not allowing herself to think about what she was about to do for fear of losing her nerve. She pulled her Maglite from her pants pocket, went to switch it on, and then thought better of it.

Not yet.

She stepped into a passageway comprised of rough-cut rock walls. Away from the meager light provided by the lantern, the darkness closed in on her, surrounded her like an invading army. The only light in the tunnel came from a lantern hanging a few hundred meters to her right, just outside the cave shared by Oliver and Coop. Pausing to listen, she heard nothing but the sound of ground water trickling down the mine's walls and the comforting din of Coop's snoring.

Gemma turned her back on the light and headed in the opposite direction, traveling away from the rest of the group, deeper into the mine. She couldn't risk her light being seen, so she stuffed the Maglite into her pocket and extended her arms out to the sides. Her fingertips trailed along damp walls comprised of coal, aged timber, and dirt. With each footstep, the gravel shattered beneath her boots like glass, and she held her breath, as if doing so would somehow stop the others from hearing and coming after her.

She shuffled forward on unsteady legs, conquering the pitch-black tunnel one precious inch at a time. It would take her hours to reach Taylor at this rate, but she couldn't bring herself to travel any faster in the dark. It wasn't only the fear of tripping over a rock or exposed root that was causing her to move slowly. It was the darkness itself. She couldn't stop thinking about the dragons from her dream. No matter how ridiculous it seemed, she kept wondering if the dream had actually been some kind of premonition. She closed her eyes, as if that would make the darkness less frightening, and her unhelpful mind produced a vivid image of a massive dragon lurking just around the next curve of the tunnel, its body coiled up and ready to devour her.

She pulled out the Maglite and switched it on, bathing the tunnel in light. She spun in a circle, searching the darkness for slimy scales and glowing eyes. Instead, the beam of her flashlight illuminated unfamiliar gangways and narrow, vertical shafts. Although she'd been in this section of the mine once before, she couldn't remember anything about it. She felt like an explorer navigating the belly of some colossal, sleeping beast. A living, breathing thing composed of dripping rock and rotting logs.

Up ahead, a petrified tree root jutted into the passageway like an outstretched leg. She maneuvered around the obstacle. She didn't remember that from the last time she'd traveled this deep into the mine. She would've remembered something protruding into the tunnel like that. Her inability to recall the tree root with any amount of certainty took up residence in her brain like a tumor, growing in size with each tentative step, until her mind succumbed completely to its presence and panic began to set in.

It didn't take this long last time. And there wasn't a tree. She was going the wrong way. Somehow, she got turned around in the darkness.

The dreadful possibilities invaded her mind like a thousand lethal spiders, each trying to inject their own poison while devouring what remained of her courage. Suddenly, the provisions in her backpack seemed meager and utterly ridiculous. A few bottles of water courtesy of Kyle, the stale granola bar from the café, her Leatherman, and a basic first-aid kit that Gavin insisted she carry at all times.

Gavin.

She stopped walking. The thought of him—and the safety he represented—made her want to go back. What had she been thinking, traveling so deep inside the mine without a heavy coat? More food? Extra batteries for her Maglite? What if she never found her way out? Surely, the group would come looking for her, but what if they didn't? Kyle's words from the group meeting came back to her.

"I wouldn't expect anyone in this room to risk his life to rescue me."

If they didn't come for her, and she never found her way out of the tunnels, how would she die? Hypothermia? Or would she live long enough to die of thirst? It definitely wouldn't be starvation. She'd lose her mind long before she starved to death. Her mind would snap like a rubber band the second the batteries in her Maglite died, plunging her into darkness.

As if in response to this terrible thought, her flashlight shuddered and blinked out.

Gemma cried and smacked it against her hand.

Once. Twice.

A faint flicker.

Then nothing.

She slapped the light three more times, her force increasing with her urgency. Finally, the light blinked and brightened and illuminated a dark shape along the left side of the cave a few feet away. Something large in the shadows, clinging to the wall.

Gemma froze. Slowly, she raised her flashlight and aimed it at the shape.

She uttered a small cry of relief.

The emergency-egress ladder.

A memory came to her: Oliver standing at the base of the ladder, one hand on the lowest rung, explaining to the group that if Task Force ever found their way into the mine—or, God-forbid, blew up the entrance, trapping them inside—these metal bars would be their lifeline. Their salvation.

No one had attempted to climb it, not even Oliver, because it was too dangerous. It wasn't so much a ladder as a series of metal rungs bolted directly into the rock, ascending straight up for twenty or so feet before the wall dramatically sloped inward, and the ladder, following the natural curve of the cave, disappeared from sight.

According to an old map of the mine that Oliver had found in a filing cabinet in the Station's basement, the egress ladder led to a steel door four-hundred feet up. The door could only be opened from the inside.

She reached out and touched one of the rungs, half-expecting it to come alive beneath her fingers and transform into some kind of massive serpent. Instead, the metal felt cold and lifeless and was coated with the same icy ground water that trickled down the granite walls and dripped from the overhead timbers.

She was going to fall and break her neck.

She would be paralyzed and die down here.

Gemma shoved the insidious thoughts away and began to climb, traveling upward at a steady clip, her confidence growing with each rung. The rungs were slippery, but they were nothing she couldn't handle. Once, she made the mistake of glancing down, and she realized that she'd reached a height where, if she fell, she'd certainly shatter bones and be unable to drag herself back to the rest of the group. But then the ladder curved in, following the natural slope of the shaft, and she found herself ascending at a more manageable angle. She tried to make up time by climbing faster, but after a few minutes, the rocks curved outward and she was climbing near-vertically once again.

Her hands felt like blocks of ice. She stopped climbing and tried blowing on her fingers and flexing them. When that didn't work, she linked one arm through the rungs and tucked her opposite hand inside her jacket. She counted to sixty in her head, giving her fingers a full minute to thaw out, before switching hands.

She resumed her climb, the Maglite clenched between her teeth. The idea of scaling the cave in total darkness was too horrible to imagine. But the physical exertion soon left her breathless, and when the flashlight nearly slipped out of her mouth, she turned it off and stuffed it into her pocket.

At some point, it all became too much. Gemma stopped ascending and clung to the ladder in total darkness, her chest throbbing from the effort. The overworked muscles in her upper arms and thighs protested every movement. But her hands were the worst. She could no longer feel her fingers, no matter how often she stuffed them inside her jacket to warm them. She couldn't risk another rung, couldn't go up or down, couldn't do anything but hang onto the ladder as her strength ebbed away. How long could she hang on until her arms gave out? Why hadn't she thought to bring a rope along? Or one of the old climbing carabiners from the gift shop? Something—*anything*—that might arrest her fall.

She closed her eyes—trading one darkness for another—and concentrated on her breathing. On not panicking. In and out. Deep, even breaths.

And then...a faint sound, echoing from below.

Metal clanging against metal.

Someone was on the ladder.

Heart pounding, Gemma held her breath and listened for the sound again. After a few seconds of silence, she removed her flashlight from her pocket and directed the beam downward. The light was dimmer than before, illuminating only a dozen or so feet below her own boots. She saw nothing but steel rungs descending into the murky darkness below. Anyone could be down there, cloaked in shadows, watching her.

Climbing up after her.

The thought propelled her, the pain in her chest and legs and the numbness in her hands all but forgotten. There was nowhere to go but up. Keeping her eyes on the ladder below her, she ascended faster than before, telling herself over and over that the sound hadn't been real. She'd imagined it. Even if she *was* being followed, it had to be someone from her group.

But why wouldn't they call out to her? Why wouldn't they tell her to stop? Why—

A dull thud followed by a sharp wave of pain that shot from the back of her head straight down to her toes. She bit down hard on her lower lip, resisting the overwhelming urge to scream. Linking one arm through the rung, she tentatively reached up and touched the back of her head. There was no dampness. No blood, thank goodness. Just a hard hit. There would be a lump. She dug the Maglite from her pocket and turned it on, directing the beam upward. Above her head, she could see a flat pane of rusted metal with an L-shaped lever.

The hatch.

"Yes!" Gemma unleashed a primal scream of victory and pounded on the hatch, her numb fingers barely registering the impact. *"I made it! You didn't get me!"* she bellowed into the air, her voice reverberating off the stone walls. She hadn't gotten lost in the

mine. She hadn't slipped off the ladder and fallen to her death. And she'd done it all by herself.

Taylor would be waiting for her on the other side of the metal door.

She yanked on the handle, but her boots slipped precariously on the wet rungs. She tightened her grip on the ladder and tried the handle again, but it wouldn't budge. "Please," she whispered, summoning every ounce of her remaining strength to force the lever open. "Please, God."

The lever jerked in her hand, and a gust of cold air blew against her cheeks. She inhaled the familiar scents of the forest—pine and fresh rain—as rotting leaves caressed her face on their journey to the bottom of the shaft. She pushed the hatch the rest of the way open, performing her great escape for an audience of trees. They towered over her, most still without their leaves, their limbs outstretched like skeletal arms toward the heavens. Beyond the trees, a smattering of stars glimmered on a dark canvas.

Freedom.

She climbed two more rungs until her head poked through the opening. The escape hatch was nothing more than a circular tube of concrete, raised a foot or so off of the forest floor and topped with a metal lid. Tossing the Maglite out of the hatch, she wrapped her fingers around the rim, the concrete rough and cold beneath her palms, and heaved herself out. Glimpsing the ground below, she lifted her boot, searching for the final rung...

Her foot slipped.

And then—

Air.

Gemma grabbed wildly at damp leaves, and then at concrete, searching for a handhold on the hatch, *anything* to arrest her fall, but her numb hands found nothing. The sky overhead disappeared and she slipped back into the shaft, nothing separating her from death except four-hundred feet of jutting rocks and open air.

A hand grabbed her arm.

She hung there, suspended in the air, like a dancer twirling in slow motion. Her left shoulder felt as if it might explode out of its socket. A grunt of pain from above. More pressure on her arm, followed by the sound of her jacket ripping. Something soared past her in the darkness—she felt the wind of it against her cheek—and then her body crashed against the ladder. Her ribcage slammed into one of the metal rungs, knocking the remaining breath from her body and silencing her pain-filled cry.

And then she was traveling upward as Taylor pulled her out of the hatch.

CHAPTER
SEVEN

Gemma collapsed to the ground, and a sharp pain ripped through her left palm. She cried out. A stick protruded from one of the old fingernail wounds. She seized it with shaking fingers and yanked it out. A gush of warm blood erupted from her palm and ran down her wrist. Then she lay on her back, clutching her injured hand to her chest, and took in the cold blanket of stars above.

There was no fire.

No dragons circling, waiting to consume her.

She'd made it.

Leaves rustled as Taylor crawled over to her. "Are you okay?" He pushed the hair away from her face.

Gemma's body began to shake. She held her trembling hands out in front of her. "What's...wrong...with me?" Even her voice sounded unsteady.

"It's just the adrenaline." Taylor took her bloody hand and examined it, his forehead wrinkling with concern. "You hit the side of the hatch pretty hard. Can you get up?" He extended a hand to help her, but when she tried to sit up, the pain in her chest drove her back to the ground.

"Ow!"

"What hurts?"

"My chest," she moaned. "It feels like someone stabbed me."

"Might be a broken rib. I need to check, okay?" When she shoved his hand away, he said, "I'll be careful. Just relax."

She nodded, steeling herself for more pain.

Taylor gently prodded the right side of her ribcage with the tips of his fingers, following the lines of her ribs, eyebrows furrowed in concentration. Finally, he pulled his hands away. "I'm not a medic, but nothing feels broken. That doesn't mean you didn't crack a rib. But it's probably just bruised." He shook his head. "I'm so sorry, Gemma."

"You're sorry? For what?"

"For not getting here sooner. You could've fallen."

Gemma placed a hand on his arm. "I *did* fall. You saved me. If it wasn't for you, I'd be dead—or worse—right now." She imagined lying at the base of the ladder—mangled but somehow still alive—surrounded by all that darkness. Her worst nightmare. "You have nothing to apologize for. How did you find me?"

Taylor rolled up his left sleeve to reveal the crude drawing on his forearm. "Your map. Between you and me, I hope you aren't considering a career in cartography."

The number tattooed on Taylor's inner wrist drew Gemma's attention, and she took his hand in her own, running her fingers along the ink, studying them as if they were a code she must decipher. She could sense he wanted to pull his hand away, but when he didn't, she quickly tried to memorize all ten digits.

5705550717

"Taylor? What's this?"

He pulled his hand away and yanked down his sleeve to cover the ink. "Nothing." He gestured toward the concrete hatch. "What is this place? You're living down there?"

And then it hit her. Despite everything she knew about Taylor —their history and the bond they shared—he was still a Task Force soldier. By agreeing to meet him, she'd compromised the safety of her entire group. Kyle and Addie. Mia. Sophia. All fast asleep, four-hundred feet beneath the surface of the earth, totally unaware that the enemy now knew the location of their camp.

When she didn't answer, he retrieved his rifle from the ground and slung it over his shoulder. "What's going on with you, Gemma? I can understand laying low for a while after everything that happened back at home. But it's been two years. Why are you still out here?"

She tried to see past the uniform and the coldhearted expression to the boy she'd once loved. *Still* loved. "Surviving. Trying to stay alive. That's what I'm doing."

"Trying to stay alive?" Taylor gawked at her as if she'd lost her mind. "What do you think is happening? Do you think the Task Force is *killing* subversives?" He shook his head, his expression softening. "We detain subversives and send them to detention centers. That's it. No one is killing anyone." He took her uninjured hand and squeezed it, a maddeningly condescending gesture that made her want to scream. "Gemma, you can't believe everything these people tell you. They're extremists."

She snatched her hand away. "I want to get up. Help me up."

"Not yet. Just take it easy..."

Extremists. She wanted to punch him. He deserved a punch for using that term. "I said, help me *up!*"

Taylor slipped an arm beneath her shoulders and lifted her.

The agony in her chest had dulled to a manageable ache. Even breathing was becoming easier, which was good because she had a lot to say.

"How do you feel?"

"What do you care?" she said. "Aren't you going to detain me?" An image flashed in her mind—metal handcuffs digging into her mother's delicate wrists—and she jammed her hands together and thrust them at him. "That's your job, isn't it? So, what are you waiting for?"

Taylor's lips tightened into a thin line, but he said nothing.

His silence infuriated her. He wasn't even trying to deny the truth in her words. She jabbed a finger at the hatch. "There are men, women, and children down there. They're cold and hungry and miserable because of you."

Something dark entered his eyes. "That's enough." His voice was cold and robotic. The voice of a mindless drone.

But she couldn't stop because he still didn't know. He still didn't understand the full extent of what he'd done. "Do you know what I saw the other day? I saw a man hanging dead on a cross. I saw a man whose only crime was providing our group with supplies. He wasn't even a *subversive*, as you call us. Just a local storeowner. An innocent man. And they hung him up and left him to rot."

Taylor ran a hand through his dark hair. "If you're implying that the Task Force murdered this man—"

"I'm not implying anything. They did it, Taylor. They *had* to have done it. Right after I found Henry's body, two of my friends got ambushed at his store. They're both gone. And if I had gone into town with them, I'd be dead, too."

Taylor closed the distance between them and gripped her arms. "Then you need to let me help you, okay? I can get you out of here. Tonight. Let me take you someplace safe and we'll figure everything out."

Despite her romantic delusions of running away with Taylor, the idea repulsed her. She pulled her arms free and took a step back. "No way. I'm not leaving my friends."

"Gemma, there are other scouts from my unit searching this mountain right now. I'm not the only one. Even if I pretend that I never located your camp, someone's going to find you. You've got a few days, at best."

"They won't find us. Not unless you tell them where we are."

"Yes, they will. I'm the only scout in this sector right now, but I found your people at the fire tower in less than two days. If I hadn't stumbled across you, I would've kept eyes on your friends in the fire tower until their shift ended. Then I would've followed them back to your camp and called in your position."

Gemma considered this. "You didn't report our location yet? Not even the fire tower?"

A short pause. "No."

"Why not?"

"Honestly?" He shook his head. "I have no idea."

Gemma gazed into Taylor's ice-blue eyes. The same eyes she'd fallen in love with so many years earlier, long before he realized it.

Then she bent to retrieve her backpack and flinched at the sharp pain in her chest. "I have to go back."

"Gemma—"

"Wait as long as you can before you tell your friends about the mine, okay? Please? A day should be enough. Just give us a head start."

She tossed the backpack over her shoulder and scanned the forest, trying to get her bearings. The mine's main entrance was a half-mile to the east of the hatch, maybe a little farther. The walk back should give her enough time to figure out what to say to Kurt and Mia when she reached the entrance. She headed in what she hoped was the right direction, furiously wiping her damp eyes on her sleeve, until Taylor's hand closed around her wrist.

"Gemma." For a moment, he looked exactly like that little boy again. The one in the oversized suit, sitting in the front row at his mother's funeral. "Please don't go."

Please don't go.

The same words he'd said to her the night she'd gone into hiding.

Gemma's eyes passed over him. His uniform. The patches bearing the strange insignia. She imagined herself saying yes. Throwing herself into his arms. Leaving with him. More than anything, she wanted to lay in his arms again and forget about the past two years. The loneliness, the darkness, the fear. She could hardly remember a time when those things weren't as much a part of her daily life as breathing. To be rid of them forever seemed impossible.

But she held back. Not for herself, but for the others. For Sophia. "I've missed you every single day since we last saw each other," she whispered. "You're always in the back of my mind. This ghost that haunts me. But I can't abandon my friends, Taylor. These people are the only family I have left."

"That's not true." His hands closed around hers. "You have me."

She thought of the last night they'd spent together, just before she'd gone into hiding. Two years later and she could still feel the pressure of his lips against hers, the delicate way his fingers grazed her neck. How many times had her treacherous mind produced that exact memory when Gavin kissed her?

"What are you thinking about?" he asked.

She went up on her tiptoes and brought her hands to his face, the stubble of his unshaven chin like sandpaper against her palms. "Do you remember the night you came to see me? After my parents were detained?"

Their lips were only inches apart now. "Of course, I do."

Everything seemed to hinge on the next few moments. Her future, Taylor's future, even Gavin's future. Three roads converging briefly in a strange and beautiful way. "That was my first kiss," she admitted, her cheeks burning with embarrassment. But it felt important for him to know the truth. "I waited for you, Taylor. I'm *still* waiting for you."

And then he closed the distance between them, his strong hands drawing her face up to meet his. Everything felt so familiar, as if the past two years had never happened. Her heart beat a steady rhythm in her ears. She tilted her head back and closed her eyes, losing herself in the familiar scent of him. The sturdiness of his body. The gentleness of his touch.

But he didn't kiss her.

Instead, he pulled back.

"What's his name?"

She blinked. "Huh? Whose name?"

Only then did she realize that Taylor's right hand was holding her left, his fingers lightly grazing the pearl ring on her finger.

"The guy who gave you this."

Although he spoke the words quietly, the force of them was like a shove. Ashamed, she lowered her gaze and focused on his nametape. How could she explain her relationship with Gavin in a way Taylor would understand? How could he ever understand the intensity of a relationship based on shared fear and loneliness? A relationship of necessity, not love. Would she understand if the situation were reversed? What if Taylor had a girlfriend waiting for him somewhere?

Maybe he did.

"Taylor—"

A sharp crack, like a massive tree branch snapping, shattered the silence of the forest. Gemma cringed against him, bracing for the impact. For the wrath of God Himself to come pouring down on her from above. Then Taylor uttered a guttural grunt of pain and pushed her roughly to the ground. Shaken and disoriented, she lifted her head in time to see Taylor hurl himself over the nearby trunk of a collapsed pine tree. He lay in the shadows, clutching his left thigh. Dark liquid seeped through his fingers. "Stay down!" he shouted, struggling to bring his rifle up. "Keep your head down!"

Something shifted in her peripheral vision.

She turned her head and saw Brie Douglas standing beside the open escape hatch, the moonlight making her appear more zombie than human. Pale skin, bloodshot eyes, blonde hair sweat-pasted to her forehead, her nose dripping blood. Enough blood to stain the front of her jacket red.

She held a pistol.

"Brie?" Gemma gasped. "You're bleeding! What happened to you?"

"I knew we couldn't trust you." Brie rubbed her nose on her sleeve. With shaking hands, she raised the gun and aimed it at Gemma's chest. "I knew you were a traitor. I knew it. That's why I followed you. I needed to see for myself. And now…you're with *him*? A soldier?"

From his position behind the tree, Taylor again shouted at Gemma to stay down, but she ignored him and lifted herself off the ground, her hands raised in a gesture of surrender. She had to explain. After all, Brie wasn't a killer. She was grieving the loss of Max, yes, but she wasn't a killer. Maybe if Gemma explained who Taylor really was, everything would be okay. Brie would put the gun down. No one else would get hurt.

"Brie? Listen to me." Gemma struggled to keep her voice steady. "He's a soldier, but he's not the enemy. He's my fr—"

"*Shut up!*" Brie screamed, her eyes wild. "*Just shut up!*"

And she pulled the trigger.

CHAPTER EIGHT

Gemma felt the wind of the bullet on her cheek, then hit the ground as the next bullet soared over her head and slammed into a nearby tree. Fragments of rotting wood and moss rained down on her, stinging her eyes and sealing them shut. Instinctively, she played dead, her face pressed into the ground, waiting for the next gunshot. For the heavy sound of Brie's approaching footsteps, followed by the hollow thump of the bullet as it impacted the flesh of her upper back.

Or the top of her head.

"Gemma."

She ignored Brie's voice and remained motionless, inhaling the musty scent of leaves. The taste of the earth on her lips reminded her of the mine—of being buried alive—but when she closed her mouth, the same dirt invaded her nostrils, making it difficult to breathe.

But she didn't move. Her spine felt as rigid and tight as a bow string.

"I know you're not dead," Brie said. "Stand up and face me, you coward."

She raised her head slightly, risking a quick glance at the hatch.

Brie stood beside the concrete lid, her chest rising and falling with slow, deep breaths. All of her attention was focused on Gemma, and she didn't appear at all concerned about the Task Force soldier crouched a few feet away, the barrel of his assault rifle trained on her.

"Brie?" Gemma's voice cracked. "Please stop."

"Why? Why did you leave him in that godforsaken town?"

"I'm sorry about Max. I'm *so* sorry. And you're right. I shouldn't have left him. I should've gone back. But please...don't make things worse."

"Worse, *Gemma?*" Brie spat her name out, as if revolted by the taste of it. "How could things get any worse? Max is gone. And you're sneaking off in the middle of the night to meet a soldier. What's really going on? Have you sold us out?"

Gemma met Taylor's eyes, saw him shake his head. She returned her attention to Brie. "No. I'd *never* sell our group out. His name is Taylor. He's my friend. Okay? That's what I was trying to tell you. I've known him since we were kids. He's not here to hurt us, and he's not going to tell anyone where we are."

Brie lowered the gun slightly, tears shining in her eyes. "I don't believe you."

Ignoring Taylor's warnings for her to stay down, Gemma climbed to her feet. A searing pain ripped through her chest. She flinched. "I swear I'm telling you the truth. I haven't seen him in years, and then we stumbled into each other earlier tonight on my way to meet Gavin at the tower."

"And I suppose he was just taking a little hike." Brie's voice dripped sarcasm. "With his assault rifle."

"No." There was no point in lying. "He was looking for us. In fact, he'd already located our guys at the tower when I ran into him.

We agreed to meet later to talk. But that's it, I swear. He hasn't told anyone our location."

"Why should I believe anything you say?" Brie demanded. "You could be lying about everything. You could be lying about what actually happened in Ash Grove. For all I know, you might've been in on it!" Her eyes widened as if she'd had a sudden understanding, and she focused on Taylor, her small hands tightening around the pistol. "Is he the one? *Did he kill Max?*"

Gemma flattened herself on the ground, and the pistol went off again. The round buried itself in the dirt halfway between Taylor and Gemma.

Brie had terrible aim. Thank God.

"Brie, stop!"

Another loud pop, like the crack of a whip, reverberated through the forest, and a bullet slammed into the ground inches from Brie's feet. She cried out and stumbled backward.

"Drop your weapon!" Taylor shouted.

"Taylor! Don't shoot her!"

"Why not?" Brie moaned, her cries progressing into chest-heaving sobs. She brought a hand up to wipe the tears from her cheeks. "Let your boyfriend kill me. At least then I'll be with—"

Gemma jumped at the sound of another hollow crack, followed by a metallic ping. The gun flew out of Brie's hand and landed on the ground a few feet away.

Brie gaped at her empty hands. "What?"

Taylor stepped out from behind the tree, limping noticeably, the barrel of his gun aimed at Brie's chest. "Put your hands in the air."

Brie stared, wild-eyed, at the rifle in Taylor's hands. "Gemma...?"

"It's okay, Brie. He's not going to hurt you. Are you, Taylor?"

Slowly, Brie raised her hands in surrender, her thin body vibrating from either the fear, the adrenaline, or the cold. Her red-rimmed eyes darted from Gemma to Taylor and back again in rapid succession. She reminded Gemma of a cornered animal. Wild. Capable of anything.

"Okay. Taylor, put the gun down so we can—"

Before Gemma could finish her sentence, Brie bolted, tripped over a rock, but somehow managed to stay on her feet. She sprinted due east toward the entrance of the mine, arms pumping at her sides, bounding over fallen branches like a spooked deer.

"Stop!" Taylor tracked Brie's escape with the sight on his weapon.

Gemma ran to him, grabbed his arm. "No! Please. Just let her go."

Brie disappeared from sight, absorbed into the darkness of the forest.

Taylor lowered the rifle. "I wasn't going to shoot her," he said, his tone icy. "But she's going to tell the rest of your group. And when they get here, I need to be somewhere else." He slung his rifle over his shoulder and held up his right hand. "And then there's this."

Black liquid stained his palm. More was smeared across the front of his uniform. There was blood everywhere. On Taylor, on the ground, even on the barrel of his weapon. The left leg of his pants was completely drenched. There was even some on Gemma's jacket. She had no idea how it got there.

He followed her gaze to his blood-soaked pants and the color instantly drained from his face. "Oh, man," he said. "That sucks."

His legs folded beneath him and he collapsed.

Gemma grabbed him, tried to slow his fall, but he was too heavy, and he landed hard on his back, his head lolling awkwardly to one side. She crouched beside him and jammed both of her hands hard against his upper thigh, ignoring the pain in her own injured palms as she applied pressure to the wound.

He moaned. "Stop."

Oliver. He needs Oliver.

"Stop," he begged, trying to pry her hands off his thigh. "Please. Stop."

"Taylor, you have to do something for me, okay? I need you to put your hands right here." She guided both of his hands to the leg wound. "Good. Now...I need you to press down hard. As hard as you can. Just for a few seconds, while I get something out of my backpack."

Once she felt him applying pressure to the wound—though very little pressure—she took her hands away and dropped her backpack. She could barely grasp the zipper; her hands were cold, covered in blood, and shaking badly. But she managed to get it open and dug to the bottom, her fingers closing around the small, zippered pouch with the red cross on the front. She unzipped the kit and dumped it onto the ground: sterile bandages, rolls of gauze, alcohol wipes, calamine lotion, tweezers, antihistamine pills, medical tape, and a small vial of acetaminophen. Everything seemed so small, like toys from a child's play kit.

So incapable of fixing anything.

The acetaminophen wouldn't touch his pain, but it was better than nothing. She unscrewed the lid and dumped four white pills into her blood-stained palm. She could've given him more, but four seemed like a safe number. "Here. Swallow these, okay? I have some water, too."

Taylor pushed her hand away. "No aspirin. The bleeding."

"It's okay. It's Tylenol."

Gemma slid a hand under his neck and lifted his head. She put the pills in his mouth, unscrewed the cap of one of the water bottles, and gave him a sip. Grimacing, he swallowed all four pills at once.

She pulled her pocket knife out of her backpack and unfolded it. The blade gleamed, reflecting the moonlight. "Okay. Take your hands away now."

Taylor raised his eyebrows at her. "What are you going to do with *that?*"

"I'm going to cut your pants to get a better look at the wound."

His head dropped backward, and he closed his eyes again. "I can't watch."

After she pried his hands away from the wound, Gemma sliced a line through his uniform and pulled the material apart, exposing the smeared gore beneath. Taking slow breaths through her nose, bracing herself for the pulverized meat of a destroyed limb, she unwrapped one of the rolls of gauze and carefully wiped the blood away, revealing two small holes in the outer part of his thigh. Entry and exit wounds. Not as bad as she'd expected. Bright-red blood seeped from the holes. She soaked up the blood with the gauze, and the flow appeared to be slowing. "It's okay," she said, exhaling. "It looks like a clean wound through the outer part of your thigh. And the bleeding is slowing down. But I should warn you—I have absolutely no idea what I'm talking about."

"Just bandage it up," he muttered. "Do the best you can."

Gemma selected the largest bandage, tore open the sterile packaging, and pressed it down on the wound. Then she unwound the gauze and wrapped it tightly around the bandage. "Everything is going to be okay." She was speaking as much to herself as Taylor. "There's a doctor in our group. A podiatrist."

"Like feet?" he said.

"Our group might be hungry and miserable, but our feet are in awesome shape. Not a bunion or ingrown toenail in the bunch."

"Funny." He didn't sound amused.

She tore a piece of medical tape from the roll. "He went to med school, okay? Just let him clean the wound and bandage it properly. And he's got antibiotics. He might be able to—"

"No." Taylor protested. "You have to get me out of here."

She rubbed the back of her neck, massaging the tense muscles. "You've been shot. My friends aren't any danger to you, Taylor."

"It's not them."

Gemma sat back on her heels and examined her work. Not bad. "Then what is it?"

"My extraction time is zero-five-hundred."

"Your *what?*"

"My unit...that's when they're picking me up. I have to be there by five."

Gemma felt her chest tighten—the familiar squeeze of anxiety, where every breath was a battle to be fought and won. "Where?"

"The old covered bridge on Swamp Road. Do you know it?"

"Yes." Two days earlier, she'd parted ways with Allen and Max at the same bridge.

Taylor grimaced as he pushed himself onto his elbows. "You have to get me there. And you've got less than..." He glanced at his watch. "...four hours to do it."

She studied her own watch, hoping to see different numbers. "But do you really *have* to go back? Why can't you stay with us? The others in my group...they'll understand. They're good people. They just need to see that you're—"

"Gemma. If I'm not at the bridge, and my unit hasn't heard from me, they'll send out more soldiers to search the mountain. They'll locate me by pinging my radio."

"Why don't you call your boss or whoever and tell them that you're not ready to be extracted yet?"

"I can't do that either."

"Why not?"

Taylor nodded toward the open hatch.

"Because my radio is at the bottom of that shaft."

CHAPTER
NINE

They had to get the radio back.

Gemma could see it in her mind, a black rectangle lying at the base of the ladder, invisible in the darkness. She remembered it now, how something had passed inches from her face when Taylor grabbed her. The radio must've continued its plunge to the bottom, eventually hitting Brie and bloodying her nose. But it hadn't knocked her off the ladder, thank God.

"How?" she managed. "How did it happen?"

Taylor gestured to a spot on his tactical vest. "The clip broke when I grabbed you. It was either you or the radio."

She felt numb. Even the pain in her chest had disappeared. "Okay. Everything's going to be okay. I'll just climb back down and get it." She tried to mean it. Tried to convince herself that she was capable of lowering her body into that black oblivion one leg at a time, boots blindly searching for the next slippery rung.

It would be even worse than climbing up...which she would *also* have to do again.

"No way," Taylor said. "It's too dangerous. You almost fell the last time."

"Okay." She wasn't about to argue *too* hard for climbing back down. "Then we'll hike to the entrance. It's not far. Oliver can patch you up while I find the radio. Then you can call your unit and tell them that you need more time and they don't have to pick you up."

He gaped at her. "And when I get back to my unit, how do I explain the gunshot wound in my leg?"

"You don't *have* to go back to your unit," she said, growing frustrated. "We'll find the radio and destroy it. Then you can stay with us."

Taylor tilted his head toward the heavens, as if searching the stars for answers. "I'd be AWOL, Gemma. If you think it's bad now, just wait until a Task Force soldier goes missing up here. My entire unit will converge on this sector. Even if you could convince your group to leave tonight, they'd find us in a few days. Probably less."

No. She couldn't accept that. There had to be another option. She couldn't bear the thought of losing him again. Not yet. If he returned to his unit, how would they ever find each other again?

"Taylor—"

"The bridge," he interrupted, his voice firm. "Just get me there by zero-five-hundred and I'll figure out the rest. That's the only chance we have."

"I can't carry you out of here," she whispered.

"You won't have to carry me. I can walk. Just help me up."

Taylor could be stubborn when he set his mind to something, so there was no point in arguing. She crouched and allowed him to sling his left arm over her shoulder. When she pulled him off the ground, he released his grip on her and slumped against a tree, both hands clutching his wounded thigh, a grimace of pain etched across his face. After a few seconds of what seemed like agony, his body relaxed. Perspiration glistened on his forehead as he leaned against the tree, eyes closed, taking deep breaths.

Gemma felt helpless. She couldn't do anything for him—only watch and wait for the pain to pass. She pictured the miles of mountainous terrain stretching between them and their destination.

The clock was ticking. She ignored the impulse to look at her watch, as if she could somehow slow time by disregarding it.

"Okay," Taylor finally said. "Let's go."

Guided by moonlight, they kept a steady pace down the mountain, exchanging few words as they raced the clock and the sun to the covered bridge. Taylor kept an arm slung over her shoulders, just as he had that night at the carnival so many years earlier. Only this time she was the rescuer, and he was the one who needed saving. With his weight unbalancing her, they stumbled often but never fell. Each time, she silently thanked God for keeping them on their feet. She wasn't sure she'd be able to get Taylor off the ground again if he went down.

In the hours before dawn, an eerie quiet settled over the mountain. No insects buzzed or chirped. No deer roamed, snapping branches beneath their thick hooves. Lower on the mountain, a thin layer of fog blanketed the forest floor, concealing obstacles and forcing them to slow down. It felt as if they were trapped in some otherworldly dimension, cut off from the rest of the world. It would've been beautiful if the fate of the others back at the Station didn't hang in the balance.

We're not going to make it.

The words repeated in her mind, over and over. As the hours passed, and they grew closer to the bridge, the words took on a mystical quality. Instead of allowing her nagging doubts to drag her down, she used them to her advantage. Turned them into a powerful cadence and kept pace with them. Fed off of them. Weaponized them. Allowed them to propel her forward, one step at a time.

Besides, it kept her from thinking about Gavin. And Sophia.

And what Brie must be telling everyone.

Every so often, when his pain became too great, Taylor would remove his arm from her shoulders, lean against a tree, and bury his face in his forearm until it passed. In those moments, she could do nothing but put her hand on his back and assure him that everything was going to be okay.

She had no idea if that was true. But she needed him to keep walking. And when he did, she resumed her cadence.

We're not going to make it.

They'd been walking for three hours when Taylor's irritated voice broke through the walls of her mind. "Can you please *stop?*"

"Stop walking?"

"No. Stop saying we're not going to make it. I feel like I'm losing my mind."

Gemma felt her face flush. How long had she been saying the words out loud? "Sorry," she muttered. "I'll stop."

"Are you sure this is the right direction?"

Was she sure? Of course not. It seemed like the right direction, but she was completely exhausted. She wasn't sure of anything anymore. Not even her own name. Her tank was empty. She was running on adrenaline.

"Of course," she lied, running her tongue along her dry lips. She was desperate for a drink of water, but there wasn't time to stop.

He pressed a button on his watch, illuminating the face. "How much longer until we reach the bridge?"

"I don't know."

"What do you mean, you don't know?"

"I mean, *I don't know*," she snapped. "Okay? I don't know. I'm hungry. I'm tired. I've barely slept in the past forty-eight hours. But I do know one thing: if we keep stopping every ten minutes so you can rest, we really aren't going to make it."

"Rest? You think I'm stopping to *rest?*"

The weight of his arm on her shoulders lessened as he tested his strength to see if he was capable of walking unassisted.

He wasn't.

"Just walk." She gripped his waist tighter. "Don't talk to me anymore."

An hour later, they reached the covered bridge.

It stood at the intersection of two roads—Aline and Swamp—both deserted and dark, their surfaces heavily-rutted from the constant barrage of poultry and logging trucks. In the distance, she could hear the sound of a tractor-trailer downshifting. Twin concrete posts jutted out of the ground in front of the old bridge like raised fingers, blocking any vehicles from driving onto the dilapidated structure. Vehicles turning onto Swamp Road crossed the creek using the adjacent concrete overpass. The two bridges stood side-by-side like bitter cousins at a family reunion, forced into close proximity with one another but not on speaking terms.

Gemma helped Taylor climb over a padlocked chain strung across the bridge's entrance. Some local official's halfhearted attempt at discouraging vandals and hormone-fueled teenagers from desecrating one of Ash County's few historical landmarks. But the chain clearly wasn't doing its job. Gemma and Taylor trudged into the darkness, their boots sending empty beer cans rolling. The beam from Gemma's Maglite passed over a slew of neon words and images spray-painted on the bridge's interior walls and roof, most of them graphic in nature.

Worst of all was the eye-watering odor of old urine.

Taylor slipped his arm off her shoulders and lowered himself carefully to the floor. He closed his eyes and leaned against the side of the bridge, running a hand through his damp hair. "The smell is giving me a headache. Why don't they just pee off the bridge into the stream? You'd think that would be more fun."

With her Maglite, Gemma inspected the interior of the bridge. She'd seen the bridge dozens of times during supply runs but had never set foot inside it. Broken beer bottles and crushed cans were strewn across the floor. Discarded fast-food bags lay everywhere, expelling their empty wrappers and rotting remnants onto the wood. Most disturbingly, what appeared to be a pair of flannel pajamas lay crumpled in the far corner of the bridge. She didn't even want to consider what might've happened to their owner.

She held her breath as her eyes drifted to the wooden beams overhead, anticipating the sight of thousands of red-glowing eyes peering down at her.

"Taylor? There aren't any bats in here, right?"

"No," he replied, without opening his eyes. "No self-respecting bat would live in here."

Gemma wasn't convinced, but she couldn't see any bats, and there were other, more pressing matters. Crouching to check

Taylor's bandage, she handed him the Maglite, and he held it steady as she unwrapped the bandage and lifted the sterile pad to inspect his wound. It wasn't bleeding anymore, but she couldn't tell what kind of damage the bullet had inflicted to the inside of his leg. Or what kind of infection might already be setting in.

Sensing Taylor's eyes on her, studying her reaction, she nodded encouragingly. "It doesn't look bad. Since we've already established that I'm terrible at drawing maps, maybe I should consider a career in the medical field?"

He didn't even crack a smile. "Yeah. Maybe."

After she finished rewrapping the wound, she dug into her backpack and pulled out a bottle of water. "Here. Drink this."

Taylor pushed it away. "Keep it. I have plenty of water in my CamelBak. Plus, you'll need it for the hike back to your camp. My guys will be here soon."

"Are you sure they're coming?"

"I'm sure."

Gemma pulled up her jacket sleeve to look at her watch.

4:37

She had to leave. Now.

Gemma leaned her head against Taylor's shoulder and closed her eyes. The only sound was the constant flow of water rushing by in the creek below. She tried to think of something to say to Taylor. Something to make them both feel better. The idea of hiking all the way back to the Station without him—and without knowing when or if she might see him again—made her chest ache. It wasn't supposed to be this way. They weren't supposed to find each other again only to be ripped apart after only a few hours.

Besides, she couldn't leave without explaining the ring.

And Gavin.

She was about to speak—to try to explain her relationship with Gavin in a way that he could understand—when Taylor's hand closed around hers. Her heart fluttered as he raised it to his lips, kissed the back of her palm, and held it firmly against his chest. "Gemma, how is it, after all this time, that you're still a complete pain in my—?"

"Hey!" She punched him playfully in the arm with her free hand. Her other hand remained pressed against his chest. She wished it could stay there forever. "Although, I'm more of a pain in your *thigh* now, wouldn't you say?"

Taylor rolled his eyes. "Your jokes haven't improved since we've been apart. Your fiancé must not have much of a sense of humor. Or—if he does—it hasn't rubbed off on you."

Gemma's eyes fell to the pearl ring, which appeared to glow as it caught and reflected the waning light of the moon. She covered it with her hand. "Taylor, it's not what you think. We're together, yes, but it's not serious. He's more of a friend than anything, and he's certainly not my fiancé."

Liar, she thought.

"You're wearing a ring, Gemma. On *that* finger."

When she said nothing—because, really, what *could* she say? — he returned his attention to the ground. "I should've given you a ring that night. If I could go back in time, I would've done things differently."

So would I, she wanted to say.

Instead, she started to ramble, the way she always did when she was nervous. "He asked me, but I didn't say yes. If anything, it's more of a promise ring..."

Taylor released her hand. "You don't owe me an explanation, Gemma. I shouldn't have said anything. The only thing that matters to me is that you make it back to your group. We'll figure the rest out later. But you need to go. We've already wasted too much time."

That was true in so many ways.

"Okay." Gemma pushed herself off the wooden planks and brushed the dirt from the seat of her pants. She wanted to believe that, deep inside, she possessed the physical and mental strength to find her way back to the Station without collapsing or making a wrong turn. But getting home wasn't her greatest concern. Leaving Taylor alone on the bridge felt wrong. What if no one came for him? What if he went into shock or bled to death waiting for them? What if she never saw him again?

No.

She couldn't think like that.

Her fingers traveled to her chest, tracing the small shape hidden beneath her jacket. "We're going to have to leave, you know.

Probably today. Not because of your radio but because of everything else. We've stayed too long."

"I know."

She opened her mouth to ask how they'd find each other again, but the words wouldn't come out. What if he didn't want to find her again? What if, when Taylor looked at her now, he saw only a liar and a cheater?

She didn't want to hear his answer, so she didn't ask.

Taylor switched off the Maglite and passed it to her. "My guys are going to be here any minute. Get your friends off this mountain."

"Okay."

She hesitated for a few more seconds, trying to think of something to say. But Taylor wouldn't even look at her, his handsome features having settled into that stubborn expression she knew too well. So, she turned and walked away, the old boards creaking beneath her boots, as if protesting her departure.

But she kept walking.

From the near-perfect darkness of the bridge, she stepped into the final gasps of an endless night about to surrender to the dawn. In the short period of time they'd been on the bridge, the sky had changed from black to charcoal. To the east, the sun smoldered a deep red just below the horizon, as if the world was about to catch fire. She stuffed the Maglite inside her backpack. Drawing in a deep breath, steeling herself for the journey ahead, she grabbed the straps of her backpack and began to walk.

And then Taylor called out to her.

"Gemma."

She turned and sprinted back into the darkness, tripping over empty beer cans as she ran toward the silhouette slumped against the side of the bridge. She fell into his outstretched arms, and although she couldn't see his features clearly, she could *feel* him. The warmth of him. The rough stubble of his cheeks, damp from sweat or tears or a combination of both. She began to cry, her tears blending with his, and he brought his lips to hers in a kiss that was nothing like the one they had shared two years earlier. That kiss had been tentative, uncertain, their minds full of more immediate concerns. But there was no uncertainty or hesitation in this kiss. It was, at once, frantic and passionate and beautiful.

And—for a moment—it stole Gemma away from her cold-and-lonely existence and promised something better.

When they finally pulled apart, the first hint of sunlight pierced the interior of the bridge, slicing the air between them like a knife intent on separating them.

She couldn't bear to look at her watch. It had to be nearly five o'clock by now. The light illuminated Taylor's features, and she could see the worry written on his face. But something else lurked there, too. Something that hadn't been present a few minutes earlier.

Determination.

Resolve.

"I'll find you, Gemma." He locked his blue eyes on hers as he used his thumbs to wipe the tears from her cheeks. "Okay? I have no idea how, but I will. I'll figure something out."

"Okay..."

"Just don't run off and marry this other guy in the meantime, okay? Wait for me."

She laughed through her tears. Of course, she would wait for him. She would wait forever for Taylor Nolan. "Do you promise? No matter what?"

"No matter what."

Then he kissed her again. And again. And again.

Until she stopped crying and believed him.

CHAPTER
TEN

An hour into her hike back to the Station, Gemma hit a mental wall.

At first, the return climb seemed to be going well. Despite her exhaustion, she was able to travel faster and quieter without an injured soldier draped over her shoulders. She stopped only once to gulp down the remainder of her water, then returned the empty bottle to her backpack and continued upward. Moving at a steady clip, she leaned into the climb, feeling reenergized and strengthened each time she remembered Taylor's promise to find her. And his kiss.

Just as doubt had fueled her descent down the mountain, hope now fueled her ascent.

But soon her eyes began to drift shut, and she shuffled forward, zombie-like, until she tripped over something and landed hard on the ground. Then she got back up, bruised and sore but wide-awake, and continued slogging along until sleep overtook her again.

Each time she drifted off to sleep, her brain generated another nightmare, graphic scenes playing out on the stage of her mind like old horror movies on a reel. In one, she returned to the mine to find everyone gone, and only after searching each tunnel did she hear the explosion. As the rocks rained down on her, she realized that the Task Force had blown the entrance to the mine, sealing her alone in the darkness forever.

In another dream, she saw Taylor lying dead on the bridge, forgotten by his unit.

In yet another, Sophia screamed Gemma's name as Task Force soldiers dragged her toward a cross planted in the middle of a cornfield.

To make matters worse, beneath the relative warmth of her blood-stained jacket, her damp clothes and undergarments clung to her like Lycra, trapping moisture against her skin and causing her to shiver uncontrollably. She considered stopping to rest for a few minutes, maybe even taking a quick nap, but then nixed the idea. She had to get back to the others as quickly as possible to get them out of the mine.

And to find out about Brie. What had she told everyone? How much did Gavin know?

And what would she do if she returned to the Station and found everyone gone?

That final thought, in particular, jarred her, and she treated it as an unwelcome visitor, shoving it out of her mind and barring the door shut behind it. They wouldn't leave without her. Not Addie or Oliver or Gavin. Especially not Gavin. Even if the others left, he would stay behind. He would wait for her.

Unless he knew about—

"Don't move."

Gemma's eyes shot open, her entire body suddenly alert courtesy of the accompanying adrenaline dump. In a breath, she had to decide whether to stop or run. Everything in her body was telling her to run. Taylor had said there were other soldiers searching the mountain. If the voice belonged to a soldier, he would be heavily-armed and well-trained. Just like Taylor, who'd shot a pistol right out of Brie's hand.

She stopped.

"Good girl. Now, get your hands in the air. And don't try anything stupid, or I'll put a bullet in your spine."

She raised her hands above her shoulders.

That voice.

It was the same voice she'd heard on the radio before Max screamed at her to run.

Come out, come out, wherever you are!

"Turn around," he ordered. "Very slowly."

A strange calm settled over her as she turned to face the soldier. The black assault rifle in his hands matched Taylor's, as did the olive fatigues and tactical vest. But he was shorter and less physically-imposing than Taylor, with closely-shorn red hair, a dash of freckles across the bridge of his nose, and narrow, humorless eyes.

There appeared to be something wrong with his eyes. Too much pupil and not enough iris. The eyes of a snake. She couldn't stand to look into them for more than a few seconds.

Her eyes plunged to the nametape on his chest.

Mullen.

He removed his dark cap and used it to wipe his brow. "What are you doing out here? It's easy to get lost on this mountain, you know. Especially for a girl."

Ignoring the jab, Gemma tried to sound nonchalant. "I'm just hiking."

He nodded at her jacket. "You injured?"

She had no idea what he was talking about, until she lowered her head and saw that her jacket was covered in Taylor's blood.

The air felt too thick for her lungs. Inhospitable, like the atmosphere of some other planet. "I tripped over a rock and cut my hand on a stick." She held up her injured palm, now matted with dried blood. "Serves me right for hiking before the sun came up."

"That's a lot of blood for a cut hand."

"Well, the cut went pretty deep. I just kept wiping it on my jacket."

"Right." Mullen cocked his head and raised a pale eyebrow. "Got any weapons on you?"

She thought of the Leatherman in her backpack, but it might as well have been on the moon. "No."

"An early-morning hike with no weapons?" Mullen huffed. "That's real bright."

"Yeah." She forced a laugh. "I suppose it's not."

"You know, my unit's tracking a group of subversives. We believe they're hiding somewhere on this mountain. In fact, they executed a man in Ash Grove a few days ago."

"They..." The words caught in her throat. "...executed someone?"

The soldier's eyes gleamed. "Sure did. Built a cross and strung him up. Looks like the old man was still alive, too. Broke a few of his fingernails in the struggle. By the time we cut the poor geezer down, the birds had stripped off most of his flesh. Hopefully he kicked the bucket before they started to eat him."

She couldn't speak. It took everything within her not to cry.

Poor Henry.

Mullen tilted his head to examine her, a smirk worming its way onto his face. "But since you're one of the people I'm looking for, I suppose you already know about the old man."

Hot bile rose into her throat as a voice inside her head screamed: He knows! He knows!

Quickly, she conjured a backstory, one she hoped sounded believable, and began to stutter it out. "Look, I don't know who you think I am. But my name is Rachel Dawson." It was the first name that popped into her mind. The name of her best friend from elementary school. "I live in Ash Grove. It's just me and my father now, since my mother passed away a few years ago. Do you have a phone with you? You can call my father to confirm, if you want."

Mullen's eyes traveled down her body as she spoke, studying every inch of her. Not even trying to hide the fact that he was barely listening. Finally, his eyes returned to hers. They were dark—the eyes of a predator. "Look, I'm just doing my job. It's possible I'm wrong about you. But I've got this little test I like to use. If you pass, I'll send you on your way. How does that sound?"

"Okay..."

"Say that Jesus was a fraud."

She reached for her throat—for the chain hidden beneath her shirt—but stopped herself just in time. "What?"

Mullen raised the rifle and aimed it directly at her face. "You heard me."

Gemma's gaze dropped from Mullen's eyes to the barrel of his rifle. From one endless darkness to another. At the other end of that long metal tube was the bullet that would end her life. She visualized its shape: silver and cylindrical, smooth like a pill. It would penetrate her skull and rip through her brain, voiding her thoughts like cancelled checks.

How stupid of me, she thought. *I never believed this day would actually come.*

And then she heard herself say, softly but firmly, "No."

"No, what?"

"I won't say that."

Mullen blinked rapidly, as if unwilling to accept what he was hearing. Then he took a step toward her and hissed, "Subversive."

She stood her ground, defiant. "I'm not a subversive. I'm not *subverting* anything. Or hurting anyone. I'm in hiding because of thugs like y——."

Mullen grabbed her jacket and twisted her roughly around. He shoved her against the tree, ripped her backpack from her shoulders, and tossed it to the ground. "Hands behind your back! Wrists together!" She felt zip-ties tighten around her wrists, the hard-plastic digging painful trenches into her skin. The soldier ran a hand down Gemma's right side, then her left, searching both of her legs and inside her boots. When he finished his search, she heard him sniff the air. "You smell disgusting. Don't you people ever bathe?"

Gemma thought of Taylor. Maybe Mullen would let her go if she admitted to knowing a soldier. The two of them might even be friends, although she couldn't imagine Taylor being friends with someone like Mullen. But when she opened her mouth to speak Taylor's name, a voice inside her mind—a quiet voice with the force of a slap—stopped her.

No.

So, she said nothing.

Mullen spun her around and brought his face to within inches of hers. How ironic that he'd commented on her smell, when the foul stench of his own breath made Gemma want to gag.

"Where's your group? I know you're not alone."

She answered quickly. Maybe too quickly. "There's no one else. Just me."

"You still want to play games?" He inspected her body again, then licked his lips. "You don't think I can make you talk?"

At those words, a fuse lit inside her. A tiny ember glowing in the darkness. She nursed it. Fed it the fuel it needed to survive. She focused on Mullen's thin lips, still moist from his tongue. She thought of the gleeful look in his eyes as he'd described Henry's agonizing death. A death he'd certainly played a part in. And she remembered watching helplessly as someone like Mullen had dragged her sobbing mother away.

The ember burst into flame.

"Go ahead, you little worm." She clenched her fists behind her back, purposefully digging her nails into her injured palms. Drawing strength from the pain. "Touch me and see what I do to you."

In an instant, Mullen's expression morphed from amusement to disbelief, and finally to unbridled rage. "You shouldn't have said that."

He brought his hands to her neck and started to squeeze.

It happened so quickly that Gemma didn't even have time to suck in a final breath. She panicked and tried to squirm away from him, but he leaned into her, holding her against the tree with his own body weight. He wasn't big, but he was strong. Frantically, she rubbed her wrists up and down on the rough bark, trying to cut through the zip-ties. If she could get an arm free, she could go for his throat. But Mullen pressed her tighter against the tree until she couldn't move her hands at all.

"When will you learn? When will you stupid people *learn?*"

After those words, every sound disappeared. She could no longer hear Mullen's heavy panting as he squeezed the life out of her. The forest grew eerily quiet, as if even the birds and animals had ceased their daily migrations in order to watch the murderous scene playing out in front of them.

Gemma looked into Mullen's eyes, hypnotized by the desolation she saw in them. It was like staring into the cold vacuum of space. When her legs gave out, the soldier held her in place with his own body. And she realized that his hideous face would be the last thing she would ever see, his voice would be the last thing she would ever hear, and his rotten breath would be the last thing she would ever smell.

I'm going to die. Right here.

This is how I die.

A loud crash broke through the eerie silence—a dead branch, maybe? —and Mullen jumped backward, releasing his grip on Gemma's neck.

She sucked in a deep breath as the light flooded back into the world.

In one liquid motion, Mullen unslung his rifle and whirled around, likely expecting to find Gemma's friends sneaking up on him. It took only a moment for him to realize they were still alone and to return his attention to Gemma.

Only a second.

But it was enough.

When Mullen turned back to her, Gemma slammed her knee squarely into his groin. His face contorted into a satisfying combination of surprise and pain. He dropped the rifle and doubled over, clutching himself and howling, a terrible, animal sound. Before he could recover from the initial blow, she ran forward and crashed into him, knocking him down. But her hands were still tied behind her back, throwing her off-balance, and she nearly fell on top of him.

Somehow, she remained on her feet... and she ran.

Ignoring Mullen's shouts for her to stop, she ran in the opposite direction of the Station, instead heading toward Ash Grove. Mullen would catch up with her—she was under no delusions about that—but she intended to draw him as far away from her friends as possible.

A final act of penance for putting everyone she loved in danger.

And for leaving Max behind.

Gemma could hear Mullen crashing through the woods behind her, bellowing curses as he narrowed the space between them. So, she opened her stride and ran faster. The forest closed around her, accepted her into its arms, protecting her like a mother protects her child.

He wasn't going to catch her.

Not on *her* mountain.

A shot rang out behind her, impossibly loud, and she ducked instinctively. The movement threw her off-balance and sent her hurtling toward the earth. With her arms tied, she could do nothing to arrest her fall, and she landed hard, knocking the air from her lungs. Her head slammed into something sharp, and the world briefly dimmed. A sickening wave of pain rolled through her body, threatening to carry her away on a sea of nothingness, but she bit down hard on her tongue, forcing herself to stay conscious.

Heavy footsteps approached, crushing fallen branches.

Gemma tried to push herself up.

Too late.

A shadow loomed. A dark figure in olive fatigues. He straddled her body, and she closed her eyes, not wanting to see anything else. He grabbed her jacket, grunting with the effort, and pulled her upper body out of the leaves.

Mullen treated Gemma to another whiff of his nauseating breath. "Open...your...eyes."

Against her will, she felt her eyelids flutter open, the brightness momentarily blinding her. But her vision cleared in time to see a fist soaring toward her face.

A jarring impact.

And then...

Nothing.

CHAPTER ELEVEN

Cold.

Pain.

Gemma swam into consciousness, fighting the current that threatened to pull her back into the murky depths of oblivion. Knowing, on some instinctive level, that she *had* to wake up, that her life depended on it. But waking meant pain. Even in those first fragile seconds of awareness, a gnawing pain built behind her eye sockets. A harbinger of things to come.

Steeling herself against the pain, she forced her eyelids open.

So bright. The light hurt her.

Everything hurt.

Still, she kept her eyes open, blinking as the world came into focus.

Where was she? What happened?

She was lying on a concrete floor in an unfamiliar room, hands bound atop her stomach. There was something soft beneath her head, cushioning it from the floor. A pillow or folded-up blanket?

She couldn't stop shivering. Whether from shock or cold, she couldn't be sure. The air tasted dry and stale—like the inside of a tomb—and she struggled to pull in each breath. To her left, a long table stretched out against a concrete wall, its surface covered with green storage containers. The wall boasted a single narrow window just below the ceiling. Much too small to squeeze through. Microscopic dust particles floated before her eyes, performing elaborate waltzes inside their slender beam of light.

Carefully, she turned her head to the right. A mustard-colored couch stood against the opposite wall, its cushions frayed and sagging. Beside the couch, twin stacks of wooden chairs nearly reached the old drop ceiling. Overhead, several of the white tiles were darkened by water stains. They reminded her of teeth.

Crooked, yellow teeth.

She swallowed, trying to force a little saliva down her raw throat, grimacing as her muscles contracted against nothing. Water. She needed water. Did she have any water left? Her head felt as though someone had placed it inside a vice and was slowly cranking it tighter and tighter. Even the meager light streaming through the window made her eyeballs pulse within their sockets.

She tried to push herself up, intending to look for her backpack, but it was no use. Everything hurt too much. Her head. Her ribcage. Even her right ankle felt swollen inside her boot. When had she injured it?

She couldn't remember.

"The roach is up, sir." A familiar voice—brimming with resentment—spoke from the far corner of the room.

An avalanche of memories crashed down on her at the sound of that voice. Mullen. She tried to flip onto her stomach to crawl away from him, but a fresh wave of agony passed through her body, and she shuddered as a thick blanket of stars fell over the room. She forced her eyes open, willed herself to stay conscious. Who knew what might happen if she passed out?

The moment her vision cleared, she lifted her head, straining to see past her feet.

At the other end of the room, Mullen stood in front of a door, regarding Gemma with his narrow, slit eyes. How much time had passed since their interaction in the forest? Yet, with his fists tightly clenched at his side, he appeared to be hanging onto his self-control by the barest of threads.

"Shall I move her to a chair for the interrogation, sir?"

Interrogation?

She felt totally helpless. A tiny worm on a big hook.

Another soldier stepped forward. A variety of patches and insignia—abundant to the point of absurdity—adorned the front of his neatly-pressed dress uniform. But his face remained obscured by shadows. "No, that won't be necessary." The man's voice sounded gritty, like sandpaper. "Get back out there, Private. Notify me as soon as you find the rest of them."

Mullen hesitated. "But, sir—"

"You're dismissed."

Gemma watched as Mullen chewed this over. Like a cat with a mouse in its jaws, he seemed unwilling to surrender his fresh kill to another cat. After a few moments, he muttered, "Yes, sir." Then he disappeared through the door, easing it shut behind him.

The older man crossed the room and knelt beside Gemma. His weathered features—a series of deep-set lines and hard edges set atop a neck as unyielding as a tree trunk—organized themselves into something resembling sympathy. However, the expression seemed strange on the man's hardened face. "Please allow me to apologize for the way Private Mullen behaved today. I assure you that he'll be disciplined harshly for his actions. In the meantime, my job is to make certain that you're safe and comfortable while we get this whole mess straightened out."

She opened her mouth to speak, produced only a dry clicking sound, then cleared her throat and tried again. "Who...are you?"

The man grinned at her, revealing a mouthful of unnaturally white teeth. "Colonel James Carver. Commander of a Special Intelligence Task Force Battalion operating out of the Gap. Private Mullen detained you under suspicion of being a subversive. He claims you admitted as much... and then tried to run from him. But —subversive or not—he had no right to cause you any pain or injuries. This particular soldier tends to be a little...overzealous...at times."

Overzealous? That was putting it mildly.

Gemma's eyes flicked to the narrow window. "Where am I?"

"Still in Ash Grove. After we finish verifying your identity, you'll be released. Your name is Rachel Dawson, correct?"

Was that the name she'd given Mullen? It sounded right. "Yes."

"Good. Would you like me to remove your restraints? I apologize for not taking them off sooner, but I had to make sure that you weren't going to be violent."

"Yes. Please."

Carver produced a small knife from his uniform pocket, lifted Gemma's hands from her stomach, and cut through the plastic zip-ties, careful to not let the knife touch her skin. "When Private Mullen brought you in, I had my medic examine you. She believes you've suffered a mild concussion. According to Mullen, you took a pretty nasty spill after you ran from him. He thinks you might've hit your head on a rock."

An image flashed through Gemma's mind: Mullen's fist, flying toward her face.

But she kept her mouth shut.

"You're going to be fine," he continued, "aside from being slightly dehydrated. My medic wanted to put you on a saline drip, but I talked her out of it. I didn't want you to wake up hooked to a bunch of tubes. Just promise me you'll drink all the water I've provided for you. How does that sound?"

She nodded her head slightly. "Okay."

Carver slid the knife back into his pocket. "Rachel, you should know that soldiers from my unit are actively searching the Dragon's Back Mountain right now for a group of subversives. Twenty-five or thirty of them. Possibly more. We believe they've been holed up there for several years, using Ash Grove as a home base, of sorts. A local storeowner recently ran afoul of them. Apparently, he'd been providing them with food and supplies for quite some time. Several of the locals suspected him of being a sympathizer but chose to look the other way. Since you're from Ash Grove, I assume you've heard about Mr. Castern?"

She rubbed at the raw skin of her wrists. "Yes. I heard."

The colonel drummed his fingers on the pews. "Terrible thing. We believe Henry made the decision to stop assisting the subversives, and they punished him by taking his life. Some people in town are pretty riled up, as you can imagine. They're talking about forming a militia to search the mountain themselves. I'm doing my best to hold them off, but I can only do so much. They're civilians, so they're not subject to my orders."

That's not possible, is it? Gemma wondered. A militia in Ash Grove?

But anything was possible now.

"It doesn't sit right with me, you know?" Carver seemed to be watching her closely. "A bunch of civilians traipsing through the woods with their hunting rifles. Feels like lynch mob justice. Things could get out of hand very quickly, if you know what I mean."

Gemma tore her eyes away from him and concentrated her attention on a water-stained ceiling tile. "The whole situation sounds very...volatile."

"It is. If we don't locate this group soon, I'll be forced to involve the town in the search. But I don't want anyone to get hurt. My top priority is protecting everyone's safety, including those who've broken the law."

She nodded. "I understand."

"Good." The colonel stood and used his palms to smooth out the wrinkles in his uniform. Then he extended his hands to her. "There's an old couch in the corner. May I help you over to it?"

"No," Gemma said quickly. She didn't want Carver or anyone else touching her. "I'm going to lay here until my head clears. But thank you for offering."

Carver withdrew his hands. "Okay. But don't try to walk right away. Take things slow. Your main issue right now is dehydration. You'll feel much better after you get some water in your system." He headed toward the exit, but hesitated when he reached the door. "The restroom is located outside in the hallway. You'll notice another door at the top of the stairwell, but that must remain locked until we confirm your identity. I apologize again for any inconvenience this has caused you, Rachel. I promise to get you home as soon as possible."

She wasn't going home. Carver would figure out her real identity soon enough. But she nodded anyway. "Thank you."

"My medic will bring your dinner in about an hour. Until then, try to drink as much water as you can. There are four jugs near the couch. If you need more water—or anything else, for that matter— just let my medic know."

"Okay."

Carver left the room, closing the door softly behind him.

Gemma watched the door for a long time. Waiting for Mullen to come bursting into the room, laughing at her and mocking her for believing Carver's lies. He would still be laughing as he dragged her back to the field and crucified her alongside Henry Castern.

But no one came.

Eventually, her fear of taking her eyes off the door gave way to an overwhelming, primal need.

Water.

Not trusting her ability to stand, Gemma slowly pushed herself onto her hands and knees, not going too fast for fear of passing out. She remained there for a few moments, breathing slowly, allowing her brain to acclimate. When her vision cleared, she crawled across the dirty floor, traveling faster when she spotted the jugs of water positioned in front of the couch.

She collapsed against the couch, grabbed one of the jugs, and brought it to her lips. Cold water flowed down her throat, reviving her. She immediately felt better. She drank until her stomach swelled and then stretched out on the couch, resting her throbbing head on the worn upholstery.

She wrapped her arms around herself and closed her eyes.

Taylor's face filled her mind, wearing the determined expression he'd worn just before she'd left him on the bridge. "*I'll find you, Gemma,*" he'd said. And she'd believed him.

Because, if anyone could find her, it would be Taylor.

He *had* to.

Or she was dead.

CHAPTER
TWELVE

With his untouched dinner cooling in front of him, Taylor gazed through his window at the doctors and nurses on the neighboring rooftop. A Life Flight helicopter appeared as a speck of blue on the horizon, and he experienced a twinge of regret as it soared toward the hospital, its rotors beating the air into submission. The heavy *whup-whup* of the blades reminded him of the old war movies he used to watch with his father. Such classics as We Were Soldiers and Black Hawk Down had inspired him to join the military, specifically the Army. Driven by a strong sense of duty to protect the weak, he'd once dreamed of becoming a helicopter pilot.

Then his mother died...and Taylor's dreams died with her.

The bird hovered over the helipad like an enormous dragonfly, its nose edging toward Taylor as the pilot oriented his landing based on the wind. Then it settled delicately onto the helipad, first one skid, then the other. The moment the pilot cut the power to the engine, the doctors and nurses converged on the helicopter, ducking to avoid being decapitated by the spinning blades.

Seconds later, they extracted a female patient from the helicopter, her blonde hair tinged with blood. She wore only jeans and a bra. A single flip-flop dangled from her left foot. Her other foot was bare. A paramedic jumped out of the helicopter and ran alongside the gurney, still bagging the intubated patient, his lips moving as he relayed information to the doctors.

Almost as a reflex, Taylor closed his eyes and began to pray for the girl. But then he caught himself and stopped.

What was the point?

The group disappeared inside the hospital, leaving the helicopter's crew to begin its post-flight checks. The co-pilot appeared to be doing most of the work: walking around the bird, opening and closing compartments, jotting down notes on a clipboard. The pilot—much older and heavier—pulled a pack of cigarettes from the pocket of his flight uniform and strolled to the roof's edge.

Taylor allowed his eyes to drift beyond this scene, to the mountain in the distance.

The Dragon's Back.

He couldn't stop thinking about Gemma.

The wound in his leg was the farthest thing from his mind, thanks to Gemma's field dressing and the excellent pain medication he'd received at Mountain View Medical Center. An ER resident had spent the better part of an hour cleaning and stitching the wounds in the outer part of his thigh, all while praising Taylor's wrapping of the wound. (Taylor hadn't mentioned Gemma, of course). Afterwards, the young doctor had prescribed a round of intravenous antibiotics to prevent infection. Before leaving the room, he'd squeezed Taylor's shoulder and thanked him for his service.

Taylor closed his eyes for what felt like the thousandth time, desperate for sleep. But his mind refused to shut down. Gemma occupied his every thought. Had she made it back to her group? What would she do if they were gone by the time she returned?

If they left her behind, it was his fault.

He got her into this.

"Knock, knock."

The door to his room swung inward and the shift nurse, Collie, poked her head through the opening. "Sorry to wake you. But it's time to check your vitals and give you more medication."

"No problem, ma'am," he replied, pushing himself up in bed. "Come on in."

Collie wheeled her cart and laptop into the room and paused at the head of Taylor's bed. "I hate bothering people when they're asleep," she said, tapping away at the keyboard, the dark skin of her hands contrasting with her bright red nails. "But I've got to do my rounds. Plus, it's important to stay ahead of the pain. Believe me when I tell you that."

"I believe you, ma'am. And it's fine. I wasn't sleeping."

The corners of her eyes wrinkled with concern. "Well, you *should* be sleeping, considering the day you've had. What's your pain like now? Scale of one to ten?"

Taylor considered this for a moment. "Maybe a two or a three, ma'am. But I was at a twelve when I checked in, so I'm happy with a three."

Collie appeared to be satisfied with that answer. "We're going to keep you on the same pain management schedule until the morning. If all goes well, I'll have the morning nurse walk your meds back a bit before you're discharged."

"And when will that be?"

"Possibly tomorrow," she said. "But I'm not making any promises. Okay?"

"Yes, ma'am."

She waved her hand as if swatting a fly. "Would you stop with the ma'am business? It makes me feel old. And I know what you're going to say next. 'But, ma'am, you *are* old!' And that's true. But it's not nice to make a chubby old nurse feel worse about herself than she already does."

"Understood..." At the last second, Taylor stopped himself from calling her 'ma'am' again. "Force of habit, I guess."

"Well, try to break that habit while you're my patient, okay?"

"Roger that."

Collie pushed two pills from their casing and handed them to Taylor along with a small glass of water. He popped them into his mouth and took a sip of water, but something stopped him from swallowing the pills. Not a voice in his head, or a premonition, or anything equally dramatic. Just a gentle tugging in his chest—one he couldn't ignore.

He slid the pills underneath his tongue and gulped down the water.

The nurse scanned his hospital bracelet and began typing information into her laptop. "I have a son who's about your age. Jackson, Jr., but we call him JJ. Been working at Wegmans for a few weeks now. Not curing cancer or anything, just bagging groceries, but it's a steady paycheck and he's not getting into trouble. His father and I are trying to convince him to join the Task Force. He could use the discipline."

Taylor's mouth filled with the bitter taste of the slowly-dissolving pills. "He'll definitely get a lot of that in the Task Force."

She closed the laptop and studied him. "Are you happy? In the Task Force, I mean?"

The question unnerved him. Was he happy in the Task Force? Before yesterday, he would've said yes without hesitation. The pay was good, and he liked the people he served with. Most of them, anyway. Plus, the job gave him the purpose he'd always been searching for. He was part of something much bigger than himself; a tiny cog in a very important wheel.

But...now?

Now he had no idea how to respond.

Finally, he shrugged. "It's a paycheck."

"A paycheck?" Collie's jaw dropped. She obviously didn't like his answer. "Without people like you, this country wouldn't stand a chance. I can hardly bear to watch the news anymore. Every night there's another horror story about these subversives. They're out there...and they're spreading like the plague."

Taylor's mind flashed back to Gemma. To their brief time together on the mountain. She'd bandaged his wound and practically carried him all the way to the bridge. She'd put her own safety at risk to help him. And for what?

What had he ever done for her?

The nurse edged closer to him, her eyes growing dark. "You know, my grandmother used to drag me to her church every Sunday. She'd forced me to be quiet and listen while the minister spewed his garbage from the pulpit. Even as a child, I knew it was wrong, but what could I do? My grandmother told me that all non-believers go to hell. It doesn't matter how good they are." She threw up her hands. "What kind of religion is that? I could've danced for joy when the government finally stopped hiding behind the First Amendment and started shutting down the churches and detaining the leaders. But they weren't content to go quietly, were they? They couldn't stop infecting others with their lies."

The words left Taylor's mouth before he could stop them. "Yes, but they're not all bad. Some are decent people."

Collie looked at him as if he'd lost his mind. "Are you kidding? The decent ones come to their senses and renounce. The other ones —the ones filling up the detention centers and *especially* the subversives—they're not decent. They're dangerous criminals. You of all people should understand that."

What was he doing? Why was he arguing with her?

"Yes, ma'am," he replied. "I suppose that's true."

The nurse's face softened, but she didn't correct him this time. "I'm sure you've seen a lot of terrible things in your line of work. Things that make you question if what you're doing is right. But I promise you: what you're doing isn't only right, it's necessary. Without people like you—" She fidgeted with the pen lying beside her keyboard. "Goodness, I don't even want to imagine what this country would look like."

Taylor wanted to say that she was right. He'd seen a lot of terrible things. And he'd done a lot of terrible things. He'd burned churches to the ground. He'd pressed the barrel of his rifle against the heads of cowering women and forced them to renounce their faith. He'd wrestled screaming children from their parent's arms and carried them away. And never once had he turned around to look back at the devastation he'd wrought. The lives he'd ruined.

He'd done so many things. Things she couldn't imagine.

She patted his legs through the blanket. "Enough talk for tonight. I can see that you're tired. Get some rest. I'll try not to bother you for a few hours." She pushed her cart toward the door. "Just press the button on your remote if you need me before then, okay?"

"Roger that."

After Collie left the room, Taylor spat the half-dissolved pills into his palm and tucked them inside his pillow case.

Outside the window, the pilot and co-pilot were gone. The hospital's dusk-to-dawn lights flickered on in the parking lot, projecting shafts of light on his window. The sun vanished beneath the horizon and night fell on the mountain, casting its inhabitants into darkness. A deeper darkness than most people would ever know. How had Gemma survived up there for two years? What had her life been like?

And who had she spent her time with?

Sleep came suddenly and without warning. He never felt his eyelids growing heavy, never felt them drifting shut. The darkness seized him and dragged him away from the hospital. Away from the bland, sterile room, with its overpoweringly antiseptic smell. Away from Collie and the pilot and the dying girl with the blood-stained hair and the single dangling flip-flop.

He slid into a nightmare, the same one he'd been having for four years.

Only this time, it was different.

The old man looks smaller somehow, his imposing height and quiet strength no longer rendering him indestructible. Standing on the porch of Taylor's childhood home, Joseph Nolan appears tired and defeated. Accusation burns within his deep-set blue eyes as he silently dares his only son to do something. To put a stop to this.

As if he could.

As if he *would*.

In the driveway, Taylor leans against the hood of an idling SUV, the engine hot against his back, his new uniform damp with sweat. He keeps his face stoic. Expressionless. Just as he's been trained to do. No good ever comes from arguing with subversives, especially ones as arrogant as his minister father. Besides, there's nothing Taylor—or anyone else—can do for him now. As the saying goes, the old man had made his proverbial bed. Now he must lie in it.

His father speaks to him. *She needs you.*

Taylor's practiced apathy falters, briefly giving way to genuine confusion. He thinks first of his mother, but she's been dead for years. *Shut up,* he mutters. And there's such a sense of freedom—of liberation—in speaking to his father this way, in saying things he never would've said when he lived under the old man's roof.

She needs you, son. You have to find her.

Something isn't right. Although he's under strict orders to not speak to the subversive while his sergeant searches the house, he can't stop himself. *Who needs me?*

You know who, son. The carnival girl.

Taylor feels his body stiffen. Anger tightens every muscle. This isn't in the script. His father never spoke about Gemma during his detention. And Taylor never told him about the carnival. He abandons the SUV and takes the porch steps two at a time, not stopping until his face is within inches of his father's. The old man flinches and steps backward, as if anticipating a punch. Taylor derives some satisfaction from this.

Don't pretend you know me. He spits the words out. *You know nothing about me.*

Hurt floods the old man's eyes. *I know you. You're my son. And you're responsible for this.* His father nods toward the house, where Taylor can hear desk drawers opening and closing. A lamp falls—or is pushed—off a desk and shatters on the floor.

But I've already forgiven you, son. I've forgiven every—

Shut up! Enraged, he grabs his father's arms and wrenches them behind his back, relishing the grunt of pain that slips from the old man's lips. *Let's go! Right now!*

Taylor pushes his father down the porch steps toward the SUV. Several cars pass by, their occupants watching with mild interest before returning their attention to the road. These detentions are nothing out of the ordinary. Not anymore.

The July air smells hot and wrong, like burnt leather. The newly-laid asphalt shimmers and bubbles beneath the roasting sun as Taylor shoves his father into the air-conditioned transport vehicle. He slams the door shut just as his sergeant emerges from inside the house, red-faced and bellowing.

SUBVERSIVE

Taylor stands at attention and takes the lecture in stride, maintaining a neutral expression as his sergeant literally spits insults in his face, calling him a worthless grunt, incapable of following orders. Taylor barely hears the shouts, the foul language, the name calling. All of it fades into the background as he locks eyes over his sergeant's shoulder with the subversive seated inside the transport vehicle.

His father's lips are moving, and although the car's windows are up and the air conditioning is blasting, Taylor hears every word.

Find her, son. The carnival girl.

Find her now.

CHAPTER
THIRTEEN

"How much farther?"

Sophia's voice roused Gavin back to consciousness. Back to the forest. Back to this endless death march. He'd fallen asleep on his feet again, his mind flashing to his final memory of his mother. Her lifeless body sprawled on the bedroom floor, an empty bottle of vodka lying just out of reach. The pills from her nightstand—*all* of the pills—gone.

He pushed the image from his mind.

The ten-year-old clung to his back like a monkey, the incessant chattering of her teeth pushing him over the edge. He didn't know how much more of this he could take. The weight of the girl. The uncertainty. The exhaustion. He was ready for it all to be over.

One way or another.

Gavin stopped walking and shifted Sophia higher on his back, trying to relieve some of the pressure on his throat. But Sophia only tightened her grip around his neck, as if afraid that he, too, might try to leave her.

"Ease up," he snapped. "You trying to kill me?"

He'd never spoken to Sophia so harshly before, but after nearly forty-eight hours with little to no sleep, he was dog-tired and miserable. Hiking all day with a sixty-pound girl clinging to his back hadn't helped matters. He felt like an old pack mule, forced to carry its final load before being led off to the slaughter.

Which, right now, didn't sound half-bad.

It would be night again soon. Almost an entire day had passed without Gemma.

"Gavin? How far?"

He scanned the unfamiliar section of forest. "I have no idea. You know as much as I do."

And that was the truth. Oliver never told him anything. It didn't matter how many supply runs he volunteered for, or how many tower shifts he pulled. He'd never be good enough to lead. Only a few select individuals were allowed into Oliver's inner circle, which included Kurt, Coop, and Mia. Those four made every decision for the group—from the food they ate, to the sleeping arrangements, to the tower rotation.

And last night, without consulting anyone, they'd decided to abandon the Station.

Gavin squinted into the distance. The tail end of the group was now a few dozen yards ahead and slowly pulling away. His neck felt a little better, and he could breathe easier. But as soon as he resumed his sluggish pace, Sophia slid back down, an anchor determined to sink him.

When Kyle had appeared at the fire tower sometime after midnight, breathless from sprinting up the mountain, he'd blurted out that Gavin and Oliver needed to get back to the Station right away. Gavin had assumed the worst. The Task Force had found them. In his mind's eye, he saw the others fleeing into the forest. Or further into the darkness of the mine.

But then Kyle had said, "It's Gemma. She's gone."

Gavin didn't remember much after that. Only running through the pitch-black woods, the beam of his flashlight bouncing along the ground, ignoring Oliver's muffled calls for him to stop. He'd tripped over fallen logs and crashed to the ground, tearing more holes in his already-tattered pants. But he'd gotten back up and continued running, desperate to reach Gemma. To find her before it was too late.

But it was already too late.

After hours of packing, the whole group had set out before dawn, bringing with them as many supplies as they could carry, keeping the rising sun to their backs as they blindly followed Oliver into the unknown. They'd stopped twice to rest and eat, but the breaks were obscenely short, lasting no more than an hour before Oliver got antsy and forced everyone, groaning and tired, back to their feet.

Kyle had offered to take turns carrying Sophia, but his attempts at prying the girl from Gavin's back had ended when she'd released a banshee-like shriek that had terrified the entire group.

But at least she wasn't screaming anymore. At least she wasn't clinging to his arm and wailing, "Gavin! Please! The Golden Girls! They'll die!" over and over into his sleeve as he dragged her away from the Station.

She'd been hysterical about leaving those chickens behind, pleading with him during the frenzied madness of packing to find something to carry them in. And he'd *tried* to figure it out—he honestly had. Because they needed the chickens...and the eggs. At the last minute, he'd run into the mine and brought back one of the old canary-cage props. But the cage wasn't big enough to fit even one of Sophia's full-bodied hens. So, they'd left the four hens behind, along with all of the cots, most of the extra clothing, and half of the food supplies.

Sharp pain radiated from his abdomen to his chest. Another side-splitting cramp. Raising his arms above his head would help to relieve the pain, but he couldn't even do that. Not with his arms wrapped around Sophia's legs. So, he trudged onward and tried to ignore the cramp. It didn't matter anyway. The physical pain paled in comparison to how dead he felt on the inside.

Sophia buried her face in his coat and started to cry again.

He should talk to her, try to comfort her...

But he couldn't bring himself to do it.

Gavin knew what Sophia was going through. He understood abandonment and the long-term issues it created. His mother had loved alcohol—and her many boyfriends—more than she'd loved him. She'd put everything else before Gavin, right up until the night she took her own life while he slept in the next room. That had been the greatest abandonment of all, and it had created a bitterness within him.

A bitterness that—until last night—he thought he'd buried and forgotten long ago.

He replayed his last moments with Gemma in his mind, searching for clues. Something he'd overlooked. But he couldn't remember anything out of the ordinary. After she brought him the jacket, they'd talked for a few minutes, they'd kissed, and she'd left. There hadn't been anything unusual about the interaction. And he distinctly remembered her saying she would see him at breakfast. Why would she say that if she was already planning on leaving him —leaving *all* of them—in the middle of the night?

Gavin continued forward, one foot in front of the other, trying to outpace the rapidly-advancing darkness. He could barely make out the silhouettes of the others up ahead, which meant he and Sophia were falling even further behind. The thought made him uneasy, being so far to the rear of the pack. Like a wounded deer, easy to pick off. As night settled upon the mountain and the shadows stalked him, he felt strange eyes on him, studying him from a distance. But each time he glanced back, he saw only trees and the sloping ridgeline. Nothing for miles.

Still...

He'd spent enough time on the mountain to know when something wasn't right.

Gavin spun around, ignoring Sophia's whines of protest as he scanned the murky darkness. And then he saw it. A glint of light as the waning sunlight to his back reflected off of something in the distance. Just a brief flash, and then it was gone. Still, he remained rooted in place, watching the spot where he'd seen the reflection, waiting for movement. For someone to emerge from the darkness.

A thought occurred to him.

What if they *were* being followed...but not by the enemy?

"Gemma?" he called out, fully aware of how pathetic he sounded. Still, he couldn't stop himself from hoping. From imagining her stepping out of the shadows, as beautiful as always, her face streaked with tears of regret.

Tears he would kiss away the moment he reached her.

Sophia lifted her head from his shoulder. "Is she back there? Do you see her?"

He waited as long as he dared, but Gemma never came forward. And he couldn't see the reflection anymore. He'd imagined the whole thing. There wasn't anyone back there. The forest was as empty and desolate as his heart.

"No." Resigned, Gavin turned around. "She's gone, Soph."

When he realized he could no longer see the others, he started to run.

CHAPTER
FOURTEEN

Just before midnight, the roaches found an abandoned farmhouse.

Laying in the prone position, the barrel of his M-4 carbine perched on a fallen tree, Private Mullen counted the roaches through his night scope. Twenty-three adults plus one whiny brat. Two of the men had hunting rifles hanging from their shoulders, but none of the others had any weapons that he could see. How did they plan on defending themselves? By throwing their illegal Bibles at him? He pictured himself shooting the Bibles out of the air like skeet before taking aim at their owners.

The property was a hot mess. Broken windows. Chipped paint. A screen door hanging off its hinges. Weeds higher than his knees. The inside of the house was probably overrun with mice and bugs. Disgusting.

A roach motel. Where roaches check in but they don't check out.

Mullen would make sure of that.

SUBVERSIVE

The group clustered around the porch. Dirty and pathetic. A few of the older ones looked so bad that he wouldn't have been surprised if they dropped over dead. They reminded Mullen of sick dogs that just needed to be put out of their misery. At fifteen, he'd put a rifle to his own dog's head and blown its brains out. He could still remember the way it had slumped to the ground, whatever made it alive...just gone.

That hadn't been murder. The dog had cancer. It was suffering.

But he didn't feel sorry for the roaches. Unlike his dog, roaches deserved to suffer.

After the female roach took off on him, he'd caught up to her and knocked her out cold. Then he'd sat beside her body for a long time, thinking over his options. He could've strangled her. That would've felt good, but only for a few minutes. Or he could've hung onto her for a little while, then strangled her. He hadn't wanted to give her up—this new plaything he'd found—but his desire to please the colonel had eventually won out, and he'd delivered the girl to Carver with pride, like a cat dropping a wounded mouse on its owner's welcome mat.

Carver had been happy but not happy enough. He wanted more.

All the other roaches.

Finding the rest of the group hadn't been difficult. Mullen had just gone to the spot where he'd found the roach and then headed in the direction she'd been traveling. That led him straight to their hideout—some kind of old mine—and from there, it had only been a matter of tracking them.

When he'd finally caught up with the roaches, they'd been moving through the woods like a herd of braindead cattle, trampling branches and brush, blazing a path a mile wide. Except for the lanky guy carrying the little girl at the back of the pack, the rest hiked all close together instead of spreading out. They thought that made them safer. Less likely to be spotted. But the idiots had obviously never heard of noise or light discipline. They wouldn't shut up, and the moment it got dark, they whipped out their flashlights.

Morons.

From his spot on the ridge, Mullen watched an old geezer climb the porch steps and give a little speech. Mullen couldn't hear what the man was saying, but the roaches didn't look impressed. The old fart was probably senile. When he finished speaking, Grandpa Roach pulled something from his pocket and used it to unlock the front door. The rest of the roaches followed him inside the house.

So, Grandpa Roach lives here. Or used to live here. Interesting.

Mullen reached for his phone, intending to call the colonel, already imagining the praise he would get for locating the other roaches so quickly. First the girl...and now all of her friends. A whole roach infestation, sir, wiped out by yours truly. But when he found Carver's number among his contacts, his thumb hovered over the call button.

Mullen knew the right thing to do. He knew what Carver would want him to do.

But...he couldn't make himself push the call button.

What was that line from the book about the Grinch?

The Grinch had an idea.

The Grinch had a wonderful, awful idea.

All of Mullen's ideas were wonderful. And awful.

But this one was *really* good.

Mullen slipped the phone back into his pocket, and his dead father spoke up inside his mind. *You know, most people have a devil on one shoulder and an angel on the other. You, son, have a devil on both.*

He remembered the day his father had spoken those words to him. He was ten years old. He'd gotten angry with his mother and shoved her down the basement stairs for not letting him watch what he wanted on television. She'd broken her arm in two places, but she'd made up some lame story for the doctors. She was a pro at making up stories by then, thanks to a dozen years of marriage to Douglas Mullen. His father had stayed calm at the hospital, but as soon as they returned home, he'd laid into his only son with the belt, lashing him until blood ran down his back and soaked into his pants.

Maybe Mullen's old man had been right all along. Maybe there wasn't any good in him. Maybe he *did* have a devil on both shoulders.

But his father was dead now. Rotting in the ground with maggots in his eyes.

Who cared what a soggy old corpse thought?

Mullen dug a protein bar out of his ruck and ate it slowly. He needed time to think. With the group tucked safely away (or so they thought) inside the house, the property appeared empty. You'd never know there were two-dozen roaches scurrying around inside, spreading disease and stealing air from a world that hated them.

He sucked water from his CamelBak. It would be *so* easy. He could make it look like an accident. No one would ever know the truth. Carver might figure it out, but he wouldn't care. Carver didn't do things the way other commanders did things. That's why he and Mullen got along so well. He might even finally get a promotion. Sergeant Mullen had a nice ring to it.

He wasn't sure what he wanted to do yet. But the choice was all his.

For now, he would just watch.

And wait.

CHAPTER
FIFTEEN

The aroma of breakfast roused Taylor from sleep.

The morning's overcast sky echoed his mood after a night spent dreaming of his father. Twelve hours of reliving one of the worst days of his life, his sleep interrupted twice when Collie woke him to administer more oxycodone. Both times, after she left, he'd spat the pills into his hand and tucked them inside his pillowcase. Then he'd closed his eyes and slipped back into the dream as if he'd never left it.

Surprisingly, his thigh didn't hurt much anymore, even without the pain meds.

A plate with a dome-shaped lid sat on his bedside table, along with a covered glass of orange juice, a carton of milk, and a bowl of mixed fruit covered in plastic wrap. His stomach growled at the smell of cooked sausage. There would be eggs, most likely scrambled, with accompanying packets of salt and pepper. He used the bed's control panel to raise himself into a seated position, reached for the orange juice, and removed the paper cover. Bringing the small glass to his lips, he gulped it down in three swallows, trying to erase the lingering acrid taste of half-dissolved pills.

The door to his room exploded inward and a familiar voice barked, "Yo, Nolan!" Sergeant Mike Yost appeared in the doorway, a Styrofoam coffee cup in each hand and a fresh uniform draped over one arm. "You alone in here?"

Taylor groaned and sank deeper into his pillows. "Thankfully, yes. And don't let the fact that this is a hospital keep you from kicking in doors."

"My hands were full." Yost crossed the room and placed one of the cups on the bedside table. Dark liquid bubbled up from beneath the cheap plastic lid. He hung the uniform on the hook next to Taylor's bed. "Don't take this the wrong way, man, but you look worse than usual. I thought a little coffee might cheer you up."

"Thanks." Taylor reached for the cup, took a sip, and grimaced. The coffee tasted stale and burnt. *Bad diner coffee,* his father would've called it. But Taylor drank it anyway, grateful for the familiar rush of energy as the caffeine hit his system. "Good to see you, man. Thanks for coming."

Yost flopped into the room's only chair and propped his feet on the bed. Tiny beads of rainwater dripped from his boots onto the linen blanket. "I would've been here a half-hour ago, but the Gestapo at the front desk stopped me. Said I had to wait until visiting hours since I'm not family." He put air quotes around the last word. "I told her that the Task Force *is* your family, but she wasn't impressed. Anyway, my shift starts at zero-nine-hundred, so I can't stay. But I wanted to talk to you before I went back out."

Something wasn't right. Taylor could feel it. "What's going on?"

Yost took a long sip of coffee. Then he removed his damp boots from the bed and leaned forward. "The guys are confused, man. To be honest, so am I. No one understands what happened to you out there. You never saw who shot you?"

Taylor crossed his arms and repeated what he'd told the two soldiers who'd picked him up at the bridge. "I heard three pistol shots from somewhere lower on the ridge. The last one grazed my leg. I never saw the guy who shot me. It could've been a subversive, or just some idiot shooting at birds."

"And you lost your radio?"

Taylor rubbed his forehead. "The stupid clip had been loose for days. It kept slipping off my belt. All of our equipment is old. Half of my stuff is held together by duct tape. Anyway, I didn't realize my radio was missing until after I got hit." The story didn't need to be perfect; it only needed to buy Gemma and her friends enough time to get off the mountain. When other Task Force scouts eventually located his radio at the bottom of the shaft, they'd know Taylor had lied, but he'd deal with that later. "Does Carver know I got shot?"

Lifting the cover off of Taylor's breakfast, Yost inspected the food briefly before he grabbed a sausage link and popped the entire thing into his mouth. "I'm sure he knows, but I doubt he cares," he spoke through a mouthful of meat. "The colonel's got too much going on right now to worry about you. You aren't going to eat this, are you?"

"Help yourself. What's going on with the colonel?"

Yost's eyes widened. "No one's told you?"

"You're the only person I've talked to since I've been here."

Yost snatched another sausage link and wagged it at Taylor. "You're not going to believe this. You really aren't. Yesterday, Colonel Carver issued an order for all scouts to collapse their searches into two main grids. Sectors three and four. Weren't you in four?"

Taylor didn't like where this was going. "Yeah."

"None of us knew what was going on. We figured Carver got a tip from a local or something." He paused to take a long swig of his coffee. A small amount dribbled onto the front of his uniform, but he didn't seem to notice. "Then we found out what *really* happened."

"Which was?"

Yost's eyes lit up with excitement. "They found one."

Taylor swallowed hard. "One what?"

"What do you think? One of *them*. A subversive. A girl from the group we've been looking for."

No. No. No.

Taylor stopped himself from grabbing Yost and shaking the story out of him by gripping a fistful of his bedsheets. "What are you talking about? What girl?"

"I have no idea. Some private from Alpha Company—Mullen —found her on the mountain yesterday morning. She was walking around alone, unarmed except for a Leatherman in her backpack. Can you believe that? How stupid can you be?"

No. This couldn't be happening.

"She tried to run, but Mullen caught her. Sounds like she almost got herself shot. From what I've heard, Mullen's a little..." Yost spun a finger next to his head in the universal symbol for crazy. "Lucky for you, this news overshadowed your little hunting accident. It was all anyone could talk about last night. I saw a picture of her on Flanagan's phone. Cute girl, but she looked pretty messed up."

Anger surged through Taylor, unlike anything he'd ever felt before. Why? Why had he asked Gemma to take him to the bridge? Why hadn't he just gone by himself? "The private who detained her..." He could barely bring himself to ask the question. "Did he...hurt her?"

"Nah. Sounds like he roughed her up a bit, but nothing major. I'm sure he was just mad that she ran." He took another sip of coffee and scowled. "This stuff is gross, even with four packets of sugar. You'd think a hospital this size could afford a decent—"

"You saw a picture of the girl, right? What did she look like?"

Yost shrugged. "I don't know. Like a normal chick, I guess. Except for the bruises. Late teens or early twenties, maybe. Definitely not leggy enough for me, and I prefer blondes, but her body was banging." He shoved the last sausage in his mouth and smirked. "I guess the subversive diet really works."

Taylor squeezed the bedsheets harder, barely restraining himself from punching Yost. The back of his throat burned as the acidic orange juice worked its way back up his esophagus. After putting herself at risk to get him to the bridge, Gemma had never made it back to the mine. A soldier had stopped her—and hurt her —and now she'd been detained. His eyes dropped to his coffee. Dark grounds stuck to the rim of the cup like specks of dirt.

Various scenarios played out in his mind. What he needed was more information. A lot more.

The same thing Carver wanted.

"Where is she?"

Yost blinked at him. "Who?"

"Who do you think?" Taylor's jaw clenched. "The girl."

Yost picked up a fork and stabbed at the pile of eggs. He scooped them into his mouth and made a face. "Your eggs are cold, man. Anyway, the girl is still in Ash Grove. I thought that was strange, you know? Why isn't Carver shipping her off to a detention center? Or to an interrogator at the Gap?"

It was obvious to Taylor. "Because *he* wants to interrogate her."

"Maybe. Especially if she's part of the group that crucified the old man. Did you hear about that?" Yost scooped more eggs into his mouth. "The locals want someone to fry for that one."

Taylor slammed his eyes shut.

Gemma had tried to tell him, but he hadn't listened to her.

He opened his eyes. "Where are they holding—"

"Sergeant Nolan?" A quiet voice interrupted him. "Good morning."

Both of their heads swiveled as a young nurse stepped into Taylor's room, her face buried in her clipboard, her blonde hair swept back into a bun. When she spotted Yost seated next to the bed, she hesitated in the doorway, her mouth dropping open. "Oh. I'm sorry to interrupt."

Yost dropped his fork and shot out of his chair. "Good morning, ma'am. You're probably here to change his bedpan or something, right? Am I in the way?"

The nurse giggled, her cheeks flushing crimson. "I'm just doing my rounds," she said breathlessly. "I didn't mean to interrupt your conversation."

"You couldn't interrupt anything if you tried."

The nurse giggled again.

Yost extended his hand. "I'm Michael, by the way. And you are...?"

"Olivia." She held a slim hand out to Yost, who shook it with a lopsided grin plastered on his face. "Olivia Wheeler. Please, take your time. I have other patients to check so I'll skip this one for now." She appeared to notice Taylor for the first time. "I'll stop back in a few minutes, Sergeant Nolan."

"Thank you," Taylor replied.

The nurse offered Yost an unabashedly flirtatious smile. "It was lovely meeting you."

"You too, ma'am."

After she left the room, Yost couldn't contain his excitement. "Oh, man. *Oh, man!* Did you see that?"

"Yeah, I saw it. And I'm sure you guys will be very happy together for the next two weeks." That was the maximum lifespan for any Yost relationship. "So, where are they holding her?"

"Huh?" Yost's eyes were glued to the doorway. "Who?"

"G—" He stopped himself from saying her name. "The girl. The subversive."

"Right. So, Carver and a few of his soldiers have commandeered the community building in Ash Grove. I heard it used to be a church. How's that for irony?"

But Taylor wasn't listening anymore. Carver must have a reason for keeping Gemma in Ash Grove instead of moving her to a detention center. Maybe he was planning on interrogating her to learn the location of the rest of her group. Or maybe he was planning something else. Something worse.

Either way, Taylor had to help her.

"You know Carver." Yost picked up the fork and demolished the last of Taylor's eggs. "He does whatever he wants. Most of the higher-ups are afraid to cross him. They treat him like some kind of god. People say he's bulletproof. He doesn't even bleed."

Taylor had heard that too, but he knew better.

Everybody bleeds.

"I almost forgot." Yost dug into the pocket of his uniform and pulled out a set of car keys. He dropped them on the bedside table next to Taylor's half-eaten breakfast. "Your Charger is parked in Lot

A. Third row. Parked it under a lamppost in the hopes that a few pigeons might take their morning dumps on it."

"You drove my car here?"

"Sure did." Yost mimed clutching a steering wheel, jerking his hands wildly back and forth. "Kept it under ninety the whole way."

"Thanks, man."

Yost crumpled his coffee cup and tossed it in the trashcan. Then he examined himself in the small mirror above the sink, using water from the faucet to smooth down a cowlick at the top of his head. "I hate to leave you, brother. But my shift starts soon, and I still have to track down that hot little nurse." He returned to the bed and thumped Taylor on the shoulder. "Don't look so depressed. This hospital thing ain't so bad. You get to watch TV all day, and hot nurses feed and bathe you. Heck, I'd shoot myself in the leg to get that kind of attention from Nurse Amelia."

"Olivia," Taylor corrected him.

"Whatever."

Yost disappeared into the hallway in pursuit of the nurse.

Taylor leaned against his pillow and returned his gaze to the window. His thigh throbbed, the pain a little worse than before, but he barely noticed it. Outside his window, the helipad was empty. A thick layer of clouds blanketed the sky, obscuring the sun from view.

There would be guards at the old church, but how many? It would help if he outranked them. He might even know a few of them. But what about Carver? How was Taylor going to get past him?

If only he could talk to Gemma. If only he could tell her that everything was going to be okay. That he would find her, no matter what. Ever since they were kids, Gemma had been the one person in his life who'd always been able to see past the bad to the good inside him. She'd never given up on him.

Find her, son. The carnival girl.

Taylor turned away from the gloomy sky, his eyes landing on his car keys.

"Hang on, Gemma," he whispered to the empty room. "I'm coming."

CHAPTER
SIXTEEN

Pale morning light streamed through the narrow window, illuminating stacks of faded storage containers. Kneeling on the floor in front of one of the open boxes, Gemma dug through its contents, pushing aside tangled strands of white lights, colored garlands, and shatterproof Christmas ornaments. Searching for anything useful. A pile of velvet bows occupied the entire bottom half of the box, and she pulled them out and dropped them to the floor, sneezing at the explosion of dust.

Nothing.

No blanket to keep her warm. No weapon with which to protect herself against the soldiers. No key to the door at the top of the stairwell. Absolutely nothing of value.

She shoved the box of decorations away. "If I'm still here at Christmas, at least I'll be able to decorate."

Her search hadn't been entirely futile, however. It *had* yielded one thing.

Information.

The soldiers were holding her in the basement of a church. Or what had once been a church. The contents of the storage containers told the story. One held nothing but Christian-themed children's books and puzzles, as well as a slew of long-expired Sunday School teacher's guides. Another held dozens of boxes of long taper candles, many showing evidence of having been burned at least once before being stored for reuse. She also found smaller, handheld candles with rings of protective plastic around the base to catch dripping wax. Gemma remembered holding candles like those during Christmas Eve candlelight vigils when she was a little girl, not long before public church services gave way to worshipping in secret.

Wiping her dusty hands on the seat of her pants, Gemma crawled to the next box and removed the lid. A cheerful lion grinned at her from the top of the pile. She picked it up by its popsicle handle and brought its face to hers, peering through its roughly-cut eye holes. A homemade mask. There were others, too. A giraffe, a kangaroo, and a zebra, their smiling faces permanently adhered to popsicle sticks. The rest of the box contained ancient craft supplies: dried-out glue sticks, broken crayons, and half-unraveled balls of yarn.

Nothing useful.

Before she piled everything back inside the container, she caught a glimpse of something at the bottom of the box, concealed beneath a pile of faded construction paper. She moved the paper aside to reveal the cover of a leather-bound book.

A Bible.

She snatched her hand away as if it had been burned.

Overhead, a door opened and boots thundered down the back stairway.

Gemma grabbed the Bible from the box and crawled to the corner of the room, wincing as her sore muscles protested the sudden movement. She shoved it into the darkness beneath the couch, and then jammed her body into the narrow gap between the couch and the wall. Cobwebs adhered themselves to her shirt and tickled the pale hairs on her skin, but she didn't brush them away.

Seconds later, the basement door swung open.

Please don't be Mullen. Anyone but Mullen.

Footsteps crossed the basement.

Gemma cringed. Something was crawling up her arm. A spider. The basement was infested with them. She could feel it moving beneath her sleeve, its legs tickling her skin, causing it to erupt into gooseflesh. But she didn't brush it away. Instead, she closed her eyes and pretended that her lips were sealed shut with glue and that her legs were bolted to the ground.

"Hey there."

Her eyes shot open.

A female soldier stood a few feet away, clutching something in her hand. She narrowed her eyes, peering into the darkness at Gemma. The soldier wasn't wearing her uniform jacket, and small but impressive muscles bulged from the sleeves of her black t-shirt. The tattoo of a scorpion occupied most of the visible real estate of her left forearm. Despite the severity of her buzzcut and the sharp lines of her face, there was something about her that put Gemma at ease. Maybe it was her eyes. They seemed kind.

"We haven't met yet. Yesterday was really crazy." The soldier's tone sounded apologetic. "I'm Private Dietrich." She gestured to the untouched turkey sandwich and thermos of chicken-noodle soup sitting on the table beneath the window. "You never ate your dinner from last night. Weren't you hungry?"

Of course, she'd been hungry. When the scent of turkey first hit her, her empty stomach had growled angrily. After the soldier who'd delivered it left, Gemma had unscrewed the lid of the thermos and determined that the chicken-noodle soup was of the overly-salty, canned variety. Easy to pass up. But the sandwich had been a different story. The bread was thick and homemade. And the turkey? Not thinly-sliced deli meat but actual, honest-to-goodness carved turkey breast.

If they want to kill you, they'll just put a bullet in your head, she'd tried to assure herself. They weren't going to poison her one turkey sandwich at a time.

But she hadn't eaten the food. Not out of fear of poisoning, but because consuming any food provided by her captors felt like giving in. Surrendering in some way. She wouldn't submit to Carver or his soldiers in any way that wasn't essential to her survival. And she wasn't starving to death...yet. Gulping down Carver's water had been a mistake, one she didn't intend to repeat. So, she'd left the tray of food untouched and slipped into the small bathroom in the hallway, where she'd placed her mouth beneath the faucet and swallowed as much of the brackish, ice-cold water as her stomach would hold. Afterwards, she'd returned to the couch and closed her eyes until her headache disappeared, taking her hunger with it.

"Can you come out of there so we can talk?" The soldier took a cautious step closer to Gemma. "I have good news. It sounds like you're going home today."

Home.

The word sounded strange to her ears, a relic from some ancient language. Was Carver actually going to release her? He couldn't have confirmed the false identity she'd given him, so why would he send her home?

Dietrich straightened up. "I know you're scared, but you have to come out of there. The colonel wants to speak with you before he lets you go. He asked me to bring you upstairs. If you don't come out on your own, I'll have to get someone to help me pull you out of there, and I really don't want to do that."

It didn't sound like a threat. It sounded like the truth. As much as Gemma hated leaving the relative protection of her spot, she couldn't risk seeing Mullen again.

Reluctantly, she slid out of the corner and stood.

"You're shorter than I expected, but these should still fit you." Dietrich tossed a pair of jeans and a black sweater to Gemma. The clothes felt warm and smelled like flowers, as if they'd come straight out of the dryer. "I thought you might want to change into some fresh clothes. Notice I said fresh, not new." She gave them a quick sniff. "But I promise they're clean. I've only worn them a few times. Go ahead and change. I'll turn around." She performed an about-face toward the far wall, slender arms crossed over her chest.

Gemma watched the door, listening for anyone coming down the stairs. But she couldn't hear anything. Hurriedly, she kicked off her boots and dropped her jacket onto the couch. With her eyes locked on the soldier's back, she slipped her shirt over her head while simultaneously pulling on the sweater, a maneuver she'd perfected in seventh-grade gym class. The sweater hung halfway to her knees, enabling her to step out of her cargo pants and pull on the jeans without exposing herself. They were a little long, so she tucked the bottoms inside her boots.

"You done? Can I turn around?"

"Yes." Gemma finished tying her bootlaces. "I'm ready."

The soldier turned to face Gemma, and her mouth fell open. "Girl, you look like a totally different person. The sweater's a little big on you, but the jeans fit great. Do you like them?"

Gemma nodded, surprised at how much better the clothes made her feel. More alive, somehow. Stronger. Despite her circumstances, she found herself wondering what Taylor would think if he could see her. "Yes. Thanks for letting me borrow them."

The soldier waved a hand at her. "You know what? Keep them. I've got plenty of cute clothes and very few opportunities to wear them."

"Really? Thank you."

"Don't mention it. I'm Amy, by the way. You ready to go upstairs?"

"Aren't you going to put those plastic ties on my wrists?"

Dietrich laughed as if she'd said something really funny. "Of course not. The colonel went out to get you something for breakfast. How will you eat with zip ties on your wrists?"

Gemma followed the soldier down a narrow hallway that reeked of fresh paint. Bulletin boards lined both walls, their surfaces littered with local newsletters, advertisements, and multicolored tacks. The papers flapped as she passed by, calling attention to themselves, and Gemma skimmed a myriad of small-town proclamations about rental apartments, used lawn mowers, and community potlucks. One advertisement for *Letty's Book Cellar* showed an older black woman standing in front of a run-down store. The paper was advertising some kind of book sale.

Gemma felt a pang of sadness.

She missed books.

She missed everything about her old life.

At the end of the hallway, Gemma and Dietrich emerged into a small foyer with red carpeting and more bulletin boards. To their right, an ornate archway curved over a pair of swinging doors. On the opposite side of the room, two chairs and a small folding table sat just inside the entryway. Several books lay on the table, and a laptop stood open, a paused movie flickering on its screen.

Beyond the table, another door. This one heavy-looking and painted red.

The exit.

Dietrich frowned at the empty table. "Brady must be on another smoke break. Awesome. Follow me."

The soldier led her through the swinging doors into what must've once been the church's sanctuary, and Gemma's breath caught in her throat.

Twelve rows of mahogany pews lined each side of the main aisle, and regal maroon carpeting covered every inch of the floor. Lavish trim in the shapes of gilded leaves and flowers formed the borders of the room's ivory ceiling. Most impressive, however, were the stained-glass windows, with Christian imagery: the star, the crown of thorns, the empty cross. The dreary sky had cleared and sunlight streamed through colored panes of glass, casting a dazzling kaleidoscope of hues on the walls. She could easily picture this place as it had once been, filled to capacity on a Sunday morning, the minister behind his pulpit, and the choir huddled in their loft, identical in their matching red gowns.

Dietrich patted her on the shoulder. "Have a seat. The colonel should be here in a few minutes."

"Okay. Thank you."

When Dietrich left the sanctuary, Gemma walked down the aisle, her hands passing over the smooth, polished wood. She lowered herself onto the pew in the first row. The altar and pulpit were gone, replaced by a long table and seven folding chairs, probably for use by the mayor or the town council during meetings. An American flag stood behind the table, topped with a soaring gold eagle. Framed photographs of the town, most of them in black and white, hung on the wall behind the table.

Not all evidence of the building having once been a church had been erased. Aside from the stained-glass windows, the mahogany communion rails remained, framing the platform where the minister had once delivered Communion to his congregants. Years of light streaming through the stained-glass windows had bleached the front wall of the sanctuary a lighter shade of ivory. Partially concealed behind the town photographs, Gemma could see a distinct shape where something large had once hung, the sunlight permanently etching proof of its existence onto the wall.

"Good morning, young lady."

Startled, Gemma swiveled in her seat.

Colonel Carver stood at the rear of the sanctuary, clutching a brown paper bag and two coffee cups. He took the aisle in several long strides, and plopped down beside her in the first row. "I brought us some chocolate croissants and lattes from the bakery down the street. How does that sound?"

Gemma's stomach growled audibly. She wanted to stick to her promise to not eat or drink anything provided by her captors. But what if Dietrich was telling the truth? What if Carver really was planning to release her today? Was it wise to be stubborn?

And she was *so* hungry...

"Thank you." She accepted the cup Carver handed her, wrapping her cold hands around it and savoring its warmth before taking a tentative sip.

Carver eyed her expectantly. "Well? What do you think?"

Gemma closed her eyes, savoring the sweetness of the drink. "It's amazing," she whispered. And it was. Nothing had ever tasted so good. "Private Dietrich said I'm going home today."

"That's the plan. But not before you eat something." He passed her the paper bag. "Have a croissant. Eat them both, if you want. The bakery in town is incredible. I've been downing two of these things every morning." He leaned back and patted his flat stomach. "It's starting to catch up with me."

Gemma inhaled her first croissant in three monster bites. She felt slightly self-conscious, but not enough to stop herself from jamming a second pastry into her mouth. Her hunger was too strong now, too overpowering. She'd grown so used to a steady diet of unripe berries and leathery venison that she'd forgotten what normal food tasted like. Henry Castern had occasionally included treats with their supplies—a few Hershey bars, a box of stale

Tastykakes—but he couldn't afford to provide nonessentials very often. Not when their group relied on him for so many of their needs and had little to offer him in return.

The sunlight pouring through the stained-glass windows vanished, and the sanctuary darkened around them. A cloud must've passed in front of the sun. "What time do you think I'll be released?" Gemma ventured, emboldened by the sudden rush of sugar.

"What did you say your name was?"

Several flaky pieces of croissant fell from her mouth onto her lap. Embarrassed, she brushed them into her hand, intending to put them inside the paper bag. But she changed her mind at the last second and slipped the crumbs into her mouth. They disintegrated on her tongue. "My name's Rachel Dawson."

The colonel's brow knitted into a frown. "No. We're past that now."

She took another sip of her latte, barely listening. "What do you mean?"

Carver placed his cup behind him on the pew and turned to face Gemma. "This is the last time I'm going to ask you, young lady. And I want the truth. What's your name?"

Gemma noticed the steely glint of Carver's eyes and the slight flare of his nostrils. Those things hadn't been there before. The atmosphere inside the room dropped like a barometer before a storm. "I don't understand what you want me to—"

Carver backhanded her across the cheek.

She cried out, her hand flying to her stinging face, the half-eaten croissant tumbling to the carpet and breaking apart.

The colonel jumped up, grabbed her sweater, and yanked her off the pew. Her feet hung in the air like a marionette, Carver's knuckles cutting ridges into her throat. Then he body-slammed her to the carpet, and her lungs popped like balloons.

Gemma gasped for air and found none. Her fingers clawed at her chest, tried to force her paralyzed diaphragm to expand. Then, remembering Carver, she curled into a ball, covered her head with both hands, and prepared for another blow. The destroyed croissant lay a few inches away, oozing chocolate onto the carpet.

Hands grabbed her shoulders and rolled her onto her back. Carver loomed over her. "No more lies. As my daddy used to say, it's time to fish or cut bait."

Gemma couldn't speak. Couldn't move. Couldn't breathe.

"You're all useless, aren't you?" Carver grabbed her sweater with two fists and wrenched her to her feet. "The whole lot of you."

She cringed, expecting another blow, but the colonel shoved her onto the pew. Her left wrist bent awkwardly beneath her body, and a sharp pain shot up her arm. But her diaphragm finally relaxed, and a rush of air filled her deflated lungs.

Carver dug into his pocket and pulled out a black phone in a heavy-duty protective case. An iPhone, similar to the one she'd left behind when she'd gone into hiding. But many of the colonel's app icons were entirely unfamiliar to her. He swiped through several screens before tapping the Photos icon, then held the phone out to her. "Perhaps this will jog your memory. This photograph was taken this morning."

Gemma's insides twisted in revulsion.

In the photograph, Max Yelchin was sprawled, barefoot and shirtless, on a blood-soaked tile floor. Someone had carved a crooked line down the left side of his face, from his forehead to his jawline. His pale arms and bare chest were covered with cuts, some still bleeding, while others had crusted over. The photographer appeared to have captured him in the act of pushing himself up, and there was a look of rage and defiance on his swollen face that made Gemma tearful with pride.

"The older gentleman died at the store, but we took the younger one alive. By your reaction, I assume this young man is a friend of yours. If so, you'll be pleased to know that he hasn't given us any useful information. Not yet, anyway." Carver cracked his neck, the sound reverberating through the empty sanctuary. "To be honest, I'm impressed he's lasted this long. Surviving two days with my interrogators is no easy feat. However, your friend isn't giving me anything to work with, which means that he's no longer useful to me. Do you understand what that means?"

Of course, she did.

"Please," she begged, unable to tear her eyes away from Max's ruined body. "Tell them to stop hurting him."

The photograph disappeared as Carver stuffed the iPhone back into his pocket. He settled onto the pew, the rage gone from his face. "The day I turned eighteen, I joined the Marines. Did two tours in the desert, fighting Islamic extremists. They were like cockroaches, hiding in their holes, coming out for scraps of food, and then—whenever the lights went on—they scattered. Over time, I came to respect them. They were willing to die for their faith. They saw martyrdom as the highest of honors. And I thought, 'If I'm going to die, why not die at the hands of someone who truly believes in what they're fighting for?' So, when the government established the Federal Task Force, I joined right away, expecting a fight similar to the one I'd faced in the desert. What I never anticipated was how easily most of you would turn away from your faith. So few of you are actually willing to suffer for it."

Gemma thought of the soldiers dragging her mother up the basement's carpeted stairs. Her mother's tearful screams. The fury on her father's face as he charged them, only to be knocked backward with the butt of a rifle.

And she thought of the others—the ones who'd been at the secret service in her parent's basement that night. How they had backed away from Gemma instead of comforting her. How they had been so quick to distance themselves from her, as if her own fate had already been sealed.

"They livestream renouncements on the internet now." Carver scratched his chin, which appeared red from a close shave. "You didn't know that, did you? The government started that program a year ago as a way for subversives to come out of hiding and clear their records. It was supposed to be an opportunity to start over, via a public mea culpa. But a lot has changed in the past year. Now, Christians line up to renounce their faith. Some even use their fifteen minutes of fame to plug their business or to get more subscribers on their YouTube channel." His lip curled into a sneer. "Using eternal damnation as a marketing tool. I wonder what your God thinks of that."

She didn't want to believe him. It wasn't possible, was it? Could so much really have changed in only two years? And why hadn't Henry Castern said anything? Why hadn't he told their group how bad things were getting?

"Each time I watch the renouncements," Carver continued, "I can't help but remember those boys in the desert with the suicide vests strapped to their chests."

Gemma closed her eyes and saw Max in the darkness. His ruined face. The tiny carvings all over his body like a roadmap of suffering. How much longer did he have? Days? Hours?

"I respect you, young lady. And I respect the young man in that photograph. Most people aren't willing to suffer for something as unimportant as their faith. But you're all still cockroaches. And when left unassailed, roaches tend to multiply."

She kept her eyes closed, unwilling to look at Carver.

God, help me, she prayed. Please protect me from him.

"You see, my soldiers are highly-trained operatives who believe in their mission and will do anything within reason to accomplish it. But the 'within reason' part has led to problems. Despite their training, many of my best soldiers remain enslaved to their ingrained principles and ethics.

"There are certain things they *absolutely will not do*. As you can imagine, this makes our unit less efficient at locating and detaining subversives. So, I handpicked a group of soldiers from my battalion's ranks for a secret assignment. These soldiers were selected for their enthusiasm for the mission, and their commitment to following orders, even if it means stepping outside the boundaries of morality." Carver leaned closer to her and lowered his voice. "The kind of soldiers who would crucify an innocent old man."

The words hit Gemma like a slap. She opened her eyes and turned to face him.

"You killed Henry."

Carver held up his hands. "Actually, it was *your* group that crucified that foulmouthed old man after he stopped providing your people with supplies. That's the official story, anyway. The one running on all of the local news outlets, as well as on social media. I wouldn't be surprised if it goes national."

Of course.

Carver had placed the blame for Henry's death on Gemma's group. What better way to smoke them out of hiding than to turn the locals against them? To ensure that no one else made the mistake of helping them—or others like them—in the future. After all, how long could they possibly survive with no link to the outside world?

Gemma slumped lower on the pew, defeated. How naïve they'd been for believing they could hide until the crisis passed. What a joke. While Gemma was in hiding, waiting for the world to get better, people like Carver were actively working to make it worse.

It was hopeless. What was she fighting for? What were *any* of them fighting for? A few more years of misery before being led off to a detention center? Or worse? It didn't matter how hard they fought...they weren't going to win this battle.

They were only prolonging their suffering.

The question escaped her lips. "What do you want?"

But she already knew.

The colonel tapped a well-manicured finger on his chest. "Everyone else, of course. The rest of your group. Their names. Where they're hiding. I also want the names of any others—aside from Mr. Castern—who have assisted your group. If you cooperate, no harm will come to you. And I'll allow your friend in the photograph to live."

Max.

A voice spoke up inside her mind. A cowardly voice, motivated by fear. *If he dies, it'll be your fault. This is your chance. You can save him. And save yourself. You could still have a good life. You could still be with Taylor. They won't kill the others. They'll just detain them.*

Carver brushed a fleck of lint from his uniform pants. "But if you refuse to help me, I'll order his immediate execution. And I'll turn you over to the residents of Ash Grove as one of the individuals responsible for the murder of Henry Castern."

Gemma buried her face in her hands. Carver would assume she was crying, but she was praying. Trying desperately to drown out the traitorous voice in her head before she did something terrible.

You have to help me, God, she prayed. I can't do this. I'm going to break.

She heard nothing. No response. But when she raised her head, her eyes landed on the church's front wall. The faint discoloration of the paint was evidence of something that had been removed and most likely destroyed. The colonel couldn't see it...but it was there.

The outline of a cross.

Not a small cross, like the one hanging in the café at the Station. But a huge cross. At least ten feet tall.

She found strength in it. Breathed it in like oxygen.

And then she said, softly but firmly, "No."

She cringed away from him, expecting another slap. But Carver didn't raise his hand. Instead, his mouth drew into a thin line, and he suddenly looked very tired. He called out: "Dietrich?"

Footsteps hurried down the aisle. Dietrich stepped in front of them, blocking Gemma's view of the cross.

The soldier's eyes landed on the ruined pastry, lingered there for a moment. Then she snapped to attention. "Yes, sir?"

"Please escort the detainee back to the basement," Carver ordered. "Let's give her a few hours to consider the consequences of lying. Not just for herself but for her injured friend. He might want to live."

"Yes, sir." Dietrich grabbed Gemma by the arm and pulled her up. "Let's go."

Carver rose from the pew, towering over both women. He put a hand on Gemma's shoulder and squeezed. "You don't have to renounce. That's not what I'm asking you to do. I only want their names and where they are. And then you can have it all back. Your life. Everything you've lost. No one has to know what you traded for it."

Gemma could feel her resolve waning. But she straightened her back and forced herself to look Carver in the eyes one more time. "I'm not going to give you what you want," she said, and tried to mean it. Desperately tried to make him believe it. "I won't. It doesn't matter what you do to me."

The colonel smiled.

"After tonight, young lady...you might change your mind."

CHAPTER
SEVENTEEN

Taylor drummed his fingers on the steering wheel as he watched the old church. He shifted in his seat, trying to get comfortable, wincing at the sharp pain in his thigh. The long walk from his hospital room to his car—plus three hours of discomfort sitting in a confined space—had taken its toll on his injured leg.

Sneaking out of the hospital hadn't been a problem, thanks to Yost. Not only had his friend provided him with a fresh uniform, but he'd also unwittingly distracted the young nurse, allowing Taylor to slip out of his room and make his way to the rear stairwell. Unfortunately, the stairwell hadn't led directly outside, and he'd been forced to cross the main lobby, passing by a hectic surgery check-in center and a coffee shop on his way to the exit. A group of doctors in green scrubs huddled together outside the shop, clutching coffees and chatting. A few nodded approvingly at him, a Task Force soldier in uniform. But none tried to stop him, despite his obvious limp and the fact that he was badly in need of a shave.

He'd taken care of the shave in the parking lot, using his rearview mirror and the electric razor he stored in his glove compartment. Then he'd driven into Ash Grove and pulled into the crowded rear lot of the local post office, backing into a spot that afforded him a great view of the church's main entrance and side parking lot.

After three hours of observation, Taylor had counted four people coming and going from the building. Three guards—two males, one female, all privates, and none of whom he recognized—plus Carver himself. One of the male privates took a smoke break every hour, leaving the building through a door that opened into the side parking lot, undoubtedly trying to avoid detection by the colonel. The door had no outside handle, so the private always propped it open with a brick before he disappeared around the back of the building.

Twice, Carver had emerged from inside and stood on the front steps, his cell phone pressed to his ear. Both times, he'd seemed irritated with whoever was on the other end of the call. Taylor had rolled his window down and strained to listen, but couldn't make out any words.

Only four soldiers. That wasn't so bad.

Of course, there could be more soldiers lurking inside the building, but Taylor didn't think so. An hour ago, the female private had driven off in a black Tahoe and returned fifteen minutes later with a large McDonald's bag and four sodas in a drink carrier. Besides, if Carver really was keeping Gemma in Ash Grove instead of taking her to the Gap for interrogation, as was protocol, he wouldn't want a lot of people knowing about it.

It took every ounce of self-control Taylor possessed to stay put. Every part of him wanted to leave his car, walk up to the front entrance, and politely ask whatever private was stationed at the door if he could speak with the colonel. Scouts were well-respected within the Task Force, so Carver would certainly agree to see him. And Taylor had the added distinction of having been injured in the field. When Carver escorted him into his office, Taylor would close the door behind him, pull his pistol on the colonel, and demand Gemma's release.

He replayed this scenario over and over in his mind, trying to make it work. Trying to foresee an ending that didn't result in his death. Or Gemma's. But with three armed and well-trained soldiers nearby, the chances of them making it out of the building alive were slim. He couldn't take that risk.

When he felt himself losing patience, he fell back on his training, relying on instruction that had been drilled and beaten into him during his six years in the Task Force. Being a scout wasn't about making emotional decisions. It required patience. Persistence. Observation. The ability to wait for the upper hand. For the perfect opportunity to strike.

And then—finally—the waiting paid off.

The church's front door swung open, and the colonel exited the building, followed by the female private. Taylor slid further down in his seat, his eyes barely clearing the driver's side window. Neither the colonel nor the private spoke as they strode down the handicapped ramp to the parking lot. Carver appeared to be texting on his phone, while the private remained a few paces behind him, her eyes on the ground. She climbed behind the wheel of the Tahoe, and the colonel jammed his phone into his pocket before pulling himself into the passenger seat. A few seconds later, the engine roared to life, and the Tahoe pulled out of the parking lot. Instead of making a left turn and heading further into town, the vehicle turned onto the highway heading out of Ash Grove.

Taylor had no way of knowing where they were going, but the closest town to the east was ten miles away. They might even be returning to the Gap, more than an hour's drive from Ash Grove.

After the SUV disappeared from sight, movement drew Taylor's attention back to the church. The side door swung open and the chain-smoking private emerged from within. Pushing the brick into place with his boot, he popped his cover on his head, lit his cigarette, and strolled behind the building.

Twelve minutes.

Taylor had timed each of the private's smoke breaks, and they usually lasted an average of twelve minutes. And the soldier always left the side door open and unguarded.

The perfect entry point.

For the next twelve minutes, only one soldier stood between Taylor and Gemma.

Taylor started the timer on his watch, then stepped out of the Charger.

He tried to look natural as he crossed the quiet street and headed for the church's unguarded side entrance. Despite hours of not stretching his leg out, he wasn't limping much, and the pain wasn't unbearable. Not yet. The adrenaline was keeping it at bay. Before leaving the hospital, he'd stuffed a few of the oxycodone pills into the pocket of his fatigues. Just in case.

Twenty feet...

Fifteen...

Taylor focused on the rear of the building, waiting for the private to step into view, a half-smoked cigarette dangling from his fingertips, his eyes widening as they landed on Taylor.

Ten feet...

Five...

But the soldier didn't appear.

When he reached the door, Taylor cast a quick glance behind him and then slipped inside the building. He removed the brick from the door and eased it shut, listening for the barely-audible click as the lock slid into place. Locking the private outside might buy him a few more seconds at a time when every second counted.

A long hallway stretched out before him, with paper-covered bulletin boards on either side. The animated voice of a sports announcer drifted to him from far away. There was still one private inside the building, and it sounded like he was listening to a baseball game.

Taylor didn't care what the kid was listening to, as long as he kept listening to it.

He proceeded down the hallway, one hand on his pistol, the other on the wall for support. His thigh was starting to throb; a dull, hammering pain, like a bad toothache. Doors flanked him on either side of the hallway, all of them closed. The rectangular windows built into the doors revealed darkened offices, probably for use by town officials.

Halfway down the hall, he noticed another door. Like every other door in the hall, it was closed. But this one had no window.

However, it *did* have two brand-new deadbolts.

Taylor eyed the end of the hallway, now only a dozen feet away. But there was no movement. No sound except for the incessant chatter of the private's radio.

He unlocked both deadbolts.

The door opened into a stairwell. He hesitated at the threshold, giving his eyes time to adjust. Shapes began to emerge out of the darkness. A small landing, only a few feet wide and crowded with cardboard boxes. Beyond that, the stairs plunged downward. There was light coming from somewhere below, and he knew—knew with absolute certainty—that Gemma was down there.

Closing the door behind him, Taylor began his descent into the basement. He couldn't help but think what a stupid plan this was. If he was discovered, the soldiers upstairs would only need to lock the deadbolts, and he would be trapped in the basement. Sure, he might be able to kick the door down or shoot his way out, but Carver's men would be ready for him. The only way this idiotic plan might work would be if he managed to sneak Gemma out of the church before the private finished his smoke break.

So that's what he would do.

He pressed the button to illuminate his watch's screen.

Seven minutes left.

He continued downward, into the dark.

CHAPTER EIGHTEEN

Gemma huddled in the corner of the basement, running her hands over her arms to generate warmth. She couldn't stop shivering. Exercise might help—doing jumping jacks or jogging in place—but she could barely summon the energy to hold her eyes open, much less stand.

After she'd refused to give Carver any information about the rest of her group, he'd sent her back to the basement, but not before confiscating her jacket and Dietrich's sweater. Now, she wore only jeans and a soiled tank top, both damp from the bucket of ice-water one of the guards had thrown on her a few hours earlier, when she'd made the mistake of falling asleep on the couch. Now the couch was soaked, and she was freezing. She'd briefly considered hanging her clothes to dry, but she couldn't stomach the idea of stripping down to her underwear.

What if Mullen came back?

She picked up the old Bible she'd found in the storage boxes and held it to her chest as if it were a shield, her shoulders heaving with silent, helpless sobs. How long could she go on like this? How long could she endure the hunger and fear and cold before her resolve snapped like an overstretched rubber band and the truth poured out? What if, at some point, she became so delirious that she confessed the location of her group without realizing she'd done so? The thought of losing control of her mind terrified her more than anything the soldiers might do to her. But it seemed entirely possible.

She cried for herself. For Sophia. For Gavin and the others. But mostly, she cried for Max. Whenever she closed her eyes, she saw him sprawled on the floor of that terrible room, blood spilling from his disfigured face and a hundred other wounds, staining the floor red. She couldn't imagine what he must be going through. The pain. The fear.

The cowardly voice broke its silence. *You can save him. You wouldn't even be putting the others in danger. They've left the Station by now. Just tell Carver what he wants to know.*

Gemma ignored the voice. Brushing a strand of damp hair from her eyes, she thumbed through the pages of the Bible, searching for a specific passage. A passage her mother had shown her after Pastor Nolan's detention.

Luke 21.

She used the neck of her tank top to wipe away her tears before they could dampen the delicate paper beneath her fingertips. Her index finger passed over the page as she squinted against the darkness to read the words of Jesus Christ to his followers. "You will be betrayed even by parents, brothers and sisters, relatives and friends, and they will put some of you to death. Everyone will hate you because of me. But not a hair of your head will perish." The words caught in her throat, but she forced herself to continue. "Stand firm, and you will win life."

The words in her mother's translation had been slightly different, but she still remembered them.

"By your endurance," she whispered, "gain your lives."

Stand firm.

Endure.

Pressing the Bible against her chest, she began to pray.

God, help me to stand firm. And help Max to endure. Don't let them kill him because of me.

Noise disrupted the silence of the basement. The sound of a boot scraping against a concrete floor.

Her eyes popped open, and she shoved the Bible under the couch as a shadow appeared beneath the window. She hadn't heard the door or any footsteps on the stairs. Someone was sneaking up on her. Or trying to. She held her breath as the shadow grew larger, revealing itself one terrifying inch at a time.

Please be Dietrich. Not Carver.

But Dietrich wouldn't be sneaking around. Neither would Carver.

A horrible realization hit her.

Mullen.

The shadow took shape, formed into a male figure in dark fatigues.

Mullen. Sneaking into the basement to finish what he'd started. Already, she could smell his foul breath, could feel his rough hand covering her mouth, silencing her scream and suffocating her.

But if Mullen was sneaking around, that meant he *had* to be quiet because he didn't want to get caught. There must be other guards upstairs. Maybe even Dietrich.

Surely, Dietrich would help her.

She opened her mouth to scream.

"Gemma? Are you down here?"

The scream died in her throat as the dark figure morphed from the soldier she feared into the one she loved. He emerged out of the shadows, clearly favoring his right leg. But he couldn't see her. His eyes hadn't adjusted to the darkness yet.

Gemma covered her mouth with her hands, worried that—in her excitement—she might cry out too loudly and someone would hear her. "Taylor?" Her voice slipped through the gaps in her fingers as little more than a squeak.

He spun in her direction, peering frantically into the dark shadows of the basement's far corner. "Gemma?" he whispered, his voice low and urgent. "Where are you?"

She pushed against the wall, propelling herself out of her hiding spot. She threw herself into his arms and clung to him, her short nails digging into his uniform jacket. Terrified that some unseen force might try to rip them apart.

Taylor staggered backward, but remained standing, somehow managing to keep both of them on their feet. He embraced Gemma and kissed her, his mouth moving from her temple, to her forehead, and finally to her numb lips.

She couldn't feel his kiss, but she could feel the warmth of his breath against her face. Her legs trembled beneath her, her body weak with relief.

Somehow, Taylor had found her.

Everything was going to be okay.

CHAPTER NINETEEN

Gemma didn't want to let Taylor go. What if she was hallucinating? If she let him go, he might disappear forever. The thought was too horrible to imagine.

But Taylor gently pried her hands from his shoulders and held her out at arm's length, studying her. "What did they do to you? Are you hurt?"

"I'm fine. How did you find me?"

Taylor fumbled with the buttons on his uniform jacket, removed it, and held it out for her to slip her arms through. "Carver and the female soldier left in a vehicle a few minutes ago, but there's a soldier still upstairs. And another one smoking a cigarette outside. We have to get out of here without either of them noticing." He gestured to his watch. "And we've got three minutes to do it."

Taylor wanted to sneak her out of the church? But what if the soldiers discovered her trying to escape? Or what if Carver returned before they made it out? Suddenly, she wanted nothing more than to

161

crawl back into her hiding spot between the couch and the wall. She tried to pull away from him. "No. We can't do this."

But he wouldn't let go of her arms. "Gemma, we don't have a choice. We have to get out of here. You don't know what Carver's capable of."

But that wasn't true. She *did* know what Carver was capable of. She'd seen evidence of it on his phone.

Taylor held her gaze, unflinching, until she managed a weak nod.

"Okay."

"Good. Stay behind me. And don't make a sound."

They left the basement and climbed the stairwell. Gemma stayed behind Taylor, one hand on his back, the other braced on the wooden railing. It felt cold and unyielding beneath her palm, and her legs shook as each step brought her closer to the top of the stairs. Anything could be waiting for them beyond that closed door. She expected it to fly open. For Carver to be standing there with an assault rifle, preparing to rain bullets down on both of them.

When Taylor reached the landing, he eased the door open, his right hand dropping to the pistol on his hip. He leaned into the corridor, checked both directions, then gave Gemma a nod and turned to the right. She followed him, and they hurried toward the closed door at the end of the corridor. Light seeped through a crack at the bottom of the door. An illuminated exit sign suspended from the ceiling flickered on and off, as if to discourage them.

They were so close. Only thirty more feet.

They were going to make it.

A hand came down over her mouth and nose, pinching them both shut. She couldn't scream or breathe. An arm wrapped around her waist and lifted her, carrying her backward down the hallway, away from Taylor and the exit.

She kicked furiously, but it did no good.

Taylor made it a few more feet before he glanced back to check on her. Their eyes met and he spun around, grabbing the pistol off his hip and aiming it over her head. *Way* over her head. "Put her down, Nowak."

"Sorry, Sarge. No can do."

An unfamiliar voice. Not Mullen.

162

Someone Taylor knew. A soldier named Nowak.

"That wasn't a request. It's an order. Put her down now."

But the soldier only chuckled, his grip loosening enough for her to pull in a quick breath. "Only one rank matters in this unit, Sarge. And it sure as heck ain't yours."

Taylor advanced slowly down the hallway, his weapon trained on Gemma's captor. "I don't want to shoot you, Private. But I will."

"No, you won't. Not when I'm using your girlfriend as a shield."

Gemma writhed in Nowak's arms, but the more she struggled, the more his grip on her mouth and nose tightened. She met Taylor's eyes and nodded, trying to communicate that he should shoot the soldier. It was their only chance. She'd watched him shoot the gun out of Brie's hand. He could do it. She trusted him.

And then, behind Taylor, a door opened.

Colonel Carver emerged from one of the dark offices, arms clasped behind his back, looking completely at ease with the situation. Perhaps even a little excited. "Afternoon, Sergeant Nolan."

Taylor spun and aimed the pistol at him, but Carver held up both of his hands. "Easy, cowboy. We're on the same team."

"Are you sure about that, sir? Because that's not what it looks like to me. It looks like you've got a little side operation going on here."

A toothpick protruded from the corner of Carver's lips. He crossed his arms over his wide chest. "I'm just doing my job, Sergeant. Speaking of jobs, it's good to see you getting around so well after your little hunting accident. Which I'm now assuming *wasn't* a hunting accident, after all. How's the leg?"

Taylor kept the pistol aimed at the colonel. "Better than ever, sir."

Carver took a step closer to Taylor. "Good. You know, when the powers-that-be at HQ assigned a bunch of unproven scouts to my unit at the last minute, I should've told them to pound sand. But I went against my instincts, and look what happened. I catch one of the newbies trying to sneak off with a detainee." The muscles in his face tightened. "Do you have any idea whose pool you just took a leak in, son?"

"If she's a detainee, sir, why are you keeping her here?" Taylor asked. "Why hasn't she been transported to the Gap? Does HQ even know about her?"

"HQ knows what I tell them—and I tell them what they need to know."

Carver sounded calm, but Gemma knew it was all an act. The expression on his face was the same one he'd worn in the sanctuary, seconds before he'd struck her.

"Keeping this nation safe from extremists isn't easy, son," the colonel continued. "Sometimes, you've got to get your hands dirty. But you wouldn't understand that, would you? You're still too wet behind the ears. You have no idea what it takes to win a war when you're fighting an ideology."

"What about the storeowner? Does HQ know you crucified him?"

Someone brushed past Gemma and inched down the hallway toward Taylor. Another soldier. Gemma recognized Dietrich's buzzcut and tattooed arms.

She had a syringe behind her back.

No!

Gemma reacted purely on instinct. She brought a knee up and slammed her boot down on Nowak's instep, feeling a sickening but satisfying crunch beneath her foot.

Thank you, Gavin.

Two things happened at once: Nowak howled, his hand falling away from her mouth, and Gemma screamed at Taylor.

"Watch out!"

Taylor's eyes darted in her direction. Capitalizing on this brief distraction, Carver lunged forward and slammed his arm against Taylor's wrist, the impact knocking the pistol to the floor. Then Carver grabbed Taylor's shoulders and slammed him into the wall. The two men grappled, and Taylor landed a solid punch on the colonel's face. Papers tore free from the bulletin board and fluttered to the carpet.

Gemma twisted in Nowak's arms, but he clamped his hand over her mouth, his iron grip on her waist tightening like a boa constrictor.

A door opened somewhere behind Gemma, and a lanky soldier sprinted past her, closing the distance between himself and the two men in four long strides. The soldier jammed the barrel of his rifle against Taylor's temple. "Are you the scumbag who locked me outside?"

Taylor tilted his head, peering at the soldier out of the corner of his eye. Then he released Carver and dropped his arms to his sides.

"Thank you, Brady." Carver straightened his uniform. He'd taken a hard punch to the face, but it didn't seem to have any effect. His nose wasn't even bleeding. "Not a moment too soon."

"Sorry, sir. He locked me—"

"Enough." Carver shot him a dangerous look. "We'll discuss it later."

Taylor's eyes flitted briefly to Gemma before returning to the colonel. "Sir, I'm willing to take the fall for everything. With the town and with HQ. I'll admit to crucifying the old man. I'll sign a confession...do whatever you want."

Gemma shouted into the damp flesh of Nowak's palm. "No!"

If Taylor admitted to murdering Henry, he'd be court-martialed. Even if it was revealed that Henry was a sympathizer, Taylor would be imprisoned for the rest of his life. Or given a death sentence.

Carver's eyes sparkled with interest. "You would do that?"

"Yes. But you have to release the girl. That's all I ask. Do we have a deal?"

Carver gnawed on his toothpick, his head bobbing slightly. Then he reached out and squeezed Taylor's shoulders. "That's noble of you, son. I might not agree with protecting a subversive, but I respect your tenacity. There's just one little problem."

"What's that, sir?"

In a lightning-fast movement, Carver snatched the syringe from Dietrich's hands and plunged it into Taylor's neck.

"I don't make deals."

Taylor's hand closed around the colonel's as he tried to pull the syringe out of his own neck. But Carver was too strong, and the struggle only lasted for a few seconds. Then Taylor's body relaxed, and his head sagged to the side, his eyes locking with Gemma's.

She watched in horror as the essence of Taylor—the beautiful soul inside of him—slowly ebbed away. She wrenched her hand free from Nowak and held it out to Taylor, but he only stared at her, confusion clouding his features. He looked as if he didn't know her.

He's dying, she thought. I'm watching him die.

Then Taylor's eyes rolled back, and his legs folded neatly beneath him. Carver dropped the syringe, caught him under the arms, and lowered his lifeless body to the carpet.

"What did you do?" Gemma screamed. *"What did you do to him?"*

The colonel crouched over Taylor and dug two fingers into the side of his neck. "Relax, young lady. Your boyfriend isn't dead. Not yet, anyway."

Gemma choked out the words. *"I hate you!"*

Carver nodded, as if he'd expected her to say that very thing. His lips drew into a thin line. "That's not very Christian of you."

But she didn't care. His words only infuriated her more.

"I'm going to kill you!"

And she meant it.

Even as she screamed at Carver, three words flashed through her mind.

Stand firm.

Endure.

Endure? She despised that word. How could God expect her to endure all of this? How could He expect anyone to suffer this much? And not just her, but everyone she loved. Her parents. Sophia. Gavin. Addie. They were all suffering.

And for what? What was the point of any of it? She wasn't going to do anything for God. She wasn't a part of His Plan. She was going to die in Ash Grove. Or spend the rest of her life in a detention center. And Taylor...if he wasn't dead yet, he would be dead soon. Carver would never allow him to live. Not after this.

Little by little, she was losing everything that mattered.

Death by a thousand cuts. Just like Max.

By your endurance, gain your lives.

No. Gemma didn't want to endure. And she didn't want to live. Not in this world. Not anymore.

She wanted to die.

CHAPTER TWENTY

Four Years Earlier

In the Sweet Street Bakery, Gemma bent over the counter, piping periwinkle blue frosting onto the last of two-dozen *Frozen* cupcakes she'd whipped up in a hurry earlier that evening. She finished boxing the cupcakes just as the bell chimed above the front door. Nancy Dugan and her puggle Destiny blew into the bakery, both panting from the unrelenting July heat.

"It feels much better in here!" Nancy exclaimed. The puggle sniffed the floor beneath one of the customer tables as Nancy sidled up to the glass display case, tugging the pink leash until the small dog trotted up beside her. "Come on, girlie. Stop looking for crumbs."

Gemma stepped out from behind the display case. "Hi, Mrs. Dugan."

Nancy's eyes immediately narrowed. "Where's Maggie?"

"In her office," Gemma said. "But I can ring you up. I just finished decorating your cupcakes. What do you think?" She placed one of the boxes on the counter next to the cash register and opened it up. She'd made simple white cupcakes with blue frosting and white sugar crystals, as Mrs. Dugan had requested. But then she'd gone rogue, creating intricate fondant snowflakes and placing one on each cupcake. "I had to rush a little, but I think they turned out really nice."

The woman's eyes darted from the cupcakes to Gemma. "*You* made these?"

"Yes, ma'am," she said proudly. Her mother had taught her to bake. It was one of the few things that still made her really happy.

Nancy rubbed at a red splotch on her fleshy neck, her nose wrinkling with concern. Or perhaps distaste. "I thought Maggie hired you to help out. I didn't realize you'd be doing any of the baking."

Gemma opened her mouth to respond, to explain that she'd taken over most of the baking duties from Maggie. But a door opened behind her, and Maggie Pendleton emerged from the kitchen.

"Of course, she's baking, Nancy. Have you seen this girl's cupcakes?" Maggie's face lit up as she peered into the box. "Gemma, you've outdone yourself again. Those snowflakes are like art. I've never been able to work with fondant. Mine always cracks."

A petite, no-nonsense woman, Maggie reminded Gemma of a grasshopper in the way she soared through the bakery, always busy, never lingering in one place for too long. Before Nancy could protest further, Maggie set to work taping the boxes shut. "So, which granddaughter are these cupcakes for? Bethy or Alissa?"

"They're...uh...for Bethy," Nancy replied. "My daughter thought I'd ordered them, and I thought she'd ordered them. We got our lines crossed, I guess."

Maggie nodded and typed numbers into the cash register. "And how old is Bethy now? Five or six?"

"She's turning six."

"That's the right age for *Frozen*, I'd say. My daughter used to be *obsessed* with those movies." Maggie stopped typing and looked up at Nancy. "Does Bethy ever sing 'Let it Go" at the top of her lungs in the car? And does her singing make you want to crash into a tree just to make it stop?"

Nancy finally broke into a smile. "All the time. I swear, every little girl thinks they sound just like Elsa."

Gemma grabbed a small bowl from beneath the sink, filled it with water, and placed it on the floor in front of Destiny, who eagerly lapped it up with her pink tongue. She patted the dog's head and then stood, wiping her hands on her apron. "Can I get you something to drink, Mrs. Dugan? An iced tea or a lemonade?"

"No." The woman's tone was sharp. "No. I don't want anything from you."

Gemma took a step back, stung. But she quickly reminded herself not to get upset. It wasn't worth it. These sorts of encounters were becoming the norm. She had to stop being so sensitive. There were much worse things happening in the world.

Like what had happened to Pastor Nolan today.

Needing a distraction, Gemma grabbed a dishrag and set to work wiping down the tables, even though most of them hadn't been used today. The bakery had once been one of the most successful businesses in Ridgefield. People always stopped in for coffee and fresh croissants or muffins on their way to work. And Maggie often bragged that she'd baked nearly every birthday cake consumed in Ridgefield for the last fifteen years.

But things were different now. Although Maggie refused to talk about it, Gemma knew that business had slowed way down after she'd been hired, and she couldn't help but worry that it was her fault.

After a few minutes of awkward chitchat, Nancy grabbed the boxes and pulled Destiny away from the nearly-empty water bowl. "I better get home before my husband watches Jeopardy without me. Thank you so much for filling this order at the last minute. You're a doll."

"Tell Bethy happy birthday for me," Maggie said.

"Will do." Nancy crossed the café and headed for the door, walking right past Gemma without acknowledging her. "Goodnight, Maggie."

"Goodnight."

The bell rang again. Gemma locked the door behind the woman and went back to work scrubbing the tables. Afterwards, she would sweep the floors. Then she would refill the sugar jars at the coffee bar. Then she would find something else to do, because she didn't want to go home. She didn't want to see her parent's devastated faces.

She didn't want to think about Pastor Nolan.

"You trying to wear a hole into that table?"

Gemma raised her head.

Maggie was watching her over the glass display case, an amused expression on her face. "Or are you just pretending that table is Mrs. Dugan?"

Gemma arched an eyebrow. "It's *really* dirty."

"I find that hard to believe. No one's sat there all day." Maggie's smile faded a little. "How are your parents?"

"They're...dealing."

But that wasn't even remotely true. After they'd learned of Pastor Nolan's detention, both of her parents had broken down. Gemma had never seen her father cry before, and she couldn't take it. So, she'd driven her mother's car to the bakery, arriving four hours early for her evening shift. Just in time to make a beautiful batch of birthday cupcakes for a woman who was probably contemplating throwing them into the trash.

"Maggie. Can I ask you a question?"

"Only if it's the kind of question that makes us both uncomfortable."

Gemma dropped the dishrag on the table. "Do you want me to keep working here? Because you've been so kind to me, and the last thing I want to do is hurt your business. I certainly don't want you to feel obligated to—"

"Gemma Alcott," Maggie interrupted, holding something up. "What is this?"

It was an extra *Frozen* cupcake, its frosting shimmering with sugar crystals. The snowflake on top more intricate than any of the others she'd designed.

"It's for my mother," Gemma said. "I always make an extra one for her."

Maggie held the cupcake up to her face. Studied the thin lines of the snowflake. Closed her eyes and breathed in its scent. *"This, my dear, is all I need to know about you. Any girl who can make something this beautiful has earned my respect. And a spot in my kitchen."*

"But I don't want to hurt your business," Gemma said. "You heard Mrs. Dugan. She was upset that I made the cupcakes. Like I've got some contagious disease or something."

Maggie waved her hand dismissively. "Trust me, Gemma. Once you reach a certain age, you stop caring what people think. And I'm *way* past that age." She dug into her purse, pulled out a stick of gum, and popped it into her mouth. "Now go home. You've been here too long already. I'll clean up."

"Are you sure? I really don't mind staying."

Maggie pulled money from the cash register and stacked it on the counter. There wasn't much there. "Absolutely not. Good grief, you're only sixteen. I'm worried I might be violating some child labor laws, here."

"I'm seventeen, Maggie. My birthday was in Apr—"

"Go home or you're fired, cupcake."

Laughing, Gemma held up her hands. "Okay, okay."

Given everything that had happened that day, it felt wrong to laugh.

But it also felt good.

She walked through the kitchen and tossed her apron into the laundry basket Maggie kept outside her office. Then she freed her auburn hair from its bun and tucked the elastic band inside her purse. Her hair always smelled like frosting at the end of her shift, whether she was working the front of the bakery, or back in the kitchen baking with Marcy.

She brought a strand of hair to her nose and inhaled.

Yup. Frosting.

"There's a garbage bag by the rear entrance," Marcy called after her. "Run that to the dumpster on your way out, would you? And don't forget your cupcake. It's on the counter."

"Okay. Night, Maggie."

"See you tomorrow."

Maggie had placed Gemma's cupcake inside a cute little box. Smiling, she picked it up and headed for the café's rear exit. She grabbed the garbage bag with her free hand and used her back to force the door open. Humid July air greeted her as she stepped outside. She walked toward the dumpster, her bicep straining against the weight of the overloaded bag as she struggled to keep it from dragging along the ground and tearing open.

A soldier stepped out of the shadows, and she almost ran into him.

She gasped, her breath snagging in her throat. "Taylor?"

Despite his Task Force uniform and everything that it implied, she wasn't afraid of him. Especially now, as he leaned on the dumpster, his eyes red and puffy, his expression haunted. He looked nothing like the boy she remembered. When had she seen him last? Two years? Three? Not since he left for his Task Force training, at least. He was several inches taller now, and he appeared much stronger and more muscular. Gone was the unruly mop of hair that always seemed to be falling into his eyes. Now, he sported a military crewcut, and a day's worth of rough stubble covered his jawline. Seemingly overnight, he'd transformed from a boy into a man.

He was even more handsome than she remembered.

"Hey, Gemma." Taylor plastered a lopsided grin on his face and ran a hand through hair that was no longer there. He appeared to notice the garbage in her hands and said, "Here. Let me get that." She reluctantly surrendered the bag to him, and he tossed it into the dumpster, swaying unsteadily on his feet.

Gemma scanned the parking lot. Her mother's Civic was parked a few rows away, beneath a lamppost. "What are you doing here?"

Taylor wobbled away from the dumpster, wiping his hands on his fatigue pants. "Remember Jake Arbogast? From school?" he asked, slurring his words. When she shrugged, he waved a hand at her. "Yeah, probably not. Anyway, I saw Jake at the gas station last week, and he mentioned that you were working at the bakery now. And I wasn't busy so..."

Hope flared inside Gemma's heart. Why would Taylor be discussing her with one of his friends? Unless...

No. She refused to tread down that dangerous path. Things were different now. *Taylor* was different now, and she had to remember that.

Gemma brushed a frosting-scented tendril of hair behind her ears. "So... you decided to wait for me by the dumpsters, on the off-chance that I was working?"

He dropped his head. "Well, yeah, it sounds weird when you say it like that. I saw your mom's car, so I knew you were inside. But I didn't want to come in, you know..." He gestured to his wrinkled uniform. "Like this."

The silence hung between them like a thick curtain. She wanted to walk away. Leave Taylor behind, along with the feelings she'd spent years trying to suppress. It took an enormous amount of self-control to not bolt for her car. "Taylor, what do you want?"

"I don't know." He jammed his hands in his pockets. "Maybe I missed you."

She blinked, certain she'd misheard him. "You what?"

He lifted his head, and their eyes met. And he must've seen some kind of invitation in her eyes because he closed the distance between them. He reached for her, his fingers tracing a path down her bare forearms, from her elbows to her hands, giving her goosebumps. "You're beautiful, Gem. You don't know it, but you are." His right hand entwined with hers, and his eyes dropped to her floral blouse. "I love your outfit."

"Really?" She snatched her hand away from his. "Because I hate yours."

Undeterred, Taylor leaned closer and pressed his forehead against hers. She could smell the sickly-sweet stench of alcohol on his breath as he whispered, "Don't say that. You love everything about me. You always have."

She blinked away hot, angry tears. How long had she dreamt of this moment? How long had she prayed that, one day, Taylor's feelings might reciprocate her own? How long had she imagined their first kiss? A kiss that would bring an end to the life she'd always known and usher in an entirely new existence. But, in all of her imaginings, the romantic scene had never played out like this. With her exhausted and cranky, and Taylor in his Task Force uniform, reeking of alcohol and regret.

"Do you want to go somewhere, Gemma? Just you and me?"

There was no mistaking what he was looking for.

She shoved Taylor away and took a step back. Needing to distance herself from his face. His hands. From every part of him. Deliberately avoiding his eyes. It was too easy to lose herself in them. She clutched the boxed cupcake tightly against her body. "I'm not going anywhere with you. Things are different now."

"They don't have to be."

"You're drunk, Taylor. You shouldn't even be drinking. You're not twenty-one yet. Where did you get alcohol? And how did you get here? So help me, if you drove drunk tonight—"

"Relax." He cut her off and returned his hands to his pockets. "I walked. You know that bar down the street? Troegs? I went there tonight, and these guys bought me shots—*a lot* of shots—to thank me for being a soldier."

She couldn't keep the sarcasm out of her voice. "How nice of them."

Taylor steadied himself with one hand on the dumpster. "You think you're better than me. And you know what, Gemma? You're right. You *are* better than me. But that doesn't give you the right to act like this."

"Like what?" she demanded, her anger swelling. "How exactly am I acting?"

He glared at her. "Like an uptight little brat."

Gemma didn't think, only reacted. She pulled the cupcake out of the box and hurled it at Taylor. He tried to swat it away, but the alcohol must've dulled his reaction time, and it hit him squarely in the face, the fondant snowflake adhering itself to his right cheek. The rest of the cupcake plummeted to the ground, leaving a bright blue streak down the front of his Task Force uniform.

Tears burned Gemma's eyes, but she wouldn't allow herself to cry. "And you don't have any right to act like *this*. You can't just show up at my job after all this time, pretend that you like me, and expect everything to be okay. Call me names if it makes you feel better, but I'm not going to let you get away with this."

He picked the snowflake off his face, dropped it to the ground, and then used his sleeve to wipe the smear of blue frosting off his cheek. "Did you seriously just throw a cupcake at me?"

"Yes, I did," she said. "I'm not just some girl you can use to make yourself feel better. I don't deserve that, Taylor."

He stared at her, all of the anger dissipating from his face. In its absence, he appeared completely broken. Then he collapsed onto the curb and buried his face in his arms.

"I know you don't," he said. "I'm so sorry."

She wanted to leave. To just get into her mother's car and drive home, leaving Taylor alone to wallow in his guilt. Because that's what he deserved. He didn't deserve an ounce of her sympathy.

But then she remembered the boy from the carnival. The one who'd stepped in and defended her when no one else would. The one who'd made sure she'd gotten home safely.

She couldn't abandon that boy. Not when he needed her the most.

Gemma sat on the curb beside Taylor. Wrapping her arms around her knees, she tried to think of something to say. Some way to comfort him. But there wasn't anything she could say. No words to undo what he'd done.

But it was Taylor who spoke first. "I turned my father in. We detained him this morning."

She put a hand between his shoulder blades. A small display of comfort. It was the best she could manage, under the circumstances. "I know."

He raised his head and looked at her, his muscles tensing beneath her hand. "How did you find out?"

"Everybody knows," she said. "Ridgefield is a small town. News travels fast."

His expression hardened. The calloused face of a soldier. Or a kid pretending to be a soldier. "Do you hate me now?"

Oh, if only she *could* hate him, her life would be so much easier. The news of Pastor Nolan's detention hadn't been surprising—they'd all known it was coming—but Taylor's involvement in the detention had been a shock. She'd been devastated. And angry. But she could never hate him, no matter what he'd done.

"I don't understand why you're doing this." She gestured to his uniform. "But I don't hate you."

He tore his eyes away from her, his face bone dry. "Just wait. You will. Someday, I'll really hurt you. And then you'll hate me, too."

In that moment, Gemma's heart felt like a bottomless lake. A lake teeming with every feeling and emotion she'd ever had for Taylor Nolan. As he slumped forward, his spine curving beneath her fingers, it was as if someone had detonated a bomb beneath the water's surface, and all of her hidden emotions came bubbling up. She scooted closer to him. Brought a hand to his unshaven cheek. Gently turned his head until he was forced to look into her eyes. "No, Taylor. As much as I might want to hate you...I never could." She hesitated a moment before adding, "And you know why."

She drew closer to him, expecting him to kiss her. *Wanting* him to kiss her. But then his tough facade crumbled, and instead of kissing her, he pulled her to him and buried his face in her shoulder. She wrapped her arms around him, and although he still refused to cry, he clung to her. Clung to her like a desperate swimmer caught in a powerful current. And she was his life preserver.

They stayed like that for a long time, holding one another, not speaking, until Taylor finally lifted his head from her shoulder.

"Will you drive me home, Gemma?" he asked. "I just want to go home."

Looking into his sad eyes, she no longer saw any trace of the soldier who'd shown up at her job intoxicated, looking for a meaningless hook-up. Instead, she saw the boy who'd walked her home one summer night, all those years ago. The boy who'd put an arm up to stop her when they reached the main road.

Her Taylor.

"Of course, I will."

Driving slowly down a tree-lined street, Gemma leaned over the steering wheel and scanned the front of each house for Taylor's address: 323 West High Street. He'd described it to her as they walked to her car, but all of the ramshackle houses on West High Street looked exactly the same. Plus, she kept missing the numbers above the entrances. She wasn't even sure that she was going in the right direction.

Taylor was no help at all. The moment he'd climbed into the passenger seat, he'd put his head against the window and promptly fallen asleep, his breath leaving a tiny circle of condensation on the glass. The whole vehicle smelled like alcohol now, and Gemma could only hope that the smell would dissipate before her mother drove the Civic to work the following morning.

She was about to wake Taylor up by punching him in the arm when she saw it. A rundown three-story grey house with black shutters, just as he'd described. Everything about the house was depressing, from the color scheme, to the rickety porch, to the overflowing garbage bins, to the Big Wheel with the missing tire on the front porch. She parked in front of the house and came around to the passenger side to help Taylor. When she slung his arm around her shoulder and pulled him out of the car, he groaned in protest, but somehow managed to support himself. They climbed the steps to the porch, passing through a door held open by a box of uncooked spaghetti noodles, then ascended two flights of stairs to Taylor's apartment on the third floor.

He dug into his pocket and handed his keys to Gemma. "I'm not sure which one it is," he said. "I'm hungry, Gem. Do you have more cupcakes?"

"No. I threw my last one at you. And you're not eating. You're going to bed."

Two minutes and several failed attempts later, she found the right key and got the door open, pulling Taylor inside and closing it behind her. She was standing in a small living room with a slanted ceiling. The room's only furnishings included a faded futon to her right and a small flat-screen television set atop a cheap wooden stand. To the left of the entryway was a narrow kitchenette with a refrigerator and stovetop but no oven. The room's only window was set low to the floor and overlooked the house's rear parking lot.

She led Taylor across the living room and into his bedroom, which was as sparsely decorated as the rest of the apartment. An unmade queen-sized bed occupied most of the room's available floor space. There was no dresser or desk to speak of, only a tall lamp by the bed that was crooked, as if it had been assembled wrong. Taylor's uniforms hung in the bedroom closet, neatly starched and pressed, while his civilian clothes were strung about the room, some tossed to the floor or haphazardly folded into overflowing storage boxes.

Gemma was pleased to see no signs of a girlfriend. No framed pictures. No discarded clothes. She wrinkled her nose. There was a musty smell to the entire apartment, but it was much worse in here. "Cleaning lady's day off?"

"Very funny." Taylor removed his arm from her shoulder and staggered toward the bed. He collapsed onto his stomach, sprawled sideways, his legs dangling off the edge of the bed. "I'm going to rest here for a minute."

Gemma left him there and went into the kitchen. Along with some dish soap and a few hand towels, she found a large Tupperware bowl beneath the sink. She returned to the bedroom and positioned it next to Taylor on the bed in case he woke up sick. Which, judging by his level of intoxication, was highly likely. Then she stuffed several pillows on either side of his body so he wouldn't be able to roll onto his back and asphyxiate. After a brief internal debate, she unlaced his boots and pulled them off, placing them on the floor in his closet. When she felt certain that Taylor was comfortable and would survive the night, she went to leave the room.

His voice stopped her.

"Gemma?"

She turned back to the bed. Taylor still lay on his stomach, but his eyes were open, searching for her. She crossed the room, stepping over faded t-shirts and torn jeans, and sat on the bed beside him. "I have to go home now. My parents are going to wonder where I am."

He reached out and touched her hand. "Thank you. For everything."

"You're welcome."

She really did need to go. If she wasn't home soon, her parents would worry. They would try her cell phone first, and she didn't want to have to lie to them about where she was. But leaving felt wrong, so she stayed with Taylor a little while longer, gently running her fingers through his almost non-existent hair until his breathing slowed, and he began to snore lightly. Then she pushed herself off the bed, careful not to wake him, and tiptoed to the doorway. She hesitated there for a few seconds, nervously tapping her fingers against the doorframe.

"I don't hate you, Taylor," she whispered. "I love you. I always have."

And then she slipped out of the apartment, locking the door behind her.

CHAPTER
TWENTY-ONE

Voices.

Many voices. Male and female. Young and old. All blending together in a nightmarish dissonance. Certain words jumped out at Taylor, rising above the din. *Sympathizer. Murderer. Traitor.* He opened his eyes, but the darkness remained, and for a horrible, panicky moment, he thought Carver had gouged his eyes out. Just like Samson in the Bible. But then Taylor realized it wasn't completely dark. He could see *something*. A haze of blurry light. Something was covering his eyes.

A blindfold.

There was fabric in his mouth, some sort of gag. It was too tight. He couldn't spit it out. A rope secured his arms to whatever he was leaning against. Another rope tightened around his calves, binding them together. He struggled, and the rope around his arms grew taut and cut into his skin. Someone grabbed his arms and wrenched them further behind his back in a surgically-precise movement that seemed designed to produce pain. He cried out in agony, his shoulders only a few millimeters away from exiting their sockets.

"Sir?" a voice said. "He's coming out of it."

Another muttered voice. This one he recognized.

Carver.

"Is he secure?"

"Yes, sir."

"Good. Let's get started." The colonel raised his voice. "Ladies and gentleman, if you would, please take your seats. We'll begin momentarily."

Silence fell over the room, broken by the shuffling of bodies and the creaking of wood. Gradually, the sound died down, save for a few random titters of nervous laughter. A woman coughed. A man cleared his throat. A cell phone rang and was quickly silenced.

Carver said, "Go ahead, son."

A pair of hands untied the blindfold, allowing it to fall away from Taylor's eyes.

He stood at the front of a church—or what had once been a church—his body secured to one of the wooden support beams. Although it was dark outside the stained-glass windows, the half-dozen gothic pendant lights that hung from the vaulted ceiling remained unlit. Instead, melting taper candles adorned every windowsill, the wax overflowing and dripping onto delicate glass plates.

Two gold candelabras stood like sentries on either side of him, the flickering candlelight illuminating dozens of faces in the pews, their features veiled in shadows, making them seem like specters from another realm. There didn't appear to be a dress code for whatever was about to happen. Some of the men sported suits, while others wore paint-splattered overalls. Most of the women wore conservative dresses and jewelry—their Sunday best—but a few looked as if they'd come straight from the gym, with their oversized sweatshirts and yoga pants and hair piled messily on top of their heads. There was nothing remarkable about any of them. Nothing that differentiated them from any other people in any other town, which made them all the more horrifying.

Over his shoulder, he glimpsed two of Carver's men—the chain-smoker, Brady, and Nowak, the beefy soldier who'd grabbed

Gemma in the hallway—standing behind him. Neither would look him in the eyes.

Taylor pulled at the ropes securing him to the post, trying to break free of his restraints. But his legs refused to respond to the messages from his brain, and his feet shifted uselessly beneath him, going nowhere. Probably a lingering result of whatever sedative Carver had injected him with.

Something crunched beneath his weight. He looked down and saw a sheet of plastic stretched out under his feet. "Wha—" he spoke against the fabric in his mouth, confused.

And then it hit him.

The plastic was to protect the carpet.

"Thank you all for coming out tonight, despite the rainy weather." Carver stepped in front of Taylor, blocking his view of the crowd. "I'm Colonel James Carver, a Battalion Commander with the Federal Task Force. I tried to speak with most of you as you arrived, to explain the necessity for tonight's somewhat unorthodox proceedings."

The colonel clasped his hands behind his back, and Taylor noticed a gold wedding band on the man's left hand. Carver was married? He tried and failed to imagine what kind of woman would marry a man like Carver. Did she have any idea where her husband was tonight? Or what he was doing?

"Ladies and gentlemen," Carver said, strolling forward. "As you know, the situation in our country is becoming dire. My soldiers and I are fighting a rebellion that continues to grow more organized and more violent with each passing day. If we have any hope of prevailing, we must be honest and transparent with each other. And that's why I asked you all here tonight. Because, as residents of Ash Grove, and as the friends and family of Henry Castern, you deserve to know the truth about what happened to him."

Taylor swallowed hard.

Henry Castern? The storeowner?

"When I first arrived in town, I vowed to get to the bottom of Henry's death. To find the perpetrators of this terrible crime and bring them to justice. Of course, we all believed he'd been murdered by a group of subversives hiding out on the Dragon's Back Mountain." Carver drew in a deep breath before continuing. "Never

183

did I imagine that the investigation would lead to one of my own soldiers."

With his heartbeat echoing in his ears, Taylor scanned the room, searching every face for Gemma's. Desperately hoping that Carver wasn't going to force her to watch this.

She wasn't there.

Thank God.

"Yesterday morning, we detained a subversive on the mountain. We're keeping her here for questioning. Based on the information she's given us, we believe she's part of the group that Henry was helping in the months prior to his murder." Carver stopped a few paces in front of Taylor, avoiding the plastic. The flickering candlelight against the commander's pale skin and sharp features made him appear even more ghastly, as if he wasn't a human being at all but some kind of ancient vampire. He crossed his arms over his chest. "Earlier today, Sergeant Nolan infiltrated this building and attempted to free the subversive. Subsequent questioning of both parties revealed that Nolan has been working with that group of subversives for quite some time. We believe he is directly responsible for the planning and execution of Henry's murder."

The crowd came alive. There were gasps, whispers, a few muttered curses. Several women dabbed their cheeks with tissues. In the second row, a burly man in a flannel shirt leaned forward and gripped the pew in front of him with both hands, his furious eyes fixed on Taylor.

Carver raised his hands, palms-out, in front of his chest. "Ladies and gentlemen, please. Quiet down. I fully intend to bring court-martial proceedings against Sergeant Nolan. However, given the brutality of the crime, I believe that you—as Henry's friends and neighbors—have the right to address him first."

Address him?

Taylor scraped his hands against the wooden support beam, sliding them back and forth, trying to cut through the rope.

But even if he managed to free his arms, his legs were still tied.

A hand shot up in the second row.

Carver pointed at him. "Yes, sir? Please state your name."

The man in the flannel shirt rose. "Carl Lovell."

"Yes, Mr. Lovell?"

"Colonel, I know the Dragon's Back like my own hand. Been hunting up there since I was a kid. There's a huge cave system. Starts just north of town. The entrance is overgrown and impossible to find, unless you know exactly where to look. It's five miles long and runs from here all the way to Stoker's Mills. There's also an old coal mine, some abandoned hunting cabins...you name it. Lots of places for a group to hide. Places your men wouldn't know about. But I'd be happy to show them, and I bet I'm not the only one." Several men seated near Lovell bobbed their heads in agreement. "If you're looking for guides, that is."

Carver uncrossed his arms. "Mr. Lovell, thank you. You raise an excellent point. If any man or woman with knowledge of the mountain is willing to help in the search, please leave your name before you head home tonight, and someone will be in touch with you."

With a satisfied smirk on his face, Lovell slumped back into his seat, the pew creaking under his weight.

"Due to the heinous nature of his crimes," Carver continued, "and because the military justice system isn't always fair or expedient, I have decided that each of you will be responsible for doling out a measure of Sergeant Nolan's punishment. One slap. One punch. One kick. Because there are so many of you, I must ask that you limit yourselves to just one."

Taylor's stomach dropped into his boots. He stopped scraping his wrists against the wood, his eyes scanning the crowd. Trying to count. There had to be a hundred people in attendance. Maybe more. All of the pews were filled. Some people were standing in the back of the sanctuary.

Could he survive such a beating?

"You're all decent, hard-working individuals," Carver continued, pacing back and forth in front of Taylor. "And I know you don't want to kill this young man. The soldiers behind me will oversee the punishment tonight. They will ensure that Sergeant Nolan survives to face a military court-martial. Also, I understand this is quite unorthodox, so if anyone feels uncomfortable or wishes to leave, now would be the time."

Those in the pews exchanged looks with their neighbors, but no one left. Several sneered at Taylor, their faces masks of barely-concealed bloodlust.

The colonel rubbed his hands together. "Very good. Thank you all for coming out this evening. Please follow the instructions of my soldiers." The colonel strolled down the aisle and disappeared through a set of double doors at the rear of the sanctuary.

The townspeople rotated in their seats and stared at Taylor, as if Carver's absence had somehow left him in charge.

He resumed scraping at his restraints.

Private Brady spoke up from behind him. "Alright. Who wants to go first?"

At first, no one stood. No one volunteered. And Taylor allowed himself to believe that his punishment would go no further. That the people in the pews were decent people, as Carver had said, incapable of carrying out this brutal penalty. After all, it was one thing to assault someone out of anger, but another thing entirely to do it when the person was gagged and bound. Defenseless.

And then a deep voice bellowed, "I'll go."

Taylor's eyes flicked in to the second row, expecting to see Carl Lovell on his feet again. Instead, a middle-aged man in a suit and tie rose from the last pew. The type of man who spent his days behind a desk in some nondescript office building, sipping nonfat lattes while reading the newspaper. The type of man who stopped at the gym every night before heading home to his wife and kids. The type of man who waved at his neighbors as he walked down his driveway to collect his mail.

Just an ordinary man.

He squeezed past several people to get to the aisle, and then strode purposely toward the front of the church. There was no hesitation in his gait. He stopped directly in front of Taylor, his eyes overflowing with hostility.

"Tell me something, kid," the man said. "Was Henry still alive when you nailed him to that cross? Because I heard he was."

But Taylor didn't respond—*couldn't* respond, because of the gag. And he saw a flicker of something pass through the man's eyes. Enjoyment.

The man would tell himself otherwise later, of course, as he removed his suit and tie and climbed into bed beside his wife. He'd tell himself that it had sickened him. That he was only doing what needed to be done. That he hadn't done it for any other reason than to avenge a wrong and to prevent further injustices from happening. After all, even heroes had to spill a little blood from time to time.

He would tell himself these things, and eventually, he would come to believe them.

Taylor knew from experience.

"This is for Henry Castern."

Taylor saw the punch coming as if in slow motion, watched the man pull his arm back like a pitcher on the mound, his slim, manicured fingers forming themselves into a surprisingly substantial fist. A series of scars adorned his knuckles—the remnants of old cuts or warts. Tiny imperfections that contrasted sharply with the man's otherwise flawless appearance.

The scars grew larger as the fist soared toward Taylor's face.

He'd had been punched once before, back in sixth grade, a week after his mom died. A zit-faced eighth-grader named Jason Pfender and a couple of his delinquent friends had cornered Taylor on his way home from school, pinning him against the side of a neighbor's garage. Taylor remembered holding back tears, not wanting to be called a sissy on top of everything else, and the way their bodies had towered over his, seeming to block out the sun. At first, they had only taunted him, smacking the side of his head and kicking him in the shins, all while calling him a Jesus-freak preacher's boy.

But what Pfender hadn't realized was that no one knows a town's dirty little secrets better than the local pastor. And—by association—the pastor's kid. Pfender didn't realize that his own mother had shown up at Taylor's house just five days earlier sporting a black eye, with streaks of mascara running down her cheeks. Taylor had listened through his father's office door as the woman had begged his father to tell her it was okay to divorce a husband who drank too much and beat her up.

Pfender and his friends had only intended to rough him up a bit that day. Nothing out of the ordinary. But Taylor's mouth had gotten the better of him, as it always did, the grief over his mother's death still a festering wound. After enduring a particularly painful smack to the face, he'd screamed, *"Who taught you how to hit, Jason? Was it your dad? Because I hear he's pretty good at beating the crap out of your mom!"*

The resulting punch had been the single worst physical pain—aside from his mother's death—that he'd ever experienced.

Until now.

The suit-and tie-man's fist landed dead-center on Taylor's left cheek, as if there had been a bulls-eye drawn there. An explosion of light and colors went off inside his brain, like fireworks, and the room seemed to expand and rotate, bright shapes coalescing into one into another like a kaleidoscope. Then the colors vanished and everything dimmed so suddenly that Taylor thought he might pass out. But something deep inside him kicked in, some primal survival instinct, and he forced himself out of the swirling blackness and back into the light.

The man massaged his fist, and then strolled out of the sanctuary.

Brady called out: "Next!"

An elderly woman with white hair stood as if her number had been called. She tucked her purse under her left arm before carefully making her way to Taylor. "Henry was a good man," she said. And then she slapped him across the cheek, the impact surprisingly jarring.

One thought kept running through his mind: A hundred people. There are at least a hundred people in here. I'm going to die.

The dam broke. They no longer came one at a time, but formed into an orderly line, each waiting for his or her turn with the prisoner. A few muttered trivialities about Henry, while others cursed Taylor loudly and openly, egging on the rest of the crowd. Most said nothing, choosing to let their fists and feet convey the message. He was slapped, punched, kicked, and spat upon so many times he lost count.

After one particularly brutal blow to the head, administered by the brute Carl Lovell, Taylor slumped forward, straining against the ropes that held him to the support beam. But the soldiers grabbed his arms, pulled him up, and held him in place.

While Lovell retreated from the sanctuary, Nowak muttered in Taylor's ear: "That was really dumb, punching the colonel. Don't you know you can't hurt him?"

Seconds later, someone kicked him in the stomach with a steel-toed boot.

Taylor slumped forward, coughing so hard it felt as if his lungs might explode. There was a vague sense of damage, of something having been done to his body which couldn't be undone, and he spat a mouthful of blood onto the plastic beneath him.

The next time he raised his head, he saw a flurry of movement high up, above the crowd. There was a balcony up there. He hadn't noticed it before. And that's when he saw her.

Gemma.

Still wearing his uniform jacket.

Duct tape covered her mouth, silencing her screams. Carver stood behind her, holding her in place. Forcing her to watch every punch. Every slap. Every kick. She fought him, struggled to break free, but the colonel grabbed a clump of her hair and yanked her head back. She flinched, and somehow, seeing Gemma in pain hurt Taylor more than any of the injuries he'd already sustained.

The soldiers hoisted him to his feet, preparing him for another blow.

A husky kid in his late teens walked to the front of the sanctuary, flanked on either side by a man and a woman Taylor assumed were his parents. The kid looked like he could play defense for Penn State, and when his thick fist careened with Taylor's temple, a bomb went off inside Taylor's head. Unconsciousness washed over him like a wave, pulling him away from the shore. Away from any hope of surviving. Far away, into a vast and deep ocean where death lurked, waiting to pull him under.

He didn't fight it this time. He allowed the current to pull him away, no longer caring where it carried him, until finally—mercifully —the floor opened up beneath him, and he plunged downward through the blood-spattered plastic.

Into hell, where he belonged.

CHAPTER
TWENTY-TWO

After the beating ended, Carver dragged Gemma down from the balcony and locked her inside a closet on the church's first floor. Her hands remained bound behind her back, the damp duct tape still covering her mouth. Outside the door, people came and went, their banal discussions drifting to her through the wood. Mindless chatter about Netflix and dance recitals and gluten-free bread recipes. All of it so infuriatingly normal that she wanted to scream.

And she did scream. For what felt like hours.

But no one cared.

Whenever she closed her eyes, she saw Taylor sprawled on the blood-spattered plastic, his body broken, his face destroyed. Carver had forced her to watch everything, right up until the soldiers cut through the ropes and allowed Taylor to crumble, lifeless, to the floor. At one point during the beating, she'd turned to the colonel and gestured to her mouth, trying to demonstrate that she would tell him anything he wanted to know, if only he would stop the crowd from hurting Taylor. But Carver hadn't given her the chance. He'd never removed the duct tape from her mouth, only held her in place and whispered into her ear, "This is all your fault. This is happening to him because of you."

Eventually, the voices died down and the closet door swung open. Private Dietrich stood in the hallway, looking pale and exhausted. Silently, she pulled Gemma off the floor and escorted her back to the basement.

At the base of the stairwell, just outside the bathrooms, Dietrich cut off Gemma's restraints and carefully peeled the duct tape away from her lips. "Are you okay?"

Gemma had no idea how to answer that question. She felt nothing.

She was totally numb.

"Is Taylor dead?"

Dietrich tilted her head toward the closed basement door, her face grim. "He's in there."

"What?"

Before Gemma could run to him, Dietrich grabbed her arm and leaned close, speaking in a low voice. "Things are going to get worse, okay? But you have to stay strong. You're a fighter. I can see that in your eyes. Just hang in there."

Gemma snatched her arm away. "Don't touch me." She opened the door and stepped into the pitch-black basement. She could hear Dietrich's boots retreating up the stairwell as she walked with her hands outstretched, trying to avoid bumping into anything. "Taylor?"

No response.

"Taylor? Are you in h—"

She tripped over something, went down hard on all fours. Beneath her palms, the floor felt wet and sticky. She brought her fingers to her nose, inhaled the coppery scent of blood.

No.

She took several deep breaths, allowing her eyes time to adjust to the darkness.

And then she saw him.

Lying on the floor a few feet away, illuminated by the moonlight coming through the narrow window, Taylor's body was concealed beneath the blood-stained plastic he'd been standing on in the sanctuary.

He wasn't moving.

"Taylor!"

Gemma crawled to him, leaving bloody handprints on the concrete. She grabbed the plastic and pulled it down, revealing dark hair stained black with blood. She saw his face and gasped. His features were abnormally large and misshapen, as if a child had crudely formed them out of clay. His eyes were swollen shut, and there was dried blood caked beneath his nostrils and ears. And his beautiful lips—lips she'd once spent hours kissing—were puffy and broken. She lowered her ear to his chest. Straining to listen, she heard nothing but the ragged sound of her own panicked sobs.

Gemma suppressed a scream, her entire body convulsing with the effort. What emerged from the depths of her throat wasn't a scream but a pitiful whimper, the death cries of a wounded animal. She gripped the fabric of his ripped t-shirt in her fists, as if holding onto Taylor would keep her entire world from spinning off its axis. Her heart felt as though someone had taken a sledgehammer to it, shattering it into a million pieces. She could feel it disintegrating within her, leaving no evidence of its existence save for the dark vacuum of empty space.

Until now, losing her parents to the Task Force had been the worst day of her life. But she couldn't survive losing Taylor.

Without him, she didn't exist.

She collapsed on top of him, burying her face in his neck. The familiar smell of him—drenched with blood—enveloped her, wrapping itself around her like a shroud. Nothing mattered anymore. Not her life or Max's or anything else. She wanted to die. To break free of this horrible world and join Taylor wherever he was.

With her head on Taylor's chest, Gemma began to formulate a plan. When Carver came back to the basement, she would attack him. Go for his gun. If she got it, she would kill him and then herself. If she didn't get the gun, she would fight the colonel, forcing him to kill her. Whatever happened, she would never leave this basement alive.

And she would never leave Taylor again.

Gently, she pulled him off the floor and cradled his upper body in her arms. Then she closed her eyes and began to pray. A desperate prayer repeated over and over. A prayer intended to drown out the horrible ideas running through her head. Ideas that weren't her own.

God, bring him back. Please, bring him back. I'm begging you. Please.

"Don't leave me," Gemma whispered into his ear. "Please don't leave me, Taylor. I love you."

She kissed his forehead and held him tightly, hunching her body protectively over his. Determined to protect whatever remained of him, even if it was only his body, from further harm. Steeling herself for the fight that lay ahead. For the footsteps that would signal Carver's return to the basement. For what she would have to do when he returned.

And then...Taylor's body shifted in her arms.

She didn't believe it; not at first. Not until she saw the steady rising and falling of his chest. His swollen eyelids flickered as if he was trying to open them.

"Gem..."

Taylor's voice.

"Taylor? Baby? I'm here." Gemma sobbed. "Thank God."

"Can't...see..." He turned his head, trying to look around. "Where...are we?"

She laughed through her tears, relief and happiness overflowing. "Your eyes are swollen shut. We're still in the church, but we're going to get out of here, okay? I promise. I won't let anything else happen to you."

Taylor's hand reached up, searching for hers. "You...okay?"

She took his ice-cold hand in hers and raised it to her lips. Kissed it. "You don't have to worry about me anymore," she said. "I'm fine."

With his free hand, Taylor gestured to his mouth.

"Water."

Gemma brushed the tears from her cheeks and leaned down to kiss his forehead. "Okay. Water." Gently, she lifted his head off her lap and lowered it to the floor. Then she removed his jacket from her shoulders and placed it underneath his head like a pillow. "I'll be right back. I'm going to get you something to drink."

When she reached the couch, all of the jugs of water were gone. Carver must've had them removed while she was in the closet as punishment for trying to escape. So, she worked her way back to the basement door and eased it open, revealing the dark corridor. At the top of the steps, light seeped through the gaps in the doorframe. She watched the door for a few seconds, one hand poised on the wall, straining to hear any approaching footsteps.

When she didn't hear anyone walking around upstairs, she stepped into the hallway and moved toward the small bathroom. Keeping her eyes on the door at the top of the stairwell, she slid her hand up and down the wall, searching for the light switch.

There.

She flipped it up, the dim lightbulb illuminating the tiny bathroom she'd only used a few times. An old toilet stood in one corner, its bowl stained yellow by years of hard water. On the opposite side of the room sat a small utility sink, its metal faucet green with corrosion. A roll of yellowing paper towels balanced precariously on the upper left ledge of the sink, next to an ancient bar of soap. There was nothing else in the room except for an extra roll of toilet paper on the back of the toilet and an empty trashcan beside the sink. The room stank of ancient disinfectant and urine.

She slumped against the wall, forcing her exhausted mind to process the situation. She needed to get water to Taylor quickly, but how?

Her eyes fell on the trashcan.

She grabbed it and placed it under the faucet, rinsing it out with scalding hot water as best she could. She considered using the bar of soap but then decided against it, as the soap looked dirtier than the trashcan itself. When she was satisfied that the trashcan was as clean as it was going to get, Gemma filled it with cold water from the tap, grabbed the roll of stiff paper towels, and carried everything back to the basement, closing the door softly behind her.

Taylor muttered, "Gemma?"

"It's me." She squatted beside him, and noticed several tiny white objects lying on the floor next to his jacket. She picked one of them up, brought it close to her face. It was a pill. "Taylor? Did you have pills in your jacket?"

He tried to nod. "From the hospital. Pain pills. I took them...in case my leg hurt."

Gemma slipped two of the pills into Taylor's mouth, and pocketed the other four for later.

Taylor raised his head as high as he could—an act that obviously caused him a great deal of pain—and Gemma tilted the small trashcan over his face, allowing the water to trickle into his open mouth. When some spilled onto the front of his t-shirt, she grabbed a few of the stiff paper towels and used them to blot the moisture from his cold skin.

He drank a surprising amount, more than she would've expected given his physical condition. Almost immediately, he appeared more alive, his features less swollen. Or perhaps Gemma was just getting used to them.

"How do you feel?" she asked.

"Terrible. But at least I can see you."

"You can?"

"A little."

"And?" She fluttered her eyelashes. "What do you think?"

"You look awful."

Gemma laughed, sliding her legs beneath him so he was resting on her lap again. Then she spread his jacket over his chest, covering his bare arms. Her fingers glided across his face, lightly passing over a laceration on his right cheek, the cut reminding her that Taylor was real. He was still *here*, injured but alive.

She leaned down and kissed him.

He winced. "Ouch."

"Sorry. I couldn't stop myself."

Taylor's hand found hers. He raised it to his swollen lips and kissed it. "I love you, Gemma," he said, his fingers passing over Gavin's ring. "I never stopped."

She bit down hard on her lip, fighting back tears. "I love you, too."

Taylor watched, silent, as she slipped Gavin's ring off her finger and tucked it inside her pocket. Then he brought a hand to her face and drew her down to him, their lips meeting in a gentle kiss that tasted of his blood and her tears.

A little while later, as the night ebbed away and Gemma felt her eyelids growing heavy, she whispered into the darkness. "Taylor? Are you awake?"

"Yeah."

"What do we do?" she asked. "When Carver comes back?"

He stayed silent for a long time. So long she thought he might've fallen asleep. When he finally spoke, his voice had taken on a hard edge. That familiar defiance she knew so well.

"We fight."

CHAPTER
TWENTY-THREE

Driven from sleep by the commingling odors of burned coffee and propane, Gavin opened his eyes to another bleak morning at Oliver's farmhouse. Their group's second—and probably final—morning at the farmhouse. They couldn't stay any longer. Not with the Task Force still out there, searching the mountain for them.

But Gavin had no idea where they might go next.

On the other side of the living room, orange flames crackled in the old fireplace, burning years of dust from the fake logs. He rolled so he was facing the living-room window, the fresh section of wood floor cold beneath his body, and stared through a narrow gap in the thick curtains. Outside, the overcast sky appeared like an insolent child on the verge of a tantrum, ready to spit rain and unleash thunder at any moment.

Another day on the run.

Another day without Gemma.

Another day of wondering where she was. And *who* she was with.

A few others still dozed in the living room, but most of the sleeping bags were already empty. Gavin winced at the cracking in his spine as he climbed to his feet. He rolled his sleeping bag, tied it together, slipped on his boots, and walked into the kitchen.

Oliver, Mia, Coop, and Kurt occupied the round kitchen table. They drank their coffee and ate their breakfasts in silence, their eyes glazed and distant, their emaciated bodies all but swallowed up by the large farmhouse kitchen. They didn't appear to notice Gavin hovering in the doorway, and that was just fine by him. He didn't want to talk to anyone. Not yet. Keeping his head down, he grabbed a cereal bar from a box on the counter and slipped out of the room.

He climbed the staircase to the farmhouse's second floor. Celia Birch passed him coming down the stairs, a frayed yellow towel wrapped around her head. Their eyes met briefly, but she didn't acknowledge him. Still stewing about the meeting, where he'd stood up to her in defense of Gemma. But Gavin didn't care. Celia was a troublemaker, and he didn't much like her.

At the top of the stairs, steam poured from the bottom of the bathroom door. Oliver and Coop had managed to get the water and gas going, and people were enjoying their first hot showers in more than two years. Through the closed door, he could hear the sound of water running, and a small voice singing *Jesus Loves Me*.

Sophia.

She hadn't recovered from Gemma's sudden disappearance, but she'd seemed a little better yesterday. Still not herself, but less clingy and more talkative. Gavin wasn't sure if the little girl wanted a mother-figure, or if she'd simply grown tired of him, but now she spent most of her time in Addie's shadow, giving him a welcome break.

He continued down the hallway in search of an empty room. Somewhere to be alone until the shower opened up. The last door on the right led into Oliver's old master bedroom—the only room with an actual bed. Kyle and Addie had slept there last night, along with Sophia and Brie and a few others. Brie still refused to talk to anyone. Each time Gavin saw her, he thought she looked thinner and paler, as if she was transforming into a ghost before his eyes.

He entered the room and stepped over unrolled sleeping bags. He just wanted to lie down. But something drew his attention to the dresser in the corner. As with everything in the farmhouse, a thick layer of dust covered the dresser's smooth wood surface. But there was a shadow in the dust, a single dark rectangle with a thinner line jutting out diagonally behind it.

On instinct, he crossed the room and pulled open the top drawer, revealing several rolls of socks, all stiff with age. Most were dress socks, thin material adorned with fancy patterns. A few even featured holiday themes—Christmas lights, four-leaf clovers, and tiny red hearts with arrows driven through them. He could easily picture Oliver wearing socks like this on a daily basis, back in his old life as a podiatrist.

Gavin reached into the drawer and pushed the socks aside, revealing the cheap particleboard bottom. And there, hidden near the back of the drawer, lay a photograph in a simple black frame.

A younger version of Oliver stood in the foreground of the picture, his arm cast across the shoulders of a strikingly-beautiful woman with sparkling eyes and strawberry-blonde curls. Both were laughing, their heads tossed back, their eyes focused not on the camera but on the sky above it. The woman held a pair of keys out in front of her, as if showing them off to the camera.

In the background of the picture was the farmhouse.

In all the time Gavin had known him, Oliver had never looked so carefree. So happy. This was an entirely different man. A man without the safety and survival of so many others weighing him down.

"We purchased this house from my grandfather."

Startled, Gavin shoved the drawer shut and spun around.

Oliver hovered in the doorway, one arm propped against the door frame. He crossed the room and slumped onto the bed, sinking into the old mattress. The bedsprings creaked beneath him. "That's my Anna. We were married for twenty-seven years. She begged me for months to renounce with her. Said the authorities would come for us sooner or later, and she wasn't going to spend our golden years in prison." He suddenly looked very old. "Telling that beautiful woman *no* was always hard for me, but it was never worse than when I said it that last time. I knew I was making a choice. Choosing my faith meant losing my Anna forever, and that's exactly what happened."

Gavin had no idea what to say. "I'm sorry, Oliver. I shouldn't have been snooping around your stuff."

The older man waved the apology away and stroked his white beard, the way he always did when he was thinking. "I want to tell you something, Gavin. But I need you to keep it between us, at least for the time being."

Gavin leaned against the dresser. "Okay?"

Oliver's gaze floated past Gavin to the window. "The Task Force has established a base of operations at an old church in Ash Grove. Yesterday, they detained one of their own soldiers for the murder of Henry Castern." He brought his eyes back to meet Gavin's. "Based on Brie's description of the soldier she saw with Gemma, it sounds like the same guy."

"What?" Gavin swallowed hard, certain he'd heard Oliver wrong. "I don't understand. You're saying *he* killed Henry? The guy Gemma was with?"

Oliver nodded grimly. "That's what the Task Force is claiming, at least. Apparently, half the town showed up at the church last night for some meeting, and they beat the guy up pretty badly."

Good.

A stab of conviction accompanied the thought, but Gavin ignored it. He rubbed at his eyes, tried to clear his mind. "I don't understand. How could you possibly know all of this?"

Oliver stared at him for a long time before lifting his shoulders in a half-shrug. "Let's just say that Henry wasn't my only friend in Ash Grove and leave it at that."

Gavin felt the walls closing in on him. He needed air. But he fought the urge to run to the window and throw it open. "What about Gemma? Where is she?"

"I don't know for sure." Oliver massaged the back of his neck. "But, at the meeting, the leader of the Task Force unit claimed they'd detained a female subversive on the Dragon's Back a few days ago. Apparently, the soldier who killed Henry tried—unsuccessfully—to break Gemma out of the church before he was captured."

Gavin clenched his fists, barely able to utter the next question. But he *had* to know. "Did they hurt Gemma, too? At this meeting?"

"As far as I know, she's okay," Oliver replied quickly. "She wasn't there. They only hurt the soldier."

Gavin dropped his head into his hands, speaking through his fingers. "Why are you telling me all of this?"

Oliver steepled his index fingers below his chin. "So you'll know where to find her."

Gavin couldn't believe what he was hearing. He'd already made up his mind to go after Gemma, but he'd expected to have to sneak away. "You'd let me go?"

Oliver winked at him. "Do I have any choice in the matter?"

"But what about the others?" Gavin felt obligated to ask, although it didn't make any difference to him. "What are you going to tell them?"

"The truth, of course." Oliver touched his beard again, his fingers lingering there. "You know, sometimes I think we're doing this whole thing wrong. Maybe we shouldn't be hiding. Maybe we should stop being cowards and put our trust in God. Maybe we'd be more useful to God out in the world, standing up for the Truth, regardless of the cost." The old man furrowed his thick brows and shrugged. "Or maybe I'm just a crazy old man."

Oliver might be right, but Gavin couldn't worry about that now. Not until he found Gemma. "What are you guys going to do today?" he asked, leaving the real question unspoken.

Oliver smiled, a strange and unfamiliar sight. "Don't worry, son. We'll wait as long as we can for you to return. In fact, today might be a good day for a worship service. We've been so preoccupied with the business of surviving, I think we've forgotten the real reason we're out here. The Lord said, '*Let my people go, so they may worship Me in the wilderness.*'" He chuckled and gestured to the window. "I hope my old barn out there will suffice."

When the old man stood, Gavin touched his arm. "Thank you."

Oliver put a wrinkled hand on Gavin's shoulder and squeezed. His damp eyes drifted to the dresser and lingered there. "If you love that girl, don't let her go. Do for Gemma what I should've done for my wife. I'll always regret giving up on her so easily. Maybe if I'd tried harder to change her mind, things would've turned out differently."

Oliver released Gavin's shoulder and turned to leave but hesitated in the doorway. He spoke without turning around. "When you go, take one of the rifles with you."

The reality of Oliver's words set in, and Gavin dropped onto the bed. Was he really going to do this by himself? What if he was captured? But being captured wasn't his biggest fear. No, his biggest fear was getting Gemma killed. If she died and he survived, how would he ever live with himself?

The answer was simple. He wouldn't.

If things didn't turn out okay...he would just have to deal with it.

Just like his mother.

Resigned, Gavin pushed himself off the bed. Before he reached the door, Kyle appeared in the hallway. "Morning, Bonnar. Did you have a nice chat with our fearless leader?"

Gavin nodded quickly. He didn't have time for Kyle today, and neither did Gemma. "Yeah. It was great." He tried to step around his friend. "I really need to—"

"You're not going to believe this, but I had a good conversation with him myself." Kyle brought an arm up, blocking Gavin's access to the hallway. He ran the tip of his finger along a crack in the doorframe. "Oliver came to see me a little while ago, when you were sleeping. We talked about everything. Our families. Our hopes. Our dreams. I think he's starting to like me."

Gavin fidgeted with his watch, checking the time. "I doubt that."

"We also talked about your little rescue mission."

Gavin looked up, shocked. A tiny bud of hope blossomed in his chest. "And?"

Kyle shrugged. "We both agreed that you're as good as dead without my help. And, for the record, that's the first time Oliver and I have *ever* agreed on anything."

Gavin clasped his hands together on top of his head. As much as he wanted—and needed—Kyle's help, he didn't feel right putting his best friend in danger. Especially when that same friend was about to become a father. "No, Kyle. Absolutely not. I'd never ask you to—"

"You didn't ask," Kyle interrupted. "And, just so we're clear, I'm not asking for your permission, Bonnar. I'm going with you."

Gavin could feel his resolve slipping. "What about Addie?"

Kyle pointed to a red splotch on the side of his face. "She didn't take it very well. She slapped me. Twice. That country girl of mine hits harder than a linebacker. I think my grandmother felt it." He shook his head, his expression turning serious. "After my face stopped hurting, we talked for a little while. And then we prayed. Eventually, she agreed that I needed to go with you." A smirk erupted on Kyle's lips. "She also agreed that you're a dead man without me."

Relieved, Gavin grabbed his friend's shoulders and hugged him. "I love you, man." He meant it. Kyle was the closest thing he'd ever had to a brother. To any family, really.

"And I think you're...swell. But let's not make this weird." Kyle gave him a quick pat on the back and then twisted out of his arms. "Be ready to go in twenty minutes. We've got a long walk ahead of us."

Kyle disappeared down the stairs, and Gavin steadied himself against the doorframe. He stood to lose so much today. His girlfriend. His best friend. His freedom. Maybe even his life. But Oliver was right. They couldn't hide out like cowards forever, waiting to be captured or killed.

It was time for a new strategy.

CHAPTER
TWENTY-FOUR

Two Years Earlier

On her living room couch, buried underneath a mountain of blankets, Gemma clutched a throw pillow to her chest. Each time her eyelids drifted shut, even for a moment, she returned to that terrible night a week earlier. To the thudding of footsteps on the first floor of the house. To the screams as the basement door burst inward and Task Force goons flooded the room, guns drawn. To the look on her father's face when one of the soldiers demanded that the homeowners step forward.

Because, that night, it had been her parents' turn to host.

Varying the days and locations of their secret worship services had only delayed the inevitable. The Task Force had found them. It was over.

When the soldiers detained her parents and led them up the basement stairs, Gemma had turned to the other worshipers, desperate, and begged them to do something. But no one had stepped forward. No hero had emerged from the cowering group.

No one would even meet her gaze.

With no other options, Gemma had charged halfway up the staircase and attacked the soldier escorting her mother. She'd pummeled his back with her fists, ignoring her mother's cries for her to stop, until the soldier spun around and gave her a hard shove.

She'd twisted her right ankle on the way down, but the basement stairs were carpeted, and two of the men from the group had caught her at the bottom, breaking her fall. Even in pain she'd fought them, tried to twist out of their arms, but they'd held her tight until the front door slammed shut and an engine revved outside.

By the time she limped to the front door, her parents were gone.

Gemma's eyes drifted to the muted television. Two women stood on a stage next to the grinning male host, obviously arguing over a skinny man with tattoos covering most of his body, including his bald head. Out of nowhere, one of the women surged forward and smacked the other in the face. A brawl ensued, complete with hair-pulling and shoe-tossing, and the host casually stepped out of the way, his grin wider than ever.

Seven days. That's how long she'd been hiding out inside her home, wrapped in blankets on the couch or buried beneath the comforter on her bed, replaying that night over and over in her mind. As if, by doing so, she could somehow change the past. Dig her way out of it. Force a different ending. The service had almost been over. If the soldiers had arrived ten minutes later, everyone would've been gone. And it wouldn't have been her parents' turn to host again for eight weeks.

Gemma grabbed the remote and changed the channel, searching for something to distract herself from thinking about her parents. What were they going through right now? She had no idea which detention center they were being housed in, but they'd probably been separated. According to the Task Force's website, until she received official notification of their location, she couldn't communicate with them. Even then, detainees weren't allowed visitors until they displayed *"sufficient evidence of progress"* in their rehabilitation process, whatever that meant.

She continued flipping through the channels until a stage filled the screen. Her finger hovered over the channel button, but she didn't press it.

Elevation Ministries with David Ogden.

The megachurch leader stood at the center of the stage, his unblemished skin, perfect hair, and expensive suit highlighted by an array of colorful spotlights. He clutched a gold microphone to his chest and spoke in a deep voice that projected both passion and power. A symphony played in the background, softly at first, then rising into a crescendo like the score of a classic movie. On the massive screen behind him, dozens of people of different colors, genders, and ages stood in a field of sunflowers, their arms reaching toward the heavens, the word ELEVATION printed in the blue sky above their outstretched hands.

"Welcome to our evening broadcast, ladies and gentlemen," Ogden began. "As always, we're coming to you live from Harrisburg, Pennsylvania. And tonight's message is very simple. It's about happiness." The word formed on the screen behind him in bold letters. "That's what our loving creator desires for your life. Happiness. Fullness. Prosperity. In his abundant mercy, he's given us this beautiful world and everything in it as a gift. An expression of his love."

Ogden's face disappeared as the camera panned to the audience. Thousands of awestruck faces gawked at the preacher, their heads bobbing up and down in agreement. Many had tears in their eyes.

"We are his children, and he is our father, and like any father, he desires the best for us. He does not want his children to suffer. He does not want them to be bound and destroyed by manmade customs or folklore. Of course, he doesn't want that! What father would? No, our loving creator wants us to live fully. To love abundantly. To rise up and journey forward together, our hands joined in peace. One world, forging a new path into the future."

The image on the screen dissolved into a new scene. The people gazing toward the heavens lowered their heads so they were looking directly into the camera. Their outstretched hands clasped together, creating an endless chain of colors and faces.

"The creator is extending his hands to you right now." Ogden reached toward the camera and closed his eyes. "It's time to let go. Surrender your burdens to him. Rid yourselves of everything that's getting in the way of your true happiness. Say it with me now. Let go." The audience rose to their feet, the sound like thunder, their hands stretching toward Ogden. A chorus of voices joined his, rising steadily in pitch and intensity.

"Let go."

"Let GO."

"LET GO!"

Gemma grabbed the remote and shut the television off.

And then she heard it.

A soft knocking coming from the back door.

No one ever used that door. And who would be knocking anyway? After her parent's were detained, she'd expected visits—or at least phone calls—from the other members of her church group. She'd expected daily deliveries of lukewarm casseroles she would never consume. Casseroles baked not out of love, but out of guilt and obligation.

But there were no casseroles. No visits. Not even any phone calls.

Nothing. Until now.

Another knock, louder this time.

"Go away," she muttered.

But the knocking continued.

Incessant. Obnoxious.

Gemma threw her pillow to the floor. No one had any right to show up unannounced, so late at night. Especially after everything she'd been through. She pushed herself off the couch, stomped through the kitchen, unlocked the deadbolt, and ripped the door open.

"LEAVE ME AL—"

The word lodged in her throat.

Taylor Nolan stood in the darkness of the backyard, hands jammed into his pockets, looking nervous and uncomfortable. His hair was slightly longer than the buzzcut he'd been sporting the last time she'd seen him, when he'd shown up unannounced at the bakery two years earlier. But, unlike that night, he wasn't dressed in his Task Force uniform. He wore a black t-shirt, faded jeans, and boots.

And he wasn't drunk.

"Gemma."

She tried to slam the door, but Taylor put up a hand to stop it. "Gemma, listen. I promise, I had nothing to do with it." His eyes landed on the basement door, hesitated over its broken hinges, before returning to hers. "Can I come in for a minute?"

Gemma studied Taylor's face for guilt and found none. He looked genuinely upset. She sighed and headed for the living room, leaving the door hanging open behind her. There was a soft click as Taylor eased the kitchen door shut and locked it.

She returned to her spot on the couch and wrapped a blanket around herself. Moments later, Taylor appeared in the entryway to the living room. She expected him to sit in her father's chair, or next to her on the couch. But he remained standing, his eyes fixed on hers. She held his gaze defiantly, waiting for the inevitable apology.

I'm so sorry, Gemma. I had no idea. Are you okay?

Meaningless words, all of them. No one truly cared. Not even Taylor. But she'd let him mutter his hollow apologies, if that's what he needed to do. When he was done, she'd thank him, assure him she was going to be okay, and politely ask him to leave. And if he didn't leave willingly, she would throw him out.

"I heard you that night."

Confused, she wrapped her blanket tighter around herself. "Huh?"

"At my apartment," Taylor continued. "The night my father was detained. I got drunk and made a fool of myself at the bakery, and then you drove me home." He returned his hands to his pockets. "I heard what you said before you left my apartment."

Gemma closed her eyes, tried to remember. She hadn't thought about that night in a long time. Like so many of her memories that involved Taylor, she'd barred it from her mind. But she remembered the highlights. Throwing a cupcake at him after he called her a brat. Driving him back to his crummy apartment. Putting him to bed. Standing in his bedroom doorway...

SUBVERSIVE

It came back to her in a flash, and her eyes snapped open, heat flushing her cheeks. "I have no idea what you're talking about," she lied. Then she grabbed the remote from the coffee table and shook it at him. "Can you please just go home? I'm busy, and you shouldn't be here——"

"I wasn't asleep," he interrupted. "You said you loved me."

Embarrassment gave way to anger. Pure, white-hot fury. She hurled the remote at him.

"Get out!"

Taylor covered his head and ducked, easily avoiding the projectile, which hit the wall behind him and broke apart. Batteries rolled under the loveseat. He straightened, eyes wide with surprise, hands raised in surrender. "Gemma, stop!"

She searched for something else to throw at him, her eyes landing on the table lamp.

"Wait." Taylor lowered his voice. "Please. Don't throw anything else. I'm not here to upset you, okay?" He pulled a folded sheet of paper from his pocket and waved it like a white flag. "I just wanted to give this to you."

Gemma crossed her arms. Whatever the paper was, she didn't want it. But Taylor stepped closer, bringing the paper within her reach, and curiosity got the better of her. She snatched the paper from his hand, unfolded it, and stared at the ten digits printed on the page.

"I don't get it. What is this?" she asked.

Taylor lowered his hands. "It's a phone number. When my father was detained, the Task Force seized most of his stuff, including the desktop computer in his office. But they never found the laptop he kept hidden in the basement. He didn't even tell me about it. I found it later, when I was cleaning out the house. My father used a different email address on that computer, and I found messages between him and this guy named Oliver. They talked about how the government was soon going to come for every Christian who refused to renounce, not just the ministers and leaders. It sounds like this Oliver guy is pretty well-connected, and he's planning on going off-the-grid with a bunch of other people to avoid detention. He wanted my father to go with him."

Gemma curled the fringes of her blanket around her index finger. "But your father was detained before he got the chance to go."

"Yes."

"I don't understand. Why are you telling me this?"

"Because I wrote to him." Taylor crossed the room and sat beside her, keeping a respectful distance between them. "I told him that my father was detained two years ago, and that I know a girl who needs help. I also told him about your parents. Their names and everything, in case he wanted to look it up. He didn't write me back for days. I was starting to think he might've already gone into hiding. But then—yesterday—I got a response."

Gemma didn't like where this conversation was going. "And?"

"He's going into hiding. Soon. A bunch of people are going with him. He wouldn't say how many. They made the decision after an unauthorized church in Minneapolis was raided, and two church elders were killed during the detention. He didn't give me any other details. Just a phone number for you to call. He said you can go with them.

A long silence followed, broken only by the soft ticking of the old grandfather clock in the hallway. Finally, Gemma whispered, "But my parents are gone, Taylor. Our church has fallen apart. Why would I need to hide?"

Taylor leaned forward, hands clasped in front of him. "Because Oliver is right. Our mission is changing. We're not just going after the leadership anymore. We can detain anyone who refuses to renounce, as long as we have sufficient evidence to bring charges against you."

Gemma's chest tightened, making it difficult to breathe. She felt on the verge of a panic attack. "What do you mean? What kind of evidence?"

Taylor counted them off on his fingers. "Your social media accounts. Your parent's tax records. Every dime your family has donated to a church. Even the purchases on your credit cards. Everything can be used against you. Your parents were in leadership, Gemma. And you're nineteen. An adult. I guarantee you're on somebody's list, and it won't be long before they come for you."

She shook her head, unwilling to believe it even though Taylor's words rang true. "No. It can't be that bad. Not yet."

"But it is," Taylor said. "I swear, it is."

Tears slipped down Gemma's cheeks. Wiping them away, she sank into the couch, wishing the worn upholstery would absorb her so she would no longer have to exist in such a world. "But...I can't leave everything, Taylor. What about this house? What about my parents? And this Oliver person...I don't even know anything about him."

Taylor reached for her hand, held it in his own. He looked more nervous than she'd ever seen him. "I get that. And I told you about Oliver because it was the right thing to do. But now I'm going to be selfish and ask you to forget everything I just said. Because I don't want you to go."

"What?" She dried her cheeks on her sleeve. "What do you mean?"

"Don't go," he whispered. "Stay with me."

And then he did something she'd pictured him doing a thousand times. He slid off the couch and dropped to one knee in front of her. One of his boots banged against the antique coffee table, sending a stack of magazines tumbling to the floor, but he didn't seem to notice as he clutched her left hand in both of his. "We could get married. There's nothing stopping us. One of the sergeants in my unit married a sub—" He stopped himself before the word slipped out. "A Christian. Everyone knows about it. She hasn't renounced, but no one cares because she's somebody's wife. If we got married, you wouldn't have to go into hiding."

Gemma wasn't sure whether to laugh or cry. She covered her mouth with her free hand and spoke through her splayed fingers. "I don't understand, Taylor. Why do you want to marry me?"

He brought his hands to her face and pulled her close, his blue eyes burning into hers. "Because I'm in love with you, Gemma. I always have been. Ever since my mother's funeral. Everyone else treated me like a ghost, like I wasn't even there. But you saw me. And that's when I fell in love with you. It just took me a while to realize it."

The blanket slipped from Gemma's shoulders, exposing the tattered flannel pajamas she'd worn like a uniform for days. But she barely noticed. She wanted to believe him. To believe he really loved her. To believe they could have a future together.

But she knew Taylor. The kind of person he'd revealed himself to be.

"No." She pushed his hands away from her face. "Don't say that. Please don't say you love me, Taylor. Because that's a lie."

The hurt in his eyes tore at her heart. "You think I'm lying about being in love with you?"

"I think you *want* to mean it, Taylor. I think you feel guilty for turning your father in, and you think marrying me and protecting me will make up for that mistake. You're still trying to use me, like you did that night at the bakery. You're just doing it in a different way."

"Gemma—"

"Please. Just go home."

She sat back and crossed her arms, waiting for Taylor to leave.

He dropped his arms to his side. Then, silently, he reached into the pocket of his jeans and pulled something out. She expected to see an engagement ring, but when he opened his hand, a silver cross strung from a delicate chain lay in the center of his palm. Five sapphire stones sparkled like memories of a different time.

Gemma hadn't seen the necklace in eight years. Not since the night the carnie tossed it into the garbage can. The following morning, she'd returned to the carnival grounds to search for the necklace. But the rides, the food trucks, even the two-story funhouse had already been torn down and shuttled away.

And all of the garbage cans had been emptied.

When Gemma opened her mouth to speak, no words emerged. Her eyes drifted between Taylor's face and the necklace several times before she managed to whisper, "How?"

He placed the necklace inside her open palm, his fingers lingering there. "I went back that night, after the carnival closed up. I'm not going to lie, digging through the garbage can wasn't fun. I even got sick once. But I kept looking. I thought I was hallucinating when I found it. Afterwards, I took it home, cleaned it up, and put it in an old shoebox in the back of my closet."

She ran her fingers over the sapphire stones. Her next question was obvious, although she thought she already knew the answer. "Why didn't you give it back to me?"

Taylor refused to look into her eyes, instead focusing all of his attention on the carpet. "Because I didn't want you wearing it. I knew the necklace would put you in danger. So, I kept it safe for you. But that was wrong. I should've given it back to you long before n—"

Gemma brought her lips to his, silencing him. Their mouths joined together perfectly, like pieces of a puzzle. Could Taylor tell this was her first kiss? She had no idea what she was doing, and the kiss felt a little awkward, but she quickly relaxed and lost herself in it. Relished every sensation. The feeling of his rough cheek against her smooth one. The way he tasted like cinnamon-flavored gum. How, beneath her fingers, his hair felt slightly damp, as if he'd recently showered. And the way her heart seemed to beat stronger and louder than it ever had before.

When they paused long enough to come up for air, she whispered, "Thank you, Taylor. Thank you so much."

He brushed a strand of hair from her face. "The chain is new. I had to get a new one because the old chain was broken. Plus, this one is longer. Easier to keep hidden." He took the necklace from her hand, undid the clasp, and draped it around her neck. "I'd do anything for you, Gemma. Just tell me what you want."

She blurted out the first thing that came to her mind. "Don't leave. Please just stay here tonight. I promise, we'll figure everything else out in the morning. Just please don't leave. Okay?"

Uncertainty flashed in Taylor's eyes, but he nodded. "Okay."

Before he could reconsider, she grabbed his hand and led him to the staircase. They climbed the steps together, silently passing by the closed door of her parent's bedroom. She hadn't been inside the room—or even opened the door—since they were detained.

The last door on the right opened into Gemma's bedroom. She flicked the overhead light on, revealing pale-grey carpeting, a canopy bed strung with fairy lights, twin purple lamps on each of her nightstands, and lavender walls plastered with posters of musicians she adored. With Taylor beside her, the decor seemed absurdly childish. The harsh overhead lighting highlighted the mess inside:

the unmade bed, the overflowing and disorganized bookshelves, the empty water glasses littering her nightstand, the pajamas and countless socks strewn across the floor.

Embarrassed, she snapped off the overhead light, leaving only the meager glow from her bedside lamps. She rushed to the bed and pulled her sheets and comforter into place. The stuffed unicorn she'd dug out of her closet two days earlier fell to the floor, and she hurriedly kicked it under the bed, hoping Taylor hadn't noticed the animal. "Sorry. My room isn't usually this messy."

Taylor remained in the doorway, appearing hesitant to cross the threshold.

"What's wrong?" she asked.

He took a step back and shook his head. "Gemma...we can't do this."

"Do what?" Only then did she realize the impression she must've given him by asking him to spend the night, and her face burned with embarrassment. She wasn't ready to take that step, not even with Taylor. "No. I know we can't do *that*. It's just that I haven't been sleeping much, and when I do, I have these awful nightmares. I know this probably sounds stupid, but since my parents..." Gemma couldn't bring herself to say it. She dropped onto the edge of her bed. "Since everything happened, I get really scared at night. I keep expecting someone to show up and drag me away. That's the real reason I asked you to stay. I'm hoping I won't be as scared with you here."

Only then did Taylor step into the room, navigating around the debris on her floor and sitting a few feet away from her on the bed. Despite her reassurances that she wasn't looking for anything romantic, he still looked uncomfortable.

She touched his arm. "Still a pastor's son, huh?"

Taylor leaned forward and unlaced his boots. "Yeah. Whether I like it or not."

Switching off the lamps, Gemma crawled beneath the sheets as Taylor slipped his boots off. Then he lay on his side so he was looking at her. The ambient light drifting in from the street made everything hazy and dreamlike. The whole night felt like a dream, from Taylor's confession of love to their first kiss. Even now, with him lying just inches away from her, she kept expecting him to disappear. To evaporate into smoke the moment she closed her eyes.

So, she kept them open.

"Taylor? Did you propose to me tonight?"

"Yeah. I think I might've done that."

"But we can't get married," Gemma said. "That would be insane. We've never even gone on a date. And we've only kissed once...and that was *after* the proposal. Don't you think that's a little weird?"

Taylor appeared to consider this for a moment. Then he nodded. "You know what? You're right. It *would* be weird to get married after just one kiss." He slid closer and put a hand on her chin, gently guiding her lips to his. All of the awkwardness was gone now, and she loved everything about their second kiss. The softness of his lips. The warmth of him beside her. How safe she felt in his arms, as if nothing bad could ever reach out and touch her again.

Kissing Taylor felt like home.

After a few minutes, he pulled away and looked at her. "How about this? If you decide to marry me, we'll go on at least one date first. Just to make sure we actually like each other, and that you don't have any annoying habits I can't get past, like snoring or chewing with your mouth open."

She laughed. "Snoring's a deal-breaker for you?"

"Absolutely." He kissed her again, lightly this time. "Why don't I take you on a real date tomorrow night? Unless you already have plans."

Gemma tapped her chin thoughtfully with her index finger. "I think I can work you into my schedule."

Taylor took her hand in his, brought it to his lips and kissed it. "Try to get some rest, okay?"

She gave him a little salute. "Yes, sir."

"I'm only a PFC, Gemma." He rolled his eyes. "Please don't salute me."

"PFC?" she repeated. "What's that stand for, anyway? Pretty freaking cute?"

Taylor slid an arm beneath her and pulled her close. "You know, I'm starting to rethink this whole marriage thing."

Gemma rested her head in the spot between his neck and his chest and closed her eyes. And, for a few hours, she didn't think about her parents. Or the Task Force. Or the terrifying world outside her bedroom. Instead, she thought about Taylor. About the promises he'd made. The kisses they'd shared. And the life they were going to build together.

She imagined lying in his arms every night, lulled to sleep by his strong, steady heartbeat.

For the first time in nearly a week, she slept.

And she didn't dream.

Hours later, Gemma lay on her back, her head nestled into the crook of Taylor's outstretched arm, watching the slowly-rotating blades of her ceiling fan. Glow-in-the-dark stars—many of them peeling away from the ceiling—shone above her head. For what felt like the hundredth time since she'd awoken and began praying an hour earlier, she brought a hand to her cheek and wiped away the tears before they could drip onto Taylor's shirt.

Family.

The word kept replaying in her mind.

She missed her family.

Glancing at her nightstand, she watched the red digital numbers on her alarm clock change from 3:59 a.m. to 4:00 a.m.

She whispered his name. "Taylor?"

No response.

Louder. "Taylor?"

He sat upright in bed, his eyes darting around the room as if searching the darkness for danger. "What? What is it?"

"Shh, it's okay." Gently, she pulled him back to the pillow. He opened his arms and she snuggled close to him, returning to his chest and the comforting sound of his heartbeat. "I'm sorry to wake you, but I really need to tell you something."

Blinking, he ran a hand through his hair. "Okay..."

Before she could change her mind, before she could talk herself out of it, Gemma forced herself to say the words. "I'm going with Oliver."

Taylor's face collapsed. That was the only way to describe it. All of the hopefulness in his eyes disappeared in an instant—she watched it go—and he looked completely broken. He opened his mouth to speak but no words came out. Finally, he managed to ask, "Why?"

She hated herself for hurting him. For leading him on, and then turning around and breaking his heart. But she needed him to know the truth. To understand why. "I woke up about an hour ago, and I couldn't get back to sleep. So, I started to pray, and I've been praying ever since." She wiped her eyes, but there was no keeping ahead of the tears now. They spilled down her face and soaked into Taylor's cotton t-shirt. "I've been begging God to tell me what to do, and now I know what He wants. He wants me to go with Oliver."

"No, no, no." Taylor's voice wavered with emotion. "Forget about God. Forget about what you think He wants. What do *you* want?"

She brought a hand to his cheek, kissed his lips. "I want to stay here with you. You're all I've ever wanted. You know that.

"Then don't go," he pleaded. "Please stay. Marry me, Gemma."

It took everything she had to shake her head, a sheer force of will. "No. I can't. I love you, Taylor, but that's not what God wants. These people—Oliver's group—I think they need me."

Anger twisted his handsome features. "But how do you *know* that? How do you know what God wants? Did He come out and tell you?"

"It's not just what God wants," she said patiently. "I want a family, Taylor."

"You can have a family...with me."

The pain in his voice made her chest ache. She wanted to be with Taylor so badly. To carve out a life with him. But it wasn't right. "No." The word slipped through her lips, barely more than a whisper. "Not like this."

Taylor shook his head. "You know what I think? I think the real reason you want to go with Oliver is because you're afraid."

"Afraid? Of what?"

"Of being with me. We both know I'm not the guy your parents would've chosen. Not a heathen like me." Taylor drew away from her and closed his eyes, pinching the bridge of his nose. "How, Gemma? How can you still believe that God exists? Look at your parents. Look at my mother. Look where their faith got them."

Taylor's words stunned her. What right did he have to mention her parents? She couldn't stand to look at him anymore, so she rolled away from him and faced the window. How could she explain her faith to him, a non-believer? How could she explain that God *had* spoken to her? Not out loud, of course, but directly into her heart. She felt totally at peace with leaving and making a life with this new family. But she didn't feel that same peace when she thought about staying behind with Taylor. And that made absolutely no sense, which is how she knew it was real. As much as she wanted to, she couldn't ignore God. The only thing she could do was trust that, someday, when the time was right, He would provide her with a path back to Taylor.

The bed shifted beneath her, and Taylor's arms encircled her from behind. "I'm sorry." He brushed her hair aside and kissed the back of her neck, making her shiver. "I'm not a good guy. You should know that by now."

Gemma flipped over to look at him, their faces centimeters apart. "Actually, you're the best guy I've ever known, Taylor Nolan. Which is why I'm in love with you. Ever since that night at the carnival, you've been my hero. And that's never going to change, no matter what you do." She choked back a sob. "I can't believe I have to leave you."

Taylor pulled her close, one hand pressing against the back of her head, and held her while she cried. He kissed her forehead. Her cheeks. Her lips. When she finally started to calm down, he whispered, "Call Oliver, okay? First thing in the morning. Go with him. But if you change your mind, even if it takes a few weeks, or a year, or five years...just come back, okay? Because I meant every word I said to you tonight."

Then he leaned down to kiss her, a passionate kiss that lasted forever, but still not long enough. "I love you, Gemma."

Would he still love her in a year? Or two?

No. Probably not.

He would find someone else by then.

But she said, "I love you, too." Because she meant it. And because she still wanted to believe in fairy tales and love stories and happy endings, even in a world filled with loss and terror and pain. She wanted hope. Because without hope, what was the point of living? And tonight, with Taylor's arms wrapped securely around her, even the improbable seemed possible.

He held her close, one hand pushing the damp hair away from her face. "I still want to marry you, Gemma," he whispered, "That's not going to change. So, try not to fall in love with anyone else. Okay?"

She curled her fingers around his wrist, so much larger than her own. "Never," she whispered against his lips as they met hers.

And she meant it.

Then.

CHAPTER TWENTY-FIVE

Carl Lovell arrived at The Sugar Shack a little after nine, squeezed his considerable girth into the only available booth, and ordered the greasy spoon's signature monster breakfast: The Sugar Slammer. Three over-easy eggs, four pancakes, home fries, and white toast. He asked the new waitress—a blonde cutie sporting hot-pink fingernails with white heart designs—to throw in a side of crispy bacon for good measure.

It had been a long morning...and he was hungry.

After concluding his business at the community building the previous night, Carl had wiped the young Task Force soldier's blood from his hands with a handkerchief, and then scribbled his name and phone number on a torn sheet of notebook paper—a makeshift volunteer form. Taking his aggression out on the soldier had felt good—the kid was a traitor, after all—but he wanted to do more. Whether they knew it or not, the Task Force needed his help with the search. They didn't know the Dragon's Back like he did. And they didn't have his instincts.

SUBVERSIVE

He'd lain awake most of the night, his cell phone plugged into its charger by the bed, just in case someone called. In his fantasies, Colonel Carver himself called, eager to talk man-to-man about the best way to take down these subversives, once and for all.

But, lo and behold, no one called.

No one had ever accused Carl of being a patient man. He'd woken early, thrown on his camouflage hunting gear, grabbed his Winchester Magnum rifle, his Smith and Wesson revolver, and was out the door before the sun came up. He searched the mountain on foot for a bit, before the inevitable pangs of hunger drove him back to town.

The waitress, Dani, delivered his food ten minutes later, dropping three plates in front of him, along with one of The Sugar Shack's famous rotating rack of syrups. Feeling adventurous, he poured a generous helping of blackberry syrup on his first pancake and devoured it in five large bites. As he'd always suspected, the blackberry syrup wasn't as tasty as the maple, but it went down alright.

He shunned the other two pancakes and moved onto the eggs, using a slice of heavily-buttered toast to mop up the mingling rivers of grease and egg yolk as he contemplated calling it quits for the day. He wasn't going to feel like hiking after an artery-clogging breakfast, anyway. And he wanted to be well-rested and ready to head back out in the morning.

Carl shook the ketchup bottle and squeezed it, dousing his home fries and eggs in a lake of ketchup. Not satisfied until a bit leaked off the edge of his plate. He speared a forkful of greasy home fries, dipped them in ketchup, and shoveled them into his mouth.

The mountain of red in front of him triggered a memory of Oliver Barnes, of all people. Boy, was that a blast from the past. He hadn't thought about the foot doc in ages. Carl had eaten breakfast with Barnes at The Sugar Shack a few times. Not because they were friends—they most certainly were *not*—but because they often ate alone on neighboring barstools. Barnes never put ketchup on anything, not even French fries, and he always seemed repulsed by the amount of ketchup Carl used.

Why bother ordering the food? Barnes had asked, the last time Carl ever saw him. *Why not just buy a bottle of ketchup and drink it?*

Carl tapped the rim of his coffee mug with a dirt-caked fingernail, remembering the self-satisfied expression on Barnes' face. How long ago had that breakfast been? Three years now? No. Only two years ago.

Right before the doc offed himself.

According to town scuttlebutt, Barnes had been conducting illegal church services in that old barn of his for quite some time, until someone finally ratted him out. When the Task Force showed up to detain Barnes, they didn't find him. Only an empty house and a suicide note.

The note was addressed to Barnes' ex-wife, Anna, who'd left him a few months earlier.

Carl drank at the Pickaxe a few nights a week with Ted Savage, a retired police officer with connections still in the force. Ted had filled him in on the details over a couple Yuenglings one night. According to Savage, Barnes' suicide note had been as short and sweet as Anna Barnes herself.

Anna, I'm sorry. But I can't do this anymore. I can't live without you.

The cops had checked Barnes' bank accounts, of course, but there hadn't been any large withdraws in the weeks leading up to his disappearance. Both of the doc's vehicles—an old pick-up truck and a Jeep Grand Cherokee—were still parked in the shed. And his cell phone was on the kitchen counter, right next to the suicide note.

The only thing missing from Barnes' house was Barnes himself.

And his bolt-action Remington rifle.

Carl downed the rest of his coffee, wincing at the bitter dregs at the bottom, then pushed the cup toward the edge of the table for the waitress to refill.

Most people in town assumed the doc had hiked up the mountain, made his way into one of the caves, and put a bullet in his skull. But his body had never been recovered, an unsettling fact that had taken up residence squarely in Carl's craw. To him, the suicide had always felt too convenient, too well-timed, given his impending detention. Carl had always believed the note was a ruse to throw the Task Force off the doc's tracks while he went off the grid.

But how far could the old man have gone on foot? Not very. The Dragon's Back was the most obvious place. Barnes' property bordered the state game lands, so he knew the area well. And his family used to own and operate the old Mammoth Mine Tour. Carl had heard rumors that Barnes' parents had died millionaires, and they'd left the coal mine and the money to their only son in the hopes that he'd continue to run the family business. But he'd gone to medical school instead, and the whole operation had shut down back in the eighties.

Carl paused, fork halfway to his mouth, as a thought struck him.

The Mammoth Mine.

He'd been there a few times as a kid. Not because it was interesting, but because it was cheap and there wasn't anything else to do in Ash Grove. Cold and boring, that's how he remembered the place. But he also remembered the tour guide talking about how the temperature inside the mine stayed in the fifties all year round.

Even in the dead of winter.

Carl took another bite of ketchup-soaked eggs. Were there still buildings up there? The land was trespassed, so he couldn't hunt on it. He hadn't been up there since the place shut down. But he remembered a gift shop and a café. As far as he knew, no one had ever torn the place down. As for the mine itself...well, that would be the perfect hideout, wouldn't it?

Plus, Barnes and Henry Castern had always been tight. Thick as thieves, as Carl's momma would've said.

Although he wasn't hungry anymore, Carl devoured the last two pancakes as God intended—drowned in local maple syrup—and allowed the pieces of the puzzle to slide into place in his mind.

The pretty waitress with the pink fingernails sidled up to Carl's booth, coffee carafe in hand. But he covered his mug with one meaty palm. "Just the check, Dani. I'll be leaving in a bit. Thanks."

Ten minutes later, Carl exited the diner and drove west out of Ash Grove, both hands tightly gripping the steering wheel. Putting a fist over his mouth, he belched up the acidic remnants of his breakfast. He squinted through the thin coating of dead bugs and bird crap on the windshield, then jammed his thumb on the button for wiper fluid. The truck responded with a hollow, grinding sound before spitting a bit of cleaner onto the glass. The wipers were junk, the metal peeking through the rubber in a few spots. When they shot across the windshield, the screeching noise made Carl want to veer off the road, rip the wipers off the truck, and snap them over his knee.

But he was too excited, so he kept his foot on the gas.

Carl pulled over just east of Barnes' old farmhouse. He intended to cover the five or six miles from the farmhouse to the coal mine on foot, as the access road that once lead from the highway to the Mammoth was overgrown and impassable. He grabbed his rifle off the passenger seat and slid out of the truck. When he started walking, he felt half-sick, his breakfast sliding around in his stomach like a greasy bowling ball.

But he pushed onward, through the mud and waist-high brambles, his breath coming in frightening, hoarse gasps. He belched again, stomach acid burning his throat, and tried not to think about the strain this little hike was putting on his already overburdened ticker. His rubber boots sunk into the muck as he headed for the concealment of the woods that surrounded Oliver's property.

Carl approached the wood line. He expected to see the farmhouse in disrepair, unable to be sold or torn down until Barnes was legally declared dead, which wouldn't happen for another few years.

But as he drew closer, voices drifted through the trees.

Carl rushed forward and huddled against a tree that provided him with a decent view of the backyard.

There were people—at least fifteen or twenty of them—milling around the property. Grungy-looking people in oversized clothes. Carl watched as an obviously-pregnant woman descended the porch steps, holding hands with a little girl with bright-red hair. Both looked dog-tired as they joined a group heading toward the barn.

Carl put a hand over his racing ticker.

Lo and behold, Barnes was there, too. Looking older and a lot scragglier.

The doc was greeting people at the barn's entrance, patting shoulders and shaking hands like a keyed-up preacher on Sunday morning. The last time Carl had seen Barnes, the man had possessed a lot less hair and a lot more belly. The stiff-necked yuppy Carl remembered was gone, as were Barnes' starched suits and penny loafers. Now, the doc's faded clothes looked like they could stand up on their own, and Carl was pretty sure he could smell them.

Barnes looked disgusting. Like he'd forgotten how to take care of himself.

They all did.

After everyone filed into the barn, Barnes remained outside. Only then did Carl notice the wooden cross in the man's left hand. An ugly thing, fashioned out of branches and tied together with some kind of rope. It looked crooked and broken, like the old doc himself.

Pathetic.

As Carl watched, the doc's chin dropped to his chest and his shoulders sagged, as if the entire weight of the world was pressing down upon him. He might've been crying. Or praying. Carl couldn't tell which, nor did he care. Finally, the doc straightened up, passed his free hand through his shaggy hair, and stepped inside, sliding the door shut behind him.

Carl held the rifle against his chest and closed his eyes, concentrating on slowing his breathing and calming his racing heart.

Despite his grandparents dragging him to church every Sunday for most of his youth, Carl never much cottoned to the idea of a holy deity floating around in the heavens, granting wishes to some and striking others down in the prime of their youth. But Carl felt like bowing and offering up prayers of thanksgiving to the Big Guy in the Sky. Maybe even dancing around a bit, or bellowing one of those obnoxious praise songs he used to doodle obscenities over in the church hymnal when his grandmother wasn't looking.

But Carl wasn't a dullard. He didn't believe in God. Or fate. Or any other ridiculous pixie-dust-and-roses notions. So, he just chalked it up to luck. Good, old-fashioned luck, along with a healthy dose of common sense. Two simple factors, joining together in perfect harmony to ensure that a resourceful man like himself ended up in the right place at the right time.

He didn't have to look inside the barn to know what they were doing. He'd heard from Ted Savage what Barnes used that barn for.

Illegal worship services. He imagined them in there now, praying or singing. Heads bowed over illegal Bibles, maybe even reading passages from their book of fairytales and lies. The thought made him want to—

A hand grabbed his arm and spun him around.

"Wha—" He grappled for his Winchester, ready to fight, until the barrel of an assault rifle wedged itself against his jaw. Then the fight left Carl's body—along with a dribble of urine.

"Hey, buddy," Carl stammered. "What's this about?"

A young Task Force soldier leaned close to him. The guy was all freckles and red-hair and acne, a slightly-older version of Alfred E. Neuman from Mad Magazine. And, ugh, the kid smelled awful— like rotten meat and body odor. So *that's* what he'd been smelling. Not Barnes and his sloppy band of Bible-bangers, after all.

The soldier looked like a ginger zombie after a four-day bender.

"Name," the kid growled. "Or I kill you right now."

"Lovell." He needed to take a leak. Badly. "Carl Lovell. And you are, friend?"

"None of your business."

"Fair enough." On any other day, Carl would've tossed this punk over his knee and beat him until he bawled for his momma. But this wasn't any other day. "Look, we're on the same side here, pal." He nodded toward the barn. "I'm not with those people. In fact, I hiked up here looking for them."

"Yeah, I figured that out myself." The kid dropped his eyes to Carl's gut and smirked. "You don't look like you've been missing any meals."

Oh, the *things* he would do to this smarmy little brat if he only had the chance. But he swallowed back his anger and said, "Your commander, Carver, asked us locals to help out with the search— since we know the area."

"Did he, now?" The kid jammed the rifle deeper into Carl's fleshy jaw. "Do I look like I need your help, boss?"

A bit more pee dribbled down Carl's leg. He hoped the soldier couldn't smell it over his own stench.

"Of course not. But I know the man who owns that property." Carl told the kid about the doc's disappearing act. "So, I came up here on a hunch, hoping you guys might've smoked the old fart out of whatever hole he's been hiding in."

The soldier's eyes narrowed into slits. "You got any identification?"

Of course! Why hadn't he thought of that sooner? Carl dropped a hand to his pocket and dug out his massive wallet. His fingers shook as he produced his identification card and handed it to the soldier. "Here. Just renewed it a month ago."

Without removing the gun from Carl's throat, the soldier took the card with his free hand and examined it closely, even turning it over to study the back. Finally, he passed the card back to Carl and lowered his rifle.

"Sorry about that, Lovell. I'm Mullen."

"Good to meet you, Mullen. And no worries. Can't fault you for doing your job." Carl gave Mullen's hand a firm shake, but imagined himself ripping the skinny punk's arm clean out of its socket and beating him with it. "So, now that you've found them, what happens next? You gonna call out the big dogs?"

The kid stared at him like he was working hard to think, the tip of his tongue sticking out of his mouth a bit. "That depends. You know how to keep your trap shut, Lovell?"

Something wasn't right with this soldier. Carl could feel it.

And he *liked* it.

"Of course." Carl nodded. "Specially when it comes to religious nut jobs."

"You got a vehicle?"

"Down the road a bit. Not far."

"Good." Mullen nodded. "Because these people are dangerous. Really dangerous. I've been watching them for days. I haven't called my unit yet because...well, they would just screw everything up. They wouldn't take care of business in the way it *needs* to be taken care of."

Carl liked where this was going. "Of course. Those government pansies would want to talk about it a bit. Take things into consideration." He clapped a hand on Mullen's shoulder. "But you look like a man of action. A man who knows his own mind."

Mullen picked at a massive whitehead on his nose. The zit looked like a volcano ready to erupt. "Listen, Lovell, I'm not comfortable letting this group out of my sights. Not even for a second. So, I need you to pick up a few things for me and bring them back here? But you'd have to be fast. I don't know how long they're going to stay in the barn. Probably less than an hour."

"Shouldn't be a problem. What do you need?"

The soldier spoke for a long time, only blinking once or twice over the course of five minutes. And Carl listened intently, committing every word to memory, excitement speeding up his heart long before he started to run.

Once again, he couldn't believe his incredible luck.

CHAPTER
TWENTY-SIX

Gemma awoke on the floor, cold and shivering, Taylor's uniform jacket draped over her like a blanket. Her hand was at her neck, her fingers curled around her cross necklace. In those first waking moments, her mind registered a single thought: I'm still here. I'm still in the basement. Hurriedly, she tucked the necklace back inside her shirt before anyone could catch her with it. Then, eager to return to the oblivion of sleep, she rolled over and pulled the jacket over her head, trying to block out the light drifting through the basement's window, her numb fingers passing over hard spots of dried blood.

Blood.

Taylor.

She sat up too quickly, clenching her teeth against the throbbing pain in her skull. Waited for it to pass as she fought the urge to panic. Because there wasn't any reason to panic. Not until it was time to panic. When the pain subsided, she stood and walked on wobbly legs toward the pale haze of morning light streaming into the basement.

Taylor stood atop one of the tables, gazing through the narrow window.

She rushed to him, arms outstretched, convinced his legs would give out at any moment. "Taylor? What are you doing up there?"

He spoke without turning around. "Thinking."

Gemma climbed onto the table and examined Taylor's face. Much of the swelling had gone down, showcasing the grayish-purple bruises that encircled both of his eyes. One of his eyes was blood-red, but the crusted blood beneath his nose and ears was completely gone. He must've snuck off to the bathroom at some point to wash it away. He didn't look great, by any means, but at least she could recognize him. "You look so much better. How do you feel?"

"Like a bunch of rednecks beat the crap out of me."

She went up on her tiptoes to peer through the grimy glass at another overcast day. Low-hanging rainclouds cluttered the gunmetal sky, unleashing the occasional low rumble of thunder. Every few minutes, a lone jogger or a dog-walker passed by the church. Normal people, living normal lives.

She wanted them to suffer for what they'd done to Taylor.

Every last one of them.

"I wonder how many of them were here last night," she asked. "I wonder how many of them hurt you."

Taylor reached for her hand, entwining his fingers with her own. "It doesn't matter."

"Yes, it does! Of course, it does. They could've killed you."

Taylor brought an index finger to his lips and pointed it at the ceiling. Then he whispered, "I need you to promise me something."

Something about his tone made her nervous. "What?"

He turned to face her, his expression hard and serious. "Promise me you'll get out of here. No matter what. If you see an opportunity to escape, even if it means leaving me behind, you take it. Don't hesitate. Don't look back. Just run."

Even before he finished speaking, Gemma was shaking her head. She'd never agree to such a ridiculous request. A powerful surge of anger washed over her. "Why? Why would you ask me to do something like that? What if I asked you to leave me behind? Would you do it?"

He stared at her, his brows creased. "You know I wouldn't."

"Then don't ask me to leave you."

"Gemma, listen to me. Carver's a psychopath...but he's also a soldier. I know exactly how his mind works. He's going to use me against you, just like he did last night. Only next time, it's going to be worse. He won't stop until you give him what he wants."

Worse? Worse than last night?

"Then I'll give the psycho what he wants," she muttered. "He wants information, right? He wants to know where my group is hiding. So... I'll lie to him. Or I'll tell him the truth. Who cares? After everything that's happened, I'm sure my friends are long gone by now." The thought ripped her up inside, so she shoved it away.

She would worry about finding Sophia and the others later.

Taylor gripped her arms with an intensity that frightened her. "No. Information is the only leverage you've got. The moment you tell Carver what he wants to know, he'll kill you." Appearing to notice his grip on her arms, he quickly released her. Then he gestured to the ceiling. "This little operation of his—it's all being done in secret. He's not working within the perimeters of the Task Force anymore. I guarantee that none of his superiors know what's going on in this town, and if they ever found out, he'd lose his command."

Gemma didn't understand. "So? What does that mean for us?"

Taylor returned his attention to the window. "It means there's no reason for Carver to let either of us leave this church alive. The moment you give up whatever information you have that he wants, you become a liability. That's why you have to be strong. Don't give him anything, no matter what he threatens to do to you. Or to me. And when he makes a stupid mistake—which he will, because he's insane—you run. Run and don't look back."

Taylor was right.

Gemma could sense Carver's inevitable return approaching, casting his shadow over them like one of the fire-breathing behemoths from her dreams. And there was nothing she could do about it.

Taylor dug into his pocket, pulled out a wad of toilet paper, and used it to dab his lip, which had started to bleed again. "I've made a lot of mistakes, Gemma. A lot of people are suffering because of the things I've done, and I'll never be able to fix that. I've dreamt about detaining my father every night for the past four years. But do you know what I dreamt about last night?

She shook her head. She hadn't dreamt at all.

He stuffed the toilet paper back into his pocket. "I dreamt about you. About that night at the carnival. You were there, sitting on the ground, muddy and crying. Only this time, it wasn't that creepy carnival guy standing over you. It was Carver. And I wasn't afraid of him, just like I wasn't afraid back then. When I woke up, I realized that I'm the one who has to take Carver down. I can't undo the bad things I've done, but maybe I can do one good thing. And if I don't make it out of here, I'm fine with that. Because I'd give my life a thousand times to save yours."

She could no longer see him through her tears. But she reached for the hazy blur that was Taylor and wrapped her arms around his neck, ignoring his muttered grunt of pain as the weight of her body hurt some hidden part of him. "I love you."

"I love you, too," he whispered into her ear. "Promise me you'll get away."

How ironic that Taylor was asking her to do the same thing she'd done on the food run, leaving Max behind to fend for himself. Could she have helped him, somehow? Or would she have just gotten herself captured? The sad truth was that she would never know because she hadn't even tried. After Max, she'd vowed she'd never leave anyone behind again. And she'd meant it.

But Taylor needed this from her.

He needed to hear her say the words...even if they were lies.

"I promise."

His body—rigid with tension—relaxed in her arms. He held her tightly and kissed her head, muttering into her hair, "Gemma, you've been a pain since the day we met."

"I know." Gemma put her hands on his chest, her eyes passing over his ripped t-shirt and landing on his forearm. And the long number tattooed there. She traced her fingers along the black ink. "What is this, Taylor? You never told me."

Surprise registered on his face, and his injured cheeks flushed red. Taylor never blushed. "A phone number."

Gemma waited for him to elaborate, but he said nothing. And then the truth leapt out at her. So simple, yet so utterly ridiculous. How hadn't she realized it sooner? The number started with the digits 5-7-0, for goodness sakes. The local area code. "You mean it's a *girl's* number?"

"Gemma..."

"Taylor Nolan, please tell me you didn't get drunk and have some girl's number tattooed on your arm!"

An amused smile appeared on his puffy lips. "You're really cute when you're angry."

"Taylor!"

"Relax." He held up his hands and backed away from her. "Please don't throw anything at me. It's the phone number I gave you for Oliver. I wanted to make sure I never forgot it, so I had it tattooed on my arm."

She blinked at him, not comprehending. And still irritated—however irrationally—at the idea of some girl's number permanently inked on her boyfriend's arm. She grabbed his wrist and scrutinized the number, searching her memories to see if the digits corresponded to the ones she'd dialed to reach Oliver.

Taylor carefully pried his wrist out of her iron grip, "After you left, I tried calling the number every few weeks, hoping for some way to keep in touch with you. I knew Oliver wouldn't be stupid enough to take a cell phone with him, but I thought maybe he'd given it to someone else. Someone he trusted. But no one ever answered. Eventually, I called and a recording said the number had been disconnected. That was a bad day."

Gemma didn't need to hear anything else. With her lips, she stopped his talking, kissing his bruised mouth gently at first, afraid of causing him more pain. But then he kissed her back, his fingers entangling in her hair, and she stopped caring about hurting him.

Taylor pressed her against the wall, and she closed her eyes, barely tasting the blood from his broken lips. The basement faded away like a bad dream. The kiss swept her back to her bedroom, on that final night before she went into hiding. She could smell the Ralph Lauren perfume she'd worn before such things became impractical. She could feel the slight breeze drifting through her open window, tickling the hairs on her neck. And she wanted to be with Taylor. Totally and completely.

She needed to tell him. "Taylor—"

The door to the basement swung open, crashed into the opposing wall, ripped through the thin layers of her daydream, and sent her hurtling back to reality.

Gemma screamed and stumbled toward the edge of the table. But Taylor grabbed her, pulling her away from the edge as Carver's soldiers burst into the basement, rifles drawn.

Brady and Nowak.

Tall and handsome, with pale skin and closely-shorn blonde hair, Brady was about as intimidating as a golden retriever. He looked more like a college fraternity brother than a soldier. Nowak was the opposite of Brady: short, stocky, and mean. With a square face, dark, unfeeling eyes, and biceps that strained against the polyester fabric of his uniform.

If Brady was a golden retriever, Nowak was a pit bull.

Brady nodded at Gemma. "Get down from there. The colonel wants to speak with you."

Wincing in pain, Taylor lowered himself down first and then helped Gemma off the table. He positioned himself between her and the doorway. "I need to speak with Colonel Carver."

Nowak scoffed, his mouth bulging with a wad of tobacco. "Yeah, that ain't gonna happen, Sarge. You're gonna have to sit this one out."

Taylor waved a hand dismissively at Gemma. "This chick doesn't know anything, man. Hasn't Carver figured that out yet? I met her at a bar a few weeks ago. After a couple drinks, she said she'd been in hiding with a bunch of subversives until they kicked her out of the group and moved on without her. Apparently, she wasn't *Christian enough*." He put air-quotes around the last two words. "I found that part out for myself when we started hooking up. I figured if I was going to use her to infiltrate the group, I might as well have a little fun in the process.

Goosebumps erupted on Gemma's arms. She knew Taylor was lying, but his story sounded so believable. And he sounded so…*awful*.

She backed into the table, feeling the need to distance herself from him.

Nowak guffawed, a trickle of tobacco juice dribbling from his mouth. He wiped it on his uniform sleeve. "Yeah, right. She admitted all that to you, with you being in the Task Force?"

"She was *drunk*." Taylor gritted his teeth "And I don't make a habit of drinking in uniform, so she had no idea I was in the Task Force." He turned to Brady. "Every day, she went back to the mountain, searching for any trace of her group. Like the roaches would ever take her back. In the meantime, she gave me a lot of good intel."

Brady's eyes flitted briefly to Gemma before returning to Taylor. Unlike Nowak, he appeared interested. "What kind of intel, Sarge?"

"Their old hideout. How many were with her. Even intel about local sympathizers. She didn't know their names—she wasn't high enough in the group for that—but she'd heard that civilians were providing supplies and opening their homes to roaches dodging the Task Force. I was this close to shutting down the entire network..." Taylor held his thumb and forefinger an inch apart. "And then the stupid roach got herself detained on the mountain and screwed everything up."

Lightheaded, Gemma used a hand to brace herself on the table. She felt like throwing up.

"You're so full of crap." Nowak spat a wad of chew on the floor. "So, why'd you try to sneak her out of here?"

"Why do you think? Because I knew she'd break, you moron. As soon as she ratted out her group, and they were captured, the rest of the network would go underground and we'd never find them." Taylor jabbed a finger in Nowak's direction. "And the next time you address me without using my proper rank, I'm going to put you on the ground."

Nowak aimed the barrel of the rifle at Taylor's stomach, his finger curling around the trigger. "I'm done listening to this. Brady, cuff the roach." Then, to Taylor: "Don't try anything, Sarge, unless you want me to gut-shot you in front of your girlfriend."

Brady scratched at his neck, his eyes darting between Nowak and Taylor. Then the lanky soldier shouldered his rifle and pulled a set of handcuffs from his utility belt. He approached Gemma hesitantly. "Hands behind your back."

"Tell Carver." Taylor ordered Brady, his voice heavy with authority. "Tell him now, soldier. If he wouldn't have been so quick to jam a needle into my neck yesterday, I would've explained everything sooner. But he needs to stop wasting his time with the girl. She's totally useless."

Maybe it was the stress. Or the lack of sleep. Or a combination of everything that had transpired over the past three days. But Taylor's words cut her deeply. It didn't matter why he was saying them. It didn't matter that he was lying. His words *felt* true, in a way he would never understand.

She's totally useless.

Gemma felt her face crumbling, and she clenched her hands into fists, struggling to hold back the tears.

Nowak's dark, squinty eyes landed on Gemma, and he lowered his rifle. "Aw, that's not nice, Sarge. You've hurt her feelings." He flashed her a lewd grin, dark flecks of tobacco adorning his yellow teeth. "Don't worry, princess. I bet I could find a use for you."

That was all it took.

"Taylor!" Gemma cried.

But it was too late. Taylor launched himself at the burly soldier. She tried to grab him but missed, snagging only a small section of his t-shirt before it ripped free from her grip. He was surprisingly fast despite his injuries.

But not fast enough.

Nowak brought his rifle up and pulled the trigger.

Gemma screamed.

A hollow click.

A fraction of a second later, Taylor slammed into Nowak full-force, knocking him to the ground. The two men wrestled for a few moments, but it was hardly a fair fight. Although injured and weak, Taylor had the benefit of being driven by a pure, animalistic rage. He straddled the soldier and began raining punches on his face, the sickening sound of flesh hitting flesh echoing throughout the basement.

Before she could reach Taylor, Brady grabbed her from behind, wrenched her arms behind her back, and snapped the handcuffs on her wrists. Then he shoved her out of the way and she fell backward, landing hard on her bottom. The younger soldier ran to the two men grappling on the floor and brought the butt of his rifle down on Taylor's head.

"No!" Gemma cried.

The strength left Taylor's body, and he collapsed on top of Nowak.

Cursing, Brady returned the rifle to his shoulder and grabbed Taylor's arm, dragging him off Nowak. Taylor landed on his back on the cement, unconscious, head lolling.

Muttering expletives, Nowak pushed himself up, blood gushing from the wrecked remains of his nose. He grabbed his rifle and cleared the chamber. The spent cartridge—the misfire that had saved Taylor's life—flew across the room and landed near Gemma's boot. Standing over Taylor's unmoving body, Nowak ran his sleeve across his face, trying to wipe away the blood, but only managing to smear the gore.

Then he raised the rifle and aimed it at Taylor's head. "You're going to put me on the ground, huh? Look who's on the ground now."

Gemma threw herself forward, trying to crawl toward Taylor. "*No!*"

"Hey!" Brady seized Nowak's arm. "Enough, man! Forget him. Let's just get the girl upstairs. Carver's waiting."

"Forget him?" Nowak screamed, gesturing to his battered face. "Look what he did to me! You don't think he should have to pay for this?" He pressed the rifle against Taylor's forehead. "He's a traitor, and he deserves to die."

"Stop!" Gemma cried. "Take me to Carver! I swear, I'll answer any of his questions. Anything he wants to know, I'll tell him. But please..." she sobbed. "Please don't kill him."

Taylor moaned and rolled onto his side, his eyes opening and closing.

Nowak snapped his head in her direction, his eyes teeming with fury. "Why do you care? Your boyfriend's a Task Force scout, princess. Do you know what that means? It means he's a hunter. Except he doesn't hunt animals. He hunts people. Has he told you how many roaches he's detained? How many he's killed?" Nowak drew a line across his throat with his index finger. "Get it? If you knew the truth, you'd be begging me to put a bullet in his head."

She opened her mouth to speak, to argue, but no words came out. Only a mournful cry that emanated from the depths of her soul. She had no strength left. No will to fight. No way to save Taylor. Nothing else to do except to give Carver exactly what he wanted.

Brady spoke up. "Let's just take her to Carver. That's our job." He nodded at Taylor, "As for him...when the time comes, Carver might let you do the honors."

Nowak took a series of deep, slow breaths, his finger poised on the trigger, a battle clearly raging within him. He looked like a bear on its hind legs, yellowed teeth bared as it tried to decide whether or not to slash its prey's throat. Finally, he slung his rifle over his shoulder. "Let's go." He grabbed her roughly by the arm and dragged her toward the basement door. "I'll deal with your boyfriend later."

Just before Nowak pulled the door shut, Gemma saw Taylor struggling to get his hands beneath him. His boots sliding weakly on the floor as he tried to stand. He turned his head, his eyes locking with hers, and gave her a tortured look before collapsing onto his stomach.

And then the door closed, separating them once again.

CHAPTER
TWENTY-SEVEN

The roaches were inside the barn.

All of them.

It was the opportunity Mullen had been waiting for.

He couldn't believe it. It was too perfect, the way everything had suddenly fallen into place. The past two nights, most of the roaches had slept in the farmhouse...but not all of them. A few men had taken rifles and walked the property line at night. The roaches were never all in the same place at one time.

And then—nearly an hour ago—he'd watched them file into the barn. Everyone went inside, even the men who were supposed to be standing guard. Dumb sheep, acting as if security were the least of their concerns.

That had solved his first problem—getting all of the roaches in one place.

But there had still been another problem. Someone needed to take the fall for this. No matter how much the general public hated subversives, what happened today was going to be a big deal. It might even make the national news. Mullen had to be sure that no one—except the people he *wanted* to know—would ever connect it to him.

And then the universe had sent him a giant, bumbling gift in the form of Carl Lovell.

Smiling to himself, Mullen leaned against a tree and popped a few sunflower seeds into his mouth. After studying the group for three days, he knew their patterns. Their schedules. Even a few of their names. Their leader was Oliver—the old man with the white hair. Another of their leaders, Coop, wore a flannel shirt and stupid bib overalls and had a face like a squirrel. There was a brunette chick—Abby or Addy or something like that—who would've been cute if she wasn't knocked up.

And the little girl, Sophia.

She had red hair, just like him.

Yesterday, when the plan first started to take shape in Mullen's mind, he'd tried to summon feelings for the girl. Guilt. Sadness. Shame. Anything. But trying to impose those foreign emotions on himself was like forcing his feet into a pair of shoes that were too small for him.

They just wouldn't fit.

It had been a long two days. He'd slept here and there but only for a few minutes at a time. Except for early this morning, when he'd accidentally dozed off for two hours. When he woke up and realized how long he'd been out, he'd been so angry with himself that he'd taken his knife from its sheath on his belt and carved a thin line into the skin of his forearm. The same way his father used to cut him when he was bad. When the blood oozed from the wound, Mullen felt his anger wane, but only a little.

Luckily, it didn't appear that he'd missed anything important during his nap.

Somewhere behind him, branches snapped. Something heavy crashing through the woods.

Spitting the sunflower shells into the dirt, Mullen turned to scan the forest. That overweight slob was back with the stuff. The moron was limping and stumbling and grunting like an injured bull that needed to be put out of its misery. Mullen returned his attention to the barn. He expected to see the door fly open and the roaches to come scattering outside, looking for the source of the noise.

But the door stayed shut.

Lovell deposited the items on the ground next to Mullen, then went down on one knee as if to propose marriage. "Sorry," he gasped between breaths. "Twisted my ankle on the way back up. Hurts like a mother."

Mullen lifted the heavy Lowe's bag from the soggy ground. Pine needles clung to its bottom. "Took you long enough." He peered inside the bag. "Did you forget we're in a hurry?"

Lovell opened his mouth to answer, but erupted into a coughing fit, hacking into his palm. Mullen imagined a chunk of lung clinging to the man's hand when he pulled it away from his face. "I had to make two stops," Lovell finally said, wiping his hand on his pants. "Gas station first, then the hardware store. There was a line at the hardware store. Must be a sale or something. Every Tom, Dick, and Harriet was out this morning."

But Mullen wasn't listening.

Somehow, against all odds, this garbage truck of a man had proven himself useful.

"Hey, man. You're bleeding."

It took Mullen a few moments to realize that Lovell was referring to the trail of dried blood protruding from his sleeve and running into the grooves of his wrist. "It's just a scratch." He scraped away some of the flakes with his fingernail. "Alright, you ready to finish the job?" He saw uncertainty flash in the fat slob's eyes, so he quickly added, "The Task Force really needs your help, sir."

That was all it took.

Lovell straightened his back, as if steeling himself for what lay ahead. "I was finishing jobs before you were standing up to pee, kid." His eyes flicked to the barn. "Carl Lovell always finishes what he starts."

SUBVERSIVE

The roaches were *singing*.

Mullen couldn't believe it. After losing a few of their own, and being forced to abandon their camp, they were still dumb enough to waste time worshipping a God who didn't exist.

If they only knew what was coming.

He huddled against the side of the barn, listening. The tune sounded familiar. Although he'd never set foot inside a church, he'd interrupted plenty of illegal worship services, and he'd started to recognize some of their songs. When the roaches started singing—well, that was the best time to make entry because they couldn't hear you coming. They rarely fought back, but the element of surprise was still important.

He reached into his fatigues, pulled out a pair of black gloves, and slipped them on.

Lovell crept around the front of the barn and leaned next to Mullen. "I checked the whole way around. Ain't no other exit." Lovell cocked a thumb toward the back of the barn. "There's a window high up in the back, just below the roof, but they ain't ever gonna reach it. Not unless their guardian angels fly 'em up there."

"Good." Mullen wished he'd brought earplugs to block out the singing. He pointed at the leather holster on Lovell's belt. "What kind of revolver you got there, pal? That a Smith and Wesson?"

"Course it is. Used to be my pop's."

Mullen conjured up his best look of admiration. "Mind if I borrow it?"

"What for?" Lovell slapped a hand on his revolver. "You've got your own gun, friend."

Despite wanting to throttle the fat pig for insubordination, Mullen kept a smile plastered on his face. He wondered if it looked as awkward as it felt. "Because I'm going to be crouching here, working on the door. If any of the roaches decide to barge through before I'm done, it's going to be hard to swing my rifle into position. I need a weapon that's a little more maneuverable." He patted Lovell on the back. "Don't worry, man. I'll give it back to you."

Lovell appeared to chew on this for a moment. And then, reluctantly, he pulled the revolver from his holster and handed it to

Mullen. "Don't you go fallin' in love with it. That's too much gun for a kid like you."

"Roger that." Mullen rolled his eyes and slipped the revolver into his waistband. "Okay, I'll handle the door. You get started with the gas. The roaches aren't going to stay in there forever."

Lovell soaked the perimeter of the barn with gasoline, and Mullen got to work on the chain, threading it through the steel door's rusty handles—quickly and quietly. The last thing he needed was for the roaches to come bursting through the double doors. He had to move fast, finish up before their song ended. It wouldn't take long for the heavy smell of gasoline to filter into the barn.

When he was satisfied with the chain, he reached into the Lowe's bag and pulled out the steel padlock. The barn had one exit, so he only needed one. He leaned close to the door—the song growing louder—and eased the padlock through the chain. One of the lines of the song came to him as clear as day.

"In life, in death, O Lord, abide with me."

He snapped the lock shut.

The story of the Grinch popped into his mind again. How the old grump's heart had grown three sizes as the Whos sang their Christmas carols. How he'd hopped on his sleigh, returned the presents and the decorations to Whoville, and then hung around to carve the roast beast.

Something was getting roasted today, but it wasn't the beast.

Lovell finally reached the door, red jug in hand, and allowed the last of the gasoline to dribble onto the age-darkened wood. Then he put the jug down and bent at the waist, palms on his thighs and breathing heavily. His face ashen and sweaty.

Mullen wondered if the man's heart was about to give out. That wouldn't be a bad thing, necessarily. Cleaner than what Mullen had in mind.

But Carl Lovell didn't fall over dead. In fact, the fat slob appeared to be recovering. His breathing was getting more normal, and he had some of the color back in his face.

Oh, well...

Mullen clapped the man on his back. "Nice work."

"Thanks, friend." Lovell pressed his ear against the side of the barn. "They've stopped singing," he whispered. "You think they smell the gas?"

"Probably. But it doesn't matter because they ain't getting out." Mullen dug into his pocket, pulled out the Bic lighter he'd used to start campfires during his overnight scout missions. He twirled the lighter in his fingers, tossed it to Lovell. "Let's get this party started."

Lovell caught the lighter with both hands, color flooding his cheeks. "Why are you giving this to me?"

"You've earned it, man," Mullen whispered. "Do the honors. If any of the roaches slip out, I'll handle it." He patted Carl's revolver on his hip.

Lovell tried to pass the lighter back to him. "This is your rodeo, kid. I'm just a spectator."

That's what you think, Mullen wanted to say.

Instead, he sidestepped Lovell's outstretched hand and pointed at the barn. "Hurry up, man. They're not singing anymore. Do it before it's too late."

Lovell threw up both of his hands. "No way!"

"Keep it down," Mullen growled.

Voices drifted through a crack in the door. Loud voices. Not church voices. Something was definitely happening inside. Either their little worship service had reached its natural conclusion, or the roaches had smelled the gasoline.

As Colonel Carver would say, it was time to fish or cut bait.

"I thought Carl Lovell always finishes what he starts," Mullen muttered, parroting Lovell's earlier words back to him. He held out his hand. "Fine. Give me the lighter."

Anger flamed in Lovell's eyes, and he closed his fist around the lighter before Mullen could take it. "That he does, kid. And don't you ever forget it." The fat man squatted and peered through the tiny gap between the doors. "They're all just standing around. I don't think they smell it yet."

Mullen pulled the revolver from his belt with a gloved hand. "That's good."

Lovell shook his head and chuckled. He wasn't even trying to be quiet now. "Oliver's up front. People are shaking his hand and hugging him, like he's some kind of kingpin. The old fool has no idea what's coming. I almost feel bad for him."

Mullen raised the revolver.

"I don't feel bad at all."

He pressed it against the right side of the man's head and pulled the trigger. A splatter of red and white, and Lovell's thick legs buckled beneath him. He crumpled to the ground, the bulk of his body landing squarely in front of the steel double doors, creating yet another obstacle—in case the roaches somehow managed to break through the chain. Which they wouldn't.

Total silence from inside the barn.

Mullen counted off the seconds in his head, made it to five before the roaches started to chatter like birds. He bent over and squinted through the gap—now speckled with Lovell's brain matter. Frightened faces stared in his direction. Metal scraped against wood as people pushed their chairs out of the way.

He listened to their voices. Fed off of their terror. It reminded him of his mother.

A woman cried, "Oliver? What *was* that?"

Their leader's voice. Powerful. Commanding. "Everyone, stay calm."

Mullen almost laughed.

Stay calm? What a joke.

The little girl—Sophia—was blubbering.

Some of them could probably smell the gasoline by now.

Mullen removed the lighter from Lovell's right hand and replaced it with the revolver, curling the sausage-link fingers around the stock. He scooted the gasoline jug a little closer to the guy's left hand and then stood and admired his work. It wasn't perfect, but it would do. Based on what he'd seen from the locals, he doubted they would kick up much of a fuss over a barnful of torched roaches.

Especially if the killer turned out to be one of their own—and he committed suicide at the scene.

A man's voice: "What's that smell? Do you smell that?"

"It's gasoline!"

The door jutted outward as someone slammed into it.

Mullen didn't jump. The door wasn't going anywhere.

SUBVERSIVE

"Oliver!" A female cried out, her voice as clear as day. She was only a few inches away from him. He could smell her shampoo. "The door won't open!"

More shouting. A few panicked screams. The pounding on the door increased, and the metal bowed outward as bodies piled against it.

Mullen scratched at his nose, felt the zit tear open. When he pulled his hand away, there was blood on his fingers.

A female voice: "There's someone outside!"

She could see him through the gap. Not that it mattered. No one would be around to say what happened here.

"Hey!" The woman cried to him through the door. She sounded young. The pregnant one. Most of the other women were older. "Please! Don't do this!"

Taking a few steps back, away from Lovell and the gasoline jug, Mullen raised the lighter and flicked his thumb. The flame ignited but flickered unsteadily, as if hesitant to play a role in this massacre. In that final moment before he dropped the lighter, Mullen thought of the little girl. The one with the red hair so much like his own. She was sobbing, her cries rising to him above all the others.

His own little Cindy Lou Who.

His dead father's voice filled his mind: *You know, most people have a devil on one shoulder and an angel on the other. You, son, have a devil on both.*

"You were right about me!" Mullen shouted toward the sky, although he held no delusions about his father's black soul ending up anywhere nice. "Just look at how right you were!"

Then the flame ignited, and with it, any doubts about hurting the girl burned up and disintegrated like ashes in the wind.

He tossed the lighter into the puddle of gasoline next to Lovell's body and watched the man catch on fire. Then the wood ignited, the flames climbing steadily higher.

The shouting and wailing coming from within the barn grew louder. More hysterical. They started pounding on the walls. Trying to smash through the wood. Someone hurled what sounded like a metal chair against the wall. It clattered to the floor.

The wood was old and dry. The fire would spread quickly.

None of them would make it out.

"I'm your god!" Mullen screamed into the flames. "I decide who lives and who dies! Worship me!"

Then he ran.

He reached the wood line and fell to his stomach, taking up a sniper's position on top of a log. He trained his rifle on the second-floor window. If any of the roaches managed to slip out that window, he would send them straight to hell with a bullet in their skulls. He wasn't worried about forensics anymore. Even if anyone cared enough to perform autopsies on the roaches—which they wouldn't—the bodies would be so badly burned that the bullets would never be traced back to him.

He watched the barn burn for a long time. Long after the screams and the coughing died down. Long after the smoke reached his own lungs, causing him to hack. Long after the flames blew out the second-floor window.

Only after the roof collapsed, and black smoke blotted out the sun, did Mullen finally pack up his rifle and go home.

CHAPTER
TWENTY-EIGHT

The soldiers led Gemma into a sparse office that smelled like vanilla air freshener and old carpet. Generic cityscapes in dusty plastic frames hung on all four walls, as if whoever decorated the office had dreamed of being anywhere else.

On the far side of the room, Colonel Carver leaned back in his chair, spit-shined boots propped on the wooden desk, paging through the contents of a manila folder. Without glancing up, he motioned for Gemma to sit in one of the chairs opposite his desk. Brady remained in the doorway, while Nowak escorted her to the chair and removed her handcuffs. Then both men snapped to attention.

With her hands freed, Gemma leaned forward and wrapped her arms protectively around her waist, her dirty hair falling around her face like a shield. The hatred radiating off Nowak felt like steam against her back. She could sense him biding his time, waiting for the opportunity to air his grievances to his commander. What would

Carver do when he saw Nowak's bloody face? When he found out what Taylor had done?

She had to protect Taylor. No matter what.

And she had to protect her friends.

Was there a way to protect them both?

Carver finally raised his head and noticed the smeared gore that used to be Nowak's nose. His brow furrowed, and his eyes drifted between Nowak and Gemma before returning to the paperwork in front of him. He waved a hand in the air. "Dismissed."

A sharp inhale from Nowak.

Brady saluted. When Carver didn't return the salute, he dropped his hand, performed an about-face, and exited the room.

But Nowak didn't move.

Stealing a quick glimpse of the soldier's battered face, Gemma saw the unnatural flare of his blood-caked nostrils. He was furious.

Nowak cleared his throat. "Sir?"

"I said dismissed."

There was no mistaking Carver's tone. He wasn't interested in Nowak or his injuries.

Gemma held her breath, waiting for Nowak to lose his patience with the colonel. To blurt out everything that had happened in the basement. But the soldier snapped into a rigid salute—one that also wasn't returned—before slipping out the door and pulling it shut behind him.

The heavy silence that followed felt like another presence in the room. Carver didn't speak to Gemma or even acknowledge her, only continued to study the contents of the mystery folder, his dark eyes gliding purposefully over every sentence. Either he was trying to unnerve her—and it was working—or whatever information the folder held was of particular interest to him.

Four minutes passed before the colonel spoke.

"Your name is Alcott." Carver gave her a pointed look before returning his attention to the paperwork. "Age: twenty-one. Originally from Ridgefield, Pennsylvania. Your parents were detained two years ago under suspicion of subversive activities. More specifically, they were conducting unauthorized, unlicensed Christian worship services within their residence." He held up a photocopied image of Gemma's driver's license. "You went missing shortly afterwards. You didn't take any money, any vehicle, not even your cell phone. Your paternal aunt, Crystal Alcott, told a local newspaper reporter that it was as if you'd just dropped off the face of the earth."

The room dimmed slightly, as if someone had turned down the lights, and static erupted in Gemma's vision. The office suddenly felt unbearably small, and so hot she couldn't seem to pull enough air into her lungs. On the verge of losing consciousness, she closed her eyes and breathed in slowly through her nose and out through her mouth, a trick she'd learned when she used to have panic attacks in middle school.

In and out.

In and out.

She heard Carver flip the page.

"The police didn't put much energy into an investigation. After all, you certainly aren't the first person to drop off the grid in the past few years. Most people in your hometown just assumed you'd ran away. Maybe took off with some boy you'd been seeing. In fact, while your aunt claimed you didn't have a boyfriend, an elderly neighbor reported seeing a young man leaving your house one morning, shortly before you disappeared."

In and out.

"Guess who else originally hails from Ridgefield?"

Gemma's eyelids snapped open.

The colonel plucked something off his desk: a green folder with various dates stamped on the front. He opened it, turning it so she could see its contents. On the right side was a thick stack of military service records. On the left side was a single paper-clipped photograph of a soldier in uniform.

"Sergeant Taylor Nolan."

The commander closed the folder and placed it on the desk before turning his dark eyes on Gemma. "Judging by the injuries on my private's face, I assume Sergeant Nolan made it through the night. I hope you thanked him for taking your punishment, young lady. I highly doubt you would've fared so well."

She hated Carver. Hated him with an intensity that surprised her. "You're a monster."

The colonel uncrossed his legs and lowered his boots to the floor. "I'm not a monster, Miss Alcott. Or a madman. I don't enjoy inflicting pain on others, despite what you might think. But I *am* a soldier. Just like your boyfriend. And my superiors expect me to produce results. Unfortunately, you're standing in the way of that. So, while it gives me no pleasure to hurt you—or the ones you love—I have absolutely no qualms about doing it." Carver leaned forward, hands clasped on the desk. "With that being said, if you care for that young man in the basement, I suggest you tell me where your friends are hiding."

Taylor's words came back to her: *The moment you tell Carver what he wants to know, he'll kill you.*

Protect them, she reminded herself. No matter the cost.

And trust in God.

Gemma shrugged. "Certainly not where I left them."

"So, you think they've moved on? Hidden someplace else?"

"Nah." Gemma leaned back in her chair and propped her boots on the desk, trying to look and sound more confident than she felt. "They're probably parading down Main Street right now. You better go check. I bet they've got a drum. And balloons."

Carver tilted his head to the side. "This isn't the time for sarcasm, young lady. If you believe your group has moved on, I see no reason for you to withhold their previous location from me."

Gemma tugged at the hem of her tank top, her thoughts drifting back to the meeting in the café, right after they lost Max and Allen. No one had wanted to leave. They had known the Task Force was closing in on them, and that the Task Force had murdered their supplier. And yet they still wanted to stay.

"Come on, Ms. Alcott," Carver prodded, his eyes gleaming. "Don't make this harder than it has to be. I don't want to hurt your boyfriend. I'm not sure how much more abuse the kid can withstand before he dies. Besides—and you've said this yourself—your group has moved on. They're safe. What have you got to lose? Giving up the location of your former camp hurts no one. But not giving it up..." He allowed the words to hang in the air.

The night her parents were detained, Gemma had watched the soldiers drag her family away. She hadn't been able to save them.

And when Max had needed her, she'd run away in fear. She'd chosen the coward's way out, as she always did.

But not now.

Not this time.

By your endurance, gain your lives.

Carver's lips curled into a smirk.

He thinks he's won, she realized. He thinks he's broken me.

That smirk fueled her. Because Carver saw her as she'd once seen herself.

Weak.

Cowardly.

Easily broken.

But not this time.

"No." A hard edge found its way into her voice. She removed her boots from the desk and straightened her back. "You can hurt me. Torture me. Kill me if you want. I don't care anymore. But I'm done playing your games. I'm done with you...your soldiers...and this town." She knew she was going too far, but she couldn't stop herself. Couldn't stop the words from pouring from her mouth. "I'm not the weak one, Carver. You are. You have guns and soldiers, but I have God. And I can do *all things* through Christ who strengthens me."

There it was.

Out in the open.

Where it belonged.

The smirk faded from Carver's face. His dark eyes bored into hers, and there was nothing behind them. Logically, the colonel was a human being. But there was no humanity in his eyes. Nothing resembling pity. Or remorse. Nothing but whatever evil drove him to do what he did.

Finally, he rose from his chair and ran his palms over the front of his uniform, smoothing out the creases. "Very well. I see you've made your decision." He strolled around the desk, pulled a pair of handcuffs from his belt, and cuffed Gemma's left hand. She offered her right hand to him, eager to return to the basement. To Taylor. To whatever came next.

They would face it together.

But Carver grabbed her shoulders and shoved her sideways, pushing her off the chair. She hit the ground hard. The colonel refused to relinquish his iron grip on her left hand, and a searing pain ripped through her shoulder as he wrenched her arm high behind her back.

"No!" she cried. "Stop!"

But Carver held that position, slowly torquing her shoulder until it felt as if it might tear loose from its socket. Nothing had ever hurt so much. Her face touched the carpet, her vision blurring into a white-hot light, so bright it was blinding. Another centimeter and her shoulder would dislocate.

But she wouldn't cry. Wouldn't beg.

Finally, seemingly satisfied with having caused her enough pain, the colonel dropped to one knee and snapped the other cuff around the thick leg of the heavy desk. It barely fit.

Her shoulder all but forgotten, Gemma yanked at the cuff. "What are you doing?"

Carver lowered his other knee to the floor and brought his face to within inches of hers. His breath reeked of stale coffee. "Relax, Miss Alcott. You don't have anything else to worry about now."

Dread washed over her, as cold and dark and bottomless as the ocean. "Why?" she demanded. "What are you going to do?"

He leaned back on his haunches and tugged at the cuff, but the desk didn't budge. She would never be able to move it on her own. He stood and headed for the door, a new jaunty lightness in his step.

He paused at the door, a monster in a Task Force dress uniform.

"I'm going to kill your boyfriend."

The door closed behind him, and Gemma began to scream.

CHAPTER
TWENTY-NINE

A boot buried itself in Taylor's ribcage, knocking the breath from his lungs.

Fresh agony, sharp and piercing, thrust him back into reality. The world came into view briefly, then exploded into a million pinpoints of light. He puked onto the concrete floor. Then, wheezing, he rolled onto his side and clutched his chest.

"Time to wake up, son."

Carver.

Fearing another kick, Taylor heaved himself onto his back. The tightness in his chest loosened a little, and he sucked in several hitching breaths. Almost immediately, his head throbbed, and he reached up and felt a tender lump above his left ear.

The soldier must've hit him with something.

Gemma.

Taylor forced his eyes open.

SUBVERSIVE

Blinding light poured through the narrow window, piercing his eyes with the sharpness of a needle. Colonel Carver stood over him, the man's broad chest rising and falling with slow, deliberate breaths.

Gemma's gone, Taylor realized. And Carver's here to kill me.

Carver pulled a clean handkerchief from his pocket, handed it to Taylor, and knelt beside him. "You're a good soldier, Nolan." He sounded apologetic. "I skimmed through your file this morning. Aside from a few minor disciplinary infractions early on, your record is spotless. You made sergeant faster than most. You even turned your father in. That took guts...and a strong dedication to the mission." His lips drew into a tight line. "You could've been useful to me."

Taylor wiped his mouth with the colonel's handkerchief, his eyes dropping briefly to the mess on the floor; a puddle of bile speckled with thin rivulets of blood.

"Are you really in this situation because of some girl from your hometown? A subversive? Who is she to you, anyway?"

"Just a girl from high school, sir," Taylor muttered. Talking hurt. Everything hurt. But the longer he talked, the longer he lived. "I barely knew her. I was using her to get information on her group."

"Is that so?"

Taylor nodded and dabbed his mouth again. Stalling for time while he tried to remember the story he'd told Nowak and Brady. "There's a network of sympathizers...in the area. Safe houses, too. An underground railroad...for roaches. That's why I tried to break her out. If your men interrogated her...she'd crack. We might get a few of her friends...but we wouldn't shut down the network."

Carver arched an eyebrow as dark and thick as a caterpillar. "That's quite a story, Nolan. But we both know it's pure fantasy."

"Colonel—"

"Stop." Carver held up a hand. "Stop lying to me, son. Whatever your connection is to this girl, she isn't worth your life. Treason is punishable by death." He brought his face closer to Taylor's. "But it doesn't have to come to that. You're a good soldier. You joined the Task Force because you believed in our mission. Religious nuts like this girl are detrimental to our society. You *know* that. She's cute...but that doesn't change what she is."

Taylor raised his eyes to meet the colonel's. "What is she?"

Carver arched an eyebrow, as if the answer should've been obvious. "The enemy, son. And you're a soldier. But I'm not asking you to kill her. Or even to hurt her. I'm asking for information. Tell me everything you know about her group. Afterward, I'll have one of my men drive you to the hospital for treatment. When you've recovered, you may return to your unit. No formal disciplinary action will be taken against you. I think we can both agree you've been punished enough."

"And the girl? What happens to her?"

The corners of the colonel's mouth ticked upward. "She won't be harmed. I give you my word. No more interrogations. No more town meetings. After you and I finish speaking, I'll arrange for her immediate transfer to the nearest detention facility, which is in Harrisburg. You could visit her often, if you desired."

Taylor stared at him. If he told Carver about the mine, Gemma would live. She'd be detained, but at least she'd be alive.

Carver brought his hand up and pointed at the gold band on his ring finger. "You aren't the first person to make this difficult decision, son. My wife, Arabella—I call her Bella—is in a detention center near Pittsburgh. I did what was best for her...and for this country. I visit her whenever I can. And I truly believe that, one day, she will change." Carver's gaze dropped to his ring. "It could be the same for you and Miss Alcott, you know? You could have a life together someday. A *real* life. Not whatever this is."

Taylor closed his eyes. Behind his closed eyelids, he saw Gemma's face. The way she'd looked this morning, before the guards had taken her away. There'd been so much love in her eyes. So much trust. Trust he didn't deserve.

He opened his eyes. "How long has your wife been in the detention center?"

"Bella? Six years now." The colonel twisted the gold band, easily sliding it off his finger. "I only see her a few times a year, but it's not as bad as it sounds. There are other women, of course, but they aren't important. They're just companions, protection against the lonely nights. I'll never give up on my Bella, as I'm sure you'll never give up on Miss Alcott. We're not so different, you and I. We both believe in the mission, and we're both in love with women who need our support—and our help—to change."

Taylor held the colonel's gaze. Looking into Carver's eyes was like catching a glimpse of his own future. One possible future, at least. But was *this* the kind of man Taylor wanted to be? A man so consumed by hatred that he would allow his own wife to rot in a detention center? Once, he would've said yes. Once, the mission had been the most important thing in the world to him. He would've done anything to strike back at God.

But now?

Everything hinged on this moment. Not just his career, but his life.

And Gemma's.

"You're right, sir," Taylor finally said. "I still believe in the mission. But you're wrong about something."

Carver slipped the ring back on his finger. "What's that?"

Lying on his back in front of Carver, Taylor felt totally exposed. Vulnerable. But he also felt powerful. Because for the first time in his life, he was going to do the right thing. He wiped his mouth one last time with the colonel's handkerchief before crumpling it and dropping it into the puddle of bile. "I'd never betray Gemma the way you've betrayed your wife."

There wasn't any anger in the colonel's eyes. None of the fury Taylor had expected. Just resignation. Maybe even a hint of sadness. Finally, he unleashed a heavy sigh and pushed himself to his feet. "Alright, son. Let's finish this. On your knees."

Carver grabbed Taylor's arms, helped him to kneel, and stepped behind him.

Kneeling on the concrete, Taylor straightened his back and raised his head as high as he could. Instead of begging for his life, he pictured his father on the day he was detained. The dignity he'd displayed in the face of ultimate betrayal. He hadn't screamed or cried or demanded release.

No. He'd quietly accepted his fate as a consequence of his faith.

But Taylor didn't have any faith. He'd lost his faith when he lost his mother. He'd been so young, and the loss had been devastating. World-destroying. But losing his mother had only been part of the devastation. The other part had been the stunning realization that

God didn't always grant wishes. He didn't always heal sick mothers. He didn't always keep His people from harm because they went to church. Or read their Bibles. Or memorized Scripture.

Sometimes, God could be cruel.

That's why Taylor had joined the Task Force. What better way to hurt God than by destroying His people's faith? He thought of the horrible things he'd done. Tearing Bibles from shaking hands and ripping them to shreds. Taunting people with Scripture verses as he led them out of their homes. Torching churches and homes. Separating families. Destroying lives.

So much pain. He'd caused so much pain to so many people.

How could he ever expect to be forgiven?

He heard Carver unsnap his pistol from its holster. He was about to die. Either heaven or hell awaited, and he knew which one he deserved.

Taylor closed his eyes and saw the faces of the people he'd hurt. Their tears. Their resolute faith.

He envied them.

The colonel's cold voice came from behind Taylor. "You don't think you're like me, but you are. I read your file. I know the things you've done."

For the first time in a decade, Taylor bowed his head, closed his eyes, and began to pray. He didn't have to struggle to remember the prayer. Even after so many years, it was as familiar to him as his own name. "Our Father, who art in heaven, hallowed be Thy name. Thy kingdom come, Thy will be done, on earth as it is in heaven. Give us this day our daily bread. And forgive us our sins, as we forgive those who sin against us..."

"You really think you deserve forgiveness?" Carver pressed the gun against the back of Taylor's head. "There's no forgiveness for you. Or for me. Or for the roaches. Don't you see, son? We're all damned. *For dust you are, and to dust you will return.* Isn't that how it goes?"

"And lead us not into temptation, but deliver us from evil..."

"There is no God to deliver you from anything." The fury radiated off of Carver like heat. "He doesn't exist. Otherwise you wouldn't be here, cowering in front of me. And I wouldn't be about to turn your head into a canoe."

"For thine is the kingdom, and the power, and the glory. Forever."

Carver drove the barrel of the gun into Taylor's skull, forcing him down on all fours. Then the colonel slipped around to Taylor's right side and aimed the gun at Taylor's temple. "I should've known. You're a roach, Nolan. Just like the rest of them." Carver spat on him and shook his head in disgust. "Dying for your faith doesn't make you a martyr. It makes you a fool."

Taylor closed his eyes again, tried to picture Gemma. Every detail of her face. The way she smelled. The way her arms felt around his neck. The way her lips felt against his. But what came to mind instead was the way her small hand had covered his as he sat before his mother's casket. He'd felt like a ship adrift on a rough sea. And this girl had given him exactly what he'd needed to survive. Not meaningless words of comfort or a sympathetic look, but a lifeline in the form of her hand. Her friendship. Her love.

She'd given him everything that day, and he loved her for it.

The bullet would come soon. It would send him to wherever he was going next.

"I'm sorry, Father," he whispered. And he meant it.

Then, from somewhere overhead, came a piercing scream.

CHAPTER THIRTY

Blood everywhere.

On her hands. On her clothes. On the carpet.

Gemma placed the letter opener, its metal tip tinged with red, back on the desk.

Carver had left the letter opener lying on his desk to mess with her. She knew that now. And it had worked. Like an idiot, she'd fallen into his trap, first trying to pick the lock on her handcuff with the metal tip. But she had no idea how to pick a lock. When that hadn't worked, she'd tried to saw through the cuff itself, metal against metal. Knowing it was ridiculous but trying anyway. But the letter opener kept slipping and jabbing into her skin. Now her wrist was covered in small cuts, all of them leaking blood.

The sight made her woozy, so she closed her eyes and leaned against the desk, her arm dangling limply at her side. What else could she do? Slipping her hand out of the cuffs hadn't worked, either. She'd only succeeded in carving a layer of skin from her wrist, leaving it red and raw. And the desk was too heavy to lift.

She'd tried. Perhaps if she could stand, she'd be able to lift it. But she was handcuffed to the floor.

Still, she couldn't stop.

She had to get free. She had to help Taylor.

Try again.

Gemma planted her boots on the floor and pushed up on the desk, trying to lift it. Using every ounce of strength remaining in her body. Sweat ran into her eyes until she couldn't see anything. She gasped for air, unable to breathe. She was hyperventilating. Pulling in too much oxygen. She felt as if she was suffocating.

But she kept pushing.

The desk lifted a little, slid backward.

Gemma let out a tiny squeal of victory. The desk hadn't moved before. Not even an inch. Rejuvenated, she used her sleeve to wipe the sweat from her eyes, and then took several slow breaths to calm herself. Glancing over her shoulder, she saw fresh indents in the carpet.

The desk *had* moved. She hadn't imagined it. It was possible. She could do this.

She pushed up again. Harder. Mostly using her thighs. Years of hiking the mountain had changed her body. Made it stronger. Instead of lifting up, the desk slid backward, and the handcuff dug into the raw flesh of her wrist. She gritted her teeth against the pain. Ignored it. Stopped breathing. Kept pushing. The desk inched upward. She could feel it lifting. Pulling away from the floor. Away from her. As if invisible hands were lifting it. She heard one of the heavy drawers slide open, and the desk lifted a fraction more.

She yanked her wrist and—amazingly—the cuff pulled free.

The desk crashed to the floor a second later.

Gemma collapsed against the desk, the handcuff hanging from her left wrist, her legs stretched out in front of her. But she didn't have time to recover. Carver was in the basement with Taylor. He'd already been gone too long. At least ten minutes. Maybe longer.

Using the desk for support, she pulled herself up and ran for the door.

Her hand closed around the knob...and the door swung open, knocking her backward into the desk.

She cried out, expecting to see Carver towering over her, his hands stained red with Taylor's blood.

But it wasn't the colonel.

"Where do you think you're going?"

Nowak stood in the doorway. He'd washed most of the smeared gore from his face, leaving the skin pink and swollen, like an ugly baby scrubbed too hard. Medical tape covered the bridge of his nose. A dark spot of blood remained where his overly-large earlobes attached to his head.

"What do you want?"

He eased the door shut and turned the latch to lock it. "Just to talk."

She scooted behind the desk, needing to put something between herself and the soldier. Not that it would stop him. "Where's Brady?"

Nowak shrugged. "Where else? Smoking. That gives us a few minutes alone."

The handcuff dangled from her left hand. She could swing it at him, try to connect with his skull. Maybe knock him out or at least disorient him.

But what if she didn't hit him? What if he grabbed her hand mid-swing?

Nowak edged his way toward her, every movement slow and deliberate. A predator stalking its prey. "Relax, princess. I just thought we could get to know each other. I think we got off on the wrong foot yesterday."

The letter opener gleamed in her peripheral vision. It was on the desk, a few inches away from her right hand. She didn't think Nowak had noticed it yet. But she didn't look at it. *Couldn't* look at it. "Come near me, and I'll scream."

The soldier tossed his head back and laughed, a guttural, barking sound that reminded her of a rabid dog. "Do you think anyone cares what happens to you?" His eyes darted between the crooked desk and her bloody left hand. "How'd you slip out of your handcuffs?"

"None of your business." Gemma searched her panicked mind for a question. A distraction. Anything. "So, is this part of your Task

Force training? Trapping women in a locked room and assaulting them?"

He froze in place and put a hand on his chest, acting offended. "Who said anything about assaulting you? I thought you had a thing for soldiers? A lot of roaches do, actually. You'd be surprised."

Gemma's chest tightened, and the words slipped from her lips before she could stop them. "You pig. Everything about you makes me sick." And she meant it. From his baby-smooth skin to his wide face to his narrow, snake-like eyes. She hated everything about him. In that moment, he was worse than the soldiers who'd detained her parents. Worse than Mullen. Worse even than Carver.

If he touched her, she would kill him.

Nowak's cheeks turned crimson. He resumed stalking her, squeezing his body between the wall and Carver's chair. "You think you're better than me, is that it? Back in school, I used to hate girls like you. Girls who thought they were too good for me."

She leaned toward Nowak, goading him, sliding her fingers along the smooth wood of the desk. The tip of her index finger touched the letter opener. "Newsflash, scumbag. Those girls *were* too good for you."

Nowak ignored the insult. "But things are different now, aren't they? I couldn't put those girls in their place because there were rules. There were consequences." He leered at her. "But not anymore. Because no one cares what we do to you subversives."

He was so close now, Gemma could smell him. He smelled like industrial soap and mint-flavored chewing tobacco. Her fingers closed around the letter opener. She imagined herself driving it into his throat and felt queasy in her stomach.

She wasn't a killer.

You have no choice, she assured herself. You have to do this.

"You think that letter opener's going to save you?" he asked. "You're not even holding it the right way."

She glanced down as a reflex, saw the blade in her right hand, exactly as it should've been—

And then Nowak slammed into her.

She hit the wall hard. All around her, foreign cities rattled in their cheap frames. The Eiffel Tower slipped off the wall and shattered on the floor. She brought her knee up, aimed for his groin, but Nowak swiveled his hips like a dancer, and she hit the outside of his muscular thigh.

"Nice try." Nowak lowered his face to hers. He seized her right arm and pinned it against the wall. Then he closed his free hand around her throat and squeezed. "But you can't stop this. Your boyfriend's dead, princess. No one's coming to save you."

Her vision narrowed into a dark tunnel with Nowak at its end. She used her free hand to grab at his hands, tried to pry them off of her neck, but they felt as immovable as tree trunks. There was something in her other hand, though—the one he was holding against the wall. Something digging into her skin. She squeezed, felt the cold blade of the letter opener. Somehow, she hadn't dropped it yet.

It was her only chance.

"Do you hear me, princess?" The soldier breathed into her ear. He kissed her on the cheek, and his grip on her right arm loosened a little.

Just a little. But it was enough.

"No one is coming to—"

She drove the blade into Nowak's thigh.

Once. Twice. Three times.

He yelped in pain—a high-pitched noise that sounded wholly unnatural coming from his gargantuan body. And then he released her throat and dropped to the floor.

Gemma staggered into the desk, gasping for air. Looked down. Saw the blood-soaked blade clutched in her hands. It slipped through her fingers and landed on the carpet.

Now.

Go.

Red bloomed on Nowak's fatigues as he struggled to his feet, his injured leg giving out. He braced himself against the wall, groped for the Glock on his belt. "Get back here!"

The radio on Nowak's belt crackled. "*Nowak? What's going on up there?*"

Carver's voice.

Gemma backed toward the door, unwilling to take her eyes off the soldier.

And the gun.

Nowak's blood-soaked hand closed around the Glock. "You're dead, princess."

Behind Gemma, the office door burst inward.

She screamed as two figures in camouflage hunting masks crashed into the room. One had a hunting rifle slung across his back. He grabbed Gemma by the shoulders, shoved her to the side, and unslung his rifle.

The other man crashed into Nowak and knocked him to the ground. The two men grappled for the Glock, and Nowak landed a good punch, slamming the man's head against the desk. The Glock flew under the desk. Instead of shooting, the man with the rifle rushed forward and kicked Nowak in the face. The soldier's head rolled backward. His nose gushed blood onto the carpet like a fountain.

Gemma dropped to the floor and reached under the desk, feeling for the Glock. Her hand closed around the cold metal. She knew about Glocks from Gavin. They have no external safety. All she had to do was aim.

And shoot.

She backed toward the doorway, keeping the Glock trained on the men.

The man with the rifle threw himself on top of Nowak. Drove the stock of his rifle into the soldier's throat, cutting off his airway. Nowak struggled to breathe, one leg kicking uselessly, before his body finally went limp.

The man pressed two fingers into the soldier's neck, and then nodded at his partner. They set to work, lifted Nowak, and dropped him roughly into the colonel's chair. They used zip-ties to secure his hands and feet to the chair. One of the men searched the desk, found a roll of duct tape in one of the drawers, and wrapped it tightly around the zip-ties before putting two final pieces over the soldier's mouth.

Gemma watched the men from the doorway, the gun extended in front of her. Prepared to kill them both. She didn't care who the intruders were. Only Taylor mattered now. If she ran to the basement, they would surely follow her, and Taylor might die. The masked men—whoever they were—had attacked Nowak. What if they wanted to kill Task Force soldiers? Would they hurt Taylor, too?

No. She couldn't risk that. Not when she still had the upper hand.

And the gun.

Her finger tightened on the trigger.

With the soldier secure, the man with the rifle turned his attention to Gemma, his chest still heaving from the exertion of the fight. He hung the rifle from his shoulder. The air around her shifted, grew warmer, as his eyes met hers.

"Gemma." His voice cracked with emotion. "It's okay."

That voice. Those green eyes.

Even before he pulled the mask off his face, she knew it was him.

"Gavin?"

She ran to him and collapsed into his arms.

CHAPTER
THIRTY-ONE

Something crashed overhead, the force of the impact rattling the basement's only window and causing the ceiling tiles to shudder. Taylor expected the whole building to collapse on top of them.

The scream died out, followed by an endless, unnerving silence.

Two seconds passed.

Three.

Still conscious of the gun aimed at his head, Taylor turned as far as he dared, trying to catch a glimpse of the colonel's face.

The colonel was gazing up at the ceiling and using his free hand to bring a radio to his lips. "Nowak? What's going on up there?"

Taylor didn't think. There was no time to think. Instead, he brought his elbow back as hard as he could, smashed it into Carver's right kneecap. Something popped as the joint bent backward at an impossible angle.

The gun went off, but the bullet went wide. It slammed into the wall.

Carver fell onto the cement. Something black flew out of his pocket and skittered across the floor.

Taylor threw himself on top of the colonel, grabbing for the pistol, but the gun exploded in his hands, the bullet zipping past his right ear. Then Carver was on top of him, his lips pulled away from his teeth into a pain-filled snarl of rage. The man's eyes brimmed with contempt, and he closed his hands around Taylor's throat. "You don't deserve a bullet," he growled.

Taylor's lungs screamed for oxygen, and he bucked his hips, throwing the colonel off-balance, but Carver pressed down harder and tightened his grip on Taylor's throat.

He went for the colonel's eyes, but Carver countered by raising his head so his eyes were just out of reach. So, Taylor dug his fingernails into the colonel's face. Sinking his meager nails into battle-hardened skin that felt as thick and tough as an elephant's hide.

His hands slid off the colonel's face as the world began to dim.

Carver's invincible, Taylor realized. He can't be killed.

And then he saw it.

High on the colonel's left cheek, a trickle of blood oozed from a fresh scratch.

A scratch made by Taylor's fingernails.

The man could bleed. It wasn't much, but it was something.

Taylor's hands came to rest on Carver's utility belt, the fingers of his right hand closing around something hard. In his mind, he could see it. The thick, textured handle of a hunting knife. He tugged weakly at it, trying to pull it free of its sheath, even as the world around him continued to fade from view. He couldn't see the colonel's face anymore, but he hung onto that tiny trickle of blood just below the man's left eye.

His thumb found the clip securing the knife to the belt, and he pushed on it, trying to pop it open. But he couldn't feel his fingers anymore. Everything was numb.

At least the pain was gone.

"Don't worry, son," the colonel said. "After you're dead, I'm going to go upstairs and kill your girlfriend. You two can be together on the other side. But don't bother waiting at the pearly gates for her to arrive. Because—and this is my promise to you—her death will be *much* more painful than yours..."

The clip popped open.

Carver, still raving, didn't seem to notice.

Taylor's hand gripped the knife and yanked it free from its case.

"And I intend to make it last for a *very* long t—"

Taylor plunged the full length of the blade into Carver's abdomen. The commander's eyes widened in surprise. His head dropped, and he regarded the knife buried up to its hilt in his gut with mild amusement. Then he coughed, a wet hacking sound. A bit of blood sprayed from his lips. His hands dropped from Taylor's neck, gripped the knife with both hands. Then he slid sideways onto the floor, his head meeting the concrete with a sickening thud.

Oxygen flooded Taylor's lungs, pushing the encroaching blackness away, and he sucked in a series of long breaths between hacking coughs. Grabbing the colonel's pistol, he crawled away from the expanding pool of blood surrounding the man's body. He crawled toward the door, and his knee came down on a hard object. He looked down to see a black cellphone. That must've been what he'd seen fall out of Carver's pocket earlier. Without knowing why, he slid the phone into his pocket.

Footsteps.

Coming down the basement stairs.

Hurriedly, he searched for a place to hide. But there was nowhere to hide. He was only a few feet from the door. And what good would hiding do anyway? They would only drag him out of his hiding place and kill him. So, he clutched the pistol against his chest and waited.

Seconds later, the basement door swung open and two men burst into the room. One was carrying a hunting rifle. The other had a Glock. The first man locked eyes with Taylor and froze in place, and the second man stumbled into him. Their eyes traveled from Taylor to the colonel's lifeless body.

Taylor tightened his grip on the pistol.

A whispered voice, but it wasn't either of the two men.

"What is it? Is he okay?"

Gemma.

She appeared behind the men in the doorway. She looked exactly like that scared girl from the carnival, so much that it took his breath away. She grabbed one of the men's arms and held it tight. Her eyes found Carver's body first, because that's where the two men were looking, and she inhaled sharply. She released the man's arm and brought a hand up to cover her mouth. Tears flooded her eyes as she looked around, desperately scanning the room.

And then she saw him.

"Taylor?"

She ran to him, sobbing, and wrapped her arms around his shoulders, her familiar scent overpowering the stench of blood and death. "You're alive. Thank God."

Over Gemma's shoulder, he saw one of the men—the one whose arm she'd grabbed—watching her, a pained expression on his face.

And Taylor knew.

That's him. The guy who gave Gemma a ring.

Then he closed his eyes and tried to forget that he'd just killed a man.

CHAPTER
THIRTY-TWO

Gemma stood in the doorway, her arm wrapped around Taylor's waist, supporting him. She bounced on her feet, her attention on the closed door at the top of the steps. She had no desire to go inside the basement ever again. Especially not with Carver's dead body only a few feet away.

But she wanted the Bible.

She called out to Gavin: "Did you find it? It's under the couch."

No answer.

She checked the door again. This was taking too long. She wanted to get out of Ash Grove now. Put as much distance between herself and the town as possible.

At least they knew Brady wasn't going to show up. Before entering the church, Gavin and Kyle had found the young guard napping at the picnic table outside, a lit cigarette smoldering between his fingers. Gavin held him at gunpoint while Kyle bound and gagged him, then they put him inside one of the empty offices.

As for Dietrich and Mullen...

Gemma had no idea where they were.

Brushing blonde hair out of his eyes, Kyle squatted over Carver's body to check for a pulse. "Well, this guy's dead."

"Was it the blade in his gut that gave it away?" Taylor muttered.

Kyle glared at him. "Gemma, who *is* this jerk? And why are we risking our lives for him, instead of locking him down here with the corpse?"

"He's a friend from back home," she said quickly. She could feel Taylor's eyes on her, but she refused to look at him. "I'll explain later. But we need to get out of here before anyone else shows up." She raised her voice: "Gavin? Forget it. We need to go."

Gavin came around the corner. He held the Bible in one hand, and Taylor's uniform jacket in the other. He handed the Bible to Gemma. "Got it. Let's get out of here."

She clutched it against her chest. "Thank you."

Taylor removed his arm from Gemma's shoulder. He accepted the jacket from Gavin with a polite nod, then slipped his arms through the sleeves and limped toward the doorway. "Let's go. We can take my car."

"Carver didn't take your keys?" Gemma asked.

"I've got a spare."

Taylor looked awful. Not quite as bad as last night—when he'd resembled a corpse—but still pretty bad. He had a new gash on his head from where Brady had hit him with the rifle, and his lips were swollen and bleeding again. But she resisted the urge to help him up the stairs. Partly because of Gavin, but also because Taylor didn't seem to *want* her help. So, she settled for following close behind him, ready to reach out and steady him if he lost his balance.

Gavin leaned close to Gemma as they climbed the stairs. "This is him, isn't it? The guy Brie saw you with?"

She didn't want to talk about it. Not now. Not ever, actually. But she couldn't lie to Gavin. "Yes. We'll talk about it later. Okay?"

"Okay."

They locked Carver's body in the basement, then checked both offices to make sure Brady and Nowak hadn't managed to free themselves. In the first office, Brady lay on his back on the floor, struggling with his restraints but not making any headway. Nowak, on the other hand, was still in the colonel's chair, not moving. He didn't even seem to be trying to break free. But when his eyes met Gemma's, the hatred she saw lurking within them reminded her so much of the carnie that she stumbled into Gavin.

He pulled the door shut.

They continued down the hallway, heading for the door that opened into the church's side parking lot. Papers flapped on the bulletin board as if bidding them adieu. One advertisement lay on the floor beneath the board, probably ripped down during the previous day's fight between Taylor and Carver. It was crinkled and dirty. Something about it drew her attention.

Gemma bent to retrieve it. It was the same advertisement she'd noticed days earlier, when Dietrich had brought her out of the basement to have breakfast with Carver.

Letty's Book Cellar – New and Used Books in Winter's Dam.
Looking for a Good Book? We've got a towering selection!
Mention this ad to save 10 percent off your purchase.
Or visit our website and use our discount code: PV1810.

Something about the ad seemed important, although she couldn't put her finger on exactly what it was. There was something vaguely familiar about it. Had she visited the bookstore with her parents at some point? She had no memory of a town called Winter's Dam, and she didn't recognize the building or the dark-skinned woman in the photograph. Still, the advertisement nagged at her.

Taylor came up beside her. "Gemma? What is it?"

"I don't know."

But she folded up the paper, stuffed it inside the Bible, and walked out the door.

She was finally going home.

Back to her family.

Outside, the town was unnervingly silent.

Gemma expected resistance. Soldiers converging on the church from all directions. An angry mob of townspeople waiting outside, torches in hand, ready to string up Gemma and the others the same way Carver's men had strung up Henry Castern.

But there were no soldiers. No townspeople. Only two elderly women in powder-blue sweatshirts, power walking across the street a few blocks away. Instead of guns, they held small weights in their hands. Neither woman seemed to notice the four people running across the street toward the post office.

When they reached Taylor's car—a black Dodge Charger—he stooped and felt around the rear wheel well and pulled a key loose. But when he reached for the driver's door, Gemma grabbed his arm to stop him. "No. Let Gavin drive." Taylor looked annoyed but didn't argue. She took the key from him and unlocked the doors. Then she crawled into the backseat and gestured for him to join her.

It was stuffy inside the car, but the vehicle smelled impossibly clean. No discarded fast-food bags or soda cans. No dust discolored the charcoal dashboard. Gemma put the Bible on her lap, then ran her hand over the seat, relishing the feeling of the smooth leather. She'd forgotten what it felt like to be inside a car.

Taylor slid in beside her.

When Gavin and Kyle climbed into the front seat, Gemma handed Gavin the key. "Can you put the windows down? We need air back here."

"Yeah. Hold on."

Gavin revved the engine. The sound made her want to cry. They'd survived. They weren't going to die in Ash Grove. She leaned back against the seat, her shoulder brushing Taylor's. She thought she felt him shift his body away from hers. But that could've been her imagination.

Gavin hit a button to lower both of the car's front windows. "Better?"

She nodded. "Much. How far is Oliver's house from here?"

"Not far. Maybe ten minutes. Less in this car."

"Yeah, but don't speed. We don't want to get pulled—"

The barrel of a pistol appeared in the open driver's window. The gun was aimed at the back of Gavin's head.

"Careful now." Private Dietrich spoke in a calm, steady voice. "Don't do anything you'll regret. Just take that key out of the ignition and hand it to me before I blow your brains all over the steering wheel."

Kyle reached for the hunting rifle propped between the front seats, but Dietrich's voice stopped him. "I wouldn't do that if I were you, buddy."

Through the rear window, Gemma met Dietrich's eyes. Keeping her hands in view, she reached across Taylor and pressed a button to lower her own window a crack. "Amy? Please don't do this."

Dietrich squinted through the gap at Gemma. Her gaze softened but only a little. "Don't make me shoot him. I don't want to do it...but I will."

But Gemma wasn't willing to give up. Not when she was so close to going home. To seeing Sophia. And Addie. "Please, Amy. Please just go away. Pretend you didn't see us. No one would ever have to know."

"Go away?" she scoffed. "And allow you guys to escape? Why would I do that?"

"Because you're not like Carver and the others. I have no idea how you ended up in this unit, but you're nothing like them, Amy. You're not."

Dietrich glanced back at the church. "What about the others? Where are they?"

"Nowak and Brady are fine. They're tied up in different offices."

"And the colonel?"

Taylor grabbed Gemma's hand and squeezed, and she knew exactly what he meant by that squeeze. But she had to tell the truth. It was their only chance. "Carver's in the basement," she said, ignoring Taylor's sharp exhale of disapproval. "He's dead."

Dietrich's mouth dropped open, and Gemma rushed to explain. "You saw what he did to Taylor last night. What he allowed the town to do. He came back this morning to kill us both. We had no choice," she said, intentionally leaving out that it was Taylor who killed the colonel.

Dietrich remained silent for a long time. Then, finally, she lowered her gun. Not all the way, but a little. "What happened to you last night wasn't right, Sergeant. I tried to talk them out of it. I want you to know that."

When Taylor said nothing, Gemma spoke up. "It's not too late to do the right thing, Amy. You helped me before. You brought me warm clothes and treated me well. Please just help me one more time."

The soldier stole another look at the church, as if hoping Carver would emerge from inside and tell her what to do. Finally, she said, "Okay. Get out of here. But Sergeant Nolan has to stay with me. He needs a hospital, and you won't be able to take him to one. That'll give the two of us time to come up with a story the higher-ups will believe."

Gavin's eyes met Gemma's in the rearview mirror, watching her reaction.

Taylor shook his head. "No way."

"Sergeant..."

"No." For the first time, he met Dietrich's eyes. "You're going to have to shoot me."

"I second that," Kyle muttered under his breath.

"We'll help him," Gemma offered. "There's a doctor in our group. And we have medicine. Antibiotics. Please, Amy."

Dietrich narrowed her eyes, clearly not wanting to reap the whirlwind of Carver's madness without a higher-ranking soldier by her side. But then she exhaled and lowered the gun all the way. "Ugh, just go. All of you. Get out of here. But you need to get far away. When they find out about Carver, they're going to be coming for everyone. Including you, Sergeant Nolan."

Taylor nodded. "Yeah. I know."

Gemma extended her hand through the open window. "Thank you." She could barely get the words out without crying. "For everything you've done for me. Thank you so much."

Dietrich slid her pistol into its holster before taking Gemma's outstretched hand. "You know what? I'm *so* ready to put this freaking town in my rearview mirror."

In the front seat, Gavin shifted the Charger into drive.

"Aren't we all?"

✝

The ride to Oliver's farmhouse felt endless. Each time a car approached them traveling in the opposite direction, Gemma squinted through the windshield, expecting to see one of the Task Force's signature black SUVs. When she wasn't watching oncoming traffic, she was turned around in her seat, staring at the highway stretching out behind them. Expecting a dark SUV to come racing up, Carver's corpse hunched over the steering wheel, the handle of the hunting knife protruding from his belly.

Of course, Nowak would be riding shotgun.

Taylor spoke into her ear, interrupting her vision. "Are you okay?"

She nodded.

"Did Nowak...do anything to you?"

Gemma knew what he meant. "No." And before he could question her further, she added, "I promise."

The deserted country road unrolled before them. She caught Gavin watching her a few times in the rearview mirror, but he quickly looked away. He hadn't said a word since they left Ash Grove. Neither had Kyle. They had both risked so much to find her, and she couldn't help but wonder if they regretted their decision to come after her.

Gemma scooted forward and put a hand on Kyle's shoulder. "How's Addie? And the baby?"

He spoke without looking back, one hand resting on the butt of the rifle. "They're both fine, as far as we can tell. The hike to Oliver's farmhouse took a lot out of Addie. I guess Oliver was going to hold a worship service this morning in the barn." He cast a look over his shoulder at Taylor. "First one we've had in a while. Addie was really excited about it."

"And Sophia? Is she okay?"

"She's fine," he said. "Just confused. We all are."

Gemma heard the disapproval in his voice. Of course, Sophia was confused. How would Gemma explain her decision to sneak off to meet Taylor? Even if her intention had been to return, Sophia wouldn't understand. She'd already been abandoned once, by her own mother. When she got back, Gemma would sit with Sophia and answer any questions she might have.

Hopefully, she hadn't lost the little girl's trust entirely.

Taylor leaned forward and pointed at the windshield. "What's that?"

At first, Gemma didn't see anything. Only an overgrown cornfield and the lush green slope of the ridge beyond.

But then she saw it.

Beyond the ridge. Thick plumes of black smoke rose up from the mountain.

A single word appeared in her mind: Dragons.

Gavin eased his foot off the gas. The car slowed. "No way. It can't be."

Gemma grabbed Gavin's shoulder. "Is that—"

"Drive!" Kyle screamed, jamming his foot on top of Gavin's. The Charger shot forward, throwing Gemma and Taylor back against the rear seat.

"The barn's on fire!"

CHAPTER THIRTY-THREE

The Charger ripped up the driveway, fishtailed on the loose gravel, and nearly spun into the overgrown yard. Gemma clung to the back of the driver's seat, her body shaking from adrenaline. She could feel Kyle's anxiety, reached for him, and got a fistful of his jacket. Before the car lurched to a stop, he pulled free of her grip and jumped, landed, and skidded on the rough driveway. In an instant, he was up and running. He bypassed the smoldering barn and sprinted toward the farmhouse, taking the porch steps two at a time and bellowing at the top of his lungs for Addie.

Gavin threw the car into park and ran to the smoking ruins, with Taylor and Gemma on his heels. They were all yelling. Even Taylor was shouting for Oliver as he limped toward the barn.

Gavin came to a sudden halt inches away from a charred body. He looked from the corpse to the barn, running his hands helplessly through his hair. "Gemma? Who *is* this?"

It wasn't any of their people. Gemma could see that for herself. The body belonged to someone much heavier than any of the men in their group. Even the heaviest among them had slimmed down many months ago.

She felt guilty for being relieved, but it was what it was.

The revolting smell of charred wood and flesh sickened her. She could taste the smoke. Could smell it on her clothes. Her nightmare come to life. Looking skyward, she expected to see massive dragons circling in the sky, patiently awaiting the opportunity to turn the rest of them into ash.

But there were no dragons.

Only devastation.

Gone. Her family was gone.

She forced herself to look at the barn. The lack of wind had prevented it from spreading to the surrounding woods, but the fire had burned hot enough to cause the barn's aluminum roof to collapse. Half of it lay inside the structure's exposed frame, while the other half extended into Oliver's old driveway. Charred support beams jutted out of the rubble, pointing skyward like skeletal fingers.

With the walls gone, Gemma could see inside the barn. She saw dozens of folding chairs, partially-melted, black and misshapen like a child's crude rendering. Aside from the support beams, only the barn's large double doors remained standing.

She saw the chains.

And the padlock.

She dropped to the ground, retching painfully, her stomach trying to eject food it hadn't consumed. She raised her head, wiping her mouth on her sleeve, and Kyle charged out of the farmhouse, the screen door slamming shut behind him.

"They're not here," he stammered, his wild eyes darting from Gemma to Gavin. "They probably went into the woods to hide, but they can't be far. We'll find them."

The sour taste of vomit lingered on Gemma's tongue. "Kyle...the barn..."

"Shut up!" Spittle flew from his lips as he jabbed a finger at her. *"Shut up, Gemma!"*

The fire was almost dead. Only a few piles of debris continued to smolder, most of them on the far side of the barn, away from the entrance. Still attached by the metal chain, the steel double doors hung partially off their hinges, leaning into one another like wounded lovers.

"We'll find them," Kyle repeated. Then his eyes landed on the body. "Who is that?"

Taylor stood over the charred remains. There was a pistol next to the body, and he nudged it with the tip of his boot. "I'm not positive, but judging by the stocky build and the hunting clothing, I think he might be a local named Carl Lovell. I had the honor of meeting him at the church last night. Looks like he shot himself." He brought a finger up and touched the padlock, then let his hand fall limply to his side. "The lock looks brand new. So does the chain."

Gavin turned to Taylor, his mouth dropping open. "You mean he locked them inside?"

"What?" Kyle took a step away from the other men, as if the idea itself was contagious. "No. Why are you listening to this guy, Gavin? He's TF!" He motioned at the long driveway. "No. Someone must've seen this Lovell guy coming and warned the others. And they all took off into the woods. Go check the house. All of our stuff is still inside. They didn't even have time to grab anything."

"Because they weren't *in* the house," Gavin said, his voice cracking. "They were in the barn. For the worship service."

Kyle lunged at Gavin, shoving him hard. Gavin stumbled into Taylor, who grabbed his shoulders to steady him.

"Do you hear yourself, man?" Kyle screamed. *"Do you hear what you're saying?"*

"Kyle, the chain..."

"Shut up about the chain!"

Gemma couldn't take it anymore. She couldn't stand the screaming. Or the fighting. Or looking at the charred wreckage of the barn. Not for one more second. She sprinted toward the farmhouse, as if she could somehow outrun the guilt. The pain. The terrible knowledge that everything was *her* fault. All of it. The loss of the only family she had left. The loss of everything that mattered.

She ran into the house, her eyes passing over drawn curtains and sleeping bags and blankets and backpacks and dirty clothes and open boxes of soup crackers and granola bars. But she didn't stop. She kept running. Up a flight of stairs. Down a long hallway. Past a bathroom and two bedrooms. Heading for the faint beam of light streaming through the open door at the end of the hall.

A bedroom.

Two sleeping bags were unrolled on the bed. Four more lay on the floor.

And there, at the foot of the bed, lay Addie's jacket, the bottom-half stretched to accommodate her growing belly.

Gemma backed away from the jacket, unable to breathe. She stumbled toward the window on the opposite wall, desperate for air. With shaking fingers, she unlocked the ancient latches and tried to push the window open, but it wouldn't budge. She pushed harder, grunting with the effort, until it finally slid upward, opening only enough for her to feel the rush of air against her face. She stuck her mouth near the opening and closed her eyes, breathing in deep mouthfuls of cool air tinged with smoke.

From her vantage point on the second story of the farmhouse, she could see the interior of the barn. Thick piles of black ash. Overturned folding chairs. And somewhere in there, buried beneath the piles of burnt wood...the huddled remains of her family.

A low moan left her lips—a harbinger of things to come—and she clamped her hands over her mouth to stop it. In her mind, she saw rising flames. Sophia's terrified face, choking on black smoke. A soundtrack of screams. The heat from the fire scorching Addie's beautiful face.

No.

She couldn't think about it.

About what it must've been like.

If she did—if she allowed herself to imagine what Addie and Sophia and all of them had endured—she wouldn't make it.

By your endurance, gain your lives.

What did that even mean?

Gemma clung to the windowsill, flakes of white paint adhering themselves to her damp palms. She watched Kyle crumple before the charred wreckage. Gavin went down beside him, placing a hand on his best friend's back. Weeping with him. *For* him.

Taylor stood a few feet away, a hand on his head, staring helplessly at the chained doors.

In that moment, more than anything, Gemma wanted her mother.

And she wanted to go home.

CHAPTER
THIRTY-FOUR

"Hey."

Gemma looked up from her spot on the floor, where she sat with her knees bent, holding Addie's jacket against her damp cheeks. The familiar smell of her friend clung to the fabric like a memory, and she could imagine seeing Addie in the doorway, smiling down at her.

But it was Gavin.

He leaned against the doorframe, face blackened by soot, hands shoved deep into his pockets. "You okay?"

She clutched Addie's jacket tighter, afraid Gavin might try to take it. "Where's Kyle?"

"Outside," he replied. "With...him."

Gemma lowered her gaze to the floor, tracing the lines in the wood with the tip of one finger. She couldn't bear to look at Gavin. Not after everything she'd done.

He left the doorway and lowered himself onto the floor beside her. She expected him to question her about Taylor, about why she ran away. But he said nothing, only rested his elbows on his knees and leaned his head against the bed frame.

Gemma broke the silence with a question.

"Can I ask you something?"

He spoke without opening his eyes. "Yeah."

"Why did you come after me? Brie must've told you everything."

He didn't respond right away, only shook his head as if struggling to find the right words. Finally, he blew out a breath. "Do you remember the first time we ever spoke to each other?"

Of course, she remembered. It was their third night at the Station. She hadn't spoken to anyone during those first three days. Not even Addie or Mia. She'd been homesick, tired, and surrounded by total strangers. She'd missed her parents and Taylor and everything else about home. She'd wanted to leave. To renounce. To forget everything about her new miserable existence.

But—that night—Gavin had sat next to her at dinner. She'd noticed him before, of course. She wasn't blind. It was impossible *not* to notice him, with his golden complexion, shy smile, and muscular build. What she hadn't noticed before were his eyes. How beautiful they were. Beautiful and full of kindness.

He hadn't said anything at first, only eaten his dinner quietly next to her. Doing nothing but making her extremely uncomfortable. She preferred to be alone. Ignored. Forgotten. That way, when she eventually slipped away in the middle of the night, no one would care.

When they both finished eating, he'd snapped his fingers at Mia, who was passing by their table. "Check, please," he'd said. "The lady's treating me tonight."

Mia had smacked the back of his head, clearly more annoyed than amused.

But Gemma had laughed. Her first real laugh in days. Maybe weeks.

Afterwards, Gavin had turned to her and extended his hand. "I'm Gavin, by the way." Something about him reminded her of her father, and she knew everything was going to be okay.

"I remember that night," she whispered. "You're the reason I decided to stay."

"I was planning on leaving, too. I hated it at the Station. Especially once I realized that our little hiding place didn't have any video games. Or electricity." Gavin ran a hand through his chestnut hair and shrugged. "My plan was to go to the bathroom in the middle of the night and then just sneak off."

Gemma stared at him. That had been her plan, too.

"I was going to walk until I hit a road," Gavin continued, "and then hitchhike home. My uncle had renounced six months earlier, and I figured I could live with him until I figured something out."

She touched the empty spot on her ring finger. Had Gavin noticed she wasn't wearing his ring? "You always seemed so comfortable at the Station. I never knew you wanted to leave."

"That's because I never told you. After we started talking, leaving wasn't an option anymore. But, in the beginning, I thought about leaving all the time. During those first few days, I kept noticing you. I knew you were trying to hide, to blend in, but I saw you everywhere. I wasn't looking for you, not at first. But you always seemed to be the first person I noticed when I walked into a room. And I started to get really worried about you."

She shifted her legs so she was facing him. "About me leaving?"

He bowed his head, tugged at the sleeve of his jacket. "After my mother killed herself, I blamed myself for a long time. I was only five, but I remember thinking that if I'd behaved better, she might still be alive. When I saw your face those first few days, you seemed so empty and lost. You reminded me a little of her. So, I asked God to make you happy. And that's when I knew."

"Knew what?"

Gavin looked at her for the first time, and she saw the hurt she'd caused him. "That I could make you happy. That God was giving me a second chance. And it wasn't because you were beautiful, which you were, or because I was looking for a reason to stay. Believe me, I wanted to leave...but I had to stay. Not for myself but for you." He rubbed at the soot on his cheeks, smearing it. "But I always knew there was someone else. I knew you weren't really in love with me."

His words felt like a slap in the face. Gavin had known—the whole time—that her heart belonged to someone else. And yet he'd remained by her side. Gemma bit down on her lip to force the tears away. "So, why did you stay with me? Why did you waste your time?"

Gavin took her hand and held it to his chest. "Isn't it obvious? Because I love you, Gemma. And I kept hoping that—one day—you'd forget him and love me back."

Gemma's gaze slid over the smooth contours of his face; a face she knew so well, better than her own. She brought a hand to his cheek, and he placed his own hand on top of hers, their fingers interlacing. Their relationship felt different now, as if the invisible barrier she'd erected between them had been torn down by the weight of his words. "Gavin," she whispered. "I'm so sorry—"

He cut her off by bringing his lips to hers in a kiss so deep, so passionate, it made her dizzy. A kiss unlike any other they had ever shared. She couldn't breathe. Couldn't think. Each brush of Gavin's familiar lips against her own felt like salve on a wound, dulling her pain. For a few moments, everything else—her time in Ash Grove, the scorched barn, the grief over the loss of her family—faded into the background.

And then Taylor's face flashed in her mind.

What was she doing?

She tried to pull away from him, but he held her tight, cradling her face in his hands. "Gavin, stop. We can't."

"Gemma...please..."

His kiss went from passionate to frantic. And Gemma could smell the smoke on his clothes. In his hair. Everything about him reminded her that the others were gone. Dead. Burned. It made her sick. She shoved his chest. Hard. *"Stop!"*

He released her, and her head snapped backward and hit the bed frame.

The impact rattled her teeth. Searing pain shot through an old wound on her head. The lump from days earlier, when she'd hit her head on the sealed door of the mine's escape hatch. Involuntary tears burned her eyes.

"Gemma!" Gavin reached for her, and then stopped himself. "I'm so sorry. I didn't mean to hurt you."

But Gemma wasn't listening. She wiped the tears away, the red-hot pain in her head fading to a dull throb. But it wasn't the pain she was thinking about anymore. Something pulled at her. Something important she'd forgotten.

Something about Henry Castern.

And the escape hatch.

Her dream came rushing back. The fire-scorched earth. The desolation. The dragons circling overhead, waiting to turn her body to a pile of ashes that would blow apart in the wind. In the dream, she'd left the safety of the mine. Climbed to the surface. Everyone else was dead, and she'd wanted to be dead, too. In the dream, she'd found Taylor...and they'd both died.

But she should've stayed put, because the world wasn't safe. The world was on fire.

But the mine had been safe.

Cool. Protected. Insulated.

Underground.

Just like—

Downstairs, the screen door slammed shut, and Taylor shouted her name.

Gemma jumped up. Her legs felt wobbly beneath her, her mind still jumbled from the impact. And from whatever had just happened with Gavin. Without thinking of why she was doing it, she slipped her arms into Addie's jacket. Then she rushed out of the room and headed for the staircase.

Gavin called after her, "Gemma, wait..."

Taylor stood at the base of the steps, ashes smeared all over his face and hands. Just like in her dream. "Are you alright? Where's—" His voice trailed off.

A hand fell on her elbow. She turned and saw Gavin standing behind her. He looked stricken.

"Gemma?" Taylor said. "What happened?"

She returned her attention to Taylor. "Did you find them?"

"Huh?"

"Bodies. Did you find any bodies?"

"No. Not yet."

"Any clothing? Anything?"

He passed an arm across his brow. "Gemma, the fire burned really hot. Even if we find them, there isn't going to be much left to —"

"Root cellars," she interrupted, hurrying down the stairs. She stopped two steps above Taylor. They were at the same height, their eyes on the same level. "Henry Castern grew a lot of root vegetables for us. Potatoes, rutabagas, radishes. We stored them inside the mine because Henry said the conditions in the mine were similar to the conditions inside his root cellar. Cool temperatures. Damp. Good ventilation to prevent mold."

Taylor tilted his head, studying her. "Okay..."

"And it never mattered how hot it got outside," she continued. "It could've been blazing hot, but our vegetables stayed cool and fresh for a *long* time in the mine."

"Gemma, what does this have to do—"

"A lot of old barns have root cellars, right?" She grabbed his shoulders and shook him. Trying to make him understand. "And root cellars need air. So, they must have—"

Gavin finished her sentence. "Ventilation pipes."

He barreled down the stairs, past Gemma and Taylor, and raced out the door.

After Gavin left, she whispered to Taylor, "Do you think it's possible?" She knew it was a long shot. But it was something to hold onto.

It was hope.

Taylor put a hand on her cheek. "Gemma, I'm starting to believe that anything's possible." He kissed her lightly on the forehead, and then sprinted after Gavin.

The screen door slammed, but Gemma remained rooted in place. She braced herself on the railing, lowered herself to the floor, and clasped her hands in front of her.

She prayed for a miracle.

Just one miracle.

"Please, God," she whispered. "Please let them be alive. Somehow."

She kept praying. Crying. Hoping. She wouldn't allow herself to stop.

Not until she heard Kyle screaming outside.

Screaming...and laughing.
And then she ran.

CHAPTER
THIRTY-FIVE

Following the sound of Kyle's laughter, Gemma found him crouched on the far side of the barn, his head tilted toward the smoldering wreckage, as if trying to eavesdrop on a conversation happening inside. Only when she drew closer did she see the rusty pipe jutting out from what remained of the charred wood.

When he noticed her, Kyle sat back on his heels, tears cutting clean tracks through the soot on his face. He gestured to the pipe. "Say *hi* to Addie."

Gemma crouched and pressed her ear against the pipe. Muffled voices drifted to her from far away. She shouted into the pipe. *"Addie!"*

The voices quieted.

And then...

"Gemma?"

At the sound of her best friend's voice, Gemma slapped a hand over her mouth to stifle a sob. At the other end of the tube, she could hear Addie crying, too.

"I've got your jacket!" Gemma cried. "I've got it, okay?"

She heard Addie laughing through her tears. "Thanks! I was worried about it!"

Gemma rested her head against the pipe. Although the fire was out, there was still a lot of heat coming off the barn. But the pipe—the lifeline carrying oxygen down to her family—felt cool to the touch. "Can I talk to Sophia?"

A few seconds later: "Gemma!"

At the faint sound of the girl's voice, Gemma's legs gave out and she slumped to the ground, her fingers still wrapped around the pipe. Kyle put a hand on her shoulder and squeezed.

"Hey, Soph! I missed you!"

If there was a reply, she didn't hear one. But she could picture Sophia down in the darkness, crying. Experiencing the same relief and joy that Gemma now felt. Because, unlike Sophia's mother, Gemma had come back. Sophia hadn't been abandoned.

Gemma raised her head toward the sky, saw the sun trying to peek through the clouds.

None of them had.

She stayed by the vent pipe, talking to the others and pressing her ear to the pipe to listen for their distant replies. She watched as Taylor and Gavin returned from Oliver's old tool shed carrying a pickax, a shovel, and a long, metal bar.

"We found the trapdoor leading into the root cellar," Taylor said, handing the metal bar to Kyle. "But part of the roof is lying on top of it. We can use this bar for leverage."

The three men crawled through the smoldering debris to the trapdoor built into the floor of the barn. A large chunk of metal roof and charred wooden beams lay on top of the door. It looked like it weighed a thousand pounds. Gemma had no idea how they would ever move it.

Surprisingly, the guys worked well together, moving quickly and efficiently, using the pickax and shovel to break apart some of the wooden beams that were still attached to the metal roof. All three men were soon drenched in sweat. The smoke drifting up from the ruins made them cough so hard that they had to take turns stepping outside for fresh air.

When they'd finally broken enough wood away from the collapsed rooftop, Gavin grabbed the steel bar and placed it on top of a pile of boards. Then he slid the other end underneath the metal roof.

Taylor gestured to Gemma. "We need you."

She left the pipe and stepped between Gavin and Taylor, wrapping her hands around the bar.

"On the count of three, push down hard," Taylor said. "Put all of your weight on the bar. We have to lift the roof up, and then slide it backward as far as we can."

Gemma looked warily at Taylor. "What if this doesn't work?"

"It'll work." Determination flashed in his eyes. "And if it doesn't, we'll try something else. But we're getting your friends out of there. They've been underground long enough."

To Gemma's right, Gavin took a deep breath and increased his grip on the bar. "You guys ready?"

Kyle nodded. "Let's get my girl out of there."

"Okay!" Taylor shouted. "On the count of three!"

Gemma closed her eyes.

"One!"

God, please.

"Two!"

We can't do this without You.

"Three!"

They fell upon the bar, all four of them grunting and straining against the incredible weight of the roof. Countering it with their own combined weight. Hunched over the bar, teeth bared, eyes watering from the smoke, they screamed at the metal slab, ordering it to rise. Disregarding the impossibility of the task in favor of faith. When it refused to budge, they dug their boots into the ashes and pushed harder. Pushing and screaming until Gemma felt certain her muscles might explode.

And then—finally—the slightest sensation of movement. A shifting. Metal and wood lifting away from the floor, little by little.

Inch by inch.

Impossible. And yet...it was happening.

"It's moving!" Taylor yelled, as if unable to believe it himself. *"Keep going! Keep pushing!"*

So they did.

And God was with them.

CHAPTER
THIRTY-SIX

No one spoke during the long drive on Summit Road. They skirted along the top of the Pisgah Mountain, the Dragon's Back's sister mountain, looking at nothing because there was nothing to see in any direction. In front of them, the single-lane dirt road stretched on for miles, rising and falling like the spine of some ancient monster. Trees surrounded their vehicle on either side, massive pines interspersed with oaks and the occasional mountain ash sporting immature spring berries.

Taylor drove the Charger, and Gemma rode shotgun. Sophia sat on her lap, her head resting on Gemma's shoulder, her eyes continually drifting shut and popping back open. Gavin shared the backseat with Addie and Kyle, who kept one hand on his wife's shoulders, the other on her belly.

Gemma kept turning around to check on Addie, needing to assure herself that her friend really was okay. When she closed her eyes, she could still smell the dank, earthy odor of the root cellar. Helping everyone climb out of its depths, watching them emerge like the dead rising from the grave, still felt like a dream. One she would never forget.

Their caravan also included Oliver's old pick-up truck. Oliver looked as happy as Gemma had ever seen him as he crawled behind the wheel of his truck. Coop was driving the other vehicle, the Jeep Grand Cherokee. Both vehicles had enough gas in their tanks to get the group a safe distance from Ash Grove for the night. After that, they would just have to figure things out.

Taylor followed Oliver's pick-up around the curves of the unimproved road, and Gemma watched the people bouncing along in the bed of the truck. They'd managed to fit everyone into the three vehicles, a feat that would have been impossible if not for the people who'd chosen to stay behind. Celia Birch had been one of them, along with Tabitha Crispin, Keith Seeley, and a handful of others. All in all, they'd lost nine people.

Not *to* the fire, but because of it.

Gemma wondered what each of them would say when they renounced.

Her mind drifted from one thought to another like a butterfly gliding between flowers, not alighting on any particular one for too long. She thought about the awesome power of God in saving her family from the fire. During their time at the Station, the mine had been their life raft. Their last resort when everything went wrong. But when they had truly needed a last resort, God had provided one in the form of a dank old root cellar.

She also thought about Colonel Carver. When the Task Force found out that one of their high-ranking officers had been killed, they would send reinforcements to search the area. They might even involve regular law enforcement in the search. Their group had no choice but to abandon the Dragon's Back—and the Station—forever.

Everything had changed.

Up ahead, the road curved sharply to the left and the forest opened around them. Oliver's brake lights flashed, and he pulled into a small gravel lot on the right side of the road. Taylor followed him into the lot and brought the Charger to a stop next to the pick-up. The Jeep pulled up behind them both.

Taylor peered through the windshield. "This is it?"

Gemma nodded. "The Altar."

All of the trees had been leveled in one spot, leaving a large, grassy clearing that offered a breathtaking view of the valley below. At the edge of the clearing, a tall cobblestone structure with two identical sets of steps led up to a narrow platform. Towering above the platform and the valley below was an iron cross.

Gemma had never been to The Altar before, but she knew about it from her parent's descriptions of the place. When her parents were kids, local churches used to hold special services on the mountain. People brought their own lawn chairs and set them up in the clearing. The minister stood on the platform during the service, the breeze rustling his vestment, the valley to his back. Because the spot was so picturesque, it hadn't only been used for church services. Teenagers used to pose for their high school photos at The Altar, and many people had gotten engaged and married there over the years.

Like most churches, The Altar had stood abandoned for years.

But, surprising enough, the site hadn't been desecrated.

The cross still stood.

With only a few hours to spare before darkness settled on the mountain, the group set up camp in the clearing, erecting small tents procured from Oliver's storage shed. In the woods nearby, several rows of wooden benches surrounded an old fire pit. Oliver gathered sticks and kindling and built a small fire. They'd stopped at a small grocery store a few miles west of Oliver's farm before linking up with Summit Road. Taylor had straightened up his uniform as best he could and gone inside for supplies, purchasing mostly bottled water and non-perishable items. But he also came back with several packs of hot dogs, rolls, chips, and all of the ingredients needed to make S'mores. When he'd mentioned the S'mores to Sophia, the girl had practically squealed with delight.

Gemma spent twenty minutes setting up the small tent she would share with Sophia. She thought she'd threaded the poles through the frame correctly, but it was lopsided and pathetic, a cartoon-version of a tent. Other tents blossomed around hers like flowers in a field, but Gemma's inability to set up her own tent made her want to hurl the thing off the side of the mountain. In fact, she was considering doing just that when Taylor appeared beside her. Without a word, he pulled the poles out of the frame and began reassembling her tent. Five minutes later, he was hammering the pegs into the ground.

"You're all set," he said.

She almost kissed him right then, as he rose and brushed the dirt from the knees of his fatigues. But she stopped herself because Gavin was standing outside his own tent, a few yards away.

Watching them.

Below the Pisgah Mountain, the valley stretched out below them. Beautiful. Uninhibited. Limitless. No towns marred the landscape. No major highways sliced across the valley. Only a smattering of houses, sprinkled here and there, along with the occasional farmhouse set along a series of connected dirt roads. Gemma found it hard to believe that anything bad could happen in such a beautiful world.

But she knew better.

Beyond the valley, in the distance, the vast expanse of the Dragon's Back rose up from the ground like a dark monument.

Or a gravestone.

Oliver stood before The Altar, the sun setting behind him. The rest of the group gathered in the clearing. Sophia stood next to Gemma, holding her hand. It was the first time their leader had appeared before them without the cross made of branches and twine.

The cross had burned in the fire.

Oliver began to cry.

"I'm so sorry," he wept, his voice barely audible. "I'm so sorry for failing all of you. You looked to me to keep you safe, and I failed. But, even worse than that, I've failed to lead you properly. We went into hiding for God, but we got so caught up in the business of surviving that we cut Him out of our lives completely."

Gemma shifted closer, listening.

"I worried constantly. About everything. I worried about keeping everyone warm enough. I worried about providing everyone with enough food. I worried about sickness. I worried about the Task Force finding us. How many times did I tell you all to trust in God to provide, and yet I didn't trust in Him myself?"

He raised his head to look at the cross. "You opened my eyes today, Father. You showed me that my next breath comes only at Your command. If you want me to eat, you'll send food. If you want me to drink, you'll send rain. But, despite all of the things you've shown me, I know that I'll continue to doubt Your sovereignty. I'll put my trust in other things, worldly things, instead of You. But when those moments come, I'll force myself to remember today. I'll close my eyes and not open them until I remember how it felt as the smoke filled my lungs and the heat blistered my face. I'll remember what it felt like to die, Lord. And what it felt like to be given new life."

Addie uttered a choked sob and buried her face in her hands. Kyle wrapped both of his arms around his wife and pulled her against his chest.

Oliver collapsed before The Altar. "You reminded us all today, Father, that iron is forged in the intense heat of a furnace. And my prayer is that, with Your patience and grace, perhaps we can be, too."

Gemma couldn't believe what she was seeing.

Beyond Oliver, the sky was on fire.

The sun descended behind the Dragon's Back, setting the low-hanging clouds ablaze with shades of crimson, orange, and violet. Painted over the backdrop of a nearly white firmament, the colors shifted and changed, recreating themselves into new hues so vibrant and diverse that Gemma could've never named them all, not if she'd had a million lifetimes to do so. And the unspeakable beauty of the waning day climaxed in a fiery vortex churning just above the horizon.

The sun's last gasping breaths.

Just like her dream.

A hand fell on Gemma's arm.

Brie Douglas stood next to her, her eyes sparkling with tears, her pixie-hair streaked black with soot. "Gemma...about the other night...I wasn't thinking straight—"

But Gemma cut her off, releasing Sophia's hand and throwing her arms around Brie's narrow shoulders. "I'm so sorry, Brie. For everything."

On the other side of the clearing, Oliver raised his head, appearing to notice the masterpiece painted in the sky behind him for the first time. "Would you look at that?"

Mia Weber approached Oliver and wrapped an arm around him. "The heavens declare the glory of God; the skies proclaim the work of His hands."

One by one, the others dropped to their knees, forming a haphazard semicircle around The Altar. Their tearful eyes focusing not on the ground but on the sky. They knelt in awestruck silence, consuming the beauty on display before them. Feeding off of it. Replenishing themselves.

The group stayed on the ground—praying and crying—until the sun completed its descent.

Only Taylor remained standing.

In the final moments before the sun disappeared, Sophia whispered in Gemma's ear. "He saved us today, didn't he?"

Gemma peered down at her. "Who?"

The girl raised her finger and pointed at the cross.

Gemma sat by the fire, her stomach swollen with the contents of two hot dogs and a bag of potato chips. Not counting Carver's croissants, it was the first real food she'd eaten in two years. With her belly full, she watched the orange flames stretch toward the sky like reaching fingers, hypnotized by the sound of the branches snapping as they succumbed to the heat.

She couldn't stop thinking about Gavin. He hadn't said a word to her since their awkward encounter at Oliver's farmhouse. She needed to talk to him, but what would she say? How sorry she was? That she cared deeply about him, even if she wasn't in love with him? He knew that already. What more was there to say?

Nothing.

There was nothing left to do but to give him back his ring, and she couldn't bring herself to do that, either. She didn't want to cause him more pain. Not yet. So, for now, she would keep it safe in her pocket until the time was right to give it back.

Gemma shifted on the log, her eyes searching the woods. Taylor had erected a tent out there somewhere, far away from everyone else. Far away from her. She couldn't even see it from the fire pit. She kept looking for him, hoping he would come and sit beside her, but he seemed intent on keeping his distance from the rest of the group.

What if he was thinking about leaving?

She had to talk to him.

Gemma stood, intending to find Taylor, but Addie arrived at the fire pit with two long sticks, the ends sharpened into points, a bag of marshmallows tucked under her arm. She lowered herself onto the log. "Beware of hot-tempered preggos bearing gifts."

Noticing the missing S'mores ingredients, Gemma gestured toward the tents. "Should I grab the chocolate and graham crackers?"

"Nope." Addie pursed her lips. "Don't need them. I just want to inhale thirty marshmallows as fast as I can."

Gemma smiled and took the sticks from Addie.

Taylor would have to wait. For now.

"How are you doing?" Gemma sat beside her friend. "Honestly?"

Addie pointed at the tears already forming in her eyes. "How do you think I'm doing? I'm all boogered up."

Wrapping her arms around Addie, Gemma couldn't help but laugh. She'd missed Addie—and all of her colorful sayings. "At least you have marshmallows."

"I know, I love them." Addie hunched over the bag of marshmallows, cradling it against her belly like a newborn baby. "But, Gem, it was so scary. When we realized what was happening. I'll never forget that *moment*, the exact second, when I smelled the smoke and realized the barn was on fire. Then the door wouldn't open. And Kyle wasn't there..." She wiped her eyes, struggling to compose herself. "What Oliver said earlier about remembering what happened today...I don't want to remember. I'd do *anything* to forget."

Gemma squeezed Addie tighter. "You're safe now. We all are."

"For now," Addie said. "But I saw a soldier through a gap in the doors when we were trying to get out."

"A Task Force soldier?" Gemma felt her body stiffen. "Did you tell Oliver?"

Addie looked down at the ground. "Not yet. I haven't even told Kyle. I couldn't see much of the soldier's face. But he was young. He had red hair. It definitely wasn't the man who'd shot himself."

A soldier with red hair?

Mullen?

As much as Gemma wanted to believe that Carl Lovell was the only person responsible for the barn fire, and that he was dead, something about Addie's story rang true. Why would Lovell go to such trouble to trap them and kill them, only to commit suicide at the scene?

What if the real murderer was still out there?

"It doesn't matter," Gemma said, more to herself than Addie. "Whoever he was, he's long gone. He can't hurt you anymore. And if he ever comes near you again, I'll break his kneecaps."

And she meant it.

Addie's eyes widened. "Sheesh, Gem. The new you is a little terrifying." Then she put a hand on her own belly. "Do you think the baby's okay? I felt him kicking earlier, when we were putting up our tents. Kyle felt it, too."

"He's fine," Gemma said. "His daddy's a wimp, but he's got a strong momma."

Addie gave her a weak smile, but it was the best Gemma could ask for.

"Alright. No more talking." Addie hoisted the bag of marshmallows into the air like a trophy. "These marshmallows aren't going to eat themselves."

✝

Night settled on the mountain, and the air grew cooler. The rest of the group slowly trickled in, gathering around the fire and roasting marshmallows on broken oak branches, and carefully avoiding the topics at the forefront of all of their minds. Instead, they talked about the sunset. They talked about God. They recalled funny stories about their time at the Station. And when the conversation began to wane, they settled into a comfortable silence, the quiet punctuated only by Gemma's frequent reminders to Addie to rotate her marshmallow before it dropped into the fire.

Later, Gemma raised her eyes from the marshmallow bubbling at the end of her stick and saw Taylor standing next to Kyle, his arms crossed over his chest. She had no idea how long he'd been standing there. The two of them had somehow made their way from the tent area to the fire without Gemma noticing. Taylor had replaced his fatigue jacket with a black hoodie. And although he appeared to be nodding in response to something Kyle was saying, his attention was obviously on Gemma.

Their eyes met.

And he smiled.

A soft smile, the corners of his mouth barely turning upward. A characteristically-understated Taylor smile, if ever Gemma had seen one, but somehow it managed to light up his entire face.

He whispered something to Kyle, then came around the fire and sat beside Gemma. Even though Gavin wasn't around, Taylor still maintained a respectful distance between them. "You look surprised to see me."

Lying was pointless. He knew her too well. She shifted closer to him, until their arms were touching, not caring what anyone thought. She wanted to bury her face in the soft fabric of his hoodie and breathe him in. "I thought you might try to leave."

"I'm AWOL," Taylor said. "Which means you're stuck with me. Although I don't know how comfortable your friends are with this whole situation."

She pulled her stick out of the fire and offered the charred marshmallow to Taylor. "They'll get used to it."

He pulled it off the stick, popped it into his mouth, and closed his eyes. "Wow. That's excellent."

"So, what were you and Kyle talking about?"

Taylor licked the marshmallow from his fingers. Then he dug into his pocket and pulled out a black cell phone. "This."

She recognized it instantly, and a wave of fear rushed over her. "That's Carver's! How did you——?"

"He dropped it," he interrupted, his voice low. "I thought we might need it."

Gemma resisted the urge to grab the phone from him and toss it into the fire. "But they could use it to track us," she whispered.

"I know. But I doubt they'd have thought of that yet. Plus, I disabled the location services and GPS, and it's turned off right now. But we still might be able to use it."

She couldn't tear her eyes away from the phone. It looked like a tiny black bomb, waiting to go off. She wished it were anywhere else but in Taylor's hands.

"There are pictures on the phone."

She nodded. "I know. That's Max."

"Yes. But that's not all." Taylor's voice took on that familiar edge of resolve. Determination. "There are text messages, Gemma. So much valuable intel. You know, for a highly-decorated officer, Carver didn't worry too much about personal security. His lock screen passcode was 1-2-3-4."

"I don't understand." She scanned the other faces around the fire. No one appeared to be paying attention to them. Not even Addie, who was lost in conversation with Mia. Only Kyle was watching them intently. "What are you saying?"

"We're going after Max," Taylor said, sliding the phone back into his pocket. "Remember what I said to you back at the church?"

Gemma said nothing...but she remembered.

Taylor stood and returned to Kyle's side.

After Addie finished her conversation with Mia, she rotated her stick, saving another blackened marshmallow a fraction of a second before it plunged into the flames. Then she scooted closer and rested her head on Gemma's shoulder. "Where do we go from here, Gem?" she asked, her voice dreamy and distant. "I mean, after everything that's happened, what are we supposed to do now?"

"Now?" Gemma's eyes met Taylor's again, and the fear in her heart was replaced by love. Love not only for him but for Addie. For Sophia. For Gavin. For Max.

For every single one of them.
But, most of all, for God. For saving the people she loved.
And maybe—just maybe—He would save one more.
With her eyes still locked on Taylor's...she nodded.
"Now we fight."

EPILOGUE

Sprawled on his stomach in the backseat of the SUV, Max Yelchin silently cheered as a massive deer fly scaled the back of the driver's seat, closing in on the exposed flesh of Lubbock's neck.

In the front seat, the two Task Force interrogators discussed Max's crucifixion.

"Are you sure Carver's coming?" Lubbock asked. "Because I ain't taking the fall for this if the higher-ups find out."

A groan from Hilton. "Relax. The colonel texted me this morning. He's going to meet us at the house. All we have to do is take the roach out to the field and hang him up. Get out before dawn, and no one's the wiser. The locals will blame the subversives."

The deer fly inched closer to Lubbock's neck. Max could've reached out and touched the fly, if his hands weren't tied. He wished he could pat its winged back, encourage it on. He had no idea how the insect had come to be inside the SUV. Especially this early in the morning, before the sun was up. He'd been bitten by enough deer flies at the Station to know that they attacked in the late afternoon, waiting in the shade to ambush their prey. They landed on the back of the neck or arms, where they would go unnoticed until they started to feed. But when they finally *did* bite your flesh, you knew it, because it was extremely painful. And the bites swelled. A lot.

Hilton let loose with a series of wet, hacking coughs. He rolled down his window and spat into the wind. The fly stopped moving, but didn't launch itself out the open passenger window. "I'm sick and tired of this chest cold, man."

Lubbock, the brute who'd administered most of Max's punishments, grunted. "Yeah? And I'm sick and tired of listening to you hack up phlegm. It's disgusting."

"Nah. Disgusting would be swallowing the stuff."

Concentrating on the fly, Max tried to tune the men out.

Lubbock and Hilton. He didn't know their first names, nor did he care. They wore no rank on their uniforms, but had identified themselves as interrogators with the Federal Task Force. Although they were both built like Mack trucks, they weren't typical Task Force drones. They wore their hair long and their beards thick, like Special Forces or Navy SEALs. But if the Task Force employed its own Special Forces Unit, intelligence clearly wasn't a prerequisite for joining. If Max had to pick the brains of the duo, Lubbock would win, but only by a non-congested nose.

But Lubbock and Hilton didn't use their brains to get people to talk.

They used their fists. And anything else they could find.

Max shifted his damaged body in an effort to find a more comfortable position. The dull ache in his lower back and shoulders was getting worse, due to the awkward position of his hands tied behind his back. But—for the first time in days—he wasn't freezing. That was something. It was a cold morning, and the soldiers were blasting the heat. He wasn't wearing any shirt or shoes, so he thanked God for the warmth. They'd also allowed him to put pants on for the drive, probably because they didn't want to be pulled over and have to explain the naked guy tied up in their backseat.

He'd spent the previous week locked inside a room with nothing but a metal bucket and fluorescent lights that stayed on 24/7. The soldiers kept the thermostat at fifty degrees because, as Hilton had said, "It's a nice, round number." The room had drains in the floor, and he soon found out why. One of their interrogation techniques had been to strip him naked and douse him repeatedly with water. Afterwards, they snapped pictures of him with their cell phones. He had no idea what they were doing with those photographs, and he didn't want to know.

When he refused to talk, they brought out the knives. Small knives, as sharp as scalpels. They carved up his body.

And his face.

The only thing worse than the knives had been the suffocation. He could still feel the thick plastic bag going over his head, cinched tight around his neck, all of the breathable air used up within seconds. Over and over again, the soldiers had suffocated him. Only when he passed out would they remove the bag. Even in his half-conscious state, his brain registered the cold oxygen flooding into every cell of his body. The blessed relief as he realized he wasn't dead yet. And then—finally—the awful realization that the whole thing was going to happen again.

And again. And again.

That's when the despair set in.

He opened his eyes and focused on the deer fly. It wasn't moving, but it was much closer to Lubbock's neck than before. Only a few inches away now, just below the headrest. Max admired its patience. The fly was waiting for the perfect moment to strike, its survival instincts overpowering its body's primal demand for blood.

When he was first captured at the store, Max's only instinct had been to survive. To do whatever was asked of him, if it meant he got to live. But they'd asked him to give up the exact location of his group. That also meant giving up his fiancé, Brie. And he couldn't do that. So, he'd refused to talk, hoping that his captors would eventually grow tired of beating him and send him to a detention center with other subversives.

But after a few days with Lubbock and Hilton—days that had felt like *years*—Max had started praying for death. They didn't plan on killing him, that much was obvious, so he prayed for an accident. Maybe they would suffocate him for too long. Or hit him too hard. Or his heart would give out. He prayed for death because he could feel himself starting to crack. Sooner or later, the interrogators were going to break him. And he would talk.

By the sound of it, God had answered his prayers.

He was going to die today.

Brie seemed so far from him now, as if his memories of her belonged to someone else. Eventually she *would* belong to someone else. Not right away, of course. She would mourn him for a long time. They were young, but the love they'd shared was real. Brie had been his first girlfriend, and she was about to become his last. Not that he was complaining. He couldn't have asked for anyone better...and she certainly could have.

He hated the thought of her mourning his death, but imagining her falling in love with someone else...well, that was like driving a steel knife into his already-decimated heart.

Hilton's voice cut into Max's thoughts. "What's your problem, Lubbs?"

"Nothing."

But something *was* wrong. Max could hear it in Lubbock's voice.

"What is it?" Hilton twisted in his seat to look at Lubbock. "You worried about the roach?"

Max snapped his eyes shut as Lubbock glanced at him in the rearview mirror. "What's he gonna do?"

"Then what is it? You don't trust Colonel Carver?"

"Of course, I trust him!" Lubbock shot back angrily, as if afraid the vehicle was bugged and his boss might be listening. "I wouldn't have volunteered for this outfit if I didn't trust the colonel. But something don't feel right. If we're just going to kill him, why couldn't we do it back at the base like the others?"

The others.

Anger flared in Max's chest, red-hot and violent. He thought of the crusted-over lacerations on his forearms. The crisscross pattern of cuts that covered most of his chest. His missing fingernails. The gash on the left side of his face. Even now, dried blood adhered the still-tender skin of his face to the leather seat.

He thought of Allen Portzline's vacant eyes. The hole in his forehead.

How many more? How many more people had they tortured? How many had they killed?

Max opened his eyes.

The deer fly was on the headrest.

Hilton barked out a laugh. "Have you ever known Carver to do things the easy way, brother? He probably thinks there's something poetic about taking the roach back to where we found him."

So, they were taking him back to Ash Grove.

But why?

The fly's wings blurred as it launched itself off the headrest and landed on the folded collar of Lubbock's uniform. Max held his breath, waiting for it to surge forward and bury its scissor-like mandibles into the brute's neck. Wishing *he* could be the one to inflict the pain. Not for himself, but for Allen Portzline, who'd been shot dead in Ash Grove. Allen was a good man, and he hadn't deserved what happened to him.

The SUV rolled to a stop. Max heard Lubbock flick on the turn signal.

"Which way?" Lubbock asked.

"Right."

The vehicle started to roll forward, then lurched to a sudden stop. Lubbock slammed his fist against the steering wheel and cursed.

The fly never moved.

"It wasn't your turn, you dumb broad!" Lubbock bellowed. *"You never seen a four-way stop before?"*

A four-way stop. They'd been driving for at least fifty minutes, most of that on the interstate. But for the last ten minutes, they'd been traveling at a much slower rate. No more than sixty miles per hour. Max remembered a four-way stop a few miles outside Ash Grove, near an old ice cream shop.

Wherever they were taking him...they were almost there.

"Carver knows what he's doing, man," Hilton continued, running his thick fingers along the inside of the passenger window. "Just relax."

Lubbock executed a right-hand turn. If Max was right about the four-way stop, they were definitely heading toward Ash Grove now. But why drive him all the way back to Ash Grove just to crucify him?

"I don't know," Lubbock said. "This seems too risky, even for Carver. I doubt the higher-ups would like it."

"The higher-ups don't care." Hilton hacked and spat out the window again. "Remember the storeowner? This operation is a junkyard, and Carver's their meanest dog. They're okay with him ripping up a few kittens here or there, as long as he does his job and protects the yard."

"Yeah, but crucifying the old geezer made sense. He was helping the roaches."

Max squeezed his eyelids together. Henry Castern. The two soldiers had spent the week taunting him about Henry's death. How painful it had been. How Henry had wet his pants and begged for mercy as they'd nailed him to the cross. They'd assured Max that he would suffer the same fate if he refused to talk.

And now it was time.

"Relax, man," Hilton said. "Our leave starts tomorrow. After we kill the roach, let's drive down to the shore, find a couple of girls, and forget all about this place."

Lubbock snorted. "That's the best idea you've had all day, Hilty." His gaze shot to the rearview mirror again, and he briefly locked eyes with Max before returning his attention to the windshield. "You getting hot back there, roachy? You look a little sweaty." He fumbled with one of the dials on the dashboard, and a blast of cold air from the vents hit Max's bare skin.

Instantly, Max began to shiver.

Hilton dug a handkerchief out of his pocket and rubbed at his nose. "Really? The air conditioning? I'm already sick. You trying to kill me?"

"Suck it up, man. We're almost there." Lubbock relaxed in his seat, and the deer fly shifted closer to his neck. "You want some music, roach? I know how much you love music."

Music. Once, Max had loved music more than anything. Especially British bands from the mid-nineties. Oasis. Blur. The Verve. Radiohead. Although Brie didn't share his love for Brit-pop —in fact, she often made fun of him for it—music was one of the things that had drawn them together. Not being able to listen to music for two whole years had been one of the worst parts of going into hiding.

But Lubbock wasn't being nice. Part of Max's torture had been sleep-deprivation, and one of the ways the soldiers had kept him awake was by blasting heavy-metal directly into his cell for eight hours every night. If Hilton intended to blast more metal through the car's speakers, that was fine. At least Max wouldn't have to spend his final minutes listening to his captor's voices.

Hilton turned on the radio. There was a flare of static, and then a man's voice filled the car.

"...listening to Elevation Ministries, with Pastor David Ogden. We're coming to you live from Harrisburg, Pennsylvania, the home of Elevation Ministries. This morning, David will be speaking with five high-school students who credit Elevation Ministries with saving their lives. Prior to meeting Pastor Ogden, each had contemplated taking his or her own life. Two had made plans to take guns to school to murder their classmates. Pastor Ogden found these lost souls through our Teen Outreach Program, known as TOP. Thanks to David's mentorship, they learned to unlock their true happiness, and they are here today to share their stories—"

"I'm not listening to this crap," Lubbock barked. He jammed the power button with his thumb and the voice disappeared as if it had never been there. "We're trying to get rid of the roaches. Not breed a new species."

"What?" Hilton sounded surprised. "You don't like Ogden?"

Lubbock grunted. "You kidding? His whole schtick is designed to appeal to the holy rollers who feel guilty for renouncing. Did you know people are calling him a prophet?" He waved a hand dismissively. "He ain't no prophet. He's a snake oil salesman with political aspirations. The dude's got friends in low places, Hilty. And I mean *really* low...like politicians. Mark my words, Ogden's going to make a Senate run next year. The media's been hinting at it for weeks."

"You think?"

"I *know*. Just wait."

Max knew nothing about David Ogden. Or Elevation Ministries. But the name seemed important, so he locked it away in his mind.

"Almost there, roach," Hilton called out. "Get your dancing shoes on."

Max couldn't stop shaking. He knew about crucifixion. Death wouldn't come from the wounds in his hands and feet, but from suffocation. The weight of his own body would kill him. His lungs would scream for air, as they had when the soldiers had put bags over his head. Relief would only come from using his feet to push himself up—an unimaginably painful act, given the spikes in his feet —and he would only have time to steal a shallow breath before his weight carried him back down. It would be like drowning...but much slower. A long and agonizing death.

Tears formed in his eyes, but he couldn't wipe them away. They ran down his face and formed wet puddles on the cold leather seat. He didn't want to die. Not today. Especially not by suffocation. There wasn't anything worse than not being able to breathe.

Was it too late to give the soldiers what they wanted?

If he told them about the Station, could he still save himself?

Max opened his mouth to make an offer...and Lubbock screamed.

The soldier jerked the wheel hard to the right—nearly sending Max rolling off the seat—and slammed a hand on the back of his neck. The deer fly rocketed off his flesh an instant before it would've become fly soup, sailing over Max and heading for the trunk.

"What—" Hilton grabbed the wheel, kept them from veering off the road. He glared into the backseat, as if Max had done something wrong.

Which...he almost had.

"What happened, man?"

Lubbock unleashed a torrent of expletives that would've made Henry Castern blush. "Something just bit me!"

Hilton stared past Max into the trunk. "I think it was just a fly. There's one buzzing around back there. A big mother, too."

"*A fly?* Felt like a dang snake!"

Hilton reached for Lubbock's neck. "Dude, it's already swelling —"

"Don't touch it, you moron!" Lubbock smacked his hand away. "It *hurts!*"

A moment earlier, Max had been contemplating giving up his friends to save his own life.

Now, he was holding back laughter.

A miserable deer fly had saved him.

He raised his head slightly, not enough to be noticed by either soldier. The sun was on the rise, the first hints of light straining to break free of the early-morning fog.

It was beautiful.

Was Brie watching it, too? If so, was she thinking about him? Sometimes, they would wake up early and sneak up to the tower to watch the sun rise. It was beautiful up there. Nothing like it in the world.

"Up ahead." Lubbock stopped rubbing the lump on his neck and pointed through the windshield. "That the right driveway?"

"Yeah." Hilton sounded nervous. "You think the locals took the old man down yet?"

"Are you serious?"

"Hey, we're out in the sticks, man. Town might've kept him up there as a scarecrow or something."

"They took him down," Lubbock said. "But the cross is still up. I texted Carver, and he confirmed."

Hilton turned the wheel to the right, and the SUV veered onto what felt like a dirt lane. Gravel crunched beneath the tires, and the vehicle shook. Through the rear passenger window, Max caught a glimpse of a white house with red shutters. Henry Castern's farmhouse. After traveling a few more yards along the long driveway, the vehicle rolled to a stop, and Hilton shut off the engine.

This is it, Max realized. It's happening.

Brie's face flashed though his mind. He was looking up at her, just as he'd done when he'd gone down on one knee to propose. What if she came to Henry's? What if she was the one who found his body?

God, please, no.

Lubbock opened his door and stepped out, stretching both arms above his head and groaning. "Doesn't look like the colonel's here, yet."

"Who cares? Let's get this done. I'm hungry." Hilton unbuckled and stepped out of the car. Then he leaned in and leered at Max through the metal cage. "Sit tight, roachy. We're going to make sure everything's all set up, and then we'll come back for you."

A shudder passed through Max's body. He tried to lift his head, intending to beg for his life, but dizziness drove him back to the seat. He was going to pass out.

No. He couldn't pass out.

What if he didn't regain consciousness until they were nailing him to the cross?

The front doors slammed shut, followed by a short beep. All of the locks clicked into place, sealing him inside the vehicle.

It was the silence that undid him. The finality of it sent him hurtling into a deep despair. He wanted to scream at them. Beg them to let him go. He had a life to go back to. A girl. Parents who loved him.

At least, he hoped they still did.

Max closed his eyes and took a few deep breaths, struggling to calm himself. The car wasn't running, which meant no heat, but at least the air conditioning was off. Still, his entire body shook. If he'd eaten anything in the last twenty-four hours, it would be making a reappearance right now. Death was close. He could feel it like a dark presence in the backseat with him, its long fingers curling around his throat.

"God..." He tried to pray, but his sleep-deprived mind wasn't functioning properly. He couldn't remember how to pray.

Raised voices came from outside the SUV, some distance away.

Max couldn't make out what they were saying, but one of them sounded like Lubbock. He was shouting. Someone was shouting back at him.

It definitely *wasn't* Hilton.

Was it Colonel Carver? The leader the two soldiers were always talking about?

Had they done something wrong?

Ignoring the pain in his lower back, Max raised his head as high as he could, trying to see what was going on. But he couldn't see anything through the fogged-up rear window, and he didn't have enough strength to hold himself up for very long. After a few seconds, he flopped back down on the seat like a dying fish, defeated.

That's what Max felt like.

A fish that had swallowed a giant hook and been dragged to shore. He'd put up a fight at first, flopping uselessly on the cold ground, trying to survive long enough to make his way back to his home. But he was tired. He had no strength left to fight.

Now he was lying still, waiting to suffocate.

Eventually, the shouting stopped.

It felt like forever before he heard anything else, but it was likely only seconds. There were voices. Several different voices. But none of them sounded like Hilton or Lubbock. He strained to listen.

The voices grew louder.

They were approaching the SUV.

Max cringed away from the door, tried to recite The Lord's Prayer before it was too late. But he was panicking, and he couldn't remember how the prayer started. He could already feel the spikes being driven into the flesh of his hands, the weight of his body pulling at the wounds, tearing them open.

The vehicle beeped again—and all four doors unlocked.

It sounded like thunder.

This is it.

This is the end.

The rear passenger door flew open.

A soldier stood there, staring in at him. Not Lubbock or Hilton but a uniformed Task Force soldier with dark hair and pale eyes. He held a pistol in one hand.

The other hand reached for Max...

"No!" Max shouted, crawling away from the soldier's grasp. He got his knees beneath him and inched along the leather seat like a slug. Aware of how pathetic he must look and not caring.

He didn't want to die.

Not like this. Not today.

"Relax, man. It's going to be—"

The soldier's hand touched his leg, just above his bare foot, and his survival instincts came rushing back. He kicked at the soldier and heard a satisfying grunt as the heel of his foot impacted flesh. Then he unleashed a guttural howl, half-laugh, half-scream, spittle flying from his lips. If they wanted to put him on that cross, they would have to fight him every step of the way. He wouldn't make it easy on them.

More hands grabbed him—trying to restrain him—but he kicked them all away and grabbed the door handle between his teeth. He pulled at it—not caring if his teeth ripped free from his gums—but the door wouldn't open. The SUV was like a police car. The rear doors wouldn't open from the inside. Frustrated, he released the handle and screamed again, the sound blocking out the soldier's shouts. His orders to stop fighting. His lies that everything was going to be okay.

A voice cut through the madness, reaching out to him as if from a far-off place. He thought he'd imagined it. But then the voice spoke again, and he stopped screaming and opened his eyes.

The soldier was gone.

"Max?"

Brie stood inside the open door, tears sliding down her pale cheeks. She was crying and smiling at the same time. Not just smiling. Laughing. And he wondered if maybe he was already dead and this was heaven.

"I knew it." She tilted her head toward the gradually-brightening sky. "Thank you."

The soldier appeared behind Brie, one hand on his chest, a pain-filled scowl on his face. He glared at Max, and Max realized this wasn't heaven.

Not yet.

"He kicked me in the chest," the soldier muttered.

Someone—a girl—put a hand on the soldier's arm. "You'll live."

Max couldn't see very well, but the voice sounded like Gemma's.

Brie turned to the soldier. "Give me the knife." And Max watched in disbelief as the soldier pulled a knife from his belt and handed it to her.

She climbed into the car, throwing her insignificant weight on top of him, and set to work cutting through the zip-ties that bound his hands together. Her hands were shaking, and she nicked his wrist a little in the process, but he barely noticed.

"Brie?"

She looked so much older than when he'd last seen her.

Had that really only been five days ago?

Brie used the knife to saw through his restraints. He could hear more voices. Voices he recognized as belonging to Gavin and Kyle. All of his friends were here. Somehow, they'd found him. He wasn't going to die. At least not yet.

He wondered what had become of Lubbock and Hilton.

After she freed his hands, Brie stretched out on the seat next to him, bringing her face next to his. He wanted to say so many things to her—declarations of love he'd thought about during his time in the interrogation room. He also wanted to ask her about the dark-haired soldier.

But none of those things seemed as important as gazing into Brie's eyes. Just being with her. Holding her. Loving her. The beautiful and crazy girl he never thought he'd see again. He watched as her eyes drifted to the left side of his face—taking in his disfiguring scar—and he instinctively turned his head, trying to block her view of it. But she stopped him with her hands, and her fingers delicately traced the jagged gash made by Lubbock's knife.

"Don't worry, babe," she whispered, bringing her lips to his. "Chicks dig scars."

ACKNOWLEDGEMENTS

Publishing a novel has been my dream for as long as I can remember. The following amazing people all played a role in making that dream a reality.

To my editor, Teresa Crumpton...thank you for taking my hand and guiding me down this yellow brick road. Your edits and suggestions made this book so much stronger. I loved our phone conversations, and I look forward to working with you on the rest of the trilogy.

Thank you to my cover designer, Rachel Rossano. I'm forever in your debt. You brought my vision to life in a way that was better than anything I could've imagined. I also appreciate you taking the time to answer all of my publishing questions. That wasn't in your job description! I'm so excited to collaborate with you in the future.

Thank you to my early readers: Judy Kissinger, Lori Thomas, Scott Rood, Amy Coleman, Joseph Mott, Joyce Mott, Gail Arbogast, and Jen Greanias. It's not easy putting your work into the world for others to read, especially before it's been edited. It's a little bit like sending your baby off to Kindergarten. Thank you for your feedback, your edits, your support, and for taking good care of my baby.

Thank you to my parents, my family, my friends, and my church family. A special thanks to my son, Ben, for your amazing cover design suggestions. I spent months agonizing over what the covers for this trilogy should look like, and you figured everything out in a fifteen-minute car ride to school. Thanks for being an all-around great kid. Also, big hugs and kisses to Sam and George. I once asked God for a chance to write full-time, and He answered that prayer in the most unexpected and wonderful way. Being a stay-at-home mom has been the greatest blessing of my life. Writing is just the icing on the cake.

To my husband, Scott...thank you for supporting our family and this crazy dream of mine. Thank you for making me laugh every day (with you and at you). Thank you for being my best friend.

Finally, all of the glory for this book goes to God, and to my savior, Jesus Christ. I made a promise to You long ago, and I'm sticking to it.

My life belongs to You.